THE FAMILY TABOR

Cherise Wolas's acclaimed first novel, *The Resurrection of Joan Ashby*, was a *New York Times Book Review* Editors' Choice and a semi-finalist for the 2018 PEN/Robert W. Bingham Prize for Debut Fiction. A native of Los Angeles, she lives in New York City with her husband. *The Family Tabor* is her second novel.

Also by Cherise Wolas

The Resurrection of Joan Ashby

THE
FAMILY TABOR

CHERISE WOLAS

THE BOROUGH PRESS

The Borough Press
An imprint of HarperCollins*Publishers*
1 London Bridge Street
London SE1 9GF

www.harpercollins.co.uk

Published by HarperCollins*Publishers* 2018
1

A catalogue record for this book is available from the British Library

ISBN: 978-0-00-820119-7

This novel is entirely a work of fiction.
The names, characters and incidents portrayed in it are
the work of the author's imagination. Any resemblance to
actual persons, living or dead, events or localities is
entirely coincidental.

Printed and bound in the UK by
CPI Group (UK) Ltd, Croydon CR0 4YY

MIX
Paper from
responsible sources
FSC **FSC™ C007454**
www.fsc.org

This book is produced from independently certified FSC™ paper
to ensure responsible forest management.

For more information visit: www.harpercollins.co.uk/green

For the girl from Port Colborne and the boy from the Bronx,

who found each other and married,

and became and remain my parents.

It was the mind that was woven, the mind that was jerked
And tufted in straggling thunder and shattered sun.
—Wallace Stevens

Put your ear down close to your soul and listen hard.
—Anne Sexton

GOOD
SAMARITAN

ONE

Tomorrow evening, Harry Tabor will be anointed Man of the Decade.

If this were the 1300s, he would be running for his life to escape savage pogroms in France, Spain, Germany, Switzerland, Austria, Belgium, or Bohemia.

If this were the 1800s, in Imperial Russia, he would be running for his life to escape savage pogroms in Odessa, in Warsaw, in Kishinev, in Kiev, in Bialystok, or in Lviv.

If this were the early 1940s, in Nazi-occupied Europe, he would be running for his life, the garish yellow Star of David on his chest, *Jew* centered in mock Hebraic, a target to be captured and deported to a savage camp to join the millions of dead going up in smoke.

It is only by a godsend that it is none of those times and none of those places, although those events, in those places, at those times, certainly clarified how one was considered by others.

Instead, it is late in the second decade of the twenty-first century, in Palm Springs, California, and on this scorching mid-August Friday night, Harry Tabor is reveling in the truth of what's coming. Man of the Decade is the desert city's exceptional honor, lofting high the special few who devotedly enrich the lives of others in astounding and uncommon ways. As Harry has been doing for thirty years, manifesting futures of promise and hope for the persecuted, the lost, and the luckless.

In March, when he received the lavish hand-delivered announcement inviting him to ascend into the very select group—only twelve such ascensions since the award's institution—he was hesitant about accepting, and had thought: *Why me?*

But now, as he embraces Roma, the love of his life and his wife of forty-four years, he thinks: *Why not me?* He commands immense respect and admiration as the highly successful head of his humanitarian enterprises, a man who effects miracles, trusting in the honey of bees, not the sting, to make those miracles happen. He shepherds all those he resettles here, thousands now, and looks after them lovingly, with care and pride.

And indeed, this moment, sheet thrown off, bodies damp, souls replenished by their Friday night union, Harry realizes there will never be a better time for this felicitous event, this proffering of esteem, this celebration of him, to which, apparently, eight hundred have confirmed their attendance. How wonderful that it has come now, when he has just begun dipping toes into the spotlight, and while he has not yet lost his hair or his teeth or his height or his hearing or his eyesight, and any notion of him shuffling off this mortal coil is far, far in the future. So far in the future, it bears absolutely no current consideration. In fact, he will not, this night, consider such an eventuality at all.

He runs a hand softly down his wife's back and says, "You're as lovely now as you were at twenty-four when we wed."

Harry says these words often to Roma, and always on Friday nights, for he still sees her as the bride she once was. And every Friday night, Roma says, "And you have matured into an emperor, my love. Enjoy your solitary hour."

Which is what she says now, smiling up at him before cloaking herself with the sheet and duvet. She is instantly asleep in the ceiling fan breeze, the blades' whirring a noise she seems never to notice.

Harry rises then for a quick shower. Under the spray, inside his head, Leonard Cohen is singing, *Hineni, hineni.* All afternoon he listened to that song in his office, its dark exultation curiously increasing his own elation. *Here I am, here I am*, he thinks as he dries off and dons the caftan Roma insisted they buy him long ago in Morocco.

When he draws the drapes, he catches his reflection. He *does* look like an emperor, and he feels like one, too, a happy emperor, a pleased potentate, a benevolent monarch.

Slipping out of their bedroom, he follows the path Roma leaves for him through the house, overheads reduced to small lighted circles, electric breadcrumbs by which she guarantees he will find his way back to her. And he always does, always wants to, always will.

In the living room, a substantial pour of brandy in a cut-crystal glass; then he is through the sliding glass doors, stepping into the late-summer night with its textured, enveloping heat, the hot air scented with life.

On his expansive back patio that smacks right up against the vast desert beyond, he stretches out on a lounge chair, and becomes one with the settled darkness that embraces his large house, that outlines the rows of towering cacti—larger than when they first moved in—silvered by moonlight, thick as terrestrial soldiers, sulfurous as ghosts. This place, this desert, *his* desert, how it stirs his insides, the grandness of everything and of every living thing mixing seductively with the fragrance of the brandy he sips.

A bat shoots by, then another one, and their soaring night search for insects to gobble up no longer gives him the slightest start. He listens to the murmurs, the rustles, the peeps, the faint calls that could mean love or despair out there, the scrabbling of creatures seeking whatever it is they need. The moon is cut in half tonight, the stars preserved rather than gleaming. He remembers when his children were young, pointing out specific stars whose names he didn't know, has never known, saying to each of them, "That star right there belongs to you, Phoebe, and that one to you, Camille, and that one to you, Simon." And they believed him; for years they believed those stars were theirs, their names attached to them in some astral registry. Perhaps he'll offer up stars to the little ones, his young granddaughters, this weekend.

This is Harry's finale on these sacred Friday nights, after he and Roma prepare a lovely dinner at home, drink a bottle of delicious wine, share news about his newest clients, her thorniest patients, their stellar children, their adorable grandchildren, and afterward, in every season, float together in the big pool until the moon appears, then make love. This solitary hour of reflection is when he considers the infinite, and the world at large, and this world of his that he thinks he created out of whole cloth.

Tonight, it's not the infinite he wants to contemplate, but the specific. And specifically, his response to one of the many questions posed by the young *Palm Times* reporter for the profile piece that will be published in Sunday's edition—highlighting, he was told, his installation as Man of the Decade.

When asked, "Do you think great things are ahead of you or behind you?" Harry had replied, "The past no longer exists, there is only the future, whatever it may hold," and something about his answer to that consideration of mystical simplicity has continued to give him pause. He studies it anew now, from multiple angles, and recognizes that the equation that has fueled him all his life is slightly different, less coy and more apt:

"The past no longer exists, but great things are always ahead in my future."

That's what he *should* have said. *That* would have been entirely accurate.

Which leads him to reconsider another of his responses during that long interview conducted in his office. His answer hadn't been at all inaccurate, but he might have fleshed it out, elaborated, said something more than, "Religious faith has nothing to do with my organization's mission. I am a historical Jew."

In the dense heat, Harry unpacks that brief explanatory offering he made to the reporter, with its pithy pearl of a phrase, a definitional near-truth, a mostly accurate shorthand to describe himself, that he thinks his brain magically deduced on its own—it didn't, but no matter.

Yes, he should have explained to the reporter that while he aligns himself with the cultural and ethical lineage of his, the Chosen People, he draws the line at, absolutely doesn't subscribe to, their belief in the power of prayer. He could have said, "Look, prayer failed all of my ancestors, everyone from whom I'm descended," and evocatively illustrated what he meant with a few quick stories:

That his great-grandparents Abraham and Minishka Tabornikov were tiny people, stoic and reverent in their religiousness, with an enormous belief that God was with them, despite the awful men on horseback who rode into their shtetl waving scimitars and swords, eagerly firebombing the place once again, leaving behind a new stack of dead Jews mangled, burned, cut down, sliced straight through. Every Shabbat and on all the big and little holidays, they prayed in the ramshackle shul that was their second home, rebuilt with *tzedakah* and reconsecrated as many times as it was left smashed and smoldering. They had three healthy sons, not strapping, but smart—the youngest, a Talmudic scholar—all marrying devoted girls who bore lovely grandchildren. Their condensed happiness was like a fragile flower cracking through bone-dry dirt, beauty found if they shut their eyes to the rough world and forced their hearts open. Paltry, pitiful gifts, taken as proof that Adonai was watching out for them, watching over them, hearing their worshipful words.

That his grandparents Aleph and Sonia Tabornikov were a little more progressive than the prior generation. They married, and with their young sons, left the shtetl for the big city, though the big city was barely a town. But with that fifty-mile migration, they reduced, to Shabbat and the top three tiers of holidays, their attendance at their newer, finer shul, whose roof did not leak, looking sideways at those who held fast to the full complement. And when their sons were old enough to understand where they came from, and that because of who they were, they were not wanted—another round of pogroms making that abundantly clear—the family sold their only inheritances, a silver Kiddush cup and menorah, packed up their meager belongings, and hightailed it out of the old country, arriving at Ellis Island, where these Tabornikovs were reborn Americans, renaming themselves Tabor. Worship did not wholly consume the totality of his grandparents' lives in their new country, but to Harry, it has seemed only by a matter of meaningless degrees. For although these new Tabors were free as they had never been before, prayer barely eased their lot in life.

That his parents, Mordechai and Lenore Tabor, were, like all the rest, dead, but after meeting at CCNY and marrying, they chose as their home a comfortable house in the Bronx within walking distance of a conservative synagogue they immediately joined. They did not attend on Shabbat or on the minor holidays, but were present at the ostensibly fun ones, like Purim and Sukkot and Hanukkah, and were always in their middle-of-the-house seats on the most holy of days, those deemed critical, young Harry seated firmly between them. And when the synagogue threw out the fusty old prayer books and adopted looser, more free-form services, with a musician to strum his guitar and a newfangled cantor who sang to the plucked notes, they went with the times. They maintained their minimized calendar of observance and their strong belief that prayer was an answer to so many things that remained, unfortunately, unanswered.

And that on Harry's own Bar Mitzvah, as he ascended the bema, reached the Torah scroll unrolled on the lectern, accepted from the well-bearded rabbi the scepter to guide him along the reversed sentences of minuscule black-inked Hebrew words, he, like all those earlier Tabors and Tabornikovs, had prayed. His prayer hadn't been for global peace, or to make Mordy and Lenore proud, or to be gifted with checks and Israeli Bonds in relatively substantial sums for 1961, but that Eve Flynn, the long-legged redhead in his homeroom, who every single Sunday attended church and sang in its youth choir under a massive crucified Christ, would finally notice him on the very day Jewish tradition declared him a man. Harry had looked out at the congregation and prayed that when everyone was at the after-party in the Tabors' tidy, well-gardened backyard, Eve, dazzled by his new manhood, might, in an enthusiastic clasping of sweaty hands, be led around the side of the house, where, under the silky fronds of the weeping willow tree, Harry would bestow upon her his first-ever kiss. He had seen his pale gingery angel among his dark-haired erstwhile tribe and sang his Torah portion as if it were a love song for her. At the party, he was knock-kneed with love for Eve, who wore a short froth of a party dress in a peach that clashed with her red hair, but exposed her slim thighs, her rounded knees, her thin calves, all that opaline skin. Despite his fervent call to God, as fervent as once intoned by his ancestors, the prayed-for kiss was not to be. Big, blond Bobby O'Ryan, a church-goer like Eve, had led her away, and in painful defeat, Harry could only imagine Eve Flynn being kissed under that weeping willow tree by a boy who, because he was no Jew, would never be a man at thirteen.

And he would have concluded by saying, "I consider myself a thoroughly modern man, standing at a vast distance from the millennia of bloodshed and obliteration and prayer, and that whatever links me to my ancestors is tenuous at best, a matter only of DNA, and not of outlook, or of temperament, or of faith. Big prayers did nothing for my ancestors, and a tiny prayer did not turn Eve Flynn's head and heart in my direction. After that, I gave up prayer entirely."

All these years, Harry has been certain that he prayed just the once and never again. Indeed, he would swear that's true.

What *is* true is that he left Eve Flynn behind, and met other girls who welcomed his kisses, and he graduated from college, and from a decent business school, and landed, surprisingly, at a hoity-toity, top-tier, gentile-owned stock brokerage firm in Manhattan, where he was the token Jew for a few years, but moved up the ladder with alacrity anyway, fell madly in love with the dazzling Jewess who deigned to become his wife, and created a life far beyond his ancestors' ken.

What is also true is that thirty-plus years ago, in what still strikes him as a miraculous decision, he moved his family to this desert and made it his mission to do good in the world.

Looking up at the moon and the stars, Harry thinks he ought to be done for the night. It's late, but not too late, and anyway the brandy is finished, and he wants to be fresh for tomorrow.

He locks the glass door, rinses the crystal, returns it to its living room tray, and snaps off the lights one by one as he winds his way through the house, back to his bed, where his wife, and the warmth of her skin, awaits him.

It is pitch-black in the bedroom, and silent once he cuts the fan's spinning entirely, and then Roma sighs her heartbroken sigh when she's dreaming about her grandmother Tatiana and her mother, Inessa. He waits until his strong and happy wife's nocturnal sadness fades away, then carefully climbs into bed, fluffs his pillows, and closes his eyes.

Soon there is an internal rush of lapping oceanic waves pulling him under, into the ruffled layers of sleep, where he will travel to places he does not know, see people he never knew, and others he once loved, traveling, he thinks, on his own, believing, as he always has, that he alone inhabits his head. Mistaken in his assumption that the past no longer exists. Mistaken, too, in his certainty that the world can be understood, that he understands the world, or, at least, that he understands his own. As his breath grows even and deep, a sensed, rather than articulated, sentiment washes over him: *I have been a very lucky man.*

And *that* is true, absolutely true. But luck is a rescindable gift.

TWO

THE HOURS PASS, AND he sleeps deeply, and then all the blood-soaked history of the Judaic people, and all the history of those to whom he is related, whose lives were cut short or resulted in his existence, and all his beliefs about the past and the future, and about faith and prayer, are fading back into the pleats of Harry Tabor's sleeping mind. It is dawn and he is waking, opening his shining brown eyes, running a large hand through his thick hair, still boisterously dark, threads of distinguished white only recently emerging, in this his seventieth year.

He is quick out of bed, the travertine marble cool under his feet, and in the bathroom, he gives his solid teeth a thorough cleaning, grinning at himself when he finishes rinsing. He picks up the razor, runs a hand over his cheeks, thinking happily of this afternoon, when his children and grandchildren will descend upon the family's substantial and striking midcentury modernist homestead, with its five bedrooms and endless other rooms, all open to the expanse of sky and desert and weather and one or the other of their two pools. He and Roma and their progeny all gathered together for this weekend of Man of the Decade pomp and circumstance.

Maybe there will be time for a hike with his son. Wouldn't Simon be surprised if he said, "I'm finally ready to do *Cactus to*

Clouds"? Really, this would be the perfect weekend to hike that tough trail he has always avoided.

He sets down the razor. He'll take the single-edge blade to his face tonight, be glisteningly smooth for the gala event celebrating him.

In his large closet, he dresses in his tennis whites, then tiptoes, socks and Tretorns in hand, out of the master bedroom with its view, when the drapes are pulled back, of the meditation pool, leaving Roma asleep, her face aglow in a shard of sunlight, dreaming, he hopes, about something pleasurable, not about Tatiana and Inessa, or the youngster she has begun treating who has ceased eating entirely.

In the sunny kitchen, the waft of espresso makes him smile again, that timer on the machine such a modern wonder. He throws back a first cup, rich and unadulterated, looking out over the large aquamarine rectangle in the main courtyard where Roma swims her daily laps before healing the children of the Coachella Valley.

Socks on, laces tied, he gulps down two more espressos, leaves the thimble-sized cup in the sink, and pulls from the freezer three bottles of water, slick as stalactites.

Out into the open-air carport, into his old convertible Mercedes coupe painted in a patina of gold, he revs the engine just a little, to feel the vroom in his being, and leaves his majestic home, which sits on a solid acre, driving past the flowering cacti and soaring palms, and the beds of mimosas, ocotillos, acacias, lemongrass, and the lilies of the Nile, after which the Tabors' street is named, turning left onto his street, onto Agapanthus Lane. He presses the gas, feels the stalwart car gather its power, gliding so easily over the smooth macadam, a hop and a skip to the courts.

He could belong to any of the private tennis clubs in the area, and his tennis pal, Levitt, would prefer playing at his own, but Harry is a man of the people, and he prefers the public courts. After all, he comes from solid stock that knew how to make do with what they had, which was nothing. And he knows how to make do, too, only he has so much more than any impoverished Tabornikov could have imagined possessing back in the Pale of Settlement, when the world was so very, very, very old. Harry Tabor may no longer be chronologically young, but he feels as if he is, lives as if he is, as if this world is a great and wonderful place, and he himself is adding to that wondrousness, waking up every day strong as a bull, his thoughts sharp and important, his very being brand-new. A man self-made, through and through. That's how he remembers his own life, up to this point.

And there is Levitt's showy Maserati cooling down when Harry pulls into his regular spot at Ruth Hardy Park. Younger than Harry by a baker's dozen, but not quite as agile a player, Levitt is a friend Harry considers "newish" since they met only a decade ago. In the desert, ten years is nothing against the antediluvian nature of the topography.

Creaky parking brake engaged, Henry swings himself easily through the car's open door, is up on his feet, retrieving his tennis bag from the backseat.

"You ready to lose again, Levitt? I'm telling you, you'd better be tough, give me your prime-A game, because today is my lucky day."

THREE

ROMA TABOR'S DREAMS ABOUT her *baba* Tatiana and her mother, Inessa, aren't about what she has suffered and lost by their absence, or the bottomless sorrow that never dissolves; instead she dreams of *their* sufferings, *their* losses, *their* sorrows that they packed away after they found a way to escape.

For many years now, when she wakes, she thinks first about luck—about the terrible steps Tatiana had to take to find a shred of it in a world that decreed she should have none, and then about its constancy in her own life. From the time she was young, those strong women defied their experiences to teach her to trust in its tangible reality. She learned the lesson, but honors their before and after by remembering that believing one deserves luck doesn't mean it won't disappear in a flash.

This morning, there is Harry's usual empty space next to her in the king-sized bed, and the sun's heat on her face, and she thinks about luck, then puts it away, and waits to see what name is in her head. Today it is Noelani McCadden, a big name for a little girl who is only eight.

In the intake session on Monday, the mother, Jeanine, said, "One day my daughter was fine, the next day not. She's an only child, and until a month ago, a couch potato. She didn't like playing games during recess, wasn't interested in taking gymnastics or ballet with her friends, or riding the bike we gave her for her birthday while her father and I took our regular after-dinner stroll. We tried to get her to go to camp this summer, where she would swim and learn how to trot on a horse, but she flat-out refused.

"Now, before dawn, she runs through our neighborhood, to the fire road, and keeps going. She's eight. It's not normal at that age to be running seven miles a day. And no matter what we do, we can't stop her. If we try to stop her, she starts screaming, so we let her go, then follow at a distance in the car. Usually it's Steve who does that, makes sure she's safe."

Roma pictured the little girl waking, dressing quickly, sneaking through the quiet house to the front door, carefully turning the locks, slipping out into air that had cooled overnight. So young, but needing to run, perhaps without any idea of why, running in the early-morning dark until light infused the sky.

"In the beginning," Jeanine continued, "she'd come in all red and sweaty, and I'd be making her breakfast and tell her to sit down at the kitchen table. And she would, but she'd keep her mouth tight and turn away from the eggs and bacon or oatmeal I'd serve her. I went out and bought sugary cereals and donuts, but nothing. And last week, when I said, 'Honey, you must drink enough water. You're running so much and we live in the desert, it's a hundred and ten and a body needs hydration,' she smacked the water glass I'd filled out of my hand. Then every time I offered her water or fruit juice or even the soft drink she used to beg me to buy and I never would, she'd smack the glass out of my hand. Glass everywhere on the kitchen floor. So I went out and bought plastic and I keep trying to get her to drink, but she won't. All day long I'm spying on my child, to see if she's drunk something or eaten something without me noticing. Hoping and hoping. I'm checking if glasses are wet. I'm counting the pieces of bread left in the loaf, crackers in the plastic sleeves, cookies in the boxes, slices of American cheese in the fridge, fruit in the crisper; I even counted the Fritos in the bag, but she's not touching a thing."

Roma met with the girl every afternoon this week, two hours each time. It is the immersive approach she prefers with a case that has developed this swiftly, to see if she can get to the essence quickly.

The questions in Noelani's case are: What has speeded this child up? Why is she running so far and so fast? Is there something monstrous she is trying to outrace, and if so, is that monstrous thing within or without? And how is a child so young overriding her natural hunger, imposing on herself an iron-willed discipline at which most adults fail?

Roma has seen elements of this many times over decades in practice, and the causes rarely reveal themselves easily. Noelani is not the youngest patient Roma has had with these symptoms, but what worked with her other patients will have no bearing here. Roma must start at the beginning, treat Noelani as she treats every patient, as the sui generis beings that they are.

When Roma asked if Noelani had any other new and uncharacteristic behaviors, Jeanine began to cry. "She lies about everything. I ask her, 'Have you brushed your teeth?' or 'Did you make your bed?' or 'Did you feed your goldfish?' and she says yes to everything, but it never turns out to be true. She lies about things that are verifiable as untrue with one glance, which Steve and I can't understand."

Naturally, the parents are scared and shaken. The cherished daughter they knew, whom they tucked into bed and kissed each night and roused in the morning with hugs, has disappeared entirely, as if she never were.

Everything Jeanine spoke about, Roma has seen in her meetings with Noelani, but she has also seen more. In addition to the girl's obsessions with running and denying herself food and liquid, she has also seen in her anxiety, anger, and impulse control.

In yesterday's session, their fifth, Roma was tough, clarifying that if Noelani does not immediately start eating and drinking, she will be hospitalized, sustaining fluids forced into her through a tube in her stomach. Roma pulled out a medical book with pictures of children in hospital beds with tubes jutting into their bellies. She pulled out from a box on her desk the medical equipment that would be used to invade Noelani's body in that way. The impact Roma had intended to create was deliberate, and there it was—the young face soon covered in sprung tears, snot dripping from the little nose. But Noelani had not given in immediately. Thirty minutes discussing the only outcome had been required before Roma was able to wring out a promise, Noelani writing her name in blocky letters on the bottom of the food plan she agreed to maintain through the weekend. Together they had chosen what she would eat: a banana and yogurt for breakfast; a tuna fish sandwich and apple for lunch; salad, chicken, and rice for dinner; and each day she would drink five glasses of water.

"Just the weekend," Roma had said, "that's all you need to promise me now." And the crying girl, her thin forearms laced with trails of mucus, had carried the handwritten food plan flat on her palms, as if it were an offering on fire, holding it out to her mother in the waiting room, who leaned forward in her chair, her cheeks as tearstained as her daughter's, until the two were face-to-face. Noelani has her mother's pretty features, although it will take a few more years for those features to fully emerge, arrange themselves on her face. But where the mother was nicely proportioned, the daughter was gaunt, nearly emaciated, and Roma was certain that Noelani has been running for far longer than only the month the parents believe it has been.

Noelani had tried smiling, a brave barely there smile, and waited for her mother to open the outer door to the parking lot, and then she was taking careful steps to their car. Jeanine had turned to Roma and said, "What now?"

"Make sure she follows the plan. She'll cry, but remind her she promised. And though she won't grasp this completely, explain she made this promise to herself, not to me or to you."

Jeanine nodded and Roma said, "Leave me a few messages over the weekend, to let me know how it's going. Remember, Jeanine, she chose those meals for herself, so give her only those meals, exactly. Of course, you and your husband, one or the other or both, will have to stand guard to make sure she eats."

Jeanine nodded again, glancing out at Noelani, still crying copious tears, her careful steps replaced by a frenzied pacing around and around the car.

"What about the running?"

"We have to figure out what the running means to her before we can alter the behavior."

"And the lying?"

"Health first," Roma said.

It had taken Jeanine McCadden so much effort to extricate her car from its tight spot, backing in, backing out, turning the steering wheel every which way, that the car seemed to be heaving, as if mimicking the tears of its unhappy cargo inside, and Roma watched until Jeanine finally broke the car free, gave her a sad little wave, and joined the quick flow of late Friday afternoon traffic.

This morning, Roma debates the odds of mother and father having the courage to keep to the plan, of Jeanine leaving the updates she requested on her office or personal voicemail. Impossible to determine, but their actions or inactions will provide her with additional information: a child's issues are rarely isolated, there is nearly always some sort of tangential cause and effect, and whatever Roma is dealing with here, with Noelani, she likely will have to address the parents' problems as well.

She rolls onto her side, stares through the gap in the drapes, at the sun spreading across the marble floor, over her body beneath the light duvet. It is Saturday, her work week finished, the morning hours hers alone. By noon, everyone will be here. Phoebe and Simon and his family arriving separately from Los Angeles, Camille from Seattle. Her family all together to celebrate the accomplishments of husband and father. She wishes she had seen Harry this morning, to kiss him, to tell him how proud she is about this honor being conferred upon him tonight. How proud that he righted his ways back then, unwound his wrongs, moved again into the light. They have never discussed that time, but this morning, she would have liked to tell him what an inspiration he is, how she marvels at his devotion to his indispensable work, the magnanimity with which he gives himself fully to everyone who needs him and to those who love him.

Noelani returns to her mind, and then Phoebe pops in. As a psychologist, Roma is used to these jumps in her thoughts, aware there is always a logic to the unconscious leaps she makes, and she considers the connection between her eight-year-old patient and her thirty-eight-year-old daughter, her eldest.

On the phone yesterday, Roma asked whether Phoebe will be bringing the new boyfriend with whom she has been taking long weekend trips since February. No one has met Aaron Green yet, not even Simon, who checks in on Phoebe's cat when this man whisks her away to the Outer Banks, to Santa Fe and Aspen and Nashville, to La Jolla and Catalina and Big Sur; last weekend's trip was to the wine country up north.

From Phoebe's descriptions, Aaron Green sounds like a paragon, but yesterday, her daughter had not been able to answer Roma's question head-on, hemming and hawing, saying only that "Aaron's hoping to be able to move some things around to free up his schedule." And Roma was quickly concerned that Phoebe has again fallen in love with the wrong man, and that the qualities this Aaron Green supposedly possesses might be colored by Phoebe's desperate desire to have a family.

Roma sighs. Oh, yes, she sees the connection now between Noelani and Phoebe. The lying the little girl is engaging in, the subterfuge Phoebe once used as a shield. Is that subterfuge, at odds with Phoebe's otherwise straightforward nature, returning? Over a man named Aaron Green?

Fifteen years since the last time, since Simon's high school graduation party, when Phoebe brought home a boy she insisted on calling her paramour. How irritated she had been with Phoebe's use of that archaic word, her refusal to employ simple language to explain the facts, her preference for befuddling. All Roma had wanted to know was whether her driven daughter was having a romance that involved physical intimacies. How she had hoped for that until meeting the paramour, the boy Roma nicknamed "the prophet," because he was actually named Elijah and seemed to have knocked Phoebe off her feet, her daughter taking Roma aside all that weekend and raising questions about the way she was living her life. She had decided to be a lawyer when she was in high school, would begin her third year of law school that fall, wanted the big firm experience after passing the bar, but, Phoebe had cried to Roma, weren't her accomplishments meaningless, her desire for her routines, her nice apartment, her pretty things wrong and shameful, her need to have everything mapped out insane?

Roma had said, "Phoebe, *we're* proud of all you've accomplished by this tender age of twenty-three, but if you're not, or if you want something different, you can always explore un-mapping yourself." By which Roma meant, *Investigate other avenues that might interest you, try being spontaneous, cull your belongings and give all that bounty to charity.*

Instead, some months later, Phoebe had nearly quit everything and run off with the prophet. In the end, at the last minute, she had pulled back and raced to the safety of home, had opened up to Roma completely, had told her mother that the love she had for Elijah had to be cut out of her heart or she would end up becoming someone she was not.

Roma sighs again. In a few hours either Phoebe will be here with Aaron Green, introducing him to her family, or she'll be here on her own. And if she is here on her own, Roma will carve out time to sit alone with Phoebe, to apply her professional expertise to her own child gently, always gently, in order to expose the truth.

It is true a mother feels something more, or different, or extra-special for her firstborn, but as a psychologist, she knows the importance of keeping things fair among siblings, and she's lucky—that touchstone word again—because her children, uniquely different, are easy to equally love.

Camille, her social anthropologist middle child, is perfectly defined by her profession, which employs flat research language and mathematical statistics to disguise its romantic and obsessive nature, and the romantically obsessive nature of those bitten by the need to explore. She was thirteen when she decided she wanted to live with tribes she could study, and she accomplished that goal, spending two years living far away, on islands in an archipelago of coral atolls off the east coast of New Guinea.

Camille will be coming alone this weekend, as always, infrequently talking about someone named Valentine. Maybe this visit Roma will ask Camille directly who Valentine is to her, what is the nature of this unexplained relationship, why she never identifies Valentine by gender. In Roma's experience with troubled children, those who are also gay and have not yet declared themselves often have a difficult time voicing the particulars of the person who has captured their attention. "They are so cool. They are really nice," is what they say to her. A conundrum her daughter has solved by always referring to Valentine as Valentine or Val. If she has ever referred to Valentine as *he* or *she*, Roma somehow missed it, which strikes her as entirely unlikely.

If it's a lesbian love relationship, it would confirm the supposition Roma's held in her heart. With her patients, Roma doesn't trade in suppositions, she asks them questions outright, knowing she will have to dig for the truth, but with Camille, a keeper of her own counsel since childhood, who even then averted her mother's deliberately casual prying with a wise smile, Roma's always had to be wary of even asking the questions, of horning in on the mental space her daughter refuses to share, of violating her fierce and innate sense of privacy. Thousands of patients and their parents have entrusted her with their secrets and fears, but not this daughter of hers.

Where Phoebe explored clothing and makeup, Camille only

explored when coerced by Phoebe. Even today, her external appearance does not command much of her attention; she's lucky in her natural beauty, somehow not tamped down by the baggy, old clothes she wears, by her refusal, most of the time, to use lipstick or mascara, a blush to brighten her cheeks.

Where Phoebe had boyfriends, Camille had friends who were boys. Roma has no idea who Camille dated in college, in graduate school, in her PhD program, or if she dated at all. Girls, boys, those who prefer the personal pronoun of *them* and *their*, or *s/he* and *he/r*, the intersex, the third gender, the transgendered—truly Roma does not care, nor would Harry, if Camille is gay, bisexual, pansexual, demisexual, or asexual. What she cares about is how Camille gates her inner life with Roma outside.

When her daughter's little-girl desire for a penis of her own did not abate, as such desire usually does, she'd wondered for the first time about Camille's sexual orientation. And then Camille convinced another little girl to remove every stitch of clothing. When Roma found them in Camille's bedroom, Camille's left hand was on the girl's flat chest, her right hand between the girl's thin legs. Roma had seen the Band-Aids on both girls' knees, and wasn't sure whether to laugh or cry, because it might only have been the kind of exploratory game children play. Despite her expertise, she's never been sure.

How old was Camille then? She was eight. Ah, the same age as Noelani.

Her youngest, Simon, worships Harry, is a lawyer like Phoebe, and somehow has become the family outlier. So young when he began college, so adaptable with intellectual heft and high emotional intelligence and the looks of a playboy—Byronic curls, soulful eyes, girls fell under his spell—Roma figured he would play the field for a long while, settle down in his forties. Instead, he is the first of her children to create his own separate family, happily married to Elena Abascal, father of her granddaughters, Lucy and Isabel. Nothing jumps out at Roma when she considers Simon in the context of Noelani, nothing ties them together, except that

Simon has been on a running jag lately, putting in the miles, he says, every morning before work, either running the hills in his neighborhood, or in a foreign park across from his hotel when he's litigating abroad. She's never asked how many miles he runs, but given how often he's out of town, and the way he works late into the nights, it seems unlikely he's running seven miles at a shot.

The clock on her nightstand reads *7:20 a.m.* Roma pulls open the drapes, smiles at the meditation pool, at the brightly colored desert flowers and the shrubs. Harry has his tennis this morning and then a stop at the tailor to pick up the new tuxedo he will wear tonight. He'll be arriving back home just before the kids show up. Everyone will be hungry. She shopped yesterday, has only to put out the spread, but all that can wait. First her hour of laps in the big pool, then coffee.

In the bathroom, she stands naked, inspecting her reflected hair. Fernando did a nice job on the color this time. Last time it was much too light, bold in an odd and punkish way. Over the years she has undergone a slow but steady transformation, from boring, uncommitted brown to lighter and lighter hues, until she gave in, said to Fernando, "I might as well admit life is more fun as a blonde. Let's do the whole head." It wasn't true that life was more fun as a blonde, but she was tired of fighting it, of facing daily the unfairness of her hair transmogrifying into old age long before Harry's. She rubber-bands the honeyed chunks, brushes her teeth, then pulls on her bathing suit. She lifts her cap and goggles from their hook in her closet and shuts the door.

IN THE MAIN COURTYARD, the pool is a sapphire under the sun, shooting liquid rainbows into the house at oblique angles. How she adores submergence. She is a healer of human cracks and fissures, her days spent dealing with her patients' struggles and agonies, the emotional and psychic often embodied in the physical. She uncovers all the states and syndromes that can spark and catch fire from infancy on, searing a being, those flames rarely sputtering out on their own. She works hard quenching the symptoms, providing parents with answers, and the toddlers, children, and teenagers with techniques to manage their frightening infernos, helping them douse the alarming heat and gain interior strength against what is burning them up. Resolutions if the sufferer and loved ones are lucky, cures if kind spirits are shining down, so that as they grow and mature their lives will be happier, sweeter, so that they will be saved from total annihilation. She gives them all of her time, but this hour belongs only to her, swimming with an uncluttered mind, feeling the expectant delight of having everyone together, remembering that however involved she will become with Noelani, she belongs by blood and love to others, and those others, by blood and love, belong to her.

How fortunate she and Harry have been that they and their children have never been afflicted with any kind of serious illness, not physical, emotional, or mental, everyone on their right paths. Closely knit all these years, enjoying being together, genuinely liking one another. Of course, there are the occasional, normal tensions and skirmishes among her children, and sometimes she wishes they didn't force her to read their faces, would simply admit to what's bothering them, but eventually, always, the issue is revealed, and she guides and advises them so judiciously they frequently think they have arrived at the solution on their own.

Head underwater, she holds her breath, then pushes off, stroking strongly to the other side of the long pool. One, two, three . . . fourteen long and solid strokes to reach the wall today before reversing course.

Half of fourteen is seven, and she's thinking of Noelani McCadden's toothpick legs racing her away from home, or toward something. In her session notebook, she had written: *Does the actual mileage hold an unconscious significance for Noelani?* Jeanine McCadden was adamant that her daughter runs exactly seven miles each morning, no more, no less, as if the girl were fitted with an internal mileage counter. Before her first meeting with Noelani,

Roma had researched the number and discovered that in numerology, seven represents the seeker, the thinker, the searcher of Truth who knows nothing is exactly as it seems and is always trying to understand the reality hidden behind the illusions. Roma had realized that definition described herself as well, born on the seventh day of June. And in astrology, seven meant—

No, she is not going to break her promise, no pondering about Noelani, about any of her patients, while swimming.

She will think about . . . She will think about . . . Okay, yes, what sort of sea creature would she be? Not a shark, not a whale. Not a seal. What's the difference between porpoises and dolphins?

Then a mental bolt to that weekend when Phoebe brought home the prophet. She heard moans coming from Phoebe's bedroom, and had breached her daughter's trust, carefully turning the knob, peeking through the crack, almost hoping to find Phoebe tangled naked in bed with that long-haired young philosopher whose pacific calm was threatening upheaval in Phoebe's life, but that's not what had been happening in there. Elijah had been at her daughter's feet, washing them. Between his knees, filled with water and suds, was the irreplaceable silver bowl passed down to Roma from Baba Tatiana.

Roma, she says sternly, silently, *no more, just swim.*

FOUR

ON CAMILLE TABOR'S THIRTEENTH birthday, when her breasts were just budding, her mother gave her a book written by a woman who had journeyed to the South Pacific to discover whether adolescence was a universally traumatic and stressful time, or whether the adolescent experience depended on one's cultural upbringing. Camille, a voracious reader, especially liked stories set in faraway places featuring the kinds of people never seen in Palm Springs.

After she unwrapped the present, her mother said, "A little explanation. The book is a vivid account of Samoan adolescent life and was incredibly popular, although eventually Margaret Mead and her research methods came under harsh attack. She was smack in the middle of a scholarly-scientific wrangling that began in the mid-1920s and has yet to be conclusively determined, the nature-versus-nurture debate. To what extent are human personality and behavior the products of biological factors, like the genetics you've inherited from Daddy and his ancestors and from me and mine, or are products of cultural factors, like where you live, how you're being raised, the school you attend, the music you listen to, the television shows you watch, the friends you have. You are now a teenager and it's important you learn to distinguish between the two so you can make thoughtful decisions from your head, rather than automatic ones, perhaps from your heart, whose underpinnings are harder to understand."

Her mother was a prominent child psychologist and often said to her children, "You can do anything you want if you have thought it through and are capable of articulating your reasoning. In other words, so long as you can show your work."

What Camille had already determined was that she wanted a life that was anything but quotidian, ordinary, middling, mediocre, words she knew and never wanted used to describe the life she would have, the person she would become. At home, she wasn't at all surrounded by the quotidian, but the fear was so deep, she was sure she'd been born with it. Who she would actually be and what she would actually do was all hazy in her head, until she devoured *Coming of Age in Samoa* by the redoubtable Margaret Mead.

She read that birthday book many times, but it was the first reading that set her on her path, when Camille knew she would become a social anthropologist, studying exotic tribes in exotic places, researching their rules of behavior, their interpersonal relations, their views on kinship and marriage, their motivations and ambitions, their language, customs, forms of currency, music, stories, and material creations, their taboos, ethos, moral codes, the nature of their self-governance, their notions and beliefs about the communal world in which they existed, the gods they prayed to, the visions that manifested in their dreams.

By the time she delivered her valedictory speech to her graduating class at Palm Springs High, she had stormed through all the ethnographies, memoirs, autobiographies, collected correspondence, and biographies by and about every female social anthropologist she could find. They became Camille's personal heroines.

She entered the University of Washington, thrilled to be facing a lengthy and arduous education. She thought fortitude should be required to become an expert in the rarest field, so temporally and spatially expansive it touched on everything in the world.

At nineteen, light-years ahead of her fellow collegians who hadn't any idea what interested them, she knew she intended to spend her life in unruly, woolly places beyond the pale, engaged in on-the-ground research, discovering, analyzing, reflecting, and publishing her own important ethnographies, adding to the understanding of humanity.

She was a natural, cruising through the intro and second-level anthropology courses, through biology, statistics, research methods, data analysis, and chose Polynesian as her first foreign language, because of Margaret Mead. She declared her major early, was admitted to the university's highly competitive and selective Anthropology Honors Program, took the 300- and 400-level courses, accomplished her yearlong honors project in ten months, graduated first in her class with a BA.

Then on to her master's, with its first-year core curriculum and evaluation, its second-year sequence of courses in ethnographic methods and research design, and the completion of a research competency paper.

Then on to her PhD, demonstrating her fluency in Polynesian and, by then, also in Abo, a Bantu language spoken in the Moungo department in southwestern Cameroon, and in Kilivila, spoken on the Trobriand Islands. She passed the general exam, acquired training and experience in teaching at the university level, and finally, nearing the summit of the mountain she'd been climbing all those years, the creation of her own research project, which, like her heroines', would birth new ways of understanding one tiny world, and, through extrapolation, the great big one.

It did not affect her that her friends, colleagues, and siblings, scholarship completed, had begun making serious salaries, were renting large and lovely apartments, acquiring the trappings of burgeoning achievement, because no matter what they accomplished, their lives were known, while hers would always be of breathtaking mystery, and that was the barometer by which she measured her personal success. The university gave her a stipend for teaching. Her tiny apartment, where she'd been since her junior undergraduate year, had an aura of impermanent student lodging warmed up with walls she frequently repainted in cheery colors, and, doing her part to reduce the rampant waste of fickle people, she filled with discarded furniture that was perfectly usable, stenciling on quaint polka dots and stripes when her brain required a break. It was home with a very small *h* and all that she needed.

And new in her life then was Valentine Osin, her Russian-Jewish lover, the two of them burning for each other from the first moment they met at the university's omni-anthropology cocktail party for doctoral candidates. She had never before been so spontaneously attracted to a man, and never to a man who was all heavy beard and worn denim. But there was an intensity between them she had never experienced, and never thought of denying. She'd had bad luck dating nonanthropologists, and that Valentine Osin was a physical anthropologist of the Leakey variety only further increased his mammoth appeal.

That he was Jewish was irrelevant—she didn't believe in any of it—she was sold, instead, by his accent, trimmed away and smoothed over, but retaining the hint of otherness she preferred, and by his upbringing in a town on the outskirts of a forest, and by their deep conversations, and by their impassioned sex, his swiftness, his directness, the way he could shake her up with the slightest touch, the way he stared at her as if she were a greater achievement than his eventually winning the Charles R. Darwin Lifetime Award. They were equally matched, in restless and driven natures, the desire to live unparalleled lives.

Their insistent love was only six months old when she began thinking about where she would go for her doctoral research. Her heart had pounded and her fingers had trembled when she pulled from the pages of *Coming of Age in Samoa*, the list she had maintained since the age of thirteen, of tribes who dwelled in untamed places. A precious list she had amended and revised, that grew smudged and torn, that reflected changes in her handwriting, the list from which she would find a people she could call her own for a while, in a place where she would put down temporary roots.

She quickly crossed out the isolated Amazon tribes. Interaction with them, the study of them, was prohibited by non-engagement policies at last put into place, to preserve their isolation and their lands; a safeguarding with the dual purpose of resisting further exploitative encroachments into the rainforest and protecting it for the environmental health of the entire planet.

But there was serious anxiety when she began crossing out contactable tribes already claimed by others.

Then near panic, until she found the name of one virginal tribe she had scribbled in pencil: the Sentineli, a Stone Age tribe on the Andaman Islands, in an archipelago in the Bay of Bengal, between India and Myanmar.

In the anthro library, she found scant research on them, which impelled her hope. All she could learn was that they were an uncontacted people who spoke an unclassified language, who used arrows for hunting, harpoons for fishing, and untipped javelins for shooting at those who dared to encroach. They had been fending off researchers since 1880, and although they weren't necessarily cannibals, they did often display heads on warning stakes. She imagined herself the first social anthropologist to befriend that protective hunter-gatherer tribe, the first to learn their unclassified language, to capture that language in what would become the seminal Sentineli dictionary.

She wrote up her findings, her intentions, the ethical and methodologically sound research she would perform in the Andaman Islands, but when her adviser, Dr. Jin, saw *Sentineli* on the cover he said, "I was hoping you wouldn't alight on them. I don't need to read anything else. The answer is absolutely not. The tribe has been classified not merely as uncontacted, but as uncontactable and too dangerous. The Indian government would likely refuse you a permit for those reasons. Choose another tribe, in another place."

She had called Valentine, and he was sympathetic, but the frequent futility of his work, of physical anthropology itself, eliminated his ability to understand that this was the first time she was experiencing such futility. She'd hung up, heartbroken to find herself in the wrong era. In the 1800s and early 1900s, when her heroines were out in the field, dozens of untouched tribes in unexplored locales were up for grabs. But in the hypermodern twenty-first century, with travel to remote places standard and Google mapping uncovering the most distant rock, there was no accessible tribe left whose existence had not already been the subject of cogent boots-on-the-ground participant observation, and somehow she, who missed nothing, had missed this cardinal piece of intelligence.

When she'd worn herself out crying bitterly, she searched her shelves for one of the books written by the lambent creator of modern social anthropology. Published in 1929, the title had a patronizing hegemonic tone that nonetheless encouraged one's prurient curiosity to see what was inside. Of course, she knew what was inside, but she sat upright on her frayed old couch and read Bronislaw Malinowski's *The Sexual Life of Savages* again, first page to last, as the hot pot of coffee by her side cooled to mud.

When she finished, she thought: So she would not be the first explorer on the Trobriand Islands. So she would not be following in any of the footsteps of those women responsible for directing her life path, but rather in *the* man's, in Malinowski's, who had established the imperative of researching a tribe, not from comfortable university library chairs, but out in the field with the people one was studying, engaging in their community, eating their food, taking part in their everyday lives, and she decided that wouldn't be so bad, not at all. (She wouldn't have admitted to her staunchly feminist friends that there was something appealing about following a pseudo father figure.) Plus, she already spoke Kilivila.

Malinowski had done all the heavy lifting there, but she would go anyway to those seemingly very happy islands in Melanesia, where sex reigned, and if luck was with her she would add to the knowledge about them her own penetrating and revelatory findings, hopefully as groundbreaking as his.

Which is what she did: two years in the Trobriand Islands, researching every aspect of the Trobrianders' lives and how those lives had been altered and impacted by the researchers who had come before her. Then fourteen months writing her dissertation, working at the anthro library, eating dinners and having sex with Valentine. Physically, she was in Seattle, but mentally, emotionally, spiritually, and psychically, she remained in Melanesia, carrying with her the Trobrianders' vibrancy, their lust for life, who *she* was there, doing the work she relished. And then she had gone topsy-turvy, crashing hard the very afternoon she successfully defended her work. After the kudos, and the back pats, and the champagne toasts with Dr. Jin and the oral-defense examiners, she walked home through campus, seeing the late-summer colors bleeding away, the greens and golds turning pale, then transparent, and by the time she reached her apartment, her life force was gone. She was no longer the Camille she had always been.

Months passed in which her bed became her safe place, her bedroom a cave, the blinds shuttered to hide the cheeriness of the walls, the phone ringing and ringing, the messages piling up and never returned, Valentine bringing her soup, singing to her, leaving reluctantly when she did not respond to his words, to his overtures, and his patience was worn. Then in late December a knock on her door, and Dr. Jin was standing there. "So you're here, Camille. I've sent you dozens of emails, left you numerous phone messages. I thought maybe you were away on a long holiday and hadn't let me know. Then I ran into Dr. Osin and he told me what's been going on. Dress and come to my office."

She managed to shower, to wash her matted hair, then stared at herself in the mirror. Her eyes were cloudy and red-rimmed, and how weird that she'd forgotten their light hazel hue. She was the only one in the family without dark, darker, or darkest brown eyes, and her father used to tease her, calling her "Witch Hazel." She'd hated that nickname as a kid, like glass shattering inside, but looking into her eyes, she finally understood what he'd been trying to teach her: that humor could coexist with seriousness, that she had needed to find the humor in herself even at that young age. She could hear him saying, "Come on, Witch Hazel, smile," and she tried smiling at her reflection, but it was impossible. Still, with her father closer to her heart, it was a little easier to pull on dusty jeans and a wrinkled shirt and, under cover of a large orange umbrella, make her way in teeming rain to Dr. Jin's office on campus.

"Sit," Dr. Jin had said, handing her a fragile cup of green tea. "This happens to the most committed social anthropologists. Your world in the Trobriand Islands, kept alive through all the work on your dissertation, it's still more real to you than this one, isn't it?"

She had nodded.

"I know how difficult it can be to reenter one's former life. I wish I had an instant fix for you. Sadly, there aren't any assistant professorships available right now. I could make a few calls, to *American Anthropologist, Anthropological Quarterly, Cultural Anthropology, Ethnology, Oceania*, see whether they have a rare vacancy. I haven't heard of any, but I'm happy to double-check."

She had shaken her head slowly because it hurt to make abrupt moves in the brightness of his clean office. "Dr. Jin, I think I just need another expedition, to be back out there. Is there a new one I could join? I don't have to lead it, just be a team member."

It had been Dr. Jin's turn to shake his head. "No university-funded expeditions here or anywhere for the next two years. But even if there was, based on what Val Osin tells me, months barely functioning, you wouldn't pass the psych eval right now.

"Here's a way you could retrench. Return to the Trobriands by diving back into your dissertation. Take yourself to the library and try turning it into a book. Not a study that, alas, few will read these days, but something for a broad audience. There are publishers who would be interested in exciting nonfiction based on the real-life adventures of a young and interesting scientist. I know a few. When you're ready, I could reach out to them on your behalf.

"It has real potential, Camille, a young woman who investigated the sexual practices of other young women living in a very different society. It's been a long time since Malinowski's *Savages*, and other than refuted Mead, with the adolescent Samoans, never investigated by a woman."

"I was more intrigued by other aspects I researched," she'd said, the words falling from her mouth one by one, and Dr. Jin nodded repeatedly. "Yes, of course. And I understand. But times are different now, not much call for ethnographies. And it's very disappointing, but sex sells. From what I've been told, it also greatly helps if the young and interesting scientist is actually *in* the book."

A nod was the most she could muster. She placed the fragile cup of untouched green tea on his uncluttered desk and left. The rain was still teeming, but the umbrella remained rolled up tight by her side. She had no energy for any project, but an exploitive tale about the Trobrianders and sex, with herself as a character? It was exactly what she couldn't do: replace the wildness of the Trobriand Islands with an airless library, reduce her vibrant experiences into a trite narrative, massage that extraordinary time—the raucous freedom, the exploration of others, the bonding with people so unlike herself—into something so frivolous.

When she reached home, she was soaked through, more hopeless than before.

Since that meeting with Jin, she hasn't so much as glanced at her dissertation, seven hundred pages of text, another two hundred of graphs, statistics, citations, and sources, thick as a tombstone gathering dust on her kitchen table. In fact, she doesn't even notice it anymore, when she drops her keys next to it, or sits down to eat a quick meal.

Although never one to ask for help, when her depression did not lift, she took herself to the university counseling office. The counselor-in-training was useless, said only, "Wow, so you lived among natives, wild. Must be great to be back in the real world," then adjusted her necklace. Camille didn't bother seeking out a different counselor. She had no confidence anyone else would understand her nature more clearly and felt only exhaustion thinking about repeating her story again, explaining all the reasons why that other world remained realer to her than this one—the Trobrianders' love for one another, their ties to the earth and the sky, their belief in rituals and magic. She decided to nurture herself with long walks every day, and applauded herself when she managed to do so sometimes.

On the last day of last year, on one of those walks, she stopped at a row of free-paper kiosks and took one she'd not read before. At home on the old couch, she flipped through it and came to a picture and article about the House of Lilac Love. She recognized the pretty lilac-painted building, not far from her apartment, but would never have guessed it was a hospice. As she read about the people cared for there, she imagined them as a tribe of the dying, and a minute amount of her vanished strength made itself known, enough to pick up the phone and inquire whether any jobs were available.

It had felt odd interviewing for a job that didn't include discussions about prior tribe contact, what the research hoped to reveal, the term of the expedition, housing accommodations, shots required for travel, but there was Patty Donaldson, the head of Lilac Love, who looked to Camille like a highly experienced team leader. She had army hair, a crew cut strictly maintained, gigantic hoops in her ears, an easy laugh. Her bulk was crammed into a well-tailored Day-Glo lime-green pantsuit, and when she shook Camille's hand, she said, "I like to be a splash of color for everyone. Now let's talk about you," and then exclaimed over Camille's background, her experience in fieldwork, expressing veneration for her accomplishments, and her certainty that someone highly trained in dedicated listening would be a great addition. With Patty's unceasing, honest smile aimed directly at her, Camille had felt the slightest renewing of what once had been her natural optimism.

Since January, for the last seven and a half months, she has been working as an end-of-life caregiver at Lilac Love. It is a job for which she needed no formal training: she does not insert needles into veins, or clear phlegm from throats, or dispense morphine, or arrange and empty bedpans. There are compassionate nurses for all of those tasks, selfless women who sail through the place like loving spirits. Now, five or six days a week, Camille wakes early, showers, dresses in clean and pressed clothes, fills up her thermos with her special coffee blend, makes a sack lunch, and walks to the hospice, to sit by bedsides, to ask questions that encourage exhausted tongues to recount their owners' stories, to write dictated letters to family and friends, sometimes loving letters, sometimes letters filled with angst, sometimes letters filled with vituperative hatred aimed like poison-tipped darts at their intended recipients—as sharp, surely, as those arrows the Stone Age Sentineli carried and Dr. Jin prevented her from viewing up close. She can honestly say she feels most at home in that small, vertical palace where futures are preordained.

When she has tried to explain this inexplicable shift in her focus to Valentine, his inquisition leaves her shrugging her shoulders, and he, increasingly frustrated by her curious new inability to express herself in terms he can understand, says, "Yes, yes, I know, the Trobrianders sucked all the life right out of you, but you've got to pull it together. And what I don't understand is your new fascination with death."

To Valentine, death has no immediacy; it has been reduced to the examination of skeletons, the unlocking of genes, the analyzing of migratory patterns, and dust. His pursuit of the dead shares nothing with her experiences, the way the process of death has parameters, permutations, crosses enigmatic boundaries. That they view death differently did not bother her, but his admonishment hurt, because the funny thing was, she thought she was starting to pull it together. That the desolate period of her life, ragged and ugly, the very definition of quotidian before she started at Lilac Love, was tapering off. She's no longer in the trough of the black depression into which she sank; the blackness is fading into a pallid gray, the depression softening into a lassitude, although when she's home by herself it reverts to inertia. It is too soon, she knows, to figure out how to resume her prior life; she still can't imagine how she once possessed such gargantuan dreams, such energy.

But she's awake every morning, sometimes before the alarm, interested in where she is going, and there is something so restful about being among the dying. Not those who are still denying, or angry, or bargaining, or depressed—the first four stages of Kübler-Ross's American model for death and dying, which she has now learned all about—but those who have reached the fifth and last stage, acceptance. Those people, who have accepted their outcome, are extraordinary. They aren't at all what she expected. She thought she'd find them huddled up to their gods, worn or new Bibles close by, and she, a disbeliever, would have nothing to say to them, would be unable to find common ground. A few do hang onto old remnants, but most have no atavistic reliance on religion, have cast away what they might have been taught in childhood, despite the crosses or Jewish stars hanging around old necks, lost beneath heavy drifts of wrinkles. Few prayers are uttered; they have left behind the realm of hope, seek no last-minute godly redemptions, no heightened revelations, are instead most interested in assessing all those years in which they put on their faces and their suits and braved the act of living. Had they lived? Truly lived? Lived enough? "*No*," they say, it is never enough, but no god is going to set things right at this late date. "Don't waste time on any of that nonsense," they tell her repeatedly. "I won't," she says.

But it's more complex than that. Her unbelieving is giving way to a belief in all the variants of the holy, those she learned from her anthropological studies, those she observed in the Trobriand Islands, those she's apprehending in these rooms listening to the multitude of ways in which these men and women found their own higher meaning in the physical and emotional world.

Those closest to death and still sensate pay scrupulous attention to schedules being precisely maintained. Breakfast at seven, lunch at twelve, dinner at five. No matter their lack of appetites, no matter if they slumber through mealtimes, they want those trays in their rooms, visible confirmation upon awakening of their continuing existence. Sometimes that small proof of life is all it takes to bring a slight smile to their faces, though often the slight smile is rictus in nature. Those lucky to have more time ahead of them are resisting the natural inclination to retreat into insularity, are instead expanding their horizons, insisting on being bundled up and wheeled down to the kitchen to watch the cook bake a delicacy that might taste in their mouths like their own Proustian madeleine, regardless that they can barely manage a second bite. One man has hired a college student to teach him to play chess, a game he once refused to learn because his father had been a competitive player. A woman has taken up knitting, despite fingers petrified by age and rheumatoid arthritis, the most minor of her afflictions. Wherever they fall on the incline toward death, they share a surprising stoicism. The nature of the stoicism ranges, but has a common denominator: an undistinguished day is welcomed, even if in their prior lives they would have bucked against such dullness. Religion for them is now art and music, gazing through dimming eyes at reproductions in heavy books, listening with fading hearing to love songs, operas, symphonies, Neil Young, Barbra Streisand, the Rolling Stones, even Metallica; one old gentleman requires fifteen minutes a day of what he calls his "nerve-settling polka music," which unsettles everyone else.

Most of them have become humanists, without calling themselves such, nearly evangelical in extolling its creed about the value and agency, individually and collectively, of human beings, advising her to waste no time worrying about the end. The end is irrelevant, it only matters what came before, during all those days when they lacked sufficient awareness of their own freedom and progress, when they were fully, but perhaps ungratefully, alive. She is grasping it all. And their need of her, the way they attempt to raise themselves a little higher on their pillows when she steps through their doors, has provided her with a modicum of the purpose she felt in the Trobriand Islands.

Sitting with them, talking with them, hearing all that they want to say, allowing herself to be the surrogate for those they once loved, for those who preceded them in death, for those who have disappeared, or abandoned them, or are too far away, or busy, or disinterested, to make their way to Lilac Love, to enter one of these quiet rooms, to hold a translucent hand that reveals its thinned blue veins, its age spots, its bird-fragile bones, its spasms—to give comfort and succor as once, surely, the fragile people shriveling away in their neatly made beds gave comfort and succor to them. Being present with the dying is a powerful draw. She is not out in the field, but she has a seat at the edge of eternal space. And it's helping her.

She has submitted an application to the Peace Corps, selecting Nepal, Peru, Vanuatu, Mongolia, and Burkina Faso as places where she would be interested in serving, because imagining herself exploring the world again helps lift the heaviness; it's what she needs to hold onto. She felt proactive executing the paperwork for this potential alternative, which could eliminate waiting two years for the next expedition. It also had the unpleasant effect of reinforcing her current unsteadiness—never before would she have doubted the security of her place on any expedition, but she was questioning herself so much that she could no longer presume her luck was not already broken. She hasn't mentioned the Peace Corps to her family or to Valentine. She tells herself it's because she hasn't yet been accepted, but the truth is, even if she's accepted, she's been thinking she's not ready to go, is far from full strength, needs more time at this final station before death, with its eschatological light, and the personal trinkets on bureaus like lucky charms overseeing what everyone hopes will be a painless transition to whatever is on the other side. Although they take nothing from their old religions, what remains is the contradictory notion that on the other side there might be some unearthly bliss.

In spite of her own state, being at Lilac Love is providing Camille with a palliative kind of earthbound bliss.

But there are bad nights when it is difficult to shake the belief that she is losing, has already lost substantial ground, in the race of life. Everyone else is moving forward, moving up, growing up. Actually, they've grown up. They have spouses and life partners. They have kids, are having kids, are actively thinking about having kids, or are already fearing they've left it too long, going for checkups and tests to determine sperm motility, egg viability. They have capital-H homes, with great aesthetics, and original art on the walls. They have window washers, housekeepers, nannies, personal trainers, and sometimes chefs. They have mutual funds and 401(k)s and stock portfolios, vacations booked in advance, clothes for every conceivable occasion. And yet lately, when she forces herself to go to a cocktail or dinner party, the favorite conversational topic is about giving everything up. These discussions, in which Camille does not participate, go on for hours while everyone drinks artisanal vodka and small-batch IPAs and eats complicated catered food.

Last week, at another such gathering, Camille listened again to her friends pronouncing they would pare down to the basics, live in some uninhabited place. They made suggestions to one another and promises and began drawing up plans. The flying rhetoric had set those friends aflame, but demonstrated only their ignorance.

She had pictured herself holding up a hand to end the inane conversation, saying: "Look at me. Look at Camille Tabor, your friend. I am a PhD. I have studied hard and done serious fieldwork. I have been named an up-and-comer in my profession, of which only a few make it to the top, which I am expected to reach. I have led a research expedition to the Trobriand Islands. I managed half a million dollars for that expedition. I did groundbreaking research there and wrote a massive dissertation deemed phenomenal. And to accomplish all of that, I have given up so much. It's demanding, consuming work, and this life of mine does not lead naturally to riches. I understand, it was my choice, but trust me, I'd like the financial freedom you take for granted. You're all pretending to pine for some nonmaterialistic, Waldenesque life, but here are the facts: none of you know what you're talking about. None of you would do well outside of your comfort zones, without your possessions. If you were really interested in a life off the grid, you would have interrogated me about my years in the Trobriands. I'm the only one whose career ensures I will live, have already lived, the very existence you now say you want. And yet you asked me nothing about the Trobrianders, about what life there is really like. If you had, I would have told you that they have a different outlook on sex, and on families, and subscribe to a collective notion of cohabitation, rather than the isolation you all expect and prefer. And they have spirits, and commune with the natural world in a way that has

nothing to do with your gardeners planting rows of organic vegetables for you to pluck and wash and show off. Gardeners you
plan to bring to your Walden when you chuck everything. Instead, you asked me the flying time to the Trobriands, and what
months are the high season, and if AmEx is accepted there? So
stop your silly bellyaching, your insulting chatter about how your
lives would be so much better if you didn't want private schools
for your children and the getaway home on one of the San Juans.
Admit you like your easy and luxurious existences in this world
you've conquered with your own drive and ambition."

Of course, she didn't say any of that.

She hasn't always judged so harshly; she knows she was lucky
growing up as she did, with loving parents and few worries, but in
her fluctuating despair, it struck her as particularly unfair that these
friends had never been halted, as she was now. And that they believed in the value of their stupid utterances, while Dr. Jin had
suggested that the purely social anthropological ramifications
of her work on those islands might not be of great interest. This
world, with its inventions and advances, would always dominate,
she understood that. But there was enormous value in exploring
her preferred worlds, which offered solutions that would allow
everyone, not only those topping the pyramid, to cohabit happily
on this planet; solutions embedded in the concept of the greater
good. Being among these people she once liked, she was outraged
by their obliviousness, and the false, transitory abandonment of
their avariciousness. They might think they wanted to be somewhere far away, but their gazes stopped at the gates of their affluent
existences.

She had refilled her glass with the expensive vodka she only
drinks at these parties, and debated whether to move back to Melanesia. If she wasn't there under the color of official research, she
would really be living there. And that meant a life trading what you
don't need for what you do—which she greatly admires—or, if you
had nothing that anyone wanted, you acquired what you needed
by paying for it with bundles of dried banana leaves. She'd be on a

Trobriand beach for the rest of her life, wearing a grass skirt on festival days, engaging in intriguing rites and rituals, and creating her own banana-leaf wealth—which she knew she could do—but banana-leaf wealth wasn't exchangeable for currency accepted anywhere other than on those islands. She wouldn't be able to explore all the other tribes she wanted to meet in their distant locales or make her way home to see her parents and sister and brother and nieces. If she returned to Melanesia, she'd be as stuck there as she was here, a difference only between the literal and the metaphoric. Stuck is stuck, wherever you may be.

She'd left that cocktail party buzzed, and angry with herself. With the depression that had flattened her and twisted her out of her life. With Valentine heading to a dig in South Africa, led by a famous physical anthropologist who had found very old bones in a system of caves. She'd seen him off at SeaTac earlier that day, and he was up in the sky on his way to a cave in a valley next to a mountain next to a river in the Cradle of Humankind, drafting the first of the several emails he's now sent her, all iterating the same thing—*Camille, to be clear, we are not taking a break. I say this with love, but you are too young to be spending your days with the dying. Don't you want us to be happy, to live a happy life together?*—while she was unsteadily heading for her front door, thinking that unlike her friends, her colleagues, her older sister, she wasn't sure about marriage or children, and those were the topics Valentine was talking about before he jetted away. Wanting her to marry him, wanting them to have children, for her to bear tiny versions of themselves. She couldn't imagine any of it, not with her life turned so juvenile. She couldn't see herself with a husband, a mate, a partner. Couldn't envision herself with children who would perhaps have her witch hazel eyes, Valentine's philosophical spirit, their shared hunger for lives filled with the rigorousness of novel experiences. If she were twenty or younger, her mother would have penetrating insights and suggestions Camille could put into effect to unravel her depression, her confusion, but she had never asked before, and at thirty-six, she's aged beyond her mother's vaunted professional expertise.

And yet that party was days ago, and what is she doing right now?

She's heading home to Palm Springs, where she could get some familial, or maternal, or psychological help figuring out how to re-claim her life. She couldn't bear if that life was now closed to her, if she never regained her strength, her tenacity.

She's thinking about all of this as she wheels her small bag from her ground-floor room, down the sidewalk, and into the lobby of the motel in San Luis Obispo, where she spent last night. Her sleep was restless and she needs coffee, and there on the laminated table sit urns of French Roast, Decaf, Hot Water, tiny tubs of dried creamers and sweetener packets, baskets of tea bags and hot cocoa packets, a tray of lopsided Danish, a stack of napkins several inches high. The purported breakfast free with a night's stay.

She's alone, the kid at the front desk busy putting keycards for the rooms into their slots, and then the glass doors spring open, and a clutch of elderly women bustles in, sporting backpacks and fanny packs, sensible walking shoes and sticks. Eight of them, bare-faced and wrinkled and happy, talking and laughing, pouring their coffees, dunking their tea bags, splitting Danish, debating whether the day's expedition should be to the Santa Lucia Range, or the La Panza Mountains, or the Montaña de Oro State Park. Maybe it's their age and their brusque warmth that reminds Camille of her heroines.

She nods and smiles and says, "Morning," to the old happy women, and the old happy women nod and smile and say, "Morn-ing," to her.

She takes it as an encouraging sign, her default into researcher mode, wanting to ask them how they've all come together, what bonds they share, where they hail from, who the leader is, who the followers, what this trip signifies, but she doesn't. She'd sound crazy to them, and so she refills her large Styrofoam cup, secures the lid, and pushes out through the lobby doors, into the already-warm air at seven twenty in the morning.

She unlocks her car, new when it was her college graduation

present, slips the cup into its holder, the bag into the back, herself into the driver's seat. She is about to start the second and final leg of her drive. In less than five hours she'll be on Agapanthus Lane.

When she left Seattle at the crack of dawn yesterday, she promised herself she would use the nearly twenty highway hours wisely. Instead, she wasted the first fifteen listening to music, to talk radio, to a popular true-crime podcast she found detestable and clicked off after ten minutes. And whenever the thoughts started churning, she shooed them away. But it's time to decide various things:

Whether or not she should end things with Val because she is no longer the person she was when they met.

Whether or not she should attempt to turn her doctoral dissertation into some kind of tell-all book, despite her abhorrence of the idea.

Whether or not she will go where the Peace Corps sends her, if they want her.

Whether she will pretend to Dr. Jin that she's back to normal, and ask him to find out when an assistant professorship in their department might come up, or in any university's soc. anthro department, and to make those calls to the journals, to learn if there is a rare opening, or might be one in the near future, and she could say, "In the meantime, let me be your research assistant, starting fall semester," a better proposition than trading distant fieldwork for research of local trends in disease, overpopulation, land use, and urban dialects. She's not interested in those areas, so why use up the little energy she has to pursue an opportunity she doesn't want—when winning would mean a chilly office, appropriate business attire, and, likely, immediately quitting. No matter that she's stalled now; she doesn't want any marks against her growing reputation. If she still had her natural energy, she knows what she would do: develop a new research proposal, submit it to her university and every anthropological organization that funds exploration, and when she had the money, she'd head off once more, seeking the exotic, with a clear and stated purpose. But figuring all of that out seems impossible, mind-boggling, and utterly exhausting.

And, finally, whether she will reveal to her family the depression she has been suffering from, severe enough that she has relegated her expensive and wide-ranging education and years of diligent, imaginative, and difficult work to a back burner, to the closet, that she is spending eight hours a day tending to those on the way out, when once she was only interested in figuring out how those most uniquely alive lived.

The interstate is quiet this early, and when she sees no police cars ahead or behind, or tucked into the verges and waiting to pounce, she sets her cruise control to eighty, then checks her watch. Last night, Phoebe left a voicemail commanding Camille to call her today. "While we're both driving to the place we seem incapable of not calling home, we can talk about things we won't be able to talk about there, or at least not easily, or at least not without Mom sitting down next to us, caressing our hair—wait, I forgot, Mom always knows everything. Shit, I hope that's not really true—" The message had ended with Phoebe's laugh.

Does she want to call her pluperfect older sister, founder of her own law firm, who rents a charming apartment, though she could, on a whim, purchase an embassy-sized house in the most expensive Los Angeles neighborhoods, who, despite trouble finding a husband, knows she absolutely wants one of those and the eventual children, who has never experienced a moment of depression or doubt or indecision, who wouldn't understand what it feels like to be dragged under the waves of one's life? Camille's kept everything from her family, including Phoebe, when they trade their infrequent telephonic confidences.

She stares down the long, straight highway. If she calls Phoebe at eleven, she has three and a half hours left to gather herself together, to sound like the Camille her sister thinks she knows, the Camille they all think they know.

FIVE

B EST OF SEVEN?" HARRY calls out to Levitt.
Levitt, already wiping sweat from his forehead with his terry-clothed wrists, says, "Why do you insist on subverting protocol? It's best of five, Harry. Best of five at the US Open. Best of five at Wimbledon. And there's no way you and I can go seven in this heat. Best of three, like we do every Saturday. Is this your attempt to psych me out, gain the upper hand?"

"Of course I know the protocol. I'm being a caring friend, offering you a shot at taking me down, because I'm feeling extraordinarily energetic today."

"Yeah, yeah, Harry. Just serve."

Harry bounces the yellow ball, six, seven, eight, nine times, to unbalance Levitt, who is bent over at the waist, at the ready, those thick tree trunks of his in a wide, imposing stance.

Harry feels the sun on his face, hears the solid thump of the ball on the warm court, the happy yips of small dogs freed from their leashes. Then, like a thunderbolt to the brain, he's thinking about King David and Queen Esther, the way they yipped happily, flicking their tails, circling around their new masters as Harry and Roma and Phoebe and Camille headed away from the great rambling house in Connecticut that was no longer their home. It belonged now to the buyers, that replacement family who was waving, the husband and wife the same ages as Harry and Roma, the little boys nearly the same ages as Phoebe and Camille, the family who took title and said yes, they would be delighted to take the Tabor family's dachshunds as well, agreeing it wouldn't be right to uproot the dogs from their puppyhood home, and impossible to travel thousands of miles with them, when the dogs couldn't tolerate speed, would be carsick within minutes.

Levitt calls out from across the court, "You going to serve in this century?" Harry hears him, but he can't respond, struck by these memories of King David and Queen Esther, dogs he gave to his girls when all four were young, by his ability to hand them over so easily to a family he knew nothing about, except that their financials were in order and they hadn't required a mortgage. He doesn't even recall their last name, despite seeing it on nearly every page of the purchase and sale agreement.

Why is he thinking about King David and Queen Esther, when he has not thought about them since 1987, since seeing them in the rearview mirror of the Caravan, as he and his family drove away to a new life. It is a memory he has never called up in all of these years, not even a memory he has ever had, but it is in his mind now. The girls were crying in the backseat, weren't they? Yes, he can hear his daughters crying, tiny hands hitting the sealed windows, yelling, "Let the dogs in, let the dogs in, we can't leave them behind." But he had left them behind. Had let his daughters cry themselves out. Had not turned to witness the emotion on Roma's face. She had, after all, sadly and reluctantly agreed to the dogs' dispensation.

"Hey, you okay over there?" Levitt calls out, rising from his competitor's crouch, loosening the grip on his racquet.

Harry's heart is pounding, like a bomb is about to go off in there, and he leans over, head between his knees, hoping those forgotten dogs aren't a very strange version of his life passing before his eyes, hoping he's not about to be ejected from his existence by a heart attack this minute, hoping he didn't put himself in the crosshairs of an evil eye last night by thinking how far he is from death.

But then it passes.

The memory is still there, but its toothy grip is easing.

He straightens up and says, "Sorry. Should have had more than coffee this morning. I'm fine. Let's go. You ready?"

SIX

H E'S SPRINTING UP A winding hill in his neighborhood, his breath loud in his ears, the asphalt black under his beating feet, black ravens flying out of the trees, an avian army buzzing his head, flapping their wings, diving at him, their beaks pecking and pecking and pecking, their claws finding purchase on his head, his neck, his arms, his legs, his back, and then Simon Tabor is awake, fetal-curled, fists clenched, hair and body as wet as if he has just emerged from an ice bath, his insides hollowed out by the certainty that something is desperately wrong. He will never get used to this, to the way he is left with voids—in his heart, as if that organ has lost mass or blood flow; in his throat, as if that narrow tube has opened wide and air is racing inside; and in his abdomen, as if he is starving to death, though it's not hunger at all that he feels. And this morning, there is a new element, unshed tears blinding his sight.

Slowly he unkinks his cramped arms and legs and turns over. The tears settle in the wells of his eyes, and he is loath to blink, loath to touch them, even more fearful than usual because he has no idea what this latest indignity means.

Lions charging at him yesterday, ravens today, during the frightening half hour of near-slumber, and now he is crying. It's Sisyphean, when he's already been laboring with his hijacked sleep, with his terror in having forgotten how to do what is natural, with his inability to figure out why this is happening, at such odds with how he otherwise perceives his life: as a mostly happy man whose marriage, young children, and professional pursuits mostly afford him pleasure and satisfaction.

A movement in the bed, Elena shifting under the striped comforter. In this year of his sleeplessness, he has learned his wife wakes in stages. He had not known that fact before. Deep sleep on her stomach until she shifts to her left side, facing away from him. Then the countdown begins. Twenty minutes until she shifts onto her back, the slightest of whistles coming through her full lips, thinned by dreams. Another twenty before she cracks one eye open, then the other.

He looks at the long line of Elena's hip. When his misbegotten nights were new, she suggested supposedly surefire ways to shut down his nonsensical thoughts: walking after dinner; meditating before bed; taking a boiling-hot shower in their unlit bathroom and crawling wet between the cool sheets. Desperate, he tried it all. Altered his diet, too—no meat, no cheese, cut back on his drinking. Increased his exercise—yoga first, then cycling instead of yoga, and now, instead of cycling, he runs hard and fast and long every morning. But what is a boon for his body has done nothing for his soul, has not altered his inability to sink down into bliss, too aware of the spirits gathering around him in the dark. Only recently has a thought begun to form, that what he needs perhaps cannot be supplied by healthy eating or abstinence or exercise.

In the beginning, in that first month when he thought his failure to sleep was a temporary malfunction, he rocked the bed in the middle of the night and palmed the perfect globes of Elena's ass, hoping sex would empty his brain, but Elena had sighed and mumbled, "I'll get the pills." A sylph in a nightgown that left her shoulders and back bare, the long yards of her black hair tight in a bun, his sleep guru refusing her mission, and when the light in the bathroom flicked on, Simon called after her, "What pills?"

Sleeping pills prescribed to Elena a year after Lucy's birth, expired before Isabel was born.

"They've expired," he'd said when she handed him the orange container. He'd looked inside and been unable to tell if, or how many, she'd ever taken.

"I think it takes decades to break down the components. They're probably as strong, or nearly as strong, as when I got them. Give it a go. Nothing lost and all that."

He had wanted to ask why she needed sleeping pills during that exciting time when Lucy was walking and laughing, her hands reaching out to the world, but Elena's eyes were already closed, her breath even and composed.

For several successive nights, he took a pill that was small as a dot and weightless on his tongue, hoping she was right, but she wasn't; potency was vanquished by time. When he told her the pills didn't work, she looked at him in frustration. "So call the doctor and get a new prescription." Which he did, and he took them for several more nights, but his body refused the sedation, simply wouldn't be knocked out.

Never again has he bothered Elena during his racked hours. Sometimes he watches her sleeping, curious about what she's dreaming, envying the way she goes under and stays under, missing how they used to wake nearly simultaneously, her first smile of the day beaming him fully alive. He's forgotten how to sleep, but something's changed in her, too, and he can't trace the alteration to any specific temporal point, to any specific event, but she no longer smiles and tucks into him or rolls onto him when she wakes. Now, when she comes to, she sits upright, her face hiding its secrets from him, and it's only when he's back from his run, when they're drinking their second cups of coffee, that she graces him with a smile, but it doesn't seem to him her same *I love and adore you so much* smile.

He could be mistaken; it could be some pathology of his sleeplessness that is causing him to blow out of proportion the changes he senses in her, the feeling he has that she's created subtle distance between them. But what he's not mistaken about is that Elena no longer dresses like the woman his heart toppled for. Gone are her gauzy skirts and ruffled blouses, her tight dresses with narrow slits and strappy, sexy heels, her fitted slacks with stiletto boots, all replaced with a uniform: jeans, button-down shirt, ballet slippers. And that soft black river that once streamed over her shoulders and down her spine, that he would gather up in his hands because she left it unbound, is now always center-parted and twisted into a knot at the nape of her neck.

There's a pretty Chinese bowl from a New York museum in the bathroom, a gift for her when he had been gone for weeks on a case, that holds Elena's stock of bobby pins. In the two years since Isabel's birth, he has often considered whether her tightly coiled hair, her adopted uniform, indicates the practicality of doubled motherhood or something far more charged—proof that the loss of her freedom is so wild within her that she must keep herself regimented and pinned together. She is a gorgeous woman no matter the clothes she wears or how she arranges her hair, but she is severe this way, and when he sees the Chinese bowl, he always wants to dump those securing pins in the garbage, shatter that bowl, bring back his sensual, loose-haired Elena, their early-morning lovemaking, her explicit love for him.

Maybe he's a coward. Maybe he already knows the answers, but he refrains these days from asking how she feels about no longer flying away as she used to. Until Lucy, Elena wrote for glossy travel magazines, and in those halcyon days, Simon occasionally went with her to those off-the-beaten-path places when he could. Her nightstand is stacked still with the latest issues of the travel magazines that published her work. When she was breastfeeding at night she read those magazines by the low rosy light, telling him she was keeping pace with what was going on in her absence, would not count herself out of the game. Naturally, their daughters changed everything. Now he's flying as much as she once did, which was a lot, and she refuses to say what it's like being unable to vanish into the excited glaze of the working day. As he does when the hollowness lifts, when he has run his daily ten miles, and drunk his coffee, and kissed his daughters. As always, he kisses Elena last before he's out the door, but where he once found the blackness of her eyes so enticing, now he is afraid to fall into them, afraid of what he will learn, or be told, fearful that if he can't fix his failure to sleep, he can't fix anything else.

And this morning, tears. Poised to spill down his cheeks. There's no way he can rise and run, not when he's this done in. Then he's smothering his face in his pillow, heaving silent sobs, freezing when Elena shifts onto her back, worrying she's woken and waiting to hear why he's crying his eyes out. What would he say? He wishes he knew, but he has no answers. And then deliverance—Elena's soft sleeping whistles.

He wipes his face against the pillowcase, then turns over again, and checks on the crack in the uneven ceiling. A hairline days ago, it has grown wider and longer and looks like it will soon split apart the paint and the plaster.

Does that crack mean the roof is going to collapse?

He needs to do something about it, call someone, make that call this morning, before they leave for Palm Springs, arrange for whatever person fixes cracks in ceilings in old houses in the hills to come Monday, first thing. He'll even forgo his start-of-the-week run to be here, to handle it, to not put another thing on his wife's list of things to take care of. He should pull out the house file, see what the agreement says about the roof, if any issues were noted. He doesn't specialize in real estate, but he is a lawyer, and he would have asked the critical questions. They've owned this ninety-three-year-old house for a mere five years; previous owners must have replaced the roof at least a few times over the last decades.

God forbid they need a new roof. How much would it cost? How long would it take? Would they have to bunk elsewhere for the duration? Where would they stay?

Phoebe's apartment in the flats of Beverly Hills Adjacent is too small to house five; her second bedroom is her study, in which there is no pullout couch.

He has an older colleague at the firm, Tim Devins, who owns some huge estate in Brentwood, is always talking about how he and his wife, childless by choice, have eight bedrooms that are never used, and a guesthouse no one has ever stayed in. Tim is a friendly, generous guy, and if Simon laid out his need, Tim would probably say, "Sure, buddy, no problem, for however long, *mi casa es tu casa*." But how awkward it would be to see Tim in a towel after a shower, or eating his breakfast, or lounging in his Jacuzzi attached to his pool, which surely is Olympic-sized, or kissing his sharp-featured wife before tootling off to the office.

Why is he thinking about asking Tim Devins if the Tabor family can move in while their roof is being fixed? Their roof will not need to be fixed; it is simply a small crack that needs to be filled, the ceiling repainted. And if they do have to fix the roof, and leave home for the duration, he would never ask Tim Devins.

They would stay in a hotel.

No, they would not stay in a hotel; they couldn't afford to stay in a hotel, not if the roof needs fixing. They'd have to stay in a motel. The four of them in a dingy room at some Motel 6, he pulling his tie tight and striding out the door, leaving his wife looking as if she might lift up their daughters and fling the three of them over the second-floor railing, pitching down into a parking lot filled with campers and vans.

Why is he picturing that?

Are the changes in Elena—in her waking routine, her delayed first smile of the day, her distance, her daily uniform—because she has postpartum depression? Lucy is five and Elena was fine after her birth. And Isabel is two—does postpartum depression last for two years? And, really, most of the time, she seems herself, with her customary intensity, occasionally humming as she brushes out Lucy's tangles, as she encourages Isabel to wear something other than the drooping purple tutu, her everyday favorite since last Halloween.

Simon pinches his arm hard. There will be no more crying. There will be no roof fixing, no motel living, no bodies hurtling to their deaths. Elena does not have any kind of depression, while he, on the other hand, cannot sleep, and whatever is keeping him up far exceeds run-of-the-mill insomnia.

But there is the crack in the ceiling, which he can arrange to be handled on Monday.

His watch says it's seven twenty. Elena won't wake until seven forty. The girls will wake up shortly thereafter. Elena's probably already packed for herself and their daughters.

He could get up now and pack what he'll need for the weekend. He could do that, and then start the coffee, make them all breakfast. Eggs? French toast? Pancakes? No, nothing hot because whatever he prepares will go cold before everyone sits down at the table. Lucy will insist on swimming in the pool before she eats, as she's been doing each day this summer, running out of her room buck naked and leaping into the water, requiring him, half dressed, to follow and sit by the pool until he can convince her his day needs to get under way. And Isabel will cry elephantine tears until Elena climbs into bed with her and reads her a story. The only kid he's heard of who prefers being read to in the morning and not at bedtime. So, no, no reason to cook a family breakfast. And what's even in the fridge? Didn't Elena say she didn't bother going to the market because they would be gone the weekend?

Most of today and all of tomorrow on Agapanthus Lane, with both of the children in tow. A babysitter will take care of the girls tonight while everyone else—Harry and Roma, Phoebe and her new beau, Camille, and he and Elena—dressed up in tuxedos and gowns, will be miles away at the resort in Rancho Mirage, sipping champagne on the Starlight Terrace rooftop, where he and Elena married in front of three hundred guests. They haven't been back to the resort since their wedding, though they considered returning on their first, and second, and third anniversaries. They never did, never even made a reservation, and up there tonight his father will be named Palm Springs Man of the Decade.

What comes with that designation? Will Harry be handed a plaque, or a sculpted piece of glass with his name inscribed, or the key to the city? In their conversations the past month, his father has played down the honor, saying, "I've just done what any other person with resources would have done to help unfortunate souls." Which isn't true, and when Simon said, "Dad, that isn't true," Harry said, "Oh, I don't know."

Simon puts his hands to his face, feels his lips turning up, and he wants to laugh because it's been such a long time since he has smiled in bed. He was crying, and now he's smiling, thinking of his father. Thinking of their spring, summer, and fall camping trips, star-studded nights, sleeping bags unrolled in the desert sand drifts just beyond the back patio, sand that was soft at first, then scratchy as the hours piled up, Harry teaching him how to converse and debate, getting into the grit of politics and free will and truth; the long hikes traversing the mountain peak, talking about manhood, and what it means to be a rare man who qualifies as a full human being. No baseball throwing, no football tossing, no Frisbee silliness, no Boy Scouts, no Pop Warner, no Little League, those activities weren't for Harry, and hence not for Simon. There'd been no sense of loss, of missing out, because they had all those special times together. How he loves his father and his inimitable qualities for probity, his infinite well of paternal love, and marital passion, and universal caring for those finding where they fit in their new world.

Sunday morning, tomorrow morning, he could say, "Dad, let's do our regular San Jacinto hike," and, on their ascent, ask his father if he ever experienced a lengthy bout of sleeplessness, and if he did, what he had done to solve it, where he had looked for the answers.

"Tell me, Dad," he would say, "help me figure out what's going on in my head."

Yes, that's what he'll do. He'll grab his father's hand and say, "I need a little father-and-son time, just you and me alone." And Harry will grin and grab Simon's face, kiss him hard first on one cheek and then the other, and say, "Did I tell you today how much I love you?"

His emotions are seesawing from happiness back to tears.

What is going on with him?

The crack in the ceiling has disappeared because his vision is again blurred. Are these new tears because when he says, "Let's you and me sneak away for some time alone," his father will exude palpable pleasure, or because his father is seventy now, robust and strong and active, but there is a sense of the hourglass, of the grains diminishing in the upper, gathering in the lower?

He tests the notion in his head of a world without Harry, and immediately swats it away. He can't imagine not being able to call his father, talking to him at length on his drives home. He blinks hard several times, forces some of the wetness away.

One thing put to rest is the fear that his sleeplessness is a presage to his own death. He's been to the doctor, had a complete physical, including a stress test, an EEG, an EKG. He is in perfect health, his blood pressure within the recommended range, his cholesterol terrific, his blood revealing no hidden issues, the electrical activity in his brain and heart as it should be. Whatever is keeping him awake, it's not his eventual demise, but something he'd better figure out soon. The one question he forgot to ask the doctor was: How long can a body go without sleep?

THE SILENCE IN THE house is growing heavier, wife and children in that place he no longer goes, a smothering silence ripped apart by the telephone ringing.

Simon's hollowed heart thumps into action, and he leaps from the bed, an errant tear running down the side of his nose, and he grabs the receiver from Elena's nightstand, steps out of their bedroom, his voice low and froggy when he says, "Yes? Hello? Do you know it's seven thirty on a Saturday morning?"

"Mr. Tabor, my apologies," says a deep male voice with a strong accent. "This is Altan Odaman, the president of the International Lawyers Association, calling from Istanbul, Turkey. If I figured the time difference incorrectly, my heartfelt regrets. Nonetheless, I am delighted to personally invite you to this year's conference. To be held in Medellín, Colombia, from September tenth through the twentieth. I am also delighted to inform you that, by special vote, you have been chosen to make a presentation. This is highly unorthodox, as you know. No first-time invitee has ever been afforded the opportunity to address the group. But your legal approach for recovering those Goya paintings is of great interest to everyone. Do you need time to determine your availability, or can I assume you will clear your schedule to attend? Spouses, of course, are invited as well."

In the small landing that leads from their bedroom to the living room, Simon stares at the photograph on the wall—Elena in the hospital bed with their first child barely an hour old, named Luz within moments of her worldly entrance and called, ever after, Lucy—and he sees nothing.

For several seconds, he is made speechless by this call to join the most elite of lawyers who handle global cases that alter the international landscape. But his eight years of experience as a cross-border litigator focused on the repatriation of stolen art, relics, religious icons, and sometimes ancient bones kicks in; he is naturally quick on his feet, able to pivot his courtroom cross-examinations as required, and he gathers his wits and his words and expresses his sincere and honest delight and grateful thanks to Altan Odaman and the nominating committee.

"Yes, of course I will attend, thank you so much for this honor," he says, and Odaman provides him with the highlights about the first-class airline tickets and the five-star accommodations, the ten-day schedule of programs and seminars and social events, telling Simon all will be set forth in a comprehensive email, and then Odaman rings off.

When he turns, Elena is behind him, tousled from sleep, her skin tawny gold, her high cheekbones flushed, her lips again full, and her smile is shot through with such love and intimacy that he doubts his sleeplessness, as if this year of sleeplessness has been itself a bad dream, doubts his concern that there's a slackening of their prior closeness, doubts himself for debating the strength of her love.

"You're not running this morning?" she asks, and when he shakes his head, she says, "Great. Lucy's already in the pool. Why don't you pack. I had your tuxedo pressed, it's in the closet. In a little while, I'll make birds in the nest for everyone."

"I . . ." Simon says.

How does he express to Elena the enormity of the high honor he has just received from the president of the ILA, that it is even more meaningful than making partner in February? How does he implore her to accompany him, to carefully suggest it is time to leave the children behind, as they have not been left since their births? How does he convince her that they'll figure out who will care for them in their absence, but going to Medellín, Colombia, is vital, not just for his career, although absolutely his attendance at this conference will thrust him forward exponentially, but so that the two of them can temporarily escape the tough daily grind, be alone together as they have not been in five years, recover themselves as the couple they once were. Ten days far away from their precious children, who are adorable pixies and love bugs, whose hugs and kisses are indescribable, as are their plaintive, plangent demands that their needs be swiftly met. Ten days far away to remember who they are: Simon Tabor and Elena Abascal, a couple happily married and in love.

"The ILA called, didn't they?" And Elena's look is that special intimate look he hasn't seen in a while, and there is a gentleness to her voice he wouldn't have predicted, and he is so surprised by both, by his awareness of how long they have been absent, that he must forcibly drag air into his lungs, recognizing with a jolt that his morning hollowness is gone. Whatever evaporates during these nights has resurfaced, reshaping his insides much earlier than usual.

Elena steps closer and closer until the tips of her breasts touch his bare chest. Sparks light up his body; if he looked down, surely he would see fireflies encircling the two of them. Her pink tongue flicks across his mouth, and in a heartbeat she's tugging at his lower lip, pressing down with increasing force, imprisoning his lip with her incisors, until he tastes blood. She steps back, grips his wide-awake cock, squeezes once, then leaves him there.

He hears the door to Isabel's room opening, and finds himself speculating, not about why ravens were trying to devour him this morning, or if Elena still loves him, or if he can induce her back into bed—it's been so long he can't recall the last time—or what implications the conference will have on his career, but whether, against all the odds, Colombia might be the place where his sleep is restored.

SEVEN

PHOEBE TABOR REPRESENTS MAJOR Los Angeles–based novelists, screenwriters, and playwrights, sculptors, painters, and video artists, musicians, bands, and composers. It's her still-minor clients, those beginning to climb the vines of recognition and success, that she worries about most, because their expectations are consistently unrealistic. They walk into her office presuming fantastic offers are on the table, and she must return them to reality. And it's always tough, because they have written the meaningful novel, the great script, the deep play, have created the phenomenal sculpture, the suite of inspired paintings, and it's her obligation to tell them no one is biting, or the bite isn't as big as they'd hoped, or the film director has rejected the neophyte composer's score, or the gallery has rescinded its offer to mount the young artist's new show. The facts are nearly as hard to deliver as to hear, but by the time Phoebe's clients hug her, they understand where they are, yet still have faith in their futures, because she is a truth teller. Honesty is the pillar upon which she has built her law practice. Inside, past the heavy door with its stylish engraved nameplate, *Phoebe Tabor, Esq.*, she commands a large retinue of lawyers, paralegals, and assistants, and insists that in all their firm activities, they heed her honest manner of transparently conducting business.

And yet recently, in her personal life, she has veered in the opposite direction, adopting subterfuge as her modus operandi, although calling it *subterfuge* is finely glossing the state of things.

At eight fifteen this Saturday morning, Phoebe, dressed in a black sundress and Grecian sandals, all of her limbs lightly tanned, stands at her closet mirror and arranges the hair her mother calls chestnut into a loose sexy braid. She assesses her image. Yes, she looks the part, will be viewed by her family as a woman in love.

She leans in close, fragmenting her pupils, and in those fragments she sees the unjustified complications she's brought into her life. She pulls back from the mirror and her pupils reassemble, black surrounded by irises of darkest brown, eyes so falsely guileless she has to turn away from herself.

She rustles through closets and drawers, delving through sedimentary layers of acquisitions, flinging out her choices, and packing them into her small rolling bag—used for all her loverly weekends away: an old one-piece bathing suit for the laps she always forgets to swim, a new bikini for chaise sprawling and oiling up next to the big pool alongside her sister and sister-in-law, another summery dress purchased to wear with a man a few years back who pursued her hard for a date and when she at last gave in stood her up, tennis shoes and shorts and a tank top from her youth for taking a walk in the heat with one or some or all of her family members, a college-era tennis skirt and shirt in case her father wants to play, silky pajamas that hold memories of an enjoyable four-week romp during law school, and the totteringly high silver heels purchased last week for the gala tonight, along with the ice-blue gown, already in its hanging bag. In go the miniature bottles of shampoo and conditioner and body lotion swiped from hotel-suite bathrooms these last six and a half months. Her lip-shaped cosmetics bag stowed inside the mesh netting.

She zips up the suitcase, sets it down on the floor. The tick-tick of the wheels on the wood puts Benny on notice. Until a moment ago, he was lounging on the unmade bed, but now lets out a quivering meow. He is her sweet affectionate thing, velvety fur hiding a small, solidly compact body. At night, he stretches out on top of her, his paws clinging to her neck, his purrs soothing her lonely heart.

Poor Benny. Her subterfuge has meant she's deserted him for many three-day weekends since February, consigned to the care of her brother. Simon is responsible, showing up morning and night, filling Benny's bowls, keeping his heating pad on the bed on high and cold water trickling from the bathroom sink faucet, playing with Benny for a few minutes before he heads to his own home, to his wife and children. When she returns from her weekends away, Benny is churlish, his outsized paws thumping when he lands on the kitchen counter, the dining room table, following Phoebe around, baying his disapproval at his most recent abandonment. When she is again in the bed that they share, Benny lets her know he's forgiven her by arranging himself on her head, lashing her cheek with his sandpaper tongue. But Simon and family will be in Palm Springs, too, and Phoebe reluctantly asked a neighbor to care for Benny.

Raquel was thrilled when Phoebe knocked on Wednesday night. "I want a cat sososo much, but I haven't pulled the trig. So how coolio. Yours. Def. No prob."

Raquel is twenty-five to Phoebe's thirty-eight, a secretarial temp slash aspiring actress slash aspiring model who might emote as well as the best but seems to Phoebe too short and curvy to model. And it irks Phoebe enormously that Raquel seems intent on believing they are nearly identical peas in a pod. This specious view of Raquel's, and the fact that Raquel annoys her, has compelled Phoebe to ward off the young woman's obvious desire to be friends. In her own defense, Phoebe would say that a friendship with any neighbor can too easily become an uncomfortable burden, and after an eventful workday, she'd rather not be accosted by anyone waving a bottle, saying, "Thought we might share this." Only twice has Phoebe relented, and both times, watching Raquel swaying back to her own front door, Phoebe assessed the avenues of employment that would afford Raquel the ability to purchase such expensive wine. Ashamed by her assumptions, she has kept her distance from Raquel the last few months.

But Raquel was her easiest choice for cat-sitting Benny, and thinking about the young woman being alone in her house unescorted, peeking into her life, Phoebe is opening and closing cabinets, sizing her things up, determining what they say about her, if she needs to find hiding places.

She scoops out of her nightstand the few books of erotica, the vibrator, the hopeful, unopened box of condoms, and in the bathroom, the nearly full container of Percocet from her wisdom teeth removal last year, and stashes the loot at the bottom of her hamper, throws in the damp towel hanging over the shower door to be safe.

In her study, she slips folders containing client information into the desk drawer, along with her personal bills and checkbooks and bank and money management statements, and locks it with the key hidden beneath.

In the living room her brother calls empty and she calls minimalistic and replete with architectural details—rounded columns leading to the dining room, pristine nonworking fireplace with a mantel holding a single blue vase filled with bright orange gerbera daisies, massive window overlooking the street—she inspects, but aside from the suede sofa and chairs the color of tangerines, the three huge paintings on the white walls she accepted as payment for legal bills owed by painter clients, bookshelves categorically organized, high-tech sound system, and her objects of art displayed in the whitewashed nooks and crannies, there is nothing revealing.

As the coffee brews, she pulls out Benny's dry cat food and cans of wet and places them on the kitchen counter. She wants to make it easy for Raquel, to keep her curtained in the kitchen, then a path straight out the front door.

She pours herself a first cup, hears her doorbell chime, and reluctantly pulls down a second cup.

"HI, FEEBS, REPORTING FOR duty," is what Raquel says when she steps in. "I'm sososo jelly, where are you going? Tell me the deets."

Phoebe hates that nickname to which she never responds, hates the way Raquel insists on shortening most everything. How much extra time does it take to say *Phoebe*, to say *jealous*, to say *details*? Is Raquel's life so jam-packed she can't waste a second, cares not a whit about being fully understood?

Phoebe gives her a big smile. "Come into the kitchen. I'll give you some coffee, show you what you need to do."

"Great, but first I want to hear about your hot and heavy weekends!"

What, Phoebe thinks, is Raquel is talking about?

"Please, please, spill the beans! I keep running into your gorgeous brother when he comes to feed Benny and he mentioned— Well, I got him to tell me why I've seen him so much. Because you have a new man in your life! Taking you away to cool places. Is he scrumptious?"

Oh. Raquel is talking about Aaron Green.

"Totally scrumptious," Phoebe instantly says.

"So where to this weekend?"

"Home for a family celebration."

"OMG, how exciting! Are you nervous? I'd be so nervous introducing my new man to family!"

Phoebe could correct Raquel's mistaken impression, but says, instead, "No, I'm not nervous at all."

"That's when you know the love is real!" Raquel squeals.

And Phoebe, who doesn't agree that's the way you know, pours coffee into the cup on the counter, and points to the sugar bowl, and wishes seeing herself through Raquel's eyes weren't so inviting.

Phoebe would never confess to Raquel that the scrumptious man spiriting her away to cool places for long weekends, and whom she has just confirmed she's taking home to Palm Springs, is fictitious.

She would never admit to Raquel that she created Aaron Green at midnight in late January, just home from the opening of a client's new art exhibition, her family's messages on her voicemail pissing her off, words throaty with exhausted hope that there might have been a man there who was "worth another look," said Roma, Harry calling out, "Love is good, honey." "Someone I would like," Simon had said in his message, with Elena adding, "Just so he knows your true value," and from Camille, "I hope he's fuckable, because that's always the point. No, I take that back, I don't know what the point is," and Phoebe, who had just hung up her short bronze dress and placed her high bronzed sandals in their box in the closet, stood nude in her bedroom.

She was tired of slicing open wedding invitations. From those she employs, selecting her dinner choices with angry checkmarks, writing the identical sweet comment on the RSVP cards about her excitement in participating in the joyful couple's bountiful happiness, and from friends whose first marriages cratered—weddings she also attended—but *their* luck had held and allowed them to expunge past erroneous choices and move forward into another future: *Please join us in an intimate celebration of our finding absolute true love—*

From her mid- to late twenties, Phoebe was first in her seat at the monthly brunch with her band of girls, Sunday afternoons of sangria and silly talk about what their futures might hold. One by one, those girls turned into women when they became wives and mothers, delighted their lives had come together so effortlessly.

"You're gorgeous and brilliant and your turn's coming," they said to her, and when Phoebe's turn never did come, they peppered her with questions: Did she *really* want to marry, have a child, make room in her industrious life for others?

Disbelieving when she said, "Professional success isn't the sum total of me, it's not all that I want, but I don't seem to be having any luck."

Her friends, *her friends*, would say, "Well, if you *really* want it, as you say you do, then—," that *then* so forbidding, undefinable, completely elusive, as if they held the secret and were unwilling to share, as if their attainment of the marital, the maternal, the pronoun replacements—from *I* to *we* and then to *us*—resulted in their crowning, their elevation, while she remained on the ground, assumed to be lacking the requisite nurturing abilities that would give rise to love and marriage and motherhood.

All day, every day, Phoebe nurtures everyone, her clients, her associates, her support staff, attending their opening nights, their launches, their engagement parties and weddings, and when dancing is required, she dances as if delighted to be there—what better proof is there that she possesses the necessary talents for success in her personal life? And yet she hasn't attained love, marriage, motherhood, the poles of the true shelter she seeks, with her wished-for family, a solid place against inclement weather, toasty inside, living each day together, making plans for the future.

As full as she has made her life, as large as it often is, that she might never again feel crazy in love, never feel her child growing inside, that she might spend the rest of her years alone—it is incalculable sadness, bottomless grief, wide and swollen rivers of self-pity. What is she supposed to do with the pulsing love in her heart, the love she has to give, if husband and baby never appear?

Raquel is still chattering, and Phoebe hears her say, "Really, that's how it works, you only introduce a real love to the family. Right?"

"Right," Phoebe immediately says.

The art opening had happened; the client was real, an ageless sprite named Zabi, with her magenta lipstick and Turkish slippers, her enormous fired-metal pieces hanging off the walls, like devices to protect the soft innards of some forgotten race of people less strong than sun-fried Los Angelenos. Zabi introduced Phoebe as her lawyerly god, and Phoebe had smiled, feeling her white teeth perfectly strung in her mouth, and all the time she was scanning the crowd, wishing for just one man who might make her laugh, who would know instinctively how to metaphorically strip her to her core. But there had been nobody. Or rather, there had been many, including attractive men who smiled at her, but none had taken even a half step in her direction.

Driving home, she'd thought about how she insists her clients identify their professional aims, and the personal problems that might hamper their achievement, and she took stock of herself. She was beautiful—an acknowledgment, rather than an assertion of vanity; she had an excellent brain, and a big heart, so why couldn't she achieve her personal aims? What was missing?

It took a quarter of an hour before she realized what was missing was luck.

When it came to love, she'd once had an abundance of compelling luck. Second grade loves that lasted an hour or a day; sixth grade boys who handed over their pencils when hers broke; high school boys with crushes she turned into boyfriends. College and law school admirers had lined up, relationships in which she determined when they started and ended. Then, well, *him*, and her luck held for a while, then sputtered and died.

It was luck she needed to rebirth, but how did one rebirth luck?

And what she thought was love begets love. There was a particular energy one exuded when in love. She'd experienced it herself long ago, the way she became a magnet for even more love, love she couldn't then use because she was already happily in love.

How could she again draw the energy of love directly to her?

That steamy, decidedly unwintery January night, Phoebe deleted her family's messages, then walked naked, as she never did, into the living room, and searched the spines of her novels, flipping through their pages, finding a name to bestow upon the man she was inventing, a love story as balm, trips to places ripened by dreams.

It was the only way she could think of to remagnetize herself, and when she found real love, no one would ever need to know that to obtain it, she had feigned being a woman in love.

Raquel has sugared her coffee and sipped—"*De-lish*"—and

Phoebe says, "Follow me. Benny's on the bed. I want him to get used to you," and Raquel follows along, beneath the kitchen arch, into the dining room and out, a left down the long, well-lit hallway, and across the transom.

"Jesus, Feebs. SOS, big time. You should get those trees cut back."

Phoebe takes in the big bosomy leaves of the rubber trees pressing against the large north-facing windows, preventing the entry of outside light, causing the dim watery atmosphere of her bedroom in which she sleeps, dreams, and dresses. She ought to call someone, but she's grown used to the intimacies of her life spent alone in this oxygenated version of being underwater.

"OMG, OMG, I always forget how totes adorb he is," Raquel says. *Always* meaning the two times she's been invited over, when Benny kept to himself, hiding away in here, behaving unlike the social creature that he is. Aware of the change in airflow, Benny, on the bed, cocks open an eye, gives Raquel a hard stare, then rolls himself tight into a ball, crosses his paws over his head. Phoebe feels proud.

She shows Raquel the heating pad, the trickle of water in the bathroom, how much dry and wet food to set out in his bowls on the black-and-white checkerboard kitchen floor bright with sunshine.

Raquel jerks her head at the coffee machine.

"Sure. Help yourself."

"Am I taking care of Benny because your brother's going to Palm Springs, too?"

Phoebe is as nonplussed by the disappearance of Raquel's usually overexcited voice as by the words Raquel has spoken.

"Yes. With his family. He's married, Raquel, with two kids."

"Oh, I know. But he's the kind of solid guy I want to end up with. I love chatting with him."

Simon chatting with Raquel? Phoebe can't imagine what they would chat about, but her brother is that kind of very nice guy, wouldn't blow off his sister's inquisitive neighbor in case he did any harm.

She looks at Raquel, takes in the wide blue eyes, the pink bowed mouth, the itsy-bitsy top from which pulchritude overflows, the extremely short shorts, the bare feet with toenails painted watermelon, for she has come into Phoebe's apartment shoeless.

Could Simon find this girl attractive? No, too obvious, too overly flirtatious. Especially compared to Elena, who is tall and lithe, a combination of sweet and tough. Her brother's eyes have never roamed since the day he met his wife.

Simon has Elena.

Camille has Valentine.

They are cozy in love, and it spears her straight through, skewers her heart.

Why is she the crescent moon waning when her siblings seem always to be waxing?

Her mother says Phoebe's the kind of woman men do not quickly release, and boys from various stages of her life still occasionally beat their man-sized wings in her direction, raising the air around her, blowing the dust off their joint old times, a checking-in, a checking-up, wanting to know if Phoebe has allowed someone to stick, to roost—not them, they know, though they had all tried hard.

But her mother also says that the men from Phoebe's past will always hang on, because she gave them up in the limerence phase, when romantic euphoria is at its peak. Maybe her mother is right; maybe that's why she has no flesh-and-blood man, only the perfect golem she dreamt up.

Raquel is holding her coffee cup and doing calf raises at the kitchen counter, and Phoebe says, "Raquel, you have to keep the dry food bowl filled, okay. And fresh water in his bowl, morning and night. And if he hasn't touched the wet, just dump it out and give him a fresh dollop or two."

"It'll be like having my own baby for a few days. I want my own, like right this minute, but I'll wait until I land my first really big role or a global campaign."

Phoebe has never asked Raquel the questions she'd ask if they were becoming friends—if she graduated from college, or went to acting school, or auditions regularly for roles, or what category she is considered to inhabit as a model—and it dawns on her that perhaps she's misjudged, that Raquel must have some measure of success because the rents in this lovely two-story building are high.

"Is there anything big on the horizon for you?" she asks.

"Yes! The Brazilians love me. I'm on billboards there selling Fanta and suntan lotion. And in a month I'll know if I'm the face and body of a hot Rio designer's clothing line."

The look on Raquel's face is absolutely honest—*she's* not telling any lies. And Phoebe is certain that life will turn out ideally for Raquel—she'll book that new campaign, find a solid man like Simon to love, be pregnant by next year.

Unfair, unfair, she thinks. Raquel will have it all. Simon already has it all. Camille seems to have no interest in marriage or a child of her own, but Phoebe wants those things. She strives and succeeds and reaps the benefits, but the rewards she desperately wants remain out of reach.

Best as she can, she abstains from thinking about a child because there are tsunamic emotions and morning hangovers. All that control exercised in her earlier years, all that prophylactic womb-protecting, when now, even if unguarded, likely nothing would stay behind, take root, reside within her walls for the duration. She is, after all, two years from forty.

Her weekends away with the imaginary Aaron Green, meant to uncover love, haven't panned out, have instead become indulgent curatives she uses to try and settle into the truth: no one is going to show up—not the man to love, nor a child, a cooing baby in her arms, fairy-tale-named Annabelle or Daisy or Giselle. When the charges appear on her credit card statement, she is always surprised that she indeed spent that weekend eating, drinking, and treating

herself at the hotel spas, and spending some amount of time researching on her laptop where she supposedly is with her lover,
noting it all down, because her family always asks for detailed
recitations of her trips.

Last month, at the Laguna Niguel Capri, she was impressed
with how adept she has become at eating by herself in sumptuous
hotel restaurants, sampling intricate cocktails perched on stools at
burnished bars or outside under the stars, and found herself having impulsive relations, loud and uninhibited, with a Philadelphia
heart surgeon there for a conference. He had been swimming laps
in the hotel's pool, and she, on her way to swim laps herself, was
diverted by the whirlpool and by the pool boy asking if she would
like a cocktail, and was lounging with a specialty drink in the hot
bubbling water when the heart surgeon joined her and struck up a
conversation. He was married, twenty years and counting, ten
years older than she, with a nice build and manner, and she had
gone with him to his room, engaged with him as she hasn't with
anyone else during these weekends away. He has since sent her several long romantic email missives, a poet misshaped as a doctor.

She responded only once because the love of her life will not
take the form of a married man. When she received his latest email,
she had nearly typed, *Best to your wife!*, then deleted it. Why raise
his infidelity when it affected her not at all, when she had no intention of ever seeing him again? Who was she to judge another, when
she had a pretend lover named Aaron Green?

Raquel hugs her tight, says, "Have a blasto time. Benny will be
fine. He'll be alive and happy when you come home. I promise I won't
lose your spare key." Then she is gone from Phoebe's apartment.

PHOEBE RINSES THEIR CUPS, locks the front door, snuggles Benny
to her chest, and rubs her forehead against his. Then she is at the
back door, hanging bag over her arm, wheeling her suitcase out,
bumping her way down the stairs, along the concrete path bordered

by the rubber trees that prosper, and the hapless, wilted flowers that struggle under the heavy shade, to the row of small single-car garages that belong to the building, where her own car is housed.

It isn't that she, as the eldest Tabor child, expected to outshine her siblings—they all heard their father's exhortations that success in life turns on elements more substantial than money. That fiery lesson he instilled when he burned the dollar bills she and Camille once fought over, saying with the force of paternal disappointment, "We do not fight about money in this family." It seemed a fortune he sent up in smoke when she was nine, especially since he bellowed when they left lights on in rooms they had vacated. She's learned Harry's lesson, about money not being everything, although at that age she'd been confused—were they poor and in danger of the lights being permanently turned off, or rich if money could be burned? It was six years before she stopped worrying, learned they "had money in the bank," as Harry said, dating back to his stockbroker days, the earnings accruing because of his deftness at trading for his own accounts, but that even with deftness, success in the market was mostly a matter of uncertain luck and the exercise of a discipline that forbade seeking out the big score. "Losing it all can happen so fast, it would make your head spin," he told her during that same conversation. "I left the stock market behind in nineteen eighty-six and have never again ventured in. You are not to enter the market at all." And she never has. She earns serious money these days heading up her own firm, and follows her father's precepts and actions for a well-balanced, useful, and honest life, doing mitzvahs, like offering her legal services pro bono to talented, impoverished artists, but she has failed anyway. She was sure by now she would have attained what her parents attained, what Simon has, the natural additions to that well-balanced life: a beloved spouse, a child or two, road-trip vacations with the kids to places they would not otherwise see, just as Roma and Harry had done with the three of them.

Objectively, she isn't, but there are times she feels like the loneliest girl in the world, and she refuses to emend the terminology, for a lonely woman seems infinitely more pathetic than a lonely girl rightfully still wrapped up in teenage angst and despair.

Still, the critical question remains: How does she keep hope alive when this solitary existence is stunting her as surely as the rubber trees stunt the flowers wriggling hard up through the dirt, only to find themselves in shade, their petals curling, browning, falling away. Death comes early to flowers, to most living things, when there is no sunlight. It's not hard for her to imagine a similar outcome for herself if love and motherhood escape her forever.

She unlocks the garage door and pushes it up. She drops the suitcase in the trunk, hangs the bagged gown on the backseat hook, and backs out of the small garage. Then she is out of the car again, pulling down the door and locking it, strapping in, checking her rearview mirror, backing out into the street, shifting into drive, reaching the long traffic light, which has just turned red.

She tries casting away the momentary descent into darkness by listing her attributes: mildly eclectic, highly educated, the owner of a voluminous vocabulary, which she flexibly mines. Lovely smile employed frequently, contagious laugh. She knows her thoughts are self-absorbed, but if not she herself, who will consider her life? Not her parents or her siblings, or her clients, who range from amenable to misanthropic, whom she handles with a preternatural ease. Given her level of engagement in their singular worlds and the busyness of her firm, it would seem right to assume that her personal life is similarly riotously full. For bursts of time it is, or has been: hours racked up in weekend exercise; in classes where she has learned the rudiments of Chinese cooking, advanced conversational French, wine appreciation, the construction of crossword puzzles for beginners; and in a multitude of rounds of internet dating. In that vein, before she constructed Aaron Green, she toyed with the notion of hiring an old-fashioned Jewish matchmaker, and briefly considered dialing up the level of Judaism she was willing to accept—from Reform, as Phoebe and the rest of the Tabors are, to the more involved Conservative branch—to enlarge the pool of possibilities. Since her college days, she has tried to remember to light Shabbat candles when she is home on a Friday night, saying the prayer in Hebrew, speaking aloud the wishes she harbors inside. And she is a good holiday Jew, driving to Palm Springs to join her parents in the preparation of Rosh Hashanah dinners, attending services at the temple they've belonged to forever, returning ten days later for Yom Kippur dinner and services and the next endless day spent in temple hungry and thirsty, breaking the fast with bagels and cream cheese and the salty types of fish her father particularly likes from his childhood in the Bronx.

When the light turns, she makes a left onto Olympic. Not far from her apartment are two Jewish neighborhoods, one thick with Orthodox, black hats and beards and ear curls, and the other, Modern Orthodox, mostly clean-shaven, identifiable by their kippahs or baseball caps, the acceptable substitute for honoring God above, appearing otherwise normal, but who require a nearby temple within walking distance and are wholly unavailable from sunset on Friday nights until after sunset on Saturdays, rendering null romantic weekends. Studying those two subsets of religious men, she had retreated entirely from the thought of a Jewish matchmaker.

There's a coven, a pride, a flock of the ultrareligious right now, walking on the otherwise empty sidewalk. The men with the sidelock curls, those dangling *peyot*, hands clasped behind their backs, bodies tilting forward, overdressed in their dully black coats that absorb the morning sun. Passing them, she uselessly admonishes herself to not dwell on what's missing in her life.

A bright red car whizzes past. *She* is like that car, carrying herself with spangle and spark, but the strength that has long held her up is weakening. In Palm Springs, she's going to disappoint everyone when she walks in alone, without Aaron Green. Should she throw out a few hints that the relationship may be experiencing a loss of acceleration?

God, no. Nothing has come of his supposed existence, except for the homework she must do and the need to keep everything straight, but she's not ready to resume her old role as the Tabor offspring unloved outside the familial circle.

Is it wrong that she wants the warmth of her family's attention, to retain their newly revived belief that love is not beyond her reach, that love has found her again?

Absolutely not.

And not telling the truth is kinder—she wouldn't want to be responsible for torching Harry's big award weekend.

That's not the real reason.

She's a coward, plain and simple, lacking the kind of bravery needed to come clean about her whale of a lie.

And that makes her think of the story from Hebrew school that she never got straight—was Jonah saved, regurgitated out of the whale's massive mouth, and into the cleansing water, as she could be if she came clean, or did he die in there? He probably died in there.

The pretend lover, the few relationship details she has coyly shared with her family about Aaron Green, illuminate what she tries to forget: the Phoebe who existed at twenty-three, in love with a long-haired boy named Elijah, who threw himself into life with abandon. The only former love who has never reached out to her.

Over the years, she has debated whether the way she let him go has been responsible for her perennial single status, the diminution, then disappearance, of that magnetism she once took for granted.

Sometimes late at night in her office she searches for Elijah's name, but no engine finds him, not even one other person with his name seems to exist in the whole great world, and she wonders if he went off the grid, as he swore he wanted to do someday. Or if he is dead.

She was a foolish young woman back then, and did him wrong, did herself wrong, too. She had lacked the courage to face him and explain she didn't possess his audacity to live an explorative life, that the idea of dropping out, even temporarily, frightened her, that the life she was living gave her the comfort and certainty she needed and desired. She had disappeared on him, shunned his calls, deleted his emails, hid in the tiny bathroom in the small apartment she then had, until he removed his finger from the buzzer, until his rapping against the door stopped—she imagined him putting his tongue to his knuckles and tasting the blood, inhaling the iron scent of confusion. It had taken four months before he gave up, before she sighed in relief, then flinched in horror, that she had murdered something so rare with silence.

It sounds like a bad country song, Phoebe thinks.

Then she thinks, *no*, it feels biblical, the resultant suffering she has endured since tossing away that long-ago love.

The mundane intrudes. Her car requires fuel and she swings into her regular station. At the pump, she listens to the rush of the gasoline, watches the gallons ratchet up. On the other side of the tanks, a man extracts himself from his low-slung convertible, runs his card through, and starts doing the same.

"Happy Saturday morning," he says to Phoebe across the concrete divide. He is rather handsome. His smile is nice, so are his eyes. But drawing love to herself would never happen at a gas station.

"*Bonjour*," she says.

"Are you French?"

"*Oui.*" And with that floating *oui* comes the thought that she's wrong about where love could happen. It could happen here, but it's too late, she's declared herself French. Why didn't she simply say *hello* in her native English?

"Are you visiting, or do you live here?"

This interest of his, surely it's been triggered by the allure of her supposed foreignness. If she'd said, "Hello," he would have said, "Lovely day, enjoy it," filled his tank and driven away.

Because it's a lost cause, she shakes her head and says, "*Je suis désolée. Je ne parle pas l'anglais.*"

"You don't speak English?"

"*Non.*" She could backpedal the lie that she doesn't speak English, but not the lie that she's French.

She feels his eyes on her as she hangs up the hose, screws on the fuel cap, enters the car, shuts the door, and starts the engine. At the exit, she glances in her rearview mirror and the man is looking in her direction, his hand raised in what could be a wave.

When she's back on the road, she yells at herself. He could have been the *one*, and what a story they could have told, about how their love ignited over premium unleaded at Shell. Real love, maybe, rather than the illusory love she shares with Aaron Green, whose invention was to find the real thing.

She cranks up the music and the first artist loud out of the speakers is like a finger wagging in her face. One of her favorites, with a stage name that's a play on Chet Baker. She's never listened to Chet Baker, but she likes Chet Faker, his cool, moody music, and she forces herself to sing along, to drown out how aptly his stage surname applies to her—faker, faker, faker.

EIGHT

H ARRY CLICKS THE TEMPERATURE button on his watch. Still early, but the heat is inching up, the norm for August, when Labor Day is still a couple of weeks away. Yesterday at five, it peaked at 114. Today, it could reach 108 by noon. He reaches into his bag for a bottle. Forty-five minutes ago, it could have been a frozen weapon; now it's just plastic holding cold water, which he swigs.

Levitt has gone out the gate, to the parking lot, has popped his trunk, seeking a dry shirt, then holds his phone up in the air. "Hey, Harry, I've got to make a call," he yells.

"Do what you need to do," Harry yells back, and sits down on the weather-worn bench on the court.

Levitt usually receives and returns one or two during their matches, always a patient querying him about her recent mammoplasty, or blepharoplasty, or rhinoplasty, or rhytidoplasty, or platysmaplasty, or abdominoplasty, or gluteal augmentation—the medical terms Levitt has taught him for breast implants, eyelid-lifts, nose jobs, face-lifts, neck-lifts, tummy tucks, and rounding buttocks that have fallen down or flattened with age. Levitt's features are slightly simian and he sweats like the hairy beast that he is not, and having some of the work he performs on others executed on his own visage and body would not be amiss, but it is impossible to feel sorry for the plastic surgeon in such demand that he is located on the court for matters involving not life or death, but vanity. He is the most pleasant doctor Harry has ever known and Levitt says it's because the work he does is nearly 100 percent elective, only a tiny smattering medically required, and as a result, he rarely tangles with insurance companies: he's paid up front and in full before he ever numbs an area or puts someone under and lifts the finest of scalpels, ready to perform his surgical-*artiste* magic. As Levitt's Maserati demonstrates, he is cleaning up in his business of smoothing and sanding and de-fatting and plumping Palm Springs women of a certain age, of which there are many. Men, too, more and more, as Levitt always reminds him.

Harry swigs again, feeling pleased with the way he's playing, keeping Levitt running, even if the memory of those dachshunds is still rolling around in his head. That might be the worst thing he's done in his life, leaving those dogs behind, tearing out his young daughters' hearts. Still, the girls survived, and all his children are healthy and happy, frequently phoning to fill him in on the progress of their lives, visiting regularly. He's done right by his children, whom he loves so much, done right by them all of the time, except for that lapse in judgment regarding King David and Queen Esther.

Levitt, leaning against his car, is speaking into his phone, one hand moving slowly up and down, as if compressing the air, a gesture Harry recognizes as *Calm down.* Some matron is worried about something. From what Levitt has told him, he's never botched a procedure or a surgery or been sued for malpractice; the tough-est thing about what he does is convincing people they need to be patient, that swelling requires time to subside, that stitches will dissolve as they should, that bruising will fade, leaving behind vulnerable pink skin as unblemished as a baby's, that they will, eventually, be exactly as they desire.

Harry understands that need people have for reassurance, to be told many times that everything will be okay.

And that's exactly what he told that young Owen Kaufmann from the *Palm Times*.

That dealing with closed countries, secretive emigration quotas, malfunctioning airports, armed military, corrupt officials, extreme weather, and all the other details that attend moving Jews from around the globe to this patch of arid heaven is often easier than providing the necessary calm to families breathlessly checking off days until they have the proper paperwork in hand, are boarding a plane, stretching their necks to view the despised countries they are finally leaving behind, itching to begin their new lives awaiting them here in Palm Springs. No matter the education provided about what to expect and no matter how clear Harry's people on the ground have been, he must calm them again when they land, are taken to their new home, and discover it is not the sprawling house plus pool of their dreams, but an acceptable apartment near to the very decent first jobs he has found them. And that when they were told they would be living in the desert, it meant a dry place that is usually hot or hotter or hottest, and the items they've packed into their bulging, double-strapped suitcases, like snowsuits and fleece-lined boots, would no longer be required. Acclimating to the heat takes time, they are all repeatedly told when still in Russia, Ukraine, Poland, Romania, Lithuania, Hungary, Slovakia, Belarus, Moldova, Bulgaria, Czechia, Slovakia, and, lately, China. And he tells them again when they arrive, but they can't really understand the notion of *desert heat* until they have lived here a while. With time comes an increase in physical stamina, the skin and vital organs recalibrating to the new temperatures. They all always do adjust, and then become happy, and then happier, and many end up with those large houses with pools, but in the beginning there is an enormous need to calm them down. The only transplants happy immediately were the Ethiopian Jews, who were used to the heat. In his thirty years of resettling Jews here, his own track record is nearly as unblemished as Levitt's. Only one family has ever returned from whence they came. And each year they send Harry a multipage letter, telling him how everyone in the family is doing, that they were hasty in turning back from their future, that one day they might give it another go, try better, harder, do it right, the second time around.

That story had impressed the young reporter, as did Harry's three-armed expansion of CST fourteen months ago, which formalized its informal dabbling in real estate, education, and lending. Now, CST Property provides affordable housing at below-market prices for the desert's newest inhabitants, and CST Educate! grants no-string funds for higher education, requiring only that the schools attended are accredited and that grantees maintain a B average each year, and CST Lend offers better and more elastic terms and rates on mortgages and business loans than any bank in California. He'd recruited new division presidents smartly, hiring a former property manager of midpriced developments in Texas, Florida, and Arizona, a former high-level administrator in the California community college system, and a former banker who retired early from a premiere asset-management firm and was looking for a new challenge. Owen Kaufmann had scribbled fiercely in his notebook, the red light on his phone steady as Harry's every word was also recorded.

And Harry had waited happily for the next interview question, pleased he'd finally heeded the advice of his new presidents about a campaign for CST, to publicize that the doors of CST Property, Educate!, and Lend were open not only to Jews who had availed themselves of the relocation services CST provides, but to anyone, whether or not strictly defined as a refugee, who was in need and newly arrived in the valley from a problematic country. He was pleased, too, that after additional meetings with his new presidents and several of his underling hires—second-generation go-getters whose Jewish-naming ceremonies and circumcisions Harry had witnessed, born to those he had brought to the new world as teenagers—he'd finally conceded that the campaign should feature its openhearted founder as the centerpiece.

How wary, hesitant, and unsure he'd been about that.

He had kept a deliberately low profile since uprooting his family from Connecticut. That long meandering journey allowing him and Roma to adjust to the realization that what they had planned for themselves was, as it never had been before, up in the air, needing those three traveling weeks to adapt to the changing nature of their future. And when they settled in Palm Springs, and he founded CST, he had still maintained that deliberately low profile, and kept his organization's mission quiet, "under the shade of a bushel," as his father, Mordy, might have said.

But his people convinced him and he finally said, "Okay, but we're going to go slow. I'm only going to dip one toe at a time into the spotlight."

He'd put one toe in, and it felt warm in the glow, and so he put in another toe, and enjoyed the meetings with deep-pocketed contributors and national businesses with large local presences about increasing their conservative donations up to seven figures, and he knew he had them when their final inquiry was whether CST might put up a wall in the lobby of its adobe building, etch donor names in stone or marble, to which Harry answered, "I think we can manage that."

And damn, it was gratifying having CST's works out there for all to admire, albeit in small articles printed in local magazines, and he wondered why he had waited, when public recognition all at once felt like his due.

He was seventy, so honestly what had he been waiting for? For his philanthropic works to be summarized in his eventual obituary?

That notion had filled him with unalloyed fear, and that was his state of mind when the *Palm Times* began aggressively pursuing him after the Man of the Decade announcement. He'd taken his time thinking about it, then relented, and in walked fervent Owen

Kaufmann, a cub with acne on his cheeks, and an overly starched shirt wearing him, and the too-wide tie probably handed down by his father, but with colorless eyes that shone with a fervor no longer seen much in the young, who said, "Mr. Tabor. I can't thank you enough. This is terrific. I have to admit I never thought you'd agree."

He swigs again and thinks how he relaxed into the new sensation of being sought after, and he'd extended his hand and, with a huge Harry Tabor smile, said, "Happy to finally meet you, Owen, after all the phone calls. Begin anywhere. I am, as they say, an open book."

Owen had asked the perfect first question: "Why did you decide to bring attention to yourself and the work you do now?"

Harry had leaned back in his chair, steepled his hands, and told a tiny white lie: "This isn't at all about me."

When Owen gave him an encouraging nod, Harry continued. "Indeed, I have never wanted our work to be public, but there comes a time to bring mitzvot into the light, and given the dire circumstances of refugees around the globe, it seemed appropriate to highlight the work we do here, to encourage others to reach out and help those in need. As is being done for the Syrians and other refugees by Mormon missionaries in Utah, by helpful citizens in Idaho, by groups of Canadians, and even, surprisingly, by the Germans. Each has different reasons for their compassionate aid, but bottom line, they are saving people. There are so many living in appalling conditions, throwing themselves into the ocean and drowning when their overcrowded boats sink or are sunk by despicable people profiting on these people's struggles and misery, that it was time to send out a call, a wish that others would step up and do what is right."

His answer was honest and ardent, and he had just a moment to bask in its fine qualities, thinking that if Owen Kaufmann said something like, "You're sort of a saint," Harry would deny that appellation forcefully, would say, "Not at all. Human nature is such that we give lip service to helping others, and then turn back to our own lives which, of course, are our priorities, but since I was in a position to do so, I simply made up my mind to follow through." But he did not have a chance to vocalize that well-formed response because Owen Kaufmann changed direction on Harry.

"Did you come to your work because you have always lived a moral, ethical life, or did you come to your work so that you would live a moral, ethical life?"

Harry had needed a moment to digest the distinction.

"Oh, I see. You're asking have I always been a principled man, or was I seeking to become such."

"Right," Owen Kaufmann said.

He'd never considered his life in those terms, and he said as much, then said, "You're still very young, but in every man's life, inevitably there are a few missteps that don't bear recollecting, so long as one has learned from those mistakes."

"Can you give an example of a mistake you've made and learned from?"

"I stole a pack of gum when I was a kid. My mother forced me back into the store, to apologize to the manager, and when we returned home, I was sent to my room and forbidden from watching my favorite cowboy show on TV. So that taught me if I took what wasn't mine, I'd end up losing something else that was dear to me. But Owen, that's off the record. My misdeeds, minor as they may have been, are not something to be shared with your readers."

Owen said, "Sure, I understand, no problem," and Harry felt they were in sync.

"So my next question is this: Is your religious faith the reason you've made it your mission to help Jews?"

Harry had swiveled his chair around and stared out at the high blue of the desert sky and thought about how he was born on May 14, 1948, the very day and year the State of Israel came into being, and how his family attended Palm Springs Synagogue's Reform High Holiday services, and the occasional Saturday morning Shabbat service, but not much more than that, and how each of his children had attended Hebrew school there, but he hadn't required they publicly attain their Jewish maturity, as he had once done under the banner of God and in view of family and friends, and how, until stepping down last year, he sat on the PSS board, helping orchestrate Jewish life for its congregants, but when he was too busy to attend a bimonthly meeting, the blast of freedom was enormous.

He had felt the young reporter's fervent stare, his restraint waiting, and he'd thought, *My religious faith, such as it is, is not the reason I resettle wandering Jews in my desert.*

Then he'd thought, *But what is the reason?*

He tried unearthing the instigating factor for his life's work these last thirty years, and couldn't find it, but found incipient panic that he tamped down hard. An answer was expected and so he had spoken a truth he realized last night he should have expanded upon: "Religious faith has nothing to do with my organization's mission. I am a historical Jew."

Owen Kaufmann had nodded again, and said, "So, I've tried researching this, Mr. Tabor, but I can't find any background on my next question. What does the acronym *CST* stand for?"

That Owen Kaufmann had been researching Harry before this interview was his first thought, quickly subsumed by the second: What *did CST* stand for? And the panic fluttered higher, because he was sure his strong brain retained every important piece of information about his life.

He'd rallied with, "It has a personal meaning, that's all, but not for public consumption."

Owen had smiled in a way that struck Harry as a little wolfish, that made him question the sort of young man Owen Kaufmann actually was, and the interview had continued, the small silver hoop in Owen's right ear winking under the lights, and when he was finally gone, Harry walked down the short white hallway to the file room. Faced with rows and rows of gray cabinets, containing information about every single person he has saved, along with his foreign on-the-ground staff, he wasn't sure where to look for anything that might tell him why he had named his organization CST. He stood and stared and then returned to his office and sat mulling that mystery with its heft of importance, combing through his life and coming up with zilch. When he took himself home, he poured a glass of smoky scotch and drank it with his feet in the courtyard pool, the water purpling as the sun lowered itself to the horizon, his eyes fixed on a cactus with one hanging red bloom, debating whether his inability to recall what those letters represented was a first sign of something going wrong, like Alzheimer's.

Does he have Alzheimer's? All week, he's tried to remember what compelled him to found CST, and what its letters stand for. His Man of the Decade honor is because of CST, and for the life of him, he can't recall. He didn't ask Roma because he wants to assess whether his memory contains other glitches before he worries her. She fears nothing in life other than either of them losing their minds.

"SORRY, HARRY, THE CALL took longer than I expected. . . . Hey, Harry!"

Harry looks up at Levitt.

"What?"

"Do you want to think or do you want to play?"

Harry's not sure.

Then he says, "Play," and trots to his baseline. Soon they're trading points, and collecting points, and Harry moves ahead four games to three, then five games to three, then he's leading in the sixth.

Levitt tosses up the ball, stretches to smack it with his racquet, and Harry instinctively moves forward to meet it, and is ambushed by the vision of Owen Kaufmann's wolfish smile, lips pulled up tight, small, sharp teeth bared. Was that the reporter's normal smile and Harry hadn't noticed, or was it cause for—Harry thwacks the ball, a blistering forehand so hard and fast that when Levitt dives for it, he's left hitting air as the ball soars right past him and lands, perfectly, just inside the line, before spinning away.

Definitely not cause for concern, Harry thinks, when that shot wins him the first set.

NINE

T HE SUN HAS UNFURLED, the freeway traffic has remained
sparse, and Camille has resolved nothing. Is it fair if out of
the blue she tells her family how things have been for her of late,
when she's given no hints, has trained them so well that when their
calls, emails, and texts went unanswered, they assumed she was
consumed with her anthropological work, read nothing into her
unresponsiveness, were grateful for the short conversations she had
with them these last months?

She's been dispiritedly depressed, and being home means entering a special realm, a kingdom where all the Tabors shine incredibly bright, that blaze a distinguishing family characteristic. She's
one of them, but her filaments have always been of a different variety, and now she's beclouded, bedimmed, the first among them
forced to brake before burning out.

If she laid bare her travails, would the fact of her seeking advice
render them speechless? At first, definitely. But they'd hide their
surprise, and she'd be hugged tight by them all. Her father would
say, "What can we do? Do you need money?" Her mother would say,
"Let's sit. We'll delve into it deeply, locate the roots together." Phoebe
would lose herself in the story of Valentine's marriage proposal,
which Camille would relay as off-the-cuff, lobbed the week he
left, though the proposal was serious, and then *Phoebe* would be

dispirited, if not a little depressed, and acting as if she weren't. And Simon, he would insist she take up yoga, or cycling, or running, would tell her the best way to get out of her own head was to get sweaty, to funnel her fear into movement.

A green truck flies past with a dog in the passenger seat, head out the window, russet-colored ears flapping in the current. He reminds Camille of her early childhood, recalled mostly through photographs. The one she's thinking of was taken in front of the Connecticut house—her young parents laughing as their very young daughters roll on the grass with the little dogs she and Phoebe adored. She can't believe she doesn't remember their names. Simon's not in that picture, was not yet born, not part of their old life, and his absence from that time-faded image makes her think of her own absence, how happy everyone will be when they see her, how happy everyone will be that the family is united when her father is honored. Does she have it in her to unsettle all that domestic pleasure?

She wishes she had picked up the phone, opened the lines of communication in advance of her return. She could have called Phoebe, given her a warning that would have spread, that all was not right with her. She had considered the notion, then discarded it, because Phoebe would have wanted to talk about what everyone was planning to wear tonight. And she hadn't wanted to hear her sister's lawyer voice, used when she means, *I know what's best for you*, telling Camille, as she often has in the past, that she wasn't to wear anything purchased from secondhand shops and flea markets, which constitutes Camille's entire wardrobe. "Go buy yourself something no one else has worn before, something wonderfully sexy. Purchase the best you can afford in a luxurious fabric with subtle draping, and a great pair of heels." That's what her sister would have said, which would have smacked Camille on the head with the truth that her sartorial challenges are the least of her problems.

Phoebe, of course, will be dressed in something expensively incomparable, highlighting her effortless radiance. All of her family will be dressed to the nines, every one of them imbued with an intuitive sense of what goes with what. She did not inherit that particular Tabor gene, but she made an effort this time. She will be wearing a white satin suit, trousers and jacket, a designer hand-me-down from the hostess of that last awful cocktail party, who said, "This will be great on you," and when Camille at first declined, Marni said, "Listen, no way I'm ever getting back to my prepregnancy weight, so either you take it or it goes with all the rest to Goodwill." Camille had taken it. And then spent money she shouldn't have spent on the kind of high heels Phoebe would approve of, bought spanking new. When she tried the outfit on Thursday, she wasn't repulsed by what she saw in the mirror, but she knows what will happen later today: she'll be dressed and Phoebe will come into her old bedroom and tilt her head and put a manicured finger to her mouth and say, "It's not bad, but it's not really you. Let's see if Mom has something better."

It's not Phoebe's fault that she likes to help, but Camille will feel doubly the failure, a child led by the hand and shown a range of choices in Roma's closet. Attending the gala for her father outfitted by her sister in her mother's clothes, that alone speaks to a life that has jumped the tracks.

Camille shakes her head. She's floundering, but she can stand firm in this one way, refuse all kindly suggestions, proudly wear the suit, view it as a small victory. The only kind available to her these days, other than those that occur inside the lilac walls of the hospice, helping those truly at the end of their roads.

How she wishes she were back in the Trobriand Islands, inhabiting herself fully. Everything was easier there. She was focused, smart, happy, and energetic. Fun to be around. She spoke Kilivila like a native, surprising everyone with her fluency. She wore shorts and tees and sandals, hiking boots in the bush, flippers in the water when she explored the coral atolls with the islanders. She helped with the annual yam crop, tended to the gardens, to the taro, the sweet potatoes, the leafy greens and beans, the squashes. She split coconuts; she ate raw sugarcane. She sat cross-legged on fertile ground, on green grass, at the edge of sugarcane fields, surrounded by Trobrianders, of all ages, of both genders, listening to everything they wanted to tell her, finding ways to get them to tell her everything else she desired to know. At the cracked feet of the old medicine women she learned about the magic spells they created for whoever came to them in good faith and with pure hearts, paid for with dried banana leaves. Magic spells for controlling the weather, for finding love, for increasing beauty, for attaining carving expertise, for growing the biggest yams, for building canoes, for sailing the ocean safely. Spells considered personal property, passed down from one generation to the next, along with the land they worked, with its coconut and areca palm trees, the gardens they tilled, the shells they collected from the beaches, the dried-banana-leaf wealth they stored away. She would like to be back on Kiriwina, on Kaileuna, on Kitava, or on Vakuta, asking one of those wise and wizened old women to conjure her a whole lot of magic spells. Spells that would solve all of her problems. Incantations, chants, herbs, sacred oils, anything, everything, perhaps even just a warm hand on her head.

Camille finds herself smiling. It's strange, but simply thinking about those magic spells has lightened her mood, cleared the bramble from her brain. She knows now that when she enters the kingdom of home, she will do so with bravery, with love in her heart, and her life under wraps.

TEN

LUCY HAS SPLASHED AROUND in the pool and Isabel has listened to Elena read her a story and Simon has packed and
everyone has eaten birds in a nest, and now the trunk of the car
is filled with his and Elena's small black carry-on bags and his
daughters' tiny suitcases awash in butterflies and glittery flowers.
But there is a ruckus in the house—Isabel again insisting on wearing
her purple tutu and Elena having none of it. Simon hears Elena's
pitched voice and Isabel's crying and, out here, Lucy's squeals as
she competes in a footrace with what might be an invented, invisible friend, running back and forth from the front door, over the
grass, to him at the car in the driveway.

She screeches to a halt and flings her golden downy arms around
him and looks up into his face. "Daddy, Daddy, Daddy, Daddy,
Daddy, Daddy . . ." And he knows she won't stop saying *Daddy*
until he does something, adjusts this stuck mode she's in. Lucy with
her repetitions of words, Isabel with her tutu, his children already
know how to dig in for the long haul.

An old woman in a red tracksuit and matching red sun visor is
huffing up their steep street, her old leashed dog behind, trotting
hard to keep up. Lucy peers around Simon to watch, then looks up
at him again and begins, "Doggy, doggy, doggy, doggy, doggy . . ."
and it goes on even after owner and animal have disappeared

around the bend in the road. Lucy often speaks like a child far older than she is, amazing both her parents by articulating abstract thoughts, but this repetitive game of hers can drive him loony.

"Honey, why don't you go find out what's keeping Mommy and Isabel."

"No," Lucy says, leaping back, folding her arms over her chest, staring him down. "Belly is dumbdumbdumb. I told her what to wear, but she doesn't listen."

Belly, the name Lucy calls her younger sister when she wants it understood how grown-up she is in comparison.

"We'll go together," Simon says, and then Elena is framed in the front door, holding Isabel, who is dressed in a purple dress and purple sandals with bows, her dark hair in a jiggling top-of-the-head ponytail, her face tearstained, clutching the purple tutu. Elena gives him a rueful look: the tutu, Isabel's version of a security blanket, will be joining them on this trip.

Forty minutes after he hoped to be on the road, the girls are in their car seats, the kiddie music they adore, like nails on a chalkboard to their parents, is on low, and they are heading down the curves to the flats. He likes the ivy tendrils and ice plants spilling from the hills, chosen to avert disastrous rain runoff and potential mudslides, the heavy boughs of tall trees arching lacily over the narrow street, the sun spilling through the foliage, the oft-patched road. They've just passed his favorite house, a white cottage covered in bougainvillea, blooming rose bushes heavily scattered about. It has a storybook quality to it that their own house lacks despite its age, with its squared-off rooms, its sliding glass doors that are not original. He knows the white cottage is deceptive. It looks quaint, but it's five bedrooms and five and a half baths, has a large pool with a waterfall, and the owners have lived there for twenty-five years. He tracks prices in their neighborhood, houses for sale, houses in escrow, enjoys looking at the floor plans posted online, knows everything about that white cottage. At some point, they'll either have to expand their own house—building up, a second floor, would be the only choice—or move. It's fine for now, with the girls so small, but when they're teenagers, filling every room with their emotions, it's going to be a disaster. But that's in the future, and at least he called a guy named Fred to come Monday morning, make the crack in the ceiling disappear before everything comes falling down.

Gas, he thinks and peers at the gauge, hoping Elena filled up her car. She doesn't always remember. The last time they went to Palm Springs, in June for Roma's sixty-eighth birthday, Elena hadn't done it, and the girls had been screaming, and the machine kept refusing to accept his card, and by the time the tank was filled and he was back in the car, he and Elena weren't speaking to each other. That whole trip a waste of valuable, hard-to-find conversational time. But the tank is miraculously full, which means they don't have to stop, which means when the girls fall asleep, as they do cruising the freeway, he and Elena will be able to talk, the first time in months that they are both in the same car with a couple hours of quiet driving ahead of them.

At the other end, Agapanthus Lane and the house in which he grew up. Even before their daughters were born, his mother led them to the lovely guest room, with the en suite bathroom and the king bed, but he always wishes for the bedroom that was his from infancy on, where he sprawled out when home from university and law school for holidays and several weeks each summer. He's never had the guts to say to his parents, "Let's switch the twin beds in my old room for the big bed in the guest room. We'll put the girls in the guest and I can sleep where I once did for years and years. Let me really come home." No matter how long Phoebe and Camille have been gone, they burst into the house and toss their belongings into bedrooms that have always been theirs, still imprinted with their teenage books and school awards, although the furniture has been replaced, is now white and modern. He endures an internal temper tantrum walking into the room intended for visitors, that holds nothing of him in the air, or the closet, or the shelves. It makes him feel like the interloper he sometimes considered himself to be—the youngest child, the last child, the only boy, an *oops*, he has often thought—those eight years between him and Phoebe, six between him and Camille. The only one born in Palm Springs. During high school, he used to climb up to the flat roof and sit with his legs hanging over the edge, drinking a Gatorade, looking out at the sunburned land, with its desert wildlife requiring no human intervention, the isolated stretches of emerald golf courses, the mountains off in the distance, imagining the reaction of his parents and sisters to this environment, so different from the bucolic Eastern town in which they had once lived, the house he has seen only in pictures, a giant maple outside the living room windows, snowstorms in the winter, snowmen in the front yard, games by the fireplace, the air tangy and blue with cold.

Enough, he thinks. He will not allow himself these petulant feelings today, not this weekend. Not with Harry's induction, not with his own phenomenal news about the ILA conference. He is a grown man no longer in need of his childhood space.

The traffic light turns green and Simon accelerates up the on-ramp, pulls onto the freeway, moves into the fast lane. Elena checks the backseat, then snaps off the kiddie music and says, "They're already asleep. Let's talk about Colombia. First, what do we do with the kids?"

Simon glances at Elena and she's smiling at him. Something has shaken loose this morning; they seem back on the same page. "That's exactly what I was thinking. Not who can take proper care of our precious children, but what do we do with them."

Elena's smile disappears. "I *didn't* mean it that way."

He was kidding. She knows she's a terrific mother and knows he thinks she's a terrific mother, so why can't she laugh about something all parents occasionally say? Better not to ask again about her losing her sense of humor. Better to take the high road, carry the conversation forward.

"Maybe we should come back to Palm Springs, leave them with Roma and Harry for the ten days?" he suggests. "I wonder if we can fly out from there, come back the same way?"

"We'd have to backtrack with a connecting flight out of LA, but that's not a big deal. The big deal is if we put Lucy in that kinder-readiness program, she'll miss a week of it. So are we enrolling her or forgetting about it and she'll just start kindergarten next year?"

This has been a regular topic all summer. Simon won't say this morning what he keeps saying—that it's Elena's decision, since she's the one home with the kids. For months, they've batted around whether Elena is ready for this part of Lucy's childhood to end. If Lucy's ready. She's nearly reading her favorite books on her own, but reverts in some ways for reasons they haven't been able to figure out—a thumb in her mouth, baby talk, extra-long naps several afternoons in a row; a couple of times she's wet her bed in the middle of the night when she's been diaper-free since Elena was five months pregnant with Isabel.

"What happens if we enroll her this year but she starts late?"

"I don't know," Elena says. "Do five-year-olds form immediate friendships? Would a latecomer be ostracized? I'd hate that for her."

He doesn't know the answers to those questions, but Roma would, and he can't understand why Elena hasn't called and asked for her input; they've talked so many times about reaching out to their own personal psychologist who specializes in toddlers, children, and teens. "I'll ask my mother this weekend," he says. "She'll give us some guidance."

When Elena says nothing, Simon changes gears. "Assuming Roma says Lucy starting late isn't a problem, or we decide to hold off on school until next year, what do you think about giving the girls quality time with their grandparents while we're gone?"

"Sure," Elena says. "But will Roma and Harry be able to handle them? Read to Isabel in the mornings, make sure they don't drown in the pool, get them both to eat a healthy breakfast?"

"Phoebe, Camille, and I survived, none of us drowned or starved, so I'll say yes to that."

"I didn't mean it that way," she says again, this time in a lighter voice. Then, "It's just that we've never—"

"I know," Simon says, and he does know. They've never left their daughters, or rather, Elena has never left their daughters anywhere

overnight without her, which includes with their maternal grandparents and great-grandparents, who live in Los Angeles, too. Their
honeymoon was the last vacation they took alone. In the beginning, she joked that motherhood had grounded her as it hadn't
grounded him—but that joke, less frequently raised by Elena these
days, feels sharper and stabs deeper when she does. A few weeks
ago, when he suggested hiring the nanny they can't really afford to
care for Isabel if they put Lucy in that readiness program, Elena
said, "What's the use right now? I can't travel somewhere and back
in four hours."

"So," she says. "I don't think Medellín has become a really hot
tourist spot yet. While you're busy, I could explore the city, see if I
can discover a fresh angle for an article, try to sell it to one of my
old editors."

"That would be great," he says, with enthusiastic surprise. When
they'd talked about whether he might receive the ILA invitation
this year, he'd suggested exactly what she's just proposed, and she
shot him down, said, "Christ, Simon, leave it alone."

"Okay, so what do we do with the kids?"

A small laugh from Elena this time. "My parents wouldn't be
able to manage the girls and the *abuelitos*, so let's see how your parents react to the idea of ten days with their granddaughters. Well,
actually, wouldn't it be twelve? A travel day on each end, the ten
days of the conference? Let's suggest we'll hire someone to care for
them while your parents are working, to take them on adventures,
sightseeing, that kind of thing."

He can't see his daughters lasting through even an hour of sightseeing, but what does it matter if Elena is considering at last leaving
them, if it means actually making the trip to Colombia together.

"Maybe the girl my mom hired for tonight will work out and
we can arrange everything while we're there."

"What if your parents say a few days is okay, but twelve is too
long? What do we do then?"

"They won't," Simon says. "They'll view time alone with their granddaughters as a gift, without the meddling of their son and daughter-in-law."

"Not very funny. But what if they do?"

"Then we'll figure something else out. But they'll agree, Elena. I promise."

He needs to change the subject before Elena questions whether Roma will alter the schedule she has the girls on. "What do you know about Colombia?"

"Cocaine and drug wars, but I'll look it up," Elena says, and pulls her phone from her purse and types away.

"Okay. Medellín, once the home of the now-defunct Medellín cartel, was known as the most violent city in the world. But now it's considered safer than Baltimore, St. Louis, Detroit, and New Orleans."

She looks over at him. "Is that saying much?"

Simon shakes his head. "I don't know."

"Well, this is encouraging. It's been named one of the best cities to live in South America. And one of the most innovative cities in the world for its advances in politics, education, social development, and sustainable urban development. So I guess we won't die there."

"I'm pretty sure we won't."

"It'd be a real pain in the ass if we did," she says, then lets out a real laugh. And he laughs, too, relieved. He thought she was going to say if there was danger there, she wouldn't go, and perhaps he shouldn't go either. But when Elena laughs again, the tone is acerbic and triggers one of his insomniac thoughts—that she's pulling away. That tone says to him she wouldn't mind if he found himself in danger.

"Also, there are fifty-one Catholic churches within the city limits. Other denominations, too, with churches of their own, including a Mormon mission."

The country is devout, he knows that, and yet the ILA selected it, when recent conferences were held in Sweden, Iceland, and

Australia, none of which he considers particularly religious. With life spiraling drastically into a hellish existence of terrorism and wars, all with religious fundamentalism at their core, was the ILA's intent to send some kind of message by choosing a place steeped in religion?

Religion has no place in the legal arena, except when it's the actual crux of a case. But lately, in his own practice, he's seeing otherwise stoic motions and briefs filled with religious attacks on the beliefs of his plaintiff clients, attacks that feel triggered when he reads them, and armed when reiterated on the stand by the museum and gallery representatives, and the registrars of missing and looted art, and the governmental bureaucrats of those defendant countries, responding as if the horrific rationales on which any particular genocide was based are still alive and well. A concomitant degradation in legal civility is occurring in other areas of international law as well: courtroom combatants lashing each other with religious slurs at The Hague, judges and lawyers powerless at reining in the hate speech, no matter how hard they try. When you've been complicit in legitimized murder, contempt of court lacks any kind of punch. He and his colleagues often lunch together in the firm's conference room, discussing these events they are witnessing, and he thinks now how curious that they all speak passionately about man's intolerance of his fellow man, but never about the concept of God. Bombings and killings in the name of God. The pope promising, with the full import of his position, that the murderers will have to answer to God. God, the cause and effect of everything. God, unseen and unheard, possibly man's deluded creation or a creation devised by some to control others. Simon doesn't know which of his colleagues are believers, which are not, where he himself falls on the spectrum, but shouldn't they at least talk about it? The crazies raise God in every hate-filled proclamation before annihilating lives they deem worthless, while the sane and balanced quash their own voices.

"Are there any synagogues?" he finds himself asking.

Elena scrolls down on her phone.

"None are listed, but I would think there must be one. On the other hand, it is a very Catholic country."

They hit a traffic snarl, a long line waiting to merge from the 405 to the 10 heading east, and she clicks her phone off, places it in her lap, her right hand on top, as if prepared to swear on a bible.

Given Simon's work, the cases he takes on, the art and everything else he recovers, often for the descendants of Jews wrongfully, forcibly, illegally dispossessed, and then sent to their deaths, it's odd how rarely he thinks about his own Jewishness. Usually he only considers it on this very drive, to Palm Springs for the High Holidays. He wonders if the same is true for Elena, if she rarely considers her former stringent adherence to the Catholicism of her youth and young womanhood. A few months ago, he read about how more people than ever were making pilgrimages—to Buddhist temples in Japan, to Lourdes in France, to Tirupati in India, to Our Lady of Guadalupe in Mexico, following the footsteps of prophets in Saudi Arabia and Jerusalem, trekking to Mecca—but he and Elena observe none of their own holidays, not by themselves, have not done so since coming together. A skirmish-free way of binding their diverse inherited religions, or really, of avoiding everything entirely.

Has that affected them? Is it affecting them? As people? As a married couple? Will it affect their children, never seeing their parents involved at home on any spiritual level? This is a new, previously unarticulated worry.

And he realizes he was thinking about those pilgrimages just this morning while trying to get a grip on his tears.

"Do you think," he says, "that the tenets with which we were raised are attached to us permanently?"

"Are you talking about religion?"

Simon nods.

"Then, yes," she immediately says.

The rapidity of Elena's response startles him, but he's shocked when she says, "These days, I make it to church maybe four times a month."

"You *do*? Since when?"

"Since always."

"Since always? I remember when you told me you were turning into a quasi-Catholic, sinning with me on Friday and Saturday nights, and taking yourself to church to repent on Sundays. And then I thought you stopped going." And what had his reaction been to this beautiful girl who stopped attending on major Catholic holidays, on saints' days that had meaning to her? Pride? Probably. Definitely. Pride that nothing in her past would get in the way of their potential future. He'd seen a future with her from the first moment they met, and then they'd bonded so quickly.

"No, I only stopped going as frequently. And when we got married, I didn't see any reason to mention it."

"Why?"

"Because it was something I did for myself. And it's become something that *doesn't* revolve around you."

That stings, and is unfair, and the litigator in Simon kicks in.

"First, I think I'm the definition of a man not at the center of his own world. I'm a husband, and a father, and a busy lawyer. My life revolves around all of you and all of that. Not around me. And, second, we share things, don't we? So why would you have kept this from me?"

"I'm entitled to have a private place for myself, aren't I?"

"Yes, but—"

"You have one, with your physical fitness stuff."

"But you know about that."

"It's *not* a big deal, Simon."

Isn't it? It's a secret she's kept the whole of their marriage.

"Really, Simon, it's not like I'm tippling in the afternoons or gambling or shopping until the credit cards are maxed out."

With those as the comparisons, of course, she's right. But they've always agreed that secrets are anathema to a healthy marriage, and going to *church* doesn't imbue her secret with holiness.

"You're right," he says.

"I know I am. So you understand?"

He nods and smiles, but he doesn't understand, not really.

"And, of course, it's different for me now than when I was a kid. Now, it's a place where I go to think. Back then, I loved reading about the saints and collecting the Holy Cards with their faces on them, that we traded like baseball cards. I loved their histories, the idea of mysteries and miracles and great acts of courage, but I didn't believe they were actual saints. I knew they were tools to guide us kids into understanding what constituted appropriate behavior, an aspirational notion of how to live our lives.

"I've told you this, how when I was young, I used to imagine marrying Jesus, who I thought was very handsome. I wanted to become a nun, live a sanctified life. I never imagined falling in love with a man who did not believe in the tapestry of my religion, in the Father, the Son, and the Holy Ghost, in confession, and the saving grace of heaven."

She's shocked him again. Simon looks over to see if she's smiling, if this is a joke. But she's staring out the windshield, her eyes aimed at that very heaven she's just mentioned. She's absolutely never told him any of this before. If she had . . . If she had, he would have backed away early in their relationship, would not have messed around with a girl's desires for her life, would not have been comfortable falling in love with a woman who dreamt of Jesus as the perfect man.

Have they ever really talked about any of this?

How have they not?

How did they bond so quickly without a forthright exchange about what might dissolve them with the same speed?

There's that question he's asked himself a few times when deep inside of her—if she ever imagines him as one of the killers of her Christ! It was the Romans, not the Jews, who committed that deicide, the historical truth ignored by too many people, and in the midst of this conversation, it unnerves and disturbs him, tightly knots his intestines, thinking how very far apart they might actually be because of their upbringings. Have always been, in their oblivion.

Elena tilts her head toward the side window. Her ears are tiny scalloped shells, the lobes bare today, as they have been for a long time. He doesn't know when she stopped wearing all the dangly earrings she used to never be without, but she has. Many were gifts from him.

She turns back to him and there is amusement in her voice when she says, "Here's another confession. When you're actually at home and watch the girls on a weekend afternoon, and I'm at that blow-dry bar down the hill, *that* can be a near-religious experience. Thirty minutes of someone washing my hair, massaging my scalp, handing me glasses of complimentary champagne, making me look pretty. Also, I feel some sense of the spiritual when Ashley comes to babysit when you're out of town or working late and I get to go to a Pilates class."

Elena's throwing him salves, but underneath that hint of amusement, he can't tell if she's actually being serious or ironic. This morning, listening to her breathing in her sleep, he had considered again when his ability to read her tonal inflections had altered, and when his astute and symbiotic knowledge of her had lapsed, and if something fundamental had changed between them, that she had changed something fundamental between them, and he's wondering about it anew.

And then that earlier, previously unarticulated worry circles back into his mind, along with another first-time consideration: whether he and Elena are creating a defective family structure by strictly observing nonobservance. Their little girls are living—will live—a secular life within the environs of home; religion happens elsewhere, belongs to others, is not yet anything that resonates in the slightest. Christmas spent with Elena's family, the huge tree the girls help decorate the night before, and all the presents underneath in the morning, and the Easter dinner with the gift baskets bigger than they are, filled up with chocolate bunnies and marshmallow chicks. And the few Jewish holidays, which only mean time with their *savah* and their *sabba*. Hanukkah latkes; Passover, with its yearly explanation about the exit of the Jews from the desert after forty long years of trudging through sand, the extra wineglass filled for what Lucy calls "the ghost." Rosh Hashanah and Yom Kippur are dinners for which they get to dress up, then a babysitter they shyly meet, then night-night kisses from everyone, while the rest of the Tabors, including him and Elena—"*la familia Tabor religiosa*," Elena says on those nights—go off to temple.

"Do you feel you and the girls are missing out? Not painting hard-boiled Easter eggs we'd hide outside around the house. That we never have a Christmas tree. We don't attend midnight masses. We don't light our own menorah for the eight nights of Hanukkah, don't pack away all the *hametz* and eat only matzoh during Passover?"

"No. I have what I need."

He expects her to ask if he feels he's missing out, but she doesn't. She says, "Palm trees in the distance."

The palm trees of home.

How will his daughters make sense of the world if they have no idea who they are, or where they come from, the traditions they would otherwise keep, if the past is lost because it is not deliberately carried forward into the present and future? His daughters won't have any spiritual gird, because their parents have made their marriage a religion-free zone to eliminate scuffling over that which cannot easily be melded.

There is a rustling behind them and Elena checks on the girls. "Isabel's pulling the tutu up to her cheek. They're both still asleep."

Elena is smiling at him now, a happy smile, and when she says, "Everything okay?" Simon wants to say *no*, but stashes away his rumbling, colliding concerns. Time for all of that at some distant point in the future. He'll focus now on speeding down the freeway with the tires making that white noise he loves, on his girls peacefully asleep in the backseat, on his wife next to him, on the two of them maneuvering—at least decently, he thinks, he hopes—through time and space.

ELEVEN

LEVITT IS AHEAD FOUR games to two in the second set because Harry's preoccupied with the meaning of *CST*. It feels like a key to everything he doesn't recall, but even trying to think of a word that begins with *C*, other than the name of his daughter, leaves him beleaguered, an image only of black zigzaggy lines, and then of Owen Kaufmann standing next to him while they waited for the elevator's slow arrival, saying, "You sure have a great origin story, Mr. Tabor, thank you for your time and your candor."

A ball whizzes by him. Levitt yells, "Yes!" And Harry looks up to find Levitt banging his palm on his racquet. Somehow, without being aware of playing any more points, Harry's given away two games and the set.

Levitt gushes water into his mouth and spits it out instantly, "Hot as hell. I've got cold in the car," and heads again to the parking lot.

The metal fence twangs against Harry's spine, shivers his heated skin, when he sits on the bench and leans back. He likes this park, with its unfussy nature, its lack of pretension. The palm trees are tall, the grass torched brown, a teenager on the pull-up bars is failing at chin-ups. Poor kid, he's a bean, count the ribs, arms and legs like twigs. Harry was never like that—he matured early, had Bronx-made biceps and triceps and quads and calves, from stickball, stoopball, punchball, and kick-the-can in his youth, the muscles slackening a hint now, but the form still mostly retained. A couple of young mothers are pushing their toddlers on the swings. A young man is jogging past the courts singing out loud to whatever's plugged into his ears. His warbling isn't half bad.

Harry checks the chin-up kid's progress, but the kid is gone. When he hears a whistling in his ears, he looks around, but there is no one nearby, no one close enough to him that if they were whistling he could hear it. No, it's not a whistling, it's more like the sound of leaves rustling hard in a heavy wind, but there's no wind this morning, not even the faintest of breezes.

Then a strange pain in his eyes and Harry throws up his hands and presses hard. When it disappears, he opens his eyes to the world, which includes, at a slight distance, a man standing on a stage in a white robe, a tallit around his neck, and a kippah atop his untamed hair.

Harry closes down his sight, but opening his eyes once more changes nothing—the man in the white robe and tallit and kippah is still there.

And now the white-robed man is moving.

He is alive and moving around on the stage.

And the stage is at the front of a room crowded with people.

Harry slams his eyes shut again, and it is echoey in his head, as if his well-organized thoughts and knowledge and memories have cleared out. He grasps the word *memories*, holds on to it for dear life.

Is this an old memory he's conjured up, something he ought to recall? Something that *means* something to him?

No, he doesn't think so.

No, he's sure not.

Harry hears, *Try again*, and his eyes flip open, hoping Levitt has returned, has said, inexplicably, "Try again," but there is no Levitt, only the white-robed man who has not disappeared, who is looking out over that crowd standing shoulder to shoulder.

Harry squints.

The stage isn't a stage; it's a bema.

The room is not merely a small room; it's a shul.

And the audience is not any audience, but a congregation, a congregation of Jews.

Where is he, seeing this? Is he inside? Outside? Dematerialized in the air and looking down? He doesn't know.

Then the white-robed man opens his mouth and releases the most spectacular voice Harry has ever heard, transporting him utterly, and lifting, it seems, the shul's low-ceilinged rafters.

The man, he's a cantor.

A Jewish cantor singing a prayer Harry recognizes.

He hears *Yom Kippur* in his head. The cantor is singing the Kol Nidre, the first prayer—a thrice-uttered statement—that ushers in the holy Day of Atonement, when the essence of the soul is fully revealed, while the Book of Life is open, until slammed shut until the next year. In the top drawer of his desk in his study at home are his family's tickets for the holidays that bookend the Ten Days of Awe; this year, Rosh Hashanah begins on the ninth of September, the twenty-four hours of Yom Kippur atonement on the eighteenth. All of that is coming, but is not here yet, and yet, here it is, in front of him, a vision in August.

Should he veil his eyes once more? Shutter them completely? Seal them up? No. No, nothing will change, he understands that now, and he gives in, gives himself over to the cantor's singing, his final phrases, watches as the cantor steps back. And then young boys and elderly men are rushing onto the bema, lifting rams' horns to their lips, letting loose the shofars' curlicuing wild cries of triumph, and joy, and pain, and suffering, and it goes on and on until the out-of-tune symphony fades, leaving a hollowness the cantor fills by singing a note so sweet that the congregation stills. The cantor's note trills and circles, and rises up and up and up, and Harry feels what the congregation is feeling, their hearts wrenched open, longing for that which sustains the community during the worst of times, encouraging them to reclaim their faith for another year, and then that perfect golden note is flying into the night sky above the shul, joining the blanket of brazen, brilliant stars twinkling above the wooden building. Harry can see all of that despite the blue sky overhead on this sunny summer morning in Palm Springs.

He stares at the cantor.

Who is he to Harry?

Why is he seeing him?

Or why is he being shown him?

The face, it seems familiar, a face he has seen before.

But where?

He hears *daguerreotype*, registers that it, too, is reverberating only in his head, spoken in a voice dry and unfamiliar to him.

Daguerreotype. He knows what that is. An early type of photograph. Yes, he has one in his possession, a single photograph, very old and wrinkled, the edges furred.

Is it of this man, this cantor?

It could be.

It might be.

He thinks it is

He stares at the vision.

Yes, he is sure it is.

The small photograph in the gilt frame passed down to Harry by Mordy. Passed down to Mordy by Aleph. Passed down to Aleph by Abraham. Then, in Harry's head, his father's guttural throat clearing, once a known sound, used to dislodge the years, and he hears Mordy say, "Time, I think, for me to recite once again the beginning of the oft-told tale . . .

"As you know, your great-grandfather's brother trained as a cantor. And when his training was complete, when his teachers determined they had nothing more to teach him, not that they ever really did, he applied for the desirable and desired position at the shtetl's one shul. Potential cantors were required to have deep knowledge of the prayers, an artistic musical delivery, a pleasing appearance, a flowing beard, and a wife. These rules were as nonnegotiable as the Russian Empire's rules for Jews that created desperation and deprivation—where and when and how they could move outside the Pale of Settlement, what they could study, what professions they might enter, how much money they might earn. When the shul's rabbi heard him sing, he took an unortho- dox stance. So what if the young man was unbearded and unmar- ried, a beard could always grow and a marriageable woman could be found, but rare was the stunning anomaly before him: a young cantor who possessed perfect pitch and impeccable delivery despite being profoundly deaf."

Harry is sitting on a bench on a tennis court in the desert and this profoundly deaf cantor to whom he's related—dead these last, what, hundred and forty years?—is, *was*, singing the Kol Nidre in the Pale of Settlement way back when. Maybe it would make sense if Harry had been there, been alive at that time, been in that shul during Yom Kippur, heard his great-uncle doing his thing, but he wasn't.

This isn't his own memory he's recalling—seeing unfold in real time 140 years ago.

It's not Mordy's memory either.

How is Harry seeing this mad bright vision?

Is this a hallucination, a harbinger of something else, a brain tumor, for instance?

No, not a harbinger, but a reminder.

Not a harbinger, but a reminder? That sentence is enunciated in the same dry voice unknown to him. But the words in his head are clear, and if he can hear them, then surely he is not about to keel over, the image of his ancestral cantor glued to his irises, his un- forgettable voice ringing in his ears, the last thing Harry Tabor sees and hears before exploding internally.

Never once in his life has he ever taken a morning shot of some- thing to neutralize his fears, but right this minute, he could use a short one, something very strong to knock back quick—that eighty- proof Croatian cherry brandy, an undrunk soldier in the drinks cabinet in the living room, a gift from a Jewish Croat family he brought here—would do the trick.

"Ice water."

Levitt's voice slips in, returning Harry to the present. Levitt's face and bulky body is in front of him, but the fading figment of the cantor is there, too, standing right next to his tennis-playing plastic surgeon friend, and just then, the idea that the dogs and the cantorial vision, the singing of that first repentant prayer, has something to do with tonight's honor sends an electrical current through him, and he thinks how that vision was set on the unordinary day when one atones for his sins—

"Harry, you look odd."

The vision is gone and Harry looks up at his friend, and searches for his voice, opens his mouth to encourage it, feels a tickle at the back of his throat, tries expelling a little air, expects to hear a little cry, but nothing, nothing at all. And he feels a fresh ripple of panic. His voice, he seems to have lost it, gone, disappeared, *kaput*.

"Drink. You look like you might be dehydrated," Levitt says.

Harry drinks deeply, and when he feels words again gathering in his throat, he says, "I'm fine. A hundred percent fine," thinking he'll phone his GP on Monday for an appointment, have his physical early, just in case. Until then, he won't speculate about what the hell is going on with him.

"CHANGEOVER," LEVITT CALLS OUT, a crowing in his voice, because he's never done this well against Harry. They meet again at the bench and Levitt reaches into his tennis bag for a fresh can of balls, peels back the plastic cap, and sticks his thumb through the pull. The unzipping of the metal lid sounds to Harry like a hard key turning in a lock, a lock on a metal-barred door, a metal-barred door of a jail cell, and there he is, inside, and that confounds him entirely, and he feels a trembling fear he's never experienced before. He recalls not at all experiencing that precise fear more than three decades ago, then getting down on his knees and praying for a way out. What he recalls is the term Owen Kaufmann had employed, his *origin story*. But it wasn't a story at all. All of it was true, properly humble tales he told Owen Kaufmann about the good man that he is.

He is that good man, isn't he?

Of course he is.

He heads to the baseline and trips, and trips again a moment later, going down on one knee. He's not hurt or scraped, but he is supremely unbalanced, as if one wrong step will undo who he is, and then a correction intrudes in his mind, a clarification he does not understand, in that same dry and unfamiliar voice: *The wrong step deserving of punishment you avoided by repairing to the desert.*

He looks around wildly, at the people in the park, at Levitt on the other side of the court, bouncing the ball, preparing to serve, and he feels that trembling fear again, a fear that feels new, a fear untied to anything he can put his finger on, but makes him think he is poised to go tumbling down.

Why is he hearing that voice?

And what does the voice mean, about the wrong step he avoided by moving to the desert?

Isn't he the same man he's always been?

The same before the desert and after stepping into it?

What wrong step? What *wrong step*?

Then Levitt's serving, a crack of the racquet, the ball fast as a bullet aimed straight at Harry.

TWELVE

S HOULD PHOEBE HAVE PURCHASED a present for her father? Did Simon and Elena? Did Camille? As the oldest, she should have called them and asked, or suggested they go in together on a gift commensurate with the honorific of Man of the Decade. She didn't, and likely they didn't, but it's not too late. It's not too late because she left LA too early, and she's got time to spare before arriving home at noon, when she said she would, and right here is the exit to the better of the two outlet malls on the way into town. Just a quick detour, a walk around to see if anything appeals to her, something her father might like.

The mall is neatly laid out and has a late-morning hush despite the families holding hands, ducking into stores, sitting on benches and eating handfuls of warm, soft pretzels out of bright yellow bags. Do those families look happy? That one does. And that one. But not that one at all, or rather the father does not look happy. Youngish and tattooed, but wearing chinos and loafers, he seems unsure of what he's become, with a wife and two toddlers. Poor guy. Well, at least he's participating, the way Harry used to, although Harry had taken, still takes, enormous delight in all their family outings.

The lingerie displayed in a window draws her close—such alluring things she might buy for herself if only there were a real Aaron

Green. She takes in the lace, the frills, the gossamer, then resumes her useless wandering search. There's really nothing she could buy for her father that he would either want or need.

She knows what she's doing—evading arriving home early and walking through the tall front doors of the house alone. Before inventing Aaron, Phoebe loved arriving in advance of Camille, with her stories of outlandish places and people, her esoteric facts, in advance of Simon, with his harem of tall and tiny princesses, having Roma and Harry to herself for those couple of hours before all the Tabors congregated. She never finds reentry an adjustment, the way Camille does. How many times has Camille called her when she's close, saying, "I always settle in, but those first hours, it's like a pitched internal battle between my selves. Who I am in Seattle versus who I am in Palm Springs." Phoebe has never understood what Camille means about an internal psychic split, because, until February, Phoebe relished returning to the hearth and bosom, seeing herself in the curve of her mother's neck, the shape of her father's hands, but she thinks she has a sense now of what Camille always feels. She doesn't want to show up without her siblings today; she needs their bodies, their voices, their lives, as a buffer from the pointed questions she will be asked about the nonexistent man in her life.

It's only eleven, an hour to go. She'll have a coffee, sit at one of the picnic tables, practice her explanation about why Aaron couldn't join her until she does not sound, at least in her own head, like the fake and the liar she is.

There is no line at the coffee place, and she nearly has her hand on the knob when her cell rings.

"Save me," Camille says.

"From what?" Phoebe says.

"From my life," Camille says.

Phoebe feels a tightening in her throat, a clenching in her gut, then says, "I'll save you if you'll save me."

"From what? Are you joking, Phoebe?"

Phoebe looks up at the sky, a high dome of blue, a flock of birds flying by in the shape of a boomerang, the black-brown mountains in the distance spackled in sun.

"Yes, I'm joking," she says. "Did you buy a present for Dad?"

"No, should I have?"

"I just thought about it. Where are you?"

"Twenty minutes from the city limits."

"Great. Come meet me at the better outlet mall. I'll call Simon, see if they're close, have them meet us here, too. We can buy a present for Dad if we decide we should, then we can do what you always want us to do, ascend the driveway in formation, storm the house like battle-ready troops."

"Last time when I suggested that, you said, 'Grow up, Camille, you don't need armor when you come home.'"

"Well, that was unkind."

"It was," Camille says. "What's going on? Why do you want to do that now?"

"Just being supportive, so hurry up. I don't want to sit here all day."

"Hey, is Aaron with—"

Phoebe hangs up.

THIRTEEN

THE HOUSE ONLY FEELS empty when Roma is waiting for her family to arrive. Twenty years since Phoebe has lived here. Eighteen since Camille. Fifteen since Simon. She loves the emptiness, the expansiveness, not finding her children's belongings strewn around. She does not miss the way the girls especially repeatedly asked her, in increasingly aggravated voices, whether she had seen whatever it was they were missing. And yet knowing everyone will soon be here, kicking off shoes at the front door, unpacking bags in their bedrooms, opening and closing the fridge, the cabinets, splashing in the pool, the smell of suntan lotion wafting on the hot air, she feels a deep pang that none of them live here anymore. No matter how often she tells herself to stay mum, she won't be able to curb herself, will ask within the first several hours if they really must all leave so soon. "Why not stay longer?" she'll say to them. "Stay the whole week, be kids again for a little while, hang out with us, your parents, who miss you so much." Of course, by tomorrow afternoon, when the dishwasher is full and no one has thought to empty it, when damp pool and shower towels are heaved onto hooks in the bathrooms so none properly dry, when squiggles of tanning oil leave impossible stains on the polished outdoor concrete, she will not mind as much that their departures are imminent. She used to feel guilty about her empty-nest teeter-tottering desires—needing them to stay, not too disappointed when they leave—but it's important her children know they are wanted, that their presence, their company, is highly prized. Never once has she barked at them during these visits regarding habits she broke them of in their youth and they trot back out when in temporary residence, as if demonstrating to their mother that they can't fully, truly be tamed. Not even by her, the psychologist miracle worker. She knows what all those bad habits exhibited only in this house mean: a deep comfort that they are home, can relax, be who they are completely, certain they will always be accepted here, that they've learned the world can be a rough place, and the roof under which they came into their own is the safest place to be.

Roma wanders through the serene rooms, stepping through rays of sunlight, making sure the bunches of flowers Esmeralda set out yesterday still look fresh, no flowers wilting, the comforters and pillows fluffed, enough clean and folded towels and rolls of toilet paper in all of the bathrooms. Yes, everything is ready for the deluge. The clock in Simon's old bedroom, where her marvelous granddaughters sleep, says it's eleven. An hour to go.

She's swum, drunk her coffee, read the morning paper, showered and dressed, taken another look at the gown and heels she will be wearing tonight, chosen her earrings, arranged the lunch on platters Saran wrapped in the refrigerator, set the outdoor table in the main courtyard next to the big pool, and put a couple of bottles of prosecco in the freezer, because although there will be much celebration at the gala tonight, she wants to have a family-only toast for Harry this afternoon.

She could check her voicemails, see if Jeanine McCadden called with an update on Noelani. It's not yet been twenty-four hours since the girl was on Roma's couch, a pillow on her lap, worrying the material between her small fingers, but maybe the mother has reached out. Yes, she will check. Office voicemail, number, code, five messages. The first from Feeno, her sixteen-year-old depressive, telling her he meditated for ten minutes yesterday and will try it again today. The second from Julie and Carlos about their seven-year-old who has settled on a new name, abandoning Mick for Michelle, and that he doesn't care if he's teased, he's wearing dresses to school when it resumes, and then Carlos is talking over Julie, asking what they ought to do if Mick, now Michelle, is made fun of or, worse, beaten up. The third from Tanya, who, at nineteen, is struggling with body dysmorphia, as she has been the last four years, making headway, then losing ground, telling Roma she needs to reschedule her appointment next week, which never bodes well. The fourth from Lane, the single father of Leo, a twelve-year-old who suffers from crippling anxiety and severe full-body psoriasis, that he's cleaned out their kitchen, gotten rid of the gluten, which the three of them decided ought to be tried first, to see if that mitigates any of Leo's symptoms. The fifth from the mother of Kimball, a six-year-old stutterer, that she has made an appointment with the pediatric speech pathologist Roma recommended to confirm there are no abnormalities in speech motor control, like timing, sensory, or coordination, which could be causing the girl's inability to speak with ease. But no call from Jeanine McCadden about Noelani.

She checks for messages on her cell phone next. No call from Jeanine. No call yet from Harry, telling her he's on his way home. Saturday morning tennis with Levitt must be running long, but he'll be here. He's never once missed being at the door when their children arrive for a weekend.

FOURTEEN

AT ONE OF THE MALL'S picnic tables, hunched over her coffee, rehearsing what she will say to explain Aaron Green's absence, Phoebe glances up and spots a woman who looks like her sister, but can't be.

Where is Camille's skull-hugging hair, shorn by a barber for ten bucks in a shop with a spinning pole outside?

Where are Camille's shapeless secondhand clothes?

Phoebe raises a tentative hand, to see if the woman waves, and she does.

It *is* Camille, but she's grown out her hair. Long now, dark and lush and straight, swinging back and forth, perfectly cut. And she's wearing jeans, not her usual three-sizes-too-large jeans, but tight jeans that make her legs look great, and a tight white muscle tee, and her stomach is flat as a pancake, and the muscles in her arms are nicely defined. Camille, who's never needed to worry about her weight, or been on a diet, or belonged to a gym, who lived on yams and coconut meat on those islands of hers, is svelte as a model. She *looks* like a model.

And what's on her feet?

Not her typical beat-up boy's sneakers, but pretty yellow sandals.

Phoebe stands and waves again, and Camille waves back; then she's walking faster, then running, then hugging Phoebe.

Well, that's changed, the force of a Camille hug usually threatens to break the ribs of the person she's embracing, but not this time.

Camille steps back and Phoebe inspects her sister close up. "What's happened to you?"

Camille frowns. "What do you mean?"

"You. Your clothes. Your hair. Your body. You're wearing sandals. Your toenails have gold polish on them. When did you get so thin?"

"What are you talking about? I'm the same as always."

"No, you're not. You're a completely different person. You didn't look like this in June. Mom's birthday weekend."

"I didn't come for Mom's birthday."

"You didn't? I would have sworn you were there."

"You're kidding, right?"

"I forgot, I'm sorry. But, Camille, come on. What aren't you telling me? How did you get so slim? So in shape?"

"Seriously, I'm the same as I've always been. Nothing's changed."

Is it possible that Camille is the same as she's always been? Is it possible that aside from longer hair and failing to hug the breath out of Phoebe, the only difference is Camille's now showing skin, wearing clothing that fits her correctly?

"You didn't buy those jeans, or the tank, or the sandals, did you?"

"No, Valentine did, why?"

"Because you actually look so put-together. Fantastic, really. How did he convince you to wear those tight jeans?"

"Are they tight?"

"Yes. I mean, no, they're just right. They look great on you. You look great."

"I swear, Phoebe, I didn't even notice. Val was shopping for stuff for his trip, and when he came over to show me what he bought, he said, 'Here you go,' and handed me a bag, and all this was inside, and everything fit, and that was that."

That gives Phoebe a sense of rightness in the world, that it wasn't Camille who selected these clothes she's wearing. It would have been too much today to grapple with such a fundamental alteration in her sister.

"Well, you should hire him as your personal shopper."

"He's gone. Left last week for six months. Maybe he'll come back madly in love with a paleontologist."

"Why would you say that? Is that what you want?" Phoebe's never met Valentine, and the details she's learned about him from Camille would barely fill a teaspoon. That's a startling difference between them: if she were in love, she'd want to tell Camille everything, absolutely everything, until Camille cried for mercy. From their few calls and email exchanges, she thought that Camille might be in love, but who knows with Camille. She refuses to allow herself to be read.

"Ignore me. I've been driving for hours. So is Aaron getting coffee?"

To sell this, Phoebe must not look away from Camille, must not hesitate. Camille, who gives nothing away herself, is an expert at picking up false vibrations, anything atonal, nearly as perceptive as their mother.

"He tried so hard, but he just couldn't reschedule his meetings. Important out-of-town clients. But he says he can't wait to meet everyone next time. And Simon and gang should be here any minute."

"Too bad. I was looking forward to meeting him," Camille says, her face wide-open, not picking up any errant vibe, and Phoebe feels a zing of alleviation. If she's passed the test with Camille, she might pass the test with her mother, make it unscathed through the rest of the Tabor gauntlet.

"Hey, Simon's here," Camille says, and there is their brother heading toward them. The tallest of all the Tabors, his brown hair too long for the uptight firm he works at, looking fit and tanned and tired.

"Where's everyone?" Phoebe says.

"Camille," Simon says, hugging her, pulling Phoebe into the mix, until the three of them are clasped together.

Camille pulls away first, as she always does. "Where are the little beauties?"

"They're in the car. Isabel's still sleeping and Lucy said, 'Bring my aunties to me.'"

"That's my girl," Phoebe says. When Lucy was born, Phoebe worried her desire for a child would keep her at a distance, that she'd actually covet her brother's children, but her love has been true since the start.

"If you mean more demanding every day, then you're right. We don't know if we're supposed to nip that sort of thing in the bud or let it go. I'm going to ask Mom about that and other stuff this weekend. Are we really here to buy something for Dad?"

"Probably not," Phoebe says. "I thought it would be fun if we all arrived home together."

"Why?" Simon asks.

"Camille always wants to, and this time I remembered, so I called her and I called you."

"I called *you*," Camille says.

"Oh, right, you did. Okay, well, we're all together now, so should we shop for Dad, or just head to Agapanthus?"

"What would we get him?" Simon says.

"Clothing maybe? A new watch?" Phoebe offers up.

"Does he expect something from us?" Camille asks Phoebe.

"I don't know. It just seemed like we ought to show how proud we are of him."

"Elena suggested a gift and I said not necessary. But maybe we should. I can't leave everyone in the car for too long. If we can find something in fifteen minutes that we all agree on, we'll buy it. If not, we leave. Deal?"

"Deal," Phoebe says.

"No?" Simon says, looking at Camille.

"It's got to be reasonable."

Phoebe looks at her sister. "You mean something he'd use all the time?'

"No, something reasonably priced. I'm on a tight budget these days."

Simon nods. "This morning, I was worrying we might need a new roof on the house. So reasonable is fine with me." He looks around. "Hey, Phoebe, where's Aaron?"

She's made a mistake. She should have formulated a few different responses to explain the imaginary Aaron Green's absence. If she responds to Simon exactly as she responded to Camille, her sister, who spends her life listening to what people say and searching out the anomalies, will know something is up.

"He had clients already booked. So next time."

"Were you able to ship me a couple of cases from Napa when you guys were up there? Because nothing's arrived."

Oh shit, Phoebe thinks, remembering sitting in her lovely suite at the Laguna Niguel Capri, trying to locate wineries in Napa, where she supposedly was with Aaron Green, trying to place a long-distance order on Simon's behalf as if she were actually there, learning that no matter how she implored, the receipt was preprogrammed to state it was an internet order, would show it was not purchased in person at the winery, and because Simon would definitely notice that, instead of buying wine for her brother anyway, who cares for Benny so well during her long weekends away, she had gone out to the pool and met the heart surgeon and went with him to his room and had really great sex.

"Don't hate me," she says to Simon. "But we were hitting so many wineries, and got more than a little tipsy, and I totally forgot. Next time, though. I promise. Aaron wants to go back up there again."

Why did she just say that? Why is she adding lies to the lies she's already told, digging herself deeper into the hole rather than figuring a way to scramble out? She's not a blusher at all, but she feels heat racing up her cheeks.

"I remember how it was, all that new love, no room for anyone else, for thoughts about anything else," Simon says, looking at her with happiness.

"Exactly," Phoebe says, thinking what a rotten person she is.

"Should we get going?" she says, grabbing Simon's hand, then Camille's, prodding them down the wide avenue of the mall, the Tabor children finding their way back into step.

"Being in love suits you, you're all rosy," Simon says, squeezing Phoebe's left hand.

"I agree," Camille says, squeezing Phoebe's right hand.

Oh, for fuck's sake, Phoebe thinks.

FIFTEEN

H ARRY'S POCKETS ARE CRAMMED with tennis balls, and one is clutched in his hand, but he has lost sight of what he is doing out here on the court in this hundred-degree heat, feels only the internal vibrations of anxiety and unnerving tension, can only keep thinking how inconceivable it is that such an innocuous exchange would have opened a secret vault in his memory he didn't know was there.

He replays again the sequence of events: he and Levitt taking a break at the bench, resting their rubbery legs, toweling off their sweaty faces and hands, Levitt saying, "I met PSS's new cantor. He's starting on Erev Rosh Hashanah. Coming in with a bang. You meet him yet? Nice guy. Young. For some reason, he reminded me of your son, Simon. I don't know what, a shared something or other."

That was it, that was all, Levitt making conversation. And yet, instantly, Harry had seen himself on a commuter plane, strapped into a tiny seat, the cabin so compact his head was nearly touching the ceiling, flying over crystal-blue water. And it wasn't a holiday he was on with Roma, for the seat next to him was empty when he looked out the window as the plane banked over the ocean and came in hard on a short runway. There had been a taxi, a driver saying, "Welcome to the Caymans."

He had been certain the recollection did not belong to him.

Neither he nor he and Roma had ever been to the Caymans, but there he was, sitting in a banker's office, being asked to select his private code.

And he'd thought, his private code? For what?

And that dry, unfamiliar voice had provided an answer: *A code for that numbered account.*

There's been a mistake, he had said to the voice in his head. He'd never needed a numbered account. Numbered accounts were secret, for deposits of large amounts of drug money, money hidden from the divorce lawyers and the forensic accountants of angry spouses, money from cash-only businesses to beat the taxing authorities, money made on illegal trades.

Money made on illegal trades?

His breath had come hard and fast. His head, perfectly still, seemed to be whipping around on his neck—money made on illegal trades?

Had he made such trades?

Impossible.

But he saw then the traders at his old firm. Saw them talking out of turn among themselves, discussing information they shouldn't have been discussing, that none of them was allowed to use, all that material, nonpublic information, all that insider information, floating into his ears. And he remembered overhearing them, listening hard.

No. He hadn't just heard, hadn't just listened hard.

He had considered.

No.

He had heard, considered, then checked things out.

He had confirmed what he heard.

Confirmed and used what he heard.

What he had seen, had seemingly recalled, it had to be wrong, but the banker had said, "Sir, the code?" And he remembered wanting to choose something no one would be able to decipher and he'd penned in *CST* where required.

And he had thought, This can't be right, but the voice had said, *It's right.*

If it was right, that he, Harry Tabor, had used illegal information to make illicit trades, and traveled to an island where bank accounts were secret, and set up such an account, where had these memories been hiding? In his head, he'd been screaming.

You obliterated them, the voice had said.

He'd obliterated them?

He hadn't understood what that meant, only that it wasn't his nature to obliterate anything. He wasn't a man capable of expunging the truth.

But he'd seen himself. In that banker's office in the Caymans. Selecting *CST* as his code.

And then there was a jump forward, into the desert, into the pool of their desert house, and he was telling Roma he liked the notion of carrying on the name of an illustrious ancestor, despite the sad irony that *Simon* meant *one who has heard*, and his ancestor, the profoundly deaf cantor, had never, not once in his life, heard a voice, a song, a single note, not even his own. Roma had resisted. She, who knew the myriad ways that the mind can work, how it can turn on its master and gobble him up, had put her palms on her stomach, their third child within, and said, "Are we sure about this? Do we want to name our final child, our only son, after a relative of yours who was deaf?" And he had said, "It's not as if we'd be giving him a *kenahora* by passing on a worthwhile name. Maybe he'll inherit a supreme talent, passed down from one generation to another."

Because Levitt innocently stirred together the words *cantor* and *Simon*, Harry, alarmingly, could now answer the question posed to him by young Owen Kaufmann last Monday: What does *CST* stand for? It stands for *Cantor Simon Tabornikov*. The man singing the gut-wrenching Kol Nidre on the Day of Atonement, risen from the dead, shown to Harry in a vision, a man after whom Simon is named, a man whose title and initials Harry used as his private code on a secret Cayman account, a man whose title and initials formed the name of Harry's organization, whose sole and altruistic purpose is to provide futures of plenty to those who have nothing, to those staring into the abyss, to those who can't conceive of futures at all.

This couldn't be his origin story. His origin story is simple: he is a man who walks the upstanding walk of the moral, the honorable, the good. But that doesn't seem to be his story at all; his story horrifies him.

THESE ARE THE THOUGHTS consuming him and then he hears that dry, unfamiliar voice once again, though it's no longer as unfamiliar:

What you've remembered is a start, Harry. But it's not nearly enough. You need to see it all. Such tales as these always start the same way. In the beginning . . .

The beginning? Wasn't this enough? More than enough?

Sorry, but no.

And with that *no*, more than three decades collapse, and Harry is kneeling on the carpet in his office at the stockbrokerage firm.

What was he doing down on his knees?

Praying for guidance, Harry. All these years, you've been so certain you prayed only once in your life. For a kiss from Eve Flynn on your Bar Mitzvah. But there came a second time when you desperately needed to believe in something greater than yourself, and it was to the notion of prayer that you turned, hauling it up from the basement of your being.

Close your eyes and you'll see it all exactly as it happened.

Harry closes his eyes and he's in his old office at Carruthers Investments, standing at his window, looking out at the tall buildings lost in the low and dense cloud bank.

It had been snowing all day—

Yes, he remembers that. It *had* been snowing all day, for days actually, and . . . and . . . and?

And the weight of the weather was just another thing pressing down upon you . . .

Yes, that weight, that awful weight—

Yes, he remembers that weight because happenings were occurring in his world of stock trading, a serious comeuppance was upon them, a coming-to-Jesus for those who subscribed to confession and resurrection, which included everyone at the firm other than himself and, by then, one other fellow Jew.

He had watched the heavy flakes and recognized he had not been a sterling Jew, not even a fair-weather synagogue Jew, but somehow he needed to prove to God, Yahweh, the Almighty, Adonai, whatever, that he was *serious* about coming clean, about doing exactly what had to be done in the name of righteousness, and to stave off an ignominious firing, a public arrest, a jury trial or plea bargain, and inevitable jail time. The issue of whether he had thoroughly covered his tracks was not at all in his mind. The only question for which he required an answer was, what exactly did he need to do?

Abject prayer then, down on his knees, not the way Jews prayed, but it hadn't been enough to sit in his soft black leather chair; he had needed a physical act to put him in touch with something so foreign. And so he kneeled, and did what he had not done since his Bar Mitzvah: he seriously prayed. Five minutes passed. Five more. Then another ten. And he wasn't aware of the passage of time as he stayed down, imploring, with his eyes shut tight, sure his ears were wide-open and that what he was hearing was nothing, or rather, was only and merely silence.

It *was* only and merely silence. There wasn't anything else.

Harry, silence is rarely the complete absence of sound: there were pressure waves in the air surrounding you, individual air molecules bouncing around; your body, too, was quietly cacophonous—your heart was beating, your breath rising and falling, your blood pumping through your veins and arteries, your stomach digesting the lunchtime hot dog you ate out in the frozen air at the stand, your joints were creaking, your ligaments were sliding, even your lashes were making a slight fluttering sound—and though you would have sworn your heard nothing at all, from on high came instructions you absorbed through your pores.

This is what you were told:

Sell your beautiful old house and your sports car and your ridiculous tchotchkes, donate all your dishonest gains to charities; then take your wife and daughters to a place where you will create a new life for your family, a life that will include atoning for your sins daily and giving thanks to me, for saving you.

But I didn't hear any of that. I didn't absorb anything.

Look at what happened next, Harry.

He sees himself rising up from his knees, his navy suit bearing the imprint of the carpet's faint pattern.

What were you thinking right then?

I was thinking that prayer was meaningless, and that if I did not do something immediately, resign from my position, walk away from my high-flying world, donate my filthy lucre to worthwhile charities, get my family out of Dodge, I would be going down, down, down, into a hell I could never crawl up from.

The same instruction you'd just been given.

And Harry presses his hands to heart and remembers his thoughts that day:

The big guns wanted the world to believe they knew how to make real money in the stock market, when no one in the whole world knew how to do that without the sorcery of a secret alchemy, the transmutation of verboten insider information into gold. Which is how *they* did it, and how Harry had done it, too—transforming verboten information he overheard into his own privately minted treasure. But he wasn't one of those whose history had always been paved with gold, regardless of the machinations by which that gold had been obtained. He had been reading about the Wall Street kings who, when caught manipulating their deep knowledge and contacts for personal gain, simply proffered lukewarm mea culpas, and sliced off a small piece of their fortunes and turned it and themselves over to the authorities for a slap on the hand, and he'd done the calculations—their fines were infinitesimal in comparison to the fortunes safely squirreled away. Once in a while, the government insisted on the proper optics, which required a few to briefly reside in low-security prisons, where they played pick-up basketball, golf, and tennis, and ate meals prepared by personal chefs. Small fish were not yet on the government's radar, so there were no articles for him to read about how the small fish were being treated, but Harry knew he was a small fish, starred with euphemistic intangibles, and hadn't history proved a million times over that it was always the small fish with those euphemistic intangibles that were yanked from the ocean and not thrown back, but gutted, broiled, and eaten? Which for him meant a cement cell in medium-security for years to come.

He had stared out at the admirable view he would be leaving behind, postcard-perfect amidst the swirling storm that was gathering power, would become a blizzard, would drop eighteen inches by morning. Then he wrote out his resignation letter, packed up his office, and drove home to Connecticut.

As he inched the car up the snowy drive, windshield wipers on triple time, his house came into view, lit windows spreading buttery golden light into the storming night, and he thought how he would miss the great old place, its untamed and rambling grounds. It was the kind of place a *Mayflower* scion might have inherited, but he'd acquired it for a song out of the bankruptcy of perhaps one of those old *Mayflower* families, whose providential fortune had finally trickled to nothing. But so things went, things were given and things were taken away, and he straightened his shoulders and walked through his front door.

Roma was in the living room, and Harry heard their daughters playing a game upstairs, Phoebe's six-year-old voice commanding, Camille, at four, heeding.

He mixed a pitcher of martinis, and when he handed his wife a glass and said, "Drink," Roma raised her lovely dark brows at him and stared into his eyes as she took a first sip. He drank, too, quickly draining his glass and refilling, then topping hers off and taking a seat on the couch. Roma sat down next to him, her thigh taut against his. Then she turned to him and said, "Tell me."

He told her everything: his misappropriation of material,

nonpublic information not passed to him specifically but overheard, and although he had violated at least an imputed duty of
trust, he had not otherwise been foolhardy, he had confirmed the
ferreted information before deploying it, but with confirmation
came deployment, serious deployment, all the arbitrage plays he
had made, the unbelievable balance that was piled up in a pseud-
onymously named bank account in the Cayman Islands.

In the movie the dry voice is showing him, he watches Roma
tilting her head, sees himself bowing his own, hears himself saying, "I did it because I wanted to be one of those to whom the rules
don't apply. The big guns, the men I manage who live on the interest their trust funds throw off, who have freedom because of their
unlimited resources, they treat the stock market like sport. To
them, it's the field, the diamond, the pitch, the slope. It's competi-
tion, a scoreboard, runs at bat, a shimmying ball through the hoop.
It's not mortgage payments and college funds, but a black-diamond
ski run, and I wanted to ski that hard and that fast, as if I, too, was
born possessing all that natural ability, all that they have. I wanted
a little of that freedom, or rather I wanted to feel, for a little while,
what that kind of freedom felt like. Would food taste differently?
Would I walk with an altered stride? Move faster, stand taller? I
thought of my father's stride, how it slowed over the years, how he
grew stooped from the weight of watching his nickels and dimes. I
was stupid and reckless. I forgot my parents' sacrifices, ignored the
danger I was putting us in, lost my gratitude for this life we have, a
life others would wish for."

How could he not have remembered any of this?

Stay focused, Harry. Watch.

And he watches himself looking into his wife's eyes, seeing her
rapidly absorbing this untenable information, this confession of
his. Her thoughts are hidden from him, but when it seems she might
speak, she hesitates, takes a very deep breath, then a very deep sip
of the icy martini, then another very deep breath, and finally says,
"I assume you have a viable plan to get yourself and us out of this
mess."

And he remembers his heart unclenching when her words did not end on an uptick, when there was no question mark finishing her sentence. His single nod was heavy and certain, because he did have a viable plan.

The plan that had come to mind as he steered his way out of snow-covered Manhattan that night: Palm Springs. Not long before, he'd read an article about how that movie stars' retreat, so fashionable in the fifties, was no longer fashionable, was instead scuffed at the heels, was a city that had lost its imagination, its pulse, its way. And he'd thought that such a place could hinder his imagination, rein in his unforeseen larcenous impulses, eliminate his unanticipated smashing of the rules.

And he remembers saying to his wife, "Yes. I'll divest myself of all the money and we'll move to the desert."

That's right, Harry. But what you can't recall because it's locked away in your unconscious is this:

That you thought it would be better to live on flat, scorched, dusty land that unconsciously reminded you of a place secreted away in your genetic code, a place where you had never been, nor given any thought to going.

He can't process what the voice is telling him, because he is staring at Roma, who is saying, "Only if you get rid of every corrupt dollar, Harry."

And he had agreed.

But then?

But then what?

Come on, Harry.

Oh my *god.*

Right.

The very next day, I revised that promise. I knew I needed to keep a small amount as our setting-up funds—for the purchase of a house, for the daily needs of our family, for her practice, for whatever I might choose to do out there—just enough to see us through. And I didn't tell her.

Your first lie by omission to Roma. Keep going, Harry.

Then I tried to donate all the rest of the money, the bulk of the money. But it was impossible. Absolutely impossible. Every 501(c) organization had complex paperwork I couldn't outsmart. I couldn't provide a paper trail proving where the money had come from and not a single charity would accept even a dollar.

And so?

I can't.

You have to.

I kept everything I'd illicitly made, along with the ever-aggregating interest. And hid that fact, too, from my wife.

Yep. Your second lie by omission. What were you thinking then?

That I had to do something to make everything all right. If I couldn't get rid of the money, I would use it to do good. And I made a vow to myself that I would execute this new strategy with the no-blest of intentions.

And that noble intention became—

That noble intention became CST.

He wants to cry, to sob, to curl up on the court and die in the sun.

I can't continue. I cannot continue.

Fine, Harry. I'll tell it.

A week later, you listed your gracious manse with a real estate broker.

A week after that, you and Roma held a yard sale, selling every-thing off. You kept only the photograph albums of your wedding, of your honeymoon in Spain, of your trip to Greece, where Phoebe was conceived, of your trip to France, where Camille was conceived, and of the passing of quick years marking the growth of your family, the artwork made by your daughters, clothes appropriate for blazing desert days, cold desert nights.

A week after that, you sold your cars. You made a tidy profit on your Jaguar XJ, selling it for three thousand more than you paid, that two-year-old silver paint job worth every cent, the way the car's mercury curves morphed into the missile dimensions of a rocket or a bullet. The fake-wood-sided family station wagon in which Roma ferried Phoebe to kindergarten and Camille to nursery school and herself to her office in a quaint old building in your smallish town you sold to the first poor schlub who came around, handing over the title and keys for the proffered hundred dollars. You didn't even balk when you stood in the car lot and selected a new white Dodge Caravan, which you thought appropriately named given the circumstances, and for which you paid cash.

In the first month of nineteen eighty-seven, when everything was done and dried, and the girls and the suitcases, one for each family member, and the four boxes of keepsakes were inside the minivan, nestled and warm, with snow drifts piled high and the sky threatening again, you drove your family away to the new life you were envisioning amidst the rocks and the sand and the snakes and the salamanders and the hard saguaros blasted in the sun.

Although only four weeks had passed since you ground your blue-suited knees into the office carpet, that some other force had provided you with an answer to your prayers was something you would have scoffed at, had you thought about it. But you never once thought about it. You never once gave credence to the idea that your words had been heard, and that every action you had taken since that stormy afternoon was because your prayers had been answered. Instead, you were certain that what was seeing you through to the other side, where life again would be honorable and worthwhile, had only to do with your inherent and inherited will to survive, your courage and strength to make the tough decisions to save your family, and even, you thought, perhaps wrongly, yourself and your soul.

All of that was thirty-one years ago, and buried so deep inside of you, Harry, that your memories of that time have long been erased; it is a point of fact that you erased those memories intentionally and deliberately. You commanded yourself to forget, and forget you did. You bifurcated your life, cut all ties, jettisoned the creeping fear of doom, the claustral notion of a fateful fall, cast away friends, colleagues, colleagues who had become friends, every totem of your prior identity and stockbrokerage success—the handmade suits, the collection of silk ties, the fancy car. You left behind the market, the

market makers, the increasing infractions gaining public attention.
You canceled your subscriptions to the Wall Street Journal, *the*
Financial Times, *to Barron's, never again read the financial pages,*
automatically turned the radio dial when marketplace reports came
on, turned off the news before you heard any announcer say, "Today
on Wall Street." The move from East Coast to West, a thorough con-
textual change, was the final piece that completed your intentional
forgetting. Gone were the dark crowded streets you once walked, the
autumn rain and winter snow you were used to. Instead, you were in
an unknown place where the foreign light was unique, and the vis-
tas, fresh to your eyes, held only the present and the future in vivid
sunshine. You brought nothing with you from that abnormal year
when you took actions at odds with your character, and the warped
philosophy you had temporarily embraced fell permanently away.
The eradication of those particular memories was easier than one
might expect: you had spoken of what you had done only once, to
Roma, and then never again, and there was no informational rush,
no overload, no load at all, to remind you of your past: the world was
not yet wired, it would be another decade before barely twelve percent
of Americans were using the World Wide Web, and you yourself
would remain unwired for much longer than that. If a functional
magnetic resonance imaging machine existed back then, the limbic
system in your brain would have reflected the magnitude of the neu-
ral changes in all that gray and white matter—proof of your total
inability to recall that particular shameful time. When you began
life anew in the desert, the future became everything, the only thing,
and since then you have believed you have always lived an endless
sequence of perfect days. You don't think in these terms, Harry, but
if you did, you would say that all of your years, all of your family's
years, thus far, have been enormously blessed.

These are your obliterated memories, Harry.

My obliterated memories. *Dear god.*

On Monday, I couldn't remember why I started CST, and now
you're telling me that my calling, what I've done for the last thirty
years, was my solution when I couldn't donate the money.

Yes, Harry.

All this time, I thought we made a considered decision to change our lives, to find a place that was hot and sunny and different from where we'd grown up. But there was no thoughtful decision, was there?

No, Harry.

I was fleeing, and Roma and the girls came with me.

Yes, Harry. You're lucky Roma loved you enough to not abandon you, but her decision, made neither lightly nor easily, was predicated upon what you promised to do.

And I didn't fulfill my promise.

That's between you and Roma, Harry. And I'm sorry to say, but there is more for you to remember. Tough stuff, too. And when you do remember, when you reach deeper into that secret vault you hid from yourself, you're going to have to decide whether you're entitled to any Man of the Decade award, and you're going to have to figure out how to atone, truly atone, this time.

Truly atone? How is he to atone for the fact that the life he thought he himself created, that he has been living all of this time, is based on heinous actions he took and carried through? How is he to atone for the fact that he has lied to Roma for most of their marriage, and that he has lied to Phoebe and Camille for most of their lives, and to Simon for all of his life, even though he had been unaware he was lying at all?

What else is there for him to remember?

Isn't this enough? It is already more than he can possibly handle.

I promise you this, the rest will come to you. Finish your match, Harry, which you ought not to be playing today anyway, considering it's Shabbos.

He cannot finish this match. The weight of his newly recalled treachery is twisting his guts, bearing down on his shoulders, and the exhaustion that overwhelms him is so complete that holding his racquet in one hand, the tennis ball in the other, is too much. Much too much. He drops his racquet, hears it rattle and settle, drops the ball, watches it roll to the net.

Levitt rises from his crouch, hurries across the length of the court, to Harry's side, says, "You're ghostly pale."

As ghostly as Harry's forgotten past, as his ancestral cantor beckoning him into that forgotten past.

"I don't have anything left in me."

"We'll call it a heat break," Levitt says. "Pick up where we're leaving off next week."

Moving his feet is nearly impossible, his body as heavy as if encased in concrete. What else can there be for him to remember? What other wrong has he done in his life and conveniently forgotten about? The dry voice had said, *I promise you this, the rest will come to you*, and he hears it now for what it is: a threat in his ears, a noose around his neck.

SIXTEEN

During the fifteen minutes Simon has allotted, the Tabor siblings wander and find themselves laughing a lot. In the parking lot, the laughter bubbles up again when they discover they have chosen spots near to one another, and grows louder when Elena waves and calls out, "I was about to unbuckle the kids and go searching for all of you."

"Sorry, we were looking for a gift for Harry," Simon says, which makes Phoebe start laughing, and that makes Camille start laughing, and then Simon is laughing again, too. And then Elena starts laughing because they are all laughing and she manages to say, "I don't understand what's so funny," and Simon says, "Because we didn't look very hard," and Camille says, "We didn't look at all," and then Lucy is yelling from inside the SUV, "Let us out, let us out," and Elena pulls open the back door, and out pops Lucy, who runs to her aunts, calling in a high-pitched voice, "Hi, hi, hi, hi, hi, hi, hi, hugs and kisses, hugs and kisses, hugs and kisses," and then Isabel is yowling even though Elena is already releasing her from the restraints of her car seat. Hanging on tight to the purple tutu, limp in the hot, still air, Isabel ricochets between her daddy and Phoebe, before shyly approaching Camille, whom she hasn't seen since May, at Harry's seventieth birthday party. She holds out the tutu to Camille, who lifts the girl up, presses her close, showers her small face with kisses, saying, "I've missed you so much." Isabel nuzzles close to Camille and then says, "Down, down."

Elena embraces her sisters-in-law. "Camille, you look great. Phoebe, where's Aaron?" and Phoebe's gaiety drains away, her heart snagging on itself, and in that split second, as she's readying her now-standard response, her siblings say in their own ways, "He couldn't make it because of work," and Elena says, "Oh, too bad. Next time."

"Absolutely," Phoebe says, and when Elena doesn't inquire further, she feels her jumpy blood calming, knows then that once she clears the hurdle of Roma, the weekend is going to be fine.

"Are we ready to go?" Simon says, and Lucy whoops and yells, and Isabel, watching her big sister, mirrors her actions, and Simon and Elena both say, "Enough," and then they are shepherding the girls back up into the SUV, back into their car seats, saying, "We'll be at Savah and Sabba's really soon."

"I'll text Mom," Camille says, and as she extracts her phone from her pocket, she, like her older sister, feels her jumpy blood calming. Typing, *The Tabor children and the two who are third generation, we're all on our way*, she is aware of an abnormal, unpredicted tranquility. Perhaps because they first met here at the mall, perhaps because she has engaged in uninhibited laughter, in short supply these days, but whatever is responsible, she'll take it willingly. How strange to have driven all these hours in a suspended state of confusion and fear, and now, at the beginning of this family gathering, to find herself happy. On so many visits home, she has functioned as the anthropologist, the participant-observer of the coalescing Tabors, applying Malinowski's cardinal rule of fieldwork—to see reality only from the natives' point of view—but now she wants only to immediately reintegrate into her animated family, to take her place as an integral member, for their realities to mesh. Have these last months of ministering to the dying freed her from the restraint she usually exercises with her family? Her need for a requisite period of reentry is entirely gone, and the sensation is a wonder, a restorative, a nearly euphoric pleasure to experience these new feelings of hers, to sense that they will last, that the weekend is going to be fine.

Simon never thought the weekend was going to be anything other than fine, and despite his bone-tired exhaustion, and those new concerns considered on the drive, he is buoyantly happy seeing his sisters, seeing his sisters with his children, seeing his wife laughing with their daughters and his sisters. Happy knowing he will soon plumb his mother's expertise. Happy knowing he will soon celebrate his father's fantastic achievements, and later, when the two of them have time alone, ask Harry for advice. Simon pictures everyone together at breakfast tomorrow, outside in the splendid desert morning—bagels and cream cheese and lox and onions, and the mimosas Harry loves, juice for the "wee ones," as Camille has called his daughters since their births, the adults still flying high from the Man of the Decade party—and then, when everyone is sated, and a little tipsy once again, he will tell them about the ILA invitation, the conference in Colombia, he and Elena taking the trip together, his parents offering, without his having to ask, "Of course, you'll bring the girls back here, leave them with us, we'll take care of everything, no, not a word, we're not going to take no for an answer," and he is smiling enormously when he says to his sisters, to his wife, to his young daughters fidgeting beneath their car seat straps, "Follow me. I'll lead the way. I'll lead us back home."

And in a few minutes, engines on, air-conditioning at full blast, Simon leads the charge in Elena's blue SUV, followed by Camille in her trusty old green Honda, followed by Phoebe in her pristine year-old black Audi coupe. The three cars exit the mall and return to the highway for a while, then coast off it, motorcading through the city, making the rights and lefts needed to reach, at last, Agapanthus Lane, a lane that is peaceful and quiet, with its large, well-kept homes set far back, protected from view by tough desert plantings.

Up the long drive to the house, at the midpoint the forty-foot palm tree that Camille, at thirteen, named Double M for Margaret

Mead, and Lucy remembers, chanting, "Double M, Double M, Double M, Double M," in a constant loop. Another few moments, and they spot Roma in the doorway, waving them in, grinning at them, her love washing over them.

"You said noon, and you're all here at noon on the dot," she calls out. "And all together, this is a first. Where are my delightful grand-daughters?"

Simon and Elena lift them out and the little girls run to their *savah*. "Oh, yes, these hugs are yummy! Who's hungry? Who wants to swim in the pool? Who needs something cold to drink?"

Suitcases and duffels and hanging bags are set at the front door, and when everyone has gathered around Roma, she says, "I'm just going to throw this out there, that I think you should all con-sider staying on, staying for the week. Nobody say no, just think about it. No one really needs to go home tomorrow. Here's what I know, what we all know, that life happens while we're away. Don't let's do that this time. Let's spend real time together. Let's be the family we have always been. I need you all here. I always need you all here."

The siblings, as in sync as a choir, begin laughing all over again, the tenth or fifteenth wave of laughter they've experienced since coming together at the mall.

"What?" Roma says. "What's funny?"

"Usually you wait a few hours before asking us to stay longer," Camille says.

"I decided not to waste time."

"Hey," Simon says. "Where's Dad?"

Roma would like to know where Harry is, too. She has texted him twice and left a voicemail, and her husband seems to have gone AWOL, which has left her with a flicker of worry. But for her children, she smiles and gives an unconcerned shrug, even as she takes in that Phoebe is alone, no Aaron Green holding her hand, that Camille is oddly aglow, that Simon's eyes are sunken, with black circles around them.

"His match probably went long. But come on, everybody, let's go in. I've made a pitcher of lemonade iced tea, and the chaises are all waiting for you around the big pool, and to eat we have . . ." And Simon, the sole man this moment among all these capable, strong women, is left collecting the bags, using his shoulder to close the tall front doors behind him.

SEVENTEEN

Harry is parked in an alley, utterly failing in a desperate attempt to reverse time, to return to this morning, when he woke in his bed as the man he was, or rather, as the man he thought he was, before this awful knowledge changed everything.

On this day that is supposed to be a red-letter day in his life, he thinks about confessing to Roma this wicked, corrupt, immoral, unscrupulous truth about himself. Will she ever believe he had no recollection of his deceit until it was revealed to him on his usual court playing his usual Saturday tennis with Levitt? Will she ever believe he had no idea that she knew all these years about his illicit trading, that he didn't know to be grateful she has never once mentioned it, or used it against him, or reminded him why they really moved to the desert? Will she ever believe there is a voice, a voice that is not his, speaking to him in his head? And how will their children respond when they learn everything they believe about their father is grounded on a bedrock of falsehoods?

Bedrock? Yes, because the swamp of his lies has long solidified. Falsehoods? That's a falsehood in itself.

What he did was not merely utter falsehoods—how he wishes it had only been that, but it wasn't. Nothing so trivial, so easy to forgive. What he did—what he did was intentional and active wrongdoing.

He, Harry Tabor, long ago in his past, executed, effected, made happen, serious wrong.

He leans against the headrest and closes his eyes. He sees himself in his relative youth, in his sharp suits, in the hallways of the stockbrokerage firm, taking advantage of the new electronic trading platform Instinet, and the new exchange-based NASDAQ system, able to make hundreds—nay, thousands—of trades based on verboten information, without having to step onto the stock market floor and dealing with the open outcry format, without the brokers' eagle eyes and ears monitoring his dishonest buy and sell orders, working instead in the shimmer of the blue glare of the computer screen in his own office, in total privacy.

And in that total privacy, one night . . . yes, he remembers.

He'd said *genug*.

The Yiddish word his mother used. Lenore didn't know many Yiddish words, her parents had saved that language for their private talk, but she knew that word, and so Harry knew that word, too. And that particular night, he's seeing it so clearly . . . he was in his office reviewing what he'd amassed from information he shouldn't have used, from which he'd created a fortune, an unbelievable accumulated profit, the spoils electronically wired to that CST account in the Cayman Islands, and he'd said *genug*.

He remembers telling himself *genug*, enough, that it was time to stop, and he had stopped.

But today, that *genug* is another hard lash against his back, for he didn't stop trading randomly, didn't pluck a number out of a hat, for the number at which he stopped himself was eighteen million.

He had blasphemed something inherently Judaic. In childhood, of course he had learned the importance of the number eighteen, that it was related to the Hebrew word for life, *chai*, and that Jews gave *chai*, financial gifts and donations in multiples of eighteen. Had he given any thought back then about why he stopped the trades there? Did he think he stopped for no apparent reason?

The reason is so apparent, for that number is sewn into his life, into his upbringing.

He thinks of the eighteen-dollar checks Mordy and Lenore gave him on his birthdays when he was a boy, a check for ninety dollars and eighteen cents when he graduated high school, a check for nine hundred and eighteen dollars when he graduated from college, a check for eighteen hundred dollars when he graduated from business school. And he thinks of himself and Roma writing heartfelt birthday cards to Phoebe, Camille, and Simon, slipping in checks in amounts that were multiples of eighteen, the checks growing larger each year from their thirteenth birthdays on. After their wrapped and bowed presents, his children opened that one special card, which held a multiple-of-eighteen check, and he had always taken them on their birthdays to stand in line at the bank, walking them up to the window, watching them release the check from their hot little hands and slide it over for depositing into the accounts he had set up for each, instructing them, as they walked out of the bank, that the check came with responsibility to not waste it on frivolous things, but rather to grow the money, to donate some part to a charity of their choice. He had been teaching them about what money could do, about the prospects for the future that it could provide. *Oh!* he thinks, how sanctimonious he was, in his certainty about himself, that he knew what was best, because he was doing his best, was a leader among men, was a carrier of flaming candles into the dark, while he had taken the truth of his memories and obliterated them.

How is he to behave now in these drastically altered circumstances, with these brutal facts known to him? It is impossible, that's what all of this is—all these feelings, this newly recovered knowledge of his propensity and talent for lying, for duplicity, impossible to be saddled with such egregious information, knowing, because the dry voice told him so, that there is more to come, that will be revealed to him, or rather, that he must reveal to himself.

Somehow he had nodded with a semblance of artificial pleasure when Levitt said, "We're going to celebrate tonight in your honor," and then managed to drive away from the park, away from Levitt standing at his Maserati, to Luigi's, where he now sits in his car with the air conditioner running.

Through the alley-side barred glass door, he sees Luigi in the back of his shop, a tailor made for the movies—short, friendly, old-world Italian—who once made fine clothes for the movie stars during that Palm Springs heyday; that heyday long gone when he brought Roma and their young daughters to this desert; that heyday now, at long last, making a comeback. This adopted city of his has changed for the better in the years since their arrival, and until this morning he was sure he was doing his part.

He had looked forward to this errand, to the tailor holding out the sharp tuxedo he made specially for Harry, donning the tuxedo for final inspection, when it still belonged more to Luigi than to him—though the bill was paid in full previously, Luigi fussing around him, over him, over the opulent suit, one last time, to make sure all met the tailor's exacting standards.

Harry bangs his head against the headrest again and again, then stops. He cannot indulge himself in this pitiful way. He is no longer entitled to savor this moment, this experience. He may have to wear that tuxedo tonight, but he can't pretend those memories are still blocked and forgotten. Not now, when he recalls the trading and the money he made from that trading.

Money he grew with smarts and talent. And when the banking laws changed, when it became harder to keep numbered accounts, he did the right thing, turned the money into Treasury notes of various durations, that he redeemed stateside as they matured, depositing the funds slowly into CST's accounts. And those accounts are all legitimate, reported each year, taxes properly paid.

But wait. *Wait, wait, wait.*

Among all those obliterated memories, this is newly recalled.

Or rather, he recollects taking those actions, of course he does, but where did he think the money came from? Had he thought he was handling his earnings from his stockbroker years? He made a lot of money back then, proper, clean, and legal money, but had he really believed he'd hard-earned eighteen million? Much more than eighteen million by then, with the accrued interest, with the way he'd managed it.

Yes, he had believed it.

He absolutely had believed it.

A double transmutation, a two-step sorcery—illicit information into unclean money, then his memory washing it clean. Under different circumstances, he could almost marvel at his brain's tenacious ability to erase.

What he knows about himself now, it's horrible.

Horrible, but was it any worse than what others were doing during those years? Horrible, but his actions had never hurt anyone. Horrible, but he has used the illegitimate money only for philanthropy, only for CST. Does it matter why he founded CST when his misdeeds funded altruism? When he has helped so many people? That's all solid and real. Shouldn't it be weighed and measured, constitute a balancing of the scales? It's a splinter of leeway, a flicker of hope instantly extinguished. He has no origin story, as the reporter phrased it, only a creation myth.

He is staring into the nothingness of the sky and then Luigi steps out through the back door, sees Harry sitting in his sporty gold Mercedes. His face lights up, and he raises a wrinkled hand with long, thin fingers as limber as a dancer's legs, and calls out in his movie-perfect Italian-accented English, "Come, come, my fine friend, come see the work of impeccability I have made for you," and Harry has no choice but to open the car door and step out into his changed world, bewildered. How is he supposed to figure out what there is left to figure out, to remember about his past?

In the shop's chilly air, the tailor points to the ebony tuxedo gleaming alone on a metal rack, casts a hard eye at Harry's tennis clothes, at his slick skin.

"Ah, Mr. Harry, you are too sweaty to try on, but I have no worries, and neither should you, my work is faultless, without any shortcuts. I'll put it in its bag, and off you can go. Come tell me next week how you felt wearing it tonight."

Then Harry is out in the alley, setting the singular suit flat in the back, climbing into the driver's seat, wondering how to handle, to manage, to correct his past, which he used to trust with conviction, when it was fixed and inviolable, a past of which he could be proud.

EIGHTEEN

ER MOTHER ACCEPTED AARON Green's absence without a questioning look, but now, stuck in the shallow end, sand- wiched between Roma and Camille on the pool steps, watching Elena bobbing up and down in the water, Phoebe is being asked to describe Aaron Green's features. She thought she'd already done this for them months ago during phone calls in which she imbued Aaron with the right physical touches to make him real, identified his hair color, its texture, but she's being asked to de- scribe him again, in more detail, while her mother stares directly at her. Phoebe looks skyward, as if thinking about her lover's many attributes.

She should simply say the relationship is over. She's sad, but not heartbroken. While it seemed they shared much in common, they didn't, not really. And she hadn't mentioned it, because it's Harry's weekend, no reason to dwell on a failed love right now.

She's sure she's going to speak words that make it clear the rela- tionship has ended, but then she says, "His eyes aren't cat eyes, per se, but not completely almond-shaped either, and they're a soft, late-summer green. And his voice. His voice is full-bodied, with a hint of some kind of twang, and he's got great, broad shoulders, and strong hands, and really, really nice teeth."

How strange that describing her nonexistent lover brings a delighted smile to her face. She wants to wipe it away. She wants to start laughing hysterically. She's dug herself deeper once again. She can't turn back now, but why does no one say he sounds like a man on the cover of a romance novel? She stares at the feet of her mother and her sister under the water, and then at her own toes, the family resemblance captured in those small digits.

Camille starts making a weird noise with her mouth, and then Roma is doing the same, and Elena follows along, two Jews and a Catholic ululating in a way that makes Phoebe think of Muslim women at a wedding, or a funeral.

"Yes, yes, he sounds great," Camille says. "But how is he in bed?"

Which startles Phoebe. Not because Camille has asked this personal question in front of Roma—their psychologist mother began talking to them about sex when they were very young, with Phoebe when Roma found her with a finger down her underpants—but because in building her creation, Phoebe hasn't once actually thought about the kind of kisser Aaron Green might be, or how they would be together in bed. Is he talented in the lovemaking arts? Gentle when called for, forceful when *that's* what she desires? She never even figured out his background. Where did he grow up? Where did he go to college? Was he an athlete, playing hockey or basketball? Does he still play basketball? Did he go to graduate school? Does he have two living parents? Are they still married or divorced? Does he have brothers and sisters? How was he raised? She never thought to decide whether or not he was Jewish. But she gave him the name Aaron Green, so he probably is. And if he is, then he's circumcised, and she pictures a statuesque circumcised penis, at the ready.

What is wrong with her? Well, she knows what's wrong with her, she's becoming a compulsive liar, but how come in her own fantasy she didn't imagine all the ways this fake lover would satisfy her? She should be able to roll out the specifics easily, but she can't think of a thing, her memorial trove of past relationships, of past doings in bed, all gone from her head; even the details of the recent sex with the heart surgeon refuse to be recollected.

She looks to Elena, hoping she'll interpret Phoebe's reticence as a lover's diplomacy, but Elena only grins, and then Camille laughs.

"When did you become so circumspect? You've told me the details about every sexual interaction you've ever had since we were teenagers."

Which is true.

It is her mother who steps in. "Let's not grill her. Sometimes sex with someone we think we might love is special and should be kept private. Is that what's going on here? Do you think you might love this Aaron Green?"

Phoebe will be easy and breezy—her mother's suspicions are so easily aroused—and she says, "Oh, it's still early days. I don't want to get ahead of myself."

But then, because she can't help herself, because she has either truly become a compulsive liar, or is verging on something worse, like becoming a pathological liar, which she knows, because of Roma, is a psychological condition, either a stand-alone disorder or a symptom blended into other mental disorders, she says, "But he really is sensational. I can't wait for you all to meet him."

"What does he do?" Elena asks.

"He's in logistics. Transportation. Moves big things around the world. Because of him I've learned, for instance, that A.P. Moller-Maersk of Denmark, the world's largest shipping concern, is operating Korean-built container ships called Triple-Es that are longer than the height of the Eiffel Tower, and though such ships carry more containers than anyone considered possible, there are drawbacks. The Triple-Es can sail only between Europe and Asia because their hulls, a hundred and ninety-four feet wide, are too large to fit into American ports, or to slip through the Panama Canal. And they must sail more slowly, cruising at sixteen or eighteen knots, instead of at twenty-two. A typical trip from Poland to China on a Triple-E takes thirty-four days, which apparently is a long time."

This is what she decided Aaron Green did, that she researched on her laptop, information she gathered in her notebook, as she sat in her suite at the Bel Onde in Santa Barbara back in February, when Aaron Green was new, when his creation seemed an intelligent way to lure real love into her life. It was overcast that Friday, the ocean wild and flipping over on itself. She had researched and followed links and written it all down, and then she was on the beach, the only person as far as she could see, the fog so soupy it altered perspective, beach and ocean a wedge of pie rather than an endless horizon. Twenty minutes out, the laces of her tennis shoes were tied together, hanging over her shoulder, her feet leaving firm imprints in the cold sand. The pockets of her jeans and her jacket were stuffed with polished black and white rocks the ocean threw out, that dotted the beach, and she remembers wondering when was the last time an educated woman could collect stones in her pockets and not contemplate the life and death of Virginia Woolf. After, she returned to her suite, ordered a bottle of champagne, requested specifically a single glass, and when it was delivered by a young bellman with down-free cheeks, she had tipped him a twenty and seen him out. She poured herself a glass, and on the suite's deck, under the awning that protected her from the drizzle then falling, she opened one of the books she had brought. Called *Fictional Family Life*, it was by the famous writer Joan Ashby, whom she'd recently read had abandoned her old life to make a new one in India. The dedication read, *Testify to the creation of lives and the requisite heroism in creating one's own*, and Phoebe had shifted nervously in her chair. The stories centered on a damaged boy stuck in his room who invented magical, mystical alter egos, boys his same age, raised dramatically in Colombia, Russia, Turkey, and the Galapagos Islands. When he dreamt, the boy transformed himself into Deo, Abel, Icarus, and Zed, and experienced all of their daring exploits, their fantastical lives he desperately wished for himself. In the beginning, Phoebe's mouth fell open when she discovered the damaged boy was also named Simon, and she tried superimposing her brother onto this teenage boy, giving him Simon's face, his voice, but it hadn't worked, the boy burst through, dispatched her brother, and inhabited all of the neurons, dendrites, and axons in her brain. When she reached the eighth story, she found herself breathless, and she had to calm herself by thinking about mundane things: whether the sun would come out while she was there, whether Benny missed her, whether her assistant had sent the engagement letters to the new clients she had met with the day before. And then her real thoughts, not at all prosaic, leaked from her heart into the damp air: whether she remembered how it felt to fall in love, if she could recall the exact last time she had been touched by someone she loved who loved her, too, aware of the uncomfortable connections the stories were encouraging her to make, between lives unwanted and lives desired, between truth and imagination. When she regained control, she refilled her glass and slipped back into those other lives, reading on and on until she finished the book and the bottle and cried for the damaged boy and for herself, before falling into a very drunken nap on the plush hotel bed.

"So he must travel a lot," Elena says wistfully.

Phoebe knows all about Elena's rock and hard place. Motherhood eliminated her sister-in-law's globe-trotting journalism work, an exchange she has told Phoebe she gladly made, and although her children are mostly soul-filling, she would welcome a path back into the world and the work she enjoyed. "Just to get away on my own," she told Phoebe recently. "With one single bag, returned to the pleasure of solitude, freed from questions about when baby teeth fall out, the difference between slugs and caterpillars, why chicken fingers taste better than the real chicken breasts I make. A span of traveling days when I'm not asked the who, what, when, where, why, and how of whatever is currently Lucy's obsession, in her mode of conversation, that Isabel is already attempting to copy with her small vocabulary, her short sentences." Elena now knows why the sky is blue, why grass is green, how flowers grow, but what's in Phoebe's mind isn't her sister-in-law's conundrum about how a mother can also be a working travel writer, but whether Elena has just given Phoebe a future way to gracefully exit from her Aaron Green relationship. She could blame the failure of their love affair on Aaron's exhausting travel schedule.

She nods at Elena.

"He does. He travels *a lot*."

Everything she needs is in those articles she read.

"Just since I've known him, he's been to Singapore twice, China once, Indonesia once."

"I've been to China and Indonesia, but never to Singapore," Elena says, and Phoebe smiles cheerfully as she deliberately places Elena and her past trips at the conversational center. And then becomes uncomfortably aware of her mother's eyes upon her. Anxiety grips her. Was her initial assumption right—that Roma accepted her explanation for Aaron's absence—or wrong, and she's about to be the object once again of the maternal spotlight? She feels her smile expanding defensively against the coming exposure, but then Roma says, "Elena, is Simon okay? His eyes don't look right," and Phoebe's anxiety dissipates.

"He's not sleeping," Elena says.

"Is it work? The new partnership?"

"I don't think so. He says nothing's wrong. He had a checkup and everything was fine."

Well, he's not fine, Roma thinks, *because he looks like hell.*

When Roma turns her gaze on Camille, Phoebe watches her sister leave their shared stair and wade backwards into the water, smiling and saying, "Mom, I'm great. I'm just fine. Life is peachy. It's perfect."

Under her breath, so quietly that Phoebe barely catches the words, Roma says, "Well, that's a load of bullshit." Then Roma's face closes down and Phoebe can't find even a hint of what her mother's thinking about.

What Roma is thinking about is that already, here at the beginning, she knows she must make private time for each of her children: to talk with Phoebe, because there's something off in her story about Aaron Green's absence, and she wonders if perhaps they quarreled, and with Simon, about why he isn't sleeping, and with Camille, because despite her feverish glow, and her anticipatory, overly bright and vague response to the question that Roma hadn't even asked, a response that did not refer at all to Valentine, well, that's a wall Roma needs to carefully demolish, brick by brick.

"Hey, Mom," Camille calls out, "remember those homemade popsicles you used to make us?"

From the middle of the pool, with Isabel sitting on his shoulders, Simon says, "Those were great. I haven't thought of them in years."

"I don't know why, but on the drive, I was thinking about how we used to gobble them up, three or four at a time, and then take naps. How'd you make them?"

"You want to know the secret ingredient?" Roma asks, and her children nod. "I made them with the leftover Manischewitz. The Passover wine. Well, except for a little water that I added, they were frozen wine on a stick. I gave them to you when I needed to work and none of you would give me a second of peace."

All three of her children stare at her, and Roma starts to laugh. She doesn't have to read their faces now to figure out what they're thinking.

"Please," she says. "Wipe those looks of horror off your faces. I didn't inflict any damage on you."

"*Mom!*" her children yell.

"*MOM!*" HARRY HEARS HIS children yell.

And those yells stop him cold as he's picking his way carefully around the side of the house, desperate not to run into anyone before somehow stapling himself back together. He waits, holding his breath, and when he hears their laughter boil up, he moves quickly, slipping in through the back door.

The kitchen is empty, and the dining room, and the den, and he peers around the living room wall, relieved that room is empty as well. Through the large windows, he sees them all out by the big pool.

Lucy is demanding an audience for her dive, Isabel is in a donut his son is swishing back and forth in the water, his daughters and daughter-in-law are arranging towels on the chaises, and his wife, seated on the pool stairs, is wearing the burgundy suit that reveals her fetching curves, bought for their trip to Hawaii last winter. Tall plastic glasses dot the small tables, the large pitcher of Arnold Palmers that Roma adores is nearly empty. He sighs.

Down the wide sunny halls, into their bedroom, where the sun has lit up all of their art, has turned their bed into a bright white cloud, where he wishes he could be, hiding beneath the soft duvet. He shuts the door quietly and debates locking it, but they haven't locked their door since they wanted private time when the children were young.

Through the bedroom to the bathroom, where he extracts the tuxedo from its black bag, tries to avoid looking at it when he hangs it in his closet, tries to avoid feeling the richness of the fabric, pulls out his swim trunks from the shelf above the hidden, heavy-duty safe, and slides the closet door closed. Roma is always after to him to close his closet door, always saying, "How hard is it, Harry, to close that damn door completely, it takes a second, so why can't you do it?" and now, finally, on this day of all days, he's done it, and vows he will keep doing it, satisfy this smallest of requests from his wife, who has carried the knowledge of what he himself did not remember until today.

Under the hard shower spray, he stands with his head down, his hands against the marble walls, the water smacking his head, his tight shoulders, his back newly bowed. He is a frozen man in the hot desert in a steaming shower, and he does not move until he clears his mind of the bad things he has done, that he remembers he has done, until he feels, not like himself, he knows those days are gone, but like a man who can paste a convincing smile on his face and welcome his children and his grandchildren, hug them all, and do what he always does with Roma when they've been apart for even an hour, which is to kiss her hard on her lips and say, "I love you."

He dries off and steps into his swim trunks, brushes his wet hair, inhales deeply, then stares at himself in the mirror. He pushes the corners of his mouth up with his hands, opens his eyes wide, waits until he manages to pull a twinkle down into them.

Then he is beyond the safety of the bathroom, and of the closed-door bedroom, is at the massive sliding glass doors in the living room, stepping out onto the sunbaked concrete, the aquamarine pool as inviting as an oasis, a mirage, calling out, "Welcome, welcome. It's wonderful to see everybody."

That's what he says, while in his head, in that dry voice from the court, he hears again, *In the beginning.* That biblical opening that spun him into a dark world.

Then his daughters are surrounding him, hugging him, Phoebe saying, "Hail to our conquering hero," and Camille saying, "You must be on top of the world," and it takes every ounce of his strength to keep his smile large and real, to mouth to Roma, "I love you."

He wishes she already knew everything he experienced this morning, but his wife's intelligent eyes hold none of that knowledge. Her eyes are bright and clear, the happiness within them uncensored and unclouded, happiness reflected in the strength of her smile, and she mouths back, "I love you, too."

When he feels tears pricking his eyes, tears he would not be able to rationally explain, he pulls free of his daughters, and leaps into the pool, tucking his head down, grabbing his knees with his arms, executing a cannonball, which he has never ever done before, not once in his life, displacing the blue water so thoroughly that his granddaughters are swamped by his wave, nearly going under, both kicking their legs hard and reaching out their arms to be saved. And when they are, their eyes are round and amazed watching their *sabba* below the surface, seemingly sitting on the bottom of the pool, and Lucy begins counting, "One, two, three, four, five, six . . ." and her numbers keep ringing out as her father, mother, grandmother, and aunts come together in a tight watery circle, Lucy and Isabel smack in the middle, everyone smiling, everyone looking down, waiting for the patriarch to rise.

EMPIRE OF KNOWLEDGE

NINETEEN

ALL OF THE TABORS frolicked in the pool. They played Marco Polo and Atomic Whirl and Octopus. Harry played Whale with the little ones, giving them round-trips on his back, from shallow end to deep. Lucy showed everyone how she swam the crawl—arms akimbo; the breaststroke—head retracted like a turtle, legs twitchy as a frog's; then called, "Sabba, Sabba, Sabba, looklooklook," to prove she could even swim staring straight at the big sun. Isabel, balanced atop Harry's shoulders, shrieked with delight each time he yelled "Ooomgaawah," before tossing her into the water and scooping her right up. He hung onto the side of the pool with his daughters, the three of them kicking their feet, sending up a huge spray that came down on the others in a rainbow of wet beads. He and Simon competed to see who could swim the longest without coming up for air, Simon beating him handily, five laps without taking a breath, throwing his arms up in triumph, yelling, "It's all the running I've been doing." Harry took Roma in his arms and she asked how his tennis went, if his string of unbroken victories remained intact, kissed him when he said he and Levitt had hung it up for the day, left the match unfinished until next week. She asked after Luigi and he said the tailor was his usual happy self. And when she said, "Are you excited about tonight," he pinched her rear to make her laugh and then swam a few hard laps, veering around his family as if they were buoys.

EVERYONE IS NOW IN dry bathing suits, shorts and shirts and sundresses, lunch set out on the long wooden table by the pool, and Harry is at the head, surrounded by those he loves, by those who love him because they think he is still the man he has always been, because they do not yet know he is no longer, has never been, that man.

His years of marriage to Roma have familiarized him with many of the psychological states her unnamed patients experience, including that of dissociation, a detachment from reality, a mind splitting free from the body, that can range from mild to pathological. Never once has he experienced such himself, at least not that he knows, but he is now, and he understands his mind is attempting to cope, seeking a mechanism, a defense to minimize the horrendous things he's learned, thus far, this day. Watching Simon loosening the cork on the prosecco, Harry feels himself rising, drifting up in the hot air, looking down at the wet heads of his family as they talk, laugh, turn their happy faces to where his body still sits in the chair, aiming smiles his way, full of pleasure and delight. The popping of the cork, the wine bubbling and spilling over the green glass of the bottle, yanks him down from the blue sky, tethers him firmly to his seat.

"Dad," Simon says, and Harry holds up a plastic flute for the golden liquid that fizzes in the sunlight, and he is utterly bereft, even as he's telling himself he can do this, be the father and husband they know. That he must, for them.

When the glasses are filled, Roma stands and waits for quiet. "This morning, I was trying to think of words that would capture my emotions, but none seemed to fit, none seemed important enough. So I'll simply say how proud I am of you, how proud we all are, how this award could not be bestowed on a more deserving man. Harry Tabor, you are a man among men. I love you with every ounce of my being."

There are cheers and calls for Harry to make a speech, and he sits with a smile on his face and his heart breaking, incapable of any utterance, and then Lucy stands and says, "Sabba, you're supposed to say something, something, something," and the laughter allows the moment to pass and all he can do is lift his glass higher, sweep his unseeing eyes around the table, and hope the gesture suffices. And it must, because then lunch is under way.

Dishes are passed; plates are filled. Lucy refuses anything from the fruit bowl. Isabel gestures to Elena's glass and then points to herself, and Roma hands over an empty flute, which Elena fills with a little water, and Isabel scuttles off her seat and goes around the table, insisting everyone clink their glasses against hers.

Conversations begin, and the Tabors, a quick-talking family, speak rapidly, and Harry, who can't put a morsel of food into his mouth, focuses on trying to listen. Relieved when he can do that, listen intently, although he is incapable of offering anything up.

Phoebe is asking Simon how it's going for him as a new partner at his firm, and he begins filling her in on the specifics, that he's working even more, not less, and Harry is impressed that his eldest refrains from telling his youngest what she really thinks about the choice he has made, thoughts she has previously, confidentially relayed to Harry, but then she doesn't stay quiet, says, "I think you made a big mistake not coming over to my firm. Your partner pay is less than what you'd be making at my shop, and I would have gladly changed the name to Tabor & Tabor, or the Tabor Firm, or even Tabor Squared, if that's what you wanted."

Simon reaches for the prosecco, finds the bottle empty, reaches for the second one perspiring on the table, pops the cork, refills his glass, drinks, and only then does he say to his sister, "Right now we love each other, but if we were working together, who knows what would happen. Did you want to take the risk we'd end up hating each other, barely remembering we're sister and brother, consumed instead only by firm business? And we don't really do things the same way. If we were partners, I'd suggest no longer accepting paintings by clients who can't pay their bills. I would tell you it sets a lousy precedent. That people have to pay for the expertise they want."

"Well," Phoebe says, frowning, "I guess you're one of the lucky ones, Simon, never finding anything a struggle. But if someone needs my help, why wouldn't I give it? A simple act of generosity can revive a flagging confidence, restore a belief in goodness. So what if I sometimes give away my expertise? It usually balances out in the end. I just sold four paintings for twenty times the value of the original legal bills. You can't take a month of your own salary and do as well as I've done."

The family's two lawyers are off, Phoebe questioning whether Simon remembers that he followed her into the law, not the other way around, and despite his dramatic trips abroad to foreign courtrooms, she doubts he has much feeling for the actual works he recovers. Simon keeps saying, "You're wrong, Phoebe, totally wrong." Harry usually functions as the voice of reason for these two, but not today. Let them battle it out; let them find their own way to an accord, without him.

At the other end of the table, Elena and Roma are talking about kindergarten, or about some program that comes before kindergarten, which Harry thought was called nursery school, but apparently is not.

Next to him, Camille is entertaining Lucy and Isabel with stories about the Trobriand Islands, telling them about how in Trobriand society it is taboo to eat in front of others: people take their food away and eat by themselves.

"So they don't, don't, don't have parties like us?" Lucy asks, and Camille says "No, not at all. Weird, right? We love having parties, don't we?"

"Wedowedowedo," Lucy chants, her voice climbing the scale, going higher and higher, and Harry wonders if her voice might reach the register heard only by dogs. Roma has mentioned to him her concern about how Lucy snatches onto a word, or a phrase, and can't stop repeating it, and Lucy is still saying, "Wedowedowedo . . ." until Camille hugs her tight. And that hug slows the words, until they stop, and his first granddaughter is quiet, sitting on his second child's lap.

"So," Camille says to the little girls, "do you want to hear about the very special old women on those islands who know how to make magic spells?"

"Savah?" Isabel says, pointing to Roma, making Camille laugh.

"Well, Savah's not old, but yes, special women just like Savah."

Roma hears Camille invoking her name and smiles, then blows a kiss to Harry. Beneath the animated conversations, words she intends only for him travel across the length of the table. "It's unbelievable, isn't it? That you and I created all this together."

He wants to cry out to Roma, "Yes, yes, my love, it is unbelievable that we created all this together." He wants to cry out to them all that he's lost, but an iciness is spreading through his insides, freezing the blood in his veins, and he is seeing only the darkness descending, the destruction when the truth about him comes to light. His thoughts reducing down to a single breathless hope: that they are all strong enough to endure whatever the future may hold.

Then Isabel is tugging at his hand, which he finds curled tight into a fist, her tiny fingers inching in until her palm is resting in his palm, warming him up. "Sabba, nap," she says, looking up at him, the feathery little-girl lashes like fans. He looks down into her deep brown eyes, and though it cannot be possible, for she is only two, he is certain they are reflecting the weight of his world.

TWENTY

I'LL TAKE HER IN," Elena says, rising from her chair, but Harry shakes his head.

"Story?" Isabel says.

"Of course," Harry says.

"Sleep well, honey," Elena says, stroking Isabel's head.

"Happy nap, sweetheart," Simon says, kissing his daughter's cheek.

Phoebe, Camille, and Lucy chime in, too, as Isabel holds tight to Harry, her small hand clutching his much bigger one, her trusting eyes heavy and ready to close.

Tallish grandfather and minute granddaughter bonded together; it is a sweet tableau, but Roma is troubled. Subdued since he came home, unnaturally serious during the water games, and even now, at lunch, Harry was so quiet amidst the chatter and jocularity. Is it exhaustion from the hours of tennis he played in the heat? Introspection because of tonight's award ceremony? She would like to suggest he take his own afternoon nap, but he would pooh-pooh the recommendation, say, "I am strong like Russian bear."

Roma watches how oddly he's holding himself as he walks toward the house with Isabel, as if his mind has detached from his corporeal form. It's the reverse of Noelani, who can gain no distance from the flesh of her being. Roma wants to follow them in, check on Harry, then check her voicemails again to see if Jeanine McCadden has left a message. Later she will wonder why she didn't heed her concern, but Lucy is undressing right where she stands, pulling off her bright yellow sundress, pulling down her bright yellow bathing suit, then running naked and yelling, "Water, water, water, water, water," a bright angel flinging herself into the pool, and Simon, watching his daughter, says, "Mom, we need some advice."

Roma turns her full attention to her son and says, "Lucy's needing to be naked is a natural trait she'll outgrow, and it's healthy neither of you makes a big deal of it. You want her to be proud of her body, not ashamed. Of course, the difference between private nakedness and public nakedness will be important to teach her."

Simon looks over again at Lucy, slick as a dolphin in the pool, then back to his mother. "We weren't worried about that, but should we be?"

"Not at all. I thought that's what you wanted to ask me about."

It's not at all what Roma thought Simon wanted to ask her about, but given the circumstances, five-year-old granddaughter stripping naked without thought or compunction, she decided to throw in a little unsolicited professional advice.

"No, but now I can't get the image of her being a naked teenager out of my head, having to lock her in her room because we've failed to teach her about when it's okay to be naked and when it's not." What he actually imagines is a line of boys snaking around their house, waiting for a glimpse of the developing nymphet.

Roma puts a hand on Simon's arm. "Society will take care of that, for better and for worse. First, she'll insist on wearing exactly what her friends wear, then she'll absorb the kind of positive and negative attention she receives if she dresses more individually, or shows more skin, or less skin. It's a tightrope you'll both learn to walk, and so long as she's raised to respect her physical being, everything will be fine. I guessed wrong, so what's on your mind?"

"That kinder-readiness program I was telling you about," Elena says. "I'm worried about what happens if she starts the program a week late? Are we setting her up to be an outsider?"

Roma has seen it so many times, young parents, new parents, worried about the wrong thing. She thought she was going to be asked about Lucy's repetitive speech pattern, which she's been studying since Lucy began to talk. She would have told them repetitive speech can be a sign of delayed development or developmental difficulties, especially if accompanied by an aversion to eye contact, a preference for viewing things from the corners of the eyes, squinting, covering ears against loud sounds, body rocking, difficulty interacting with others, which typically results in difficulty relating to peers. Roma hasn't seen Lucy display any of those behaviors associated with the kind of self-talk she engages in, and she seems, at times, to be cognitively advanced; still, if they were parents in her office, not her son and daughter-in-law, she would suggest they remain on the alert to Lucy making unnatural and sustained body movements, or shying away from looking at people, or developing an inability to relate to other children, or evincing an overly strong resistance to change, or if her desire to be naked continues and she begins complaining that she hates the feel of cloth on her skin.

"I wouldn't worry about her joining the class a week late," Roma says. Lucy's speech pattern could make her a prime target for bullying, but why worry them now about something that might happen whether she joined the class on time or late? Children were cruel to those perceived as different, but in the early weeks, most were too stunned by the shock of school to become aggressors immediately. The conflicts, the aggression, and the bullying usually took time to emerge.

"That's reassuring," Simon says, and Roma looks to Lucy, on the step in the pool, uttering, "Swim, swim, swim, swim." She would like to ask whether their efforts at redirecting Lucy's repetitive speech are working, then thinks: *Keep your mouth shut. One piece of unwanted advice a day is enough.* It's a double-edged sword

Roma feels at her neck: relating to her children and grandchildren as mother and grandmother, while incapable of not viewing them all through her highly trained psychological lens.

"But why would she have to join the class late?" she asks.

Simon smiles at his mother. "You'll have to wait until tomorrow to hear about it."

"You're being very mysterious."

"Being mysterious is good, isn't it?"

Roma laughs. "Being mysterious is sensational, honey. Life is always more interesting when it's filled up with mysteries."

TWENTY-ONE

Isabel insists on her pajamas. Harry places her butterfly suitcase on the twin bed she sleeps in and unzips it. "Do you think they're on the top or the bottom?" and Isabel answers by tossing out the neatly packed clothes until she finds tiny blue-flowered pajamas.

She holds up her arms so Harry can lift her sundress over her head, and then holds her arms up again, so he can slip the pajama top down. He holds up the bottoms and she holds out her hands and says, "Me, Sabba."

He drapes the clothes over one of the dressers, sets the suitcase on the floor, folds back the duvet, and Isabel climbs in. She fluffs her pillow the way he does, then turns on her side, looks at him with her enormous eyes, and says, "Story."

Harry said of course to a story when his granddaughter asked him outside, but can he calm himself sufficiently to tell one? Does he have in his head any story to tell? He hears his father's smoke-graveled voice again, his opening for the tale about Cantor Simon Tabornikov, the name that Harry inexcusably used, that he heard in part this morning, that always began with the words "Your great-grandfather's brother trained as a cantor"— and Harry, his body cricked and tight from fear and fright, tries to stretch out next to his granddaughter on the twin bed Simon slept in for years. He puts his big hand on his granddaughter's small head, aware that Isabel is surely too young to remember anything he might say. But if by some chance in the future she recollects being cradled in her *sabba*'s arms at the age of two and hearing his words, he ought to tell her a story worth remembering. A story of blind derring-do, and flawed wisdom, and the fallible human need to believe in only the best version of oneself. A true story. And he understands the story he should tell, and he opens his mouth to usher forth that story, though he doesn't know it yet in full, and then his voice is spilling into the quiet room.

"Your *sabba* is, at his core, a fine man, a serious man, a man who always wants to do the right thing, which means that he wants to be good, and do good, and offer goodness and succor to those in need, and that's nice to say and it's nice to hear, but it's possible the story begins in a different way.

"Your grandfather, your *sabba*, me, Harry, known in childhood as Hiram, grew up being taught the ways of our people, learning right from wrong. And for many years, I did no wrong, until the day I lost track of myself, and became a man unshackled from the Commandments. And with that unshackling came my worship of the wrong things, the graven images, the false idols. My father, and his father, and his father before him, they would have said I was practicing *nachesh*, taking actions based on signs and portents, using my own version of charms and incantations. And that I was practicing *kisuf*, magic, using herbs and stones, for which I substituted their modern form—information. They also would have said that I consulted the *ovoth*, the ghosts, and the *yid'onim*, the wizards, to attain what wasn't mine to attain. And they would be right. I trampled upon our ancient six hundred and thirteen mitzvot, not every one of them, not those no longer applicable in our time, but those that remain as powerful as they ever were. I failed to trust that if I heeded what was right, what I knew to be right, and if I did right, I would have ended up exactly where I am, but without the stink of disgrace, the taint of dishonor, the ignominy of shame. Oh, my sweet child, it happened so fast, so easily, and some of the details have yet to be revealed, and I don't know the ending—"

TWENTY-TWO

"T HESE ARE THE LAST of the dishes," Camille says, coming into the kitchen, plates piled up to her chin. They rattle on the stone island when she sets them down.

"What are they talking about out there?" Phoebe asks. Her mother, brother, and sister-in-law are still at the table, chairs pulled close.

"About Lucy's preference for being naked. Mom said she'll outgrow it."

Phoebe sighs. "I think it's sad life is all about outgrowing things."

At the mall, and at the table, when she was sparring with Simon, which the two of them love to do, Phoebe's eyes were bright and clear, but now they look dull. Camille can't remember ever seeing her sister's eyes dull, filled with any kind of pain. But *pain* is what crosses her mind.

"Is everything okay?" Camille asks.

"I'm just remembering being a kid. How easy things were." Phoebe looks at the glass in her hand, then loads it into the dishwasher.

How easy things *were*? Things have *never* not been easy for Phoebe.

Camille tells herself to stay quiet, but out it comes. "Phoebe, things are easy for you now, like they've always been. You were the perfect child and the perfect teenager and now the perfect adult, with a life that works perfectly. Some people just get lucky. You got lucky."

Phoebe shakes her head. Camille is wrong. Phoebe does not have a golden life, not in the ways that matter, the way her siblings have lives that matter. Simon has a golden life, not because of his genius, his going off to college young, graduating first in his law school class, making equity partner at thirty, but because he found true love. Because he's happily married with gorgeous children. And Camille has a golden life, not because of her brilliance, or all her awards and honors, but because she has always followed her own path.

"Maybe it would have been better if everyone hadn't thought of me as a golden child," she finally says.

Such a Phoebe response, Camille thinks. "I said perfect, not golden. There's a difference."

Phoebe starts laughing, and the laughter brightens her eyes.

"There *is* a difference," she says. "You're right. I'd rather have what you and Simon have, golden lives."

Camille thinks how wrong Phoebe is, then turns on the faucet and slides the plates into the sink.

They work quietly for a while—Phoebe rinsing and stacking the dishwasher, Camille wrapping the leftovers, putting them into the fridge.

"Are you lonely now that Valentine's gone?"

"It's fine," Camille says.

"Are you going to visit him?"

"I don't think so."

"You don't have any problem with being apart for six months, with all that distance between you?"

"In the world of any kind of anthropology, six months isn't even a grain of sand."

Phoebe stares at Camille and nearly says to her sister that if their situations were reversed, she'd be on a plane to South Africa in a heartbeat. She nearly says to her sister that a handsome man at the gas station wanted to talk to her and she pretended she was French, without any command of the English language. She nearly says to her sister that the last time she went on a date, more than a year ago, she sat across from the man with a frozen smile on her face, aware she had completely lost the concept of conversational rhythm. She nearly says to her sister that all she wants is a future with marriage and children, but there won't be either with Aaron Green, because he doesn't exist, because she made him up in an inane appeal to the god of love.

Camille stares at Phoebe and nearly says to her sister that she thinks she might have had some kind of nervous breakdown, a possibility unacknowledged until this minute standing here in the kitchen at home in Palm Springs, and she can't understand her collapse when once she considered herself invincible. She nearly says to her sister that since the start of the year, she's been working as a caregiver to the dying, spending her days in a lilac house on a steep hill, and even though it's helping her, she's still not herself. She nearly says to her sister that she doesn't want to visit Val in South Africa, because he wants to marry her, and the notion is so paralyzing that she's trying to pretend he never asked, because all she imagines is having to act as if the depression is nearly gone, when it's not. She nearly says to her sister that she can't picture the future when the most she can handle right now is barely living the most hateful of all things, a quotidian life.

"You want to—?" Phoebe asks.

"Yeah. Let's go float in the pool."

Phoebe drops in the soap packet and turns the dishwasher on. "So," she says, searching for a safe topic, "what are you wearing tonight?"

"Oh, Phoebe," Camille says. "Don't ruin everything."

Ruin everything? Phoebe thinks, as she follows Camille outside, where their mother now sits alone at the table, watching Lucy dunking herself madly. Why would asking Camille what she's wearing tonight *ruin everything*? Low-level anger roils inside of her, a slight raising of her hackles; then it all drains away. Why is she pretending she doesn't know what she was doing? She knows perfectly well. She asked Camille what she's wearing tonight to shift the balance of power back to herself. Because it's spectacularly maddening that Camille can so easily slough off the very idea of a man who loves her, hasn't given a thought to going to visit Val. Why should her sister have love in her life if she cares so little about it? And that's why she asked that supposedly casual question, to put Camille on edge, make her uncomfortable, force her to face something, maybe that no one gets everything in their life, a truth Phoebe has been dealing with every single day for years. Camille has everything that is unconventional—the top-notch degrees, the fantastic career that has her living on distant islands with fascinating people, her scintillating Russian lover—and what does Phoebe have? The known and familiar life she opted for when she abandoned Elijah, and an enviable lover who is completely made up. But her phenomenal fashion sense, that's where she reigns over her sister. And because she's become a small-souled liar, because she's jealous that Camille set high-flying goals for herself and has achieved them all, she wanted to hurt Camille just a little, and it was wrong and childish and she needs to find her natural better nature this moment.

She reaches out and touches her sister's shoulder, smiles a true and loving sisterly smile at Camille. "Maybe we should stay here past tomorrow, like Mom said. Hang out just us in the pool, spend time together like we never get to do anymore. Really talk."

"Maybe," Camille says, nodding her head in a way that might qualify as an answer in Camille's world, but doesn't qualify as one in Phoebe's.

"Just so you know, Phoebe, I'm wearing a gorgeous white satin suit tonight. There's no way you're not going to think it's fabulous."

Camille instantly wants to slap her own face because she sounds ridiculously defensive, because *fabulous* is not a word in her regular vocabulary, because Phoebe is not going to think the white satin suit is fabulous, because she wishes she had what Phoebe has, a future that is solid and real.

"I've no doubt," Phoebe says.

And in her sister's intonation, Camille can't find any of Phoebe's usual sarcasm when it comes to Camille and fashion. But she's hurt Phoebe, she sees that, and she should throw her sister a bone.

"Hey," she says, "do you remember those dogs we used to have?"

"Yeah. Our hot dog dogs."

Camille nods. "Do you remember their names?"

Phoebe wrinkles her forehead. "Royalty."

"Royalty?"

"No, I mean they were named after royalty. Yes. King David and Queen Esther. Why?"

"I saw a dog on the drive and thought of them. Whatever happened to them?"

Phoebe stares at Camille, though it's clear she's looking into the past, then shakes her head, and Camille watches her sister's chestnut curls flying, finding sharp old envy inside, over those curls, over that seductive color of hair.

"I don't know," Phoebe says. "But I remember we loved those dogs so much."

Then their mother is waving them over and they kneel at her chair and she puts her hands on their heads. "I love seeing my daughters together. Will you watch Lucy? Simon and Elena went to unpack and I need to check messages. I'll bring out a fresh pitcher of Arnold Palmers when I'm done."

Lucy, grinning and waving her arms, yells, "Pleasepleasepleaseplease. Bewithme, bewithme, bewithme."

God, how Phoebe wishes she had her own Lucy.

"We're right here," Camille says, stepping into the water, holding out her arms to her niece.

TWENTY-THREE

I FORGOT *NAPTIME* COULD have another meaning," Elena says.

They are at the far end of the house, in the guest room down its own separate hallway, distant from his sisters' perennial bedrooms, distant from his childhood bedroom into which his father disappeared with Isabel for her story and nap, distant from the big pool in the courtyard where Lucy is splashing under Roma's watchful eye, where Phoebe and Camille are probably drifting on rafts. Here in this secluded airy room that he has wrongly resented, that he has not recognized as the private domain that it is, he and Elena are completely alone.

The view through the large windows makes him think of the inception of the world, flat desert, cacti, two rabbits running across the shrubby sand, and when Elena says, "Any interest?" he turns and finds her stretched across the inviting king bed, the agapanthus violet of the duvet and pillows arresting against her tanned skin, beckoning him with a seductive hand.

As always, her hair is a thick coil pinned at her nape, but she's wearing only her silver bikini, the fabric imprinted to resemble the scales of a snake. She reaches up, unties the knot at the back, lets the strings fall.

"Yes? No?" she asks.

He can't recall the last time they made love in the middle of the day, can't recall the last time she initiated anything more than a kiss, other than that quick grasping of him early this morning at home, and he says, "Yes. Definitely, yes," his reaction to her as ardent as the first time he saw her at a friend's party, seated on a low stone wall, her hair loose and moonlit, her long legs brown and bare, her summer dress exceedingly short, her sexy, slightly accented voice telling a ribald story to the keen men circling like birds of prey. When her wineglass was empty, he'd swooped in with a fresh one and a smile. What were the first words he spoke to the woman who would become his wife? He was sure he'd never forget them, but they become irrelevant when her breasts are in the palms of his hands.

AT FIRST, THEY WERE trying too hard, and then the real thing kicked in, their bodies acclimating to genuine physical desire, rediscovering something close to the carnality that existed before the children came along. Now, sweaty and depleted, with Elena's skin flush against his, Simon thinks it was nearly wild, and he wants to ask what brought on this unpredicted pleasure, but something is carving away at the air, returning them to their own spheres, separating them once again into dissimilar components, though moments ago they were fully united. Truly, he doesn't know whether the divide between them is in his mind or real. And if it's real, how he might cross it. And then he says what he has not said in a very long time: "I think it's time for a story."

Elena shifts in his arms, glances up at his face, and he smiles; he's chosen well. She seems ready to speak, then refrains, something she's been doing for too long, and it bothers him, but he's gentle when he says, "What are you thinking?"

Looking down at the totality of his wife's beauty, he realizes he spends part of each sleepless night watching her without really seeing her, merely aware of her outline, of the fact of her, this woman he is bound to, with whom he has two young children, who seems less interested in their love day by day. He wonders when that happened, and why this moment, against the positive evidence that should refute his apprehension, he is again contemplating the lessening of her love.

"I was thinking that five short years ago, I was the travel writer, but you were always the storyteller, illuminating emotions people hide from themselves and from others. Even at our wedding, you told a story that had everyone tearing up. In the past few years, other than humorous recitations about your day, your stories have dried up and disappeared, and I was considering what's different about today, to bring a story on."

"I haven't a clue," he says, unsure if he's speaking the truth, knowing he's not when a sudden pressure builds behind his sternum. He waits for her to probe, the way she has always done, or rather did. In their past, she would have asked questions, unraveled his *I haven't a clue*, but this afternoon, in their postcoital embrace, she doesn't, and he reluctantly lets it go. But there is again that sense of loss he experienced when she didn't ask if he feels he's missing out by not having religion as part of their lives.

When did they, their relationship, life, or some combination, become so complicated? Or has it always been, and it's taken additional maturity and fatherhood to recognize it?

And the idea comes to him that maybe it isn't complicated at all, maybe it's merely a matter of finding the right stories to tell, the right stories to live.

He feels the heat where their skin is in contact, and though only the vaguest idea is forming, he begins.

"Once upon a time, a couple took a trip to a place of mountains and valleys and many churches. One day, during a visit to a very old church, the man took the woman's hand and hurried them past the other sightseers, through the sacred dimness, until they were beyond the weighty doors, back in the world where people walked the sunshiny streets, peered into shop windows, strolled into galleries. At the top of the church steps, the woman asked, 'Why are we leaving?' and the man said, 'It's time we had an afternoon drink.'

"What do you think they drink in Colombia?"

"Is that what the man says to the woman?" Elena asks.

"No, that's what I'm asking you."

"*Aguardiente*, definitely, and Cuba libres, probably."

"What are they?"

"The nickname for *aguardiente* is 'firewater,' sugarcane spirit flavored with aniseed. And Cuba libres are made with rum."

"Okay. So the man led the woman to a table at a charming outdoor café, their hands soldered together. When the woman sat, the sun mysteriously shadowed her face, her exposed shoulders, turned her into a Giacometti sculpture, rare and elongated, a distance contained in her core, a coolness shimmering across the warmth of her skin, and the woman said, 'We're to drink Cuba libres.'

"In no time, the young waiter was upon them, so tall he made the man feel as if God was staring down upon him. The man said, '*Hola, por favor, dos cuba libres*,' and the waiter, named Victor, smiled and said, '*Inmediatamente*.'"

"Why is the waiter named Victor?"

"I don't know, that's what jumped into my head."

"Okay. Continue."

"When Victor the waiter was gone, the woman lifted her face to the sun, and the man was enthralled by the pulse beating at the base of her long slim neck, his heart hammered by love.

"The silvery drinks arrived—"

"Not silvery," Elena says. "They're made of light or dark rum and cola."

"The golden-brown drinks arrived, ice cubes tinkling, and the man held up his glass and toasted the woman, and having her attention made him realize he had missed the force of her stare, her heart displaying itself to him."

He feels Elena press harder against him, watches as she drapes an arm across his chest.

"The woman sipped and then she said, 'That old basilica reminded me of my family's neighborhood church, much larger of course, but the same cruciform shape identifiable only by birds with their aerial view. It made me think of my years in pews, in catechism classes, dreaming of a God who was handsome. Did you hear me whispering the church parts into the cool air?'

"And the man said, 'No, I didn't hear that at all,' and the woman said, 'This is how it goes . . .'" And Simon pauses.

Elena looks up at him again and quietly says, "High altar, transept, nave, vestry, chancel, apse, font."

Simon nods. "And after the woman chanted the parts of the church, the man said to her, 'When I looked at the church's stained glass windows, I was reminded of sitting in synagogue when I was young, happy to have something to look at, wishing for something to read beyond the prayer book, wondering what my older sisters meant when they whispered with glee, 'Atone, little brother, atone!'

"For a while, the couple sat companionably, drinking their drinks, absorbed in their separate thoughts. The woman was thinking that when the visceral pleasures of life revealed themselves to her, she had intended to marry a man just like Jesus, never imagined that the man who would make her laugh and tremble would be a Jew. The churchgoers sitting on the wooden benches reverentially beholding their Christ on the cross made her wistful for those afternoons when she used to shiver figuring out her tame girlhood sins, waiting to confess, playing with the tiny crucifix that once dangled around her neck on a thin chain. She thought of that crucifix and chain tucked away in her jewelry box beside a Chinese bowl the man gave her as a gift.

"And the man was thinking about his enforced Hebrew school years, being taught the Hebrew alphabet and enduring lessons about Judaic history he likely forgot while still in the classroom. He remembered the Abba-Zaba bars he bought at the temple store before every class, long and flat and slightly squishy when firmly pressed. He would stretch out the white taffy until it finally splintered, surreptitiously placing a wad in his cheek, letting it slowly dissolve until he tasted the peanut butter inside. How that candy made those tortured hours spouting '*Aleph, Beit, Gimel, Dalet, Hey, Vav*' slightly more palatable, and responsible for the numerous cavities he incurred when he was a boy."

Simon pauses, wondering what comes next, and when Elena looks up at him, he holds up his hand, closes his eyes, and thinks until it comes to him, it all comes to him in a blinding deposit of knowledge, and when he opens his mouth, the pressure in his sternum dissolves.

"Sitting at that outdoor café, the man wanted to tell the woman a story, needed to tell her a story, a very Jewish story that he thought of as a coming-to-Jesus story, that would be, in some undefined way, *his* coming-to tale. And he decided to tell her about the ancestor after whom he was named. He said to her, 'Unlike me, past generations of my family prayed fervently. In my father's family, there was a great-uncle born and raised in the Pale of Settlement, who studied long and hard to become a cantor, and then was in search of a position. The young cantor had been profoundly deaf since birth, but when the rabbi heard him sing, the rabbi thought, *God is wise and caring, for although He made the cantor this way, He provided by giving him a magnificent voice, and a personal story that would draw large worshipping crowds,* guaranteeing both the young man's livelihood and an increase in the shul's congregation, and it didn't hurt at all that the deaf cantor's name contained an inherent irony, for although he could not hear, his name meant *one who has heard.*

"The rabbi hired the young cantor, who began his career singing through all the Shabbats and holidays. Many years passed, and in the cantor's sixtieth year, at the onset of Rosh Hashanah, when the Days of Awe began and the Book of Life was opened, he raised his celestial voice to the heavens and continued singing the prayers until the sun was setting on the tenth day. With Yom Kippur drawing to a close, the cantor stood in front of the open ark, singing his heart out, and when his prayerful words reached a godly place, the cantor, without warning, fell silent. It was said that the silence was startling, vicious, reminded people of the decimations they had experienced in the past, continued to experience at the hands of those who wanted their kind turned forever to dust. And then, the cantor toppled over, and the congregation inhaled, a hundred sets of lungs pulling in consecrated air as he crumpled onto the bema, its red carpet shabby and worn. The rabbi leaped to the cantor's side, dropped to the ground, pressed a hand to the neck of his ersatz son, his longtime friend and colleague, and felt no pulse. With eyes overflowing, he turned to the congregation and shook his head, and all those bated breaths released in a hard *whoosh*—" And Simon hears Elena sharply inhale.

"Had God determined that the cantor should expire just at that moment? During the days and nights of Awe evoking his people's fate with the deep melodies only he could carry, had the cantor missed the fact that his own name was not inscribed in the Book of Life for the coming year? Perhaps. Or perhaps an aneurysm exploded in the deaf cantor's brain and ended his life just as the Book of Life snapped shut. Who knows whether the cantor died in such a poignant way, or whether the carpeting on the bema was actually red. The only thing truly known was that the cantor had lived a worthy life, had been part of an ancient line, had carried the ancient forward in his heart and in his head and in all his sung prayers, had brought sustaining faith to his people and himself."

"Simon?"

"Yes?"

"What are you saying?"

He's not sure what he's saying, but this morning in bed, and on the drive as the miles sped by, there was a spiraling thought that there *is* something missing in him, in his life, which can't be rectified by the methods he's chosen to date. How strange if all his various fitness regimens, and his running the last six months, as if preparing for marathons, as if aiming to become one of those punishing distance runners, were for naught, because what's missing has nothing to do with the physical realm at all.

And the thought spirals faster and faster and faster, then blows apart, leaving behind something pure, something infinitely ageless.

And it hits him, his chaotic nights, they aren't about insomnia at all, but about something much deeper, about how he is living his

life without any awareness of what lies beneath, without any awareness of his historical past, without any unifying theme rooted in
the ageless to ground his present actions.

He is astonished to find his Jewishness bubbling up, seeking release, when he has never much adhered to his religion.

And it is precipitous, and overwhelming, this powerful sudden
wish to be perfectly aligned with his own people, for his daughters
to know the cantor's tale, to know all the other mystical tales,
for them to live their forward-looking lives bathed in a magical
past that is hard as nails.

He wants for them what he once fought against, including the
years spent in Hebrew school. He imagines each daughter playing
Queen Esther in a temple Purim Day parade. In his own past, a
handmade float carried the queen, a pretty teenage girl named
Laurel. He can't remember whether Mordechai the Savior or Ha-
man the Jew-Hater sat next to her, but he remembers Laurel wearing a diaphanous blue gown with a gold crown on her head, and the
float circling and circling the temple parking lot, snagging against
parking-space bumpers. He remembers his father holding his hand,
telling him that Simon's grandfather was named after Mordechai
the Savior, and that Harry's name, Hiram, meant *high-born and
lofty*, the name of the king of Tyre who supplied building materials
and workers to build King David's palace, and to Solomon, to build
the temple of YHWH, and that Simon was named after the rarest
of rare men, an ancestor who was a deaf cantor, the single time his
father explained where Simon's name had come from.

He wants that knowledge and more threaded into his daughters'
lives.

He wants them to learn their Bat Mitzvah H'aftorah portions
in the warm confines of a cantor's study, as he did not, but his
father did, and all the men who preceded his father, when they were
still Tabornikovs. He wants his daughters on the bema in adorable dresses, the Torah unwound in front of them, speaking aloud
the Hebrew words in clear, sweet voices that would wash over the
family and friends come to celebrate that passage with them.

He realizes that he wants his children to be Jewish.

Which they are not.

With Elena as their mother, there has been a hiccup in the matrilineal blood.

He realizes he is again questioning the boundaries he and Elena unthinkingly crossed to effect their union, a questioning that began on the drive, but perhaps earlier than that, and there's more, so much more now in his head.

He realizes he is contemplating changing the terms of their marriage, asking Elena to allow him to bring religion into their lives, and not in some fair way. He does not want equal time for the church, not when there are more than a billion Roman Catholics and less than fifteen million Jews in the entire world, not when Elena has said her own needs are fulfilled by her secret visits to church. He wants to insist on Hebrew school for the girls, the acquisition of a temple membership. He wants to host the High Holidays at their house, and attend Friday night Shabbat services. He wants the girls to light the Hanukkah candles, one for each night, until the whole thing is ablaze. He wants them all to eat matzoh for eight days, to read the Four Questions aloud at the Passover table, to taste the sweet honeyed nut of the *haroset*, the sharpness of horseradish slivers.

Would Elena agree to any of it, to all of it, to forfeiting equal time for Catholicism?

Would he and Elena still fit, or mostly fit, or fit as they've been fitting of late, if he were to become an observant Jew?

He imagines himself the opposite of a person who abandons spouse and children; he wants to bind what he has created, cohere this Tabor unit while still in its relative infancy.

He sees it now. The literal hole in his soul. That is not at all new. That has, instead, been within him for a very long time. This is why the spirits gather around him each night and refuse him his sleep. This is why he feels his Jewishness bubbling up, seeking release.

He is trembling inside, as he stares at the pure, at the infinitely ageless, at the revelations that exploded into being before his eyes.

He needs to be perfectly aligned with his own people.

He needs to sink himself into the loamy earth of his ancestors, to learn their ways, to make their ways his.

And another tremor runs through him, for it's not only a need; it's a want.

He *wants* to sink himself into the loamy earth of his ancestors.

And it's the kind of shock that comes after the fact, when looking back with hindsight, one says, *Of course, how did I not understand this before?*

Elena is staring at him, but he keeps his eyes focused at the view beyond the large picture windows, takes in the blue fabric of the sky, the rays of hot sun beaming down upon the tall, strong cacti, the endless rolling sand, how everything is one out there in the desert.

The conversion of his own nonobservant philosophy into something else, the potential tossing away of how he has lived his life up to now—it has happened this fast, in an instant.

"I'm just telling a story," he finally says.

Elena pulls away from him, covers herself with the sheet. "Simon—"

He reaches for her hand, tells himself to say nothing more, but when he looks at her, his heart refuses to heed.

"I think I want to be a Jew."

TWENTY-FOUR

ROM HER STUDY, ROMA hears the laughter of her daughters and granddaughter, their individual characters captured in those different trilling sounds.

No calls from Jeanine McCadden on either voicemail. Should she be the one to initiate, to see how things are going today? Or will it interfere with the therapeutic process? It is a debate she always has; sometimes she preempts a patient's parents, sometimes not. She doesn't have much of a handle on Jeanine yet, and none at all on the father, so she'll let it play out.

She peeks into Simon's old room, expecting only to find Isabel deep in her nap, but Harry has her curled up in his arms, the two of them sound asleep. She tiptoes past, then pivots, retrieves her cell phone from her study, opens its camera, and snaps a photo. Such a precious moment ought to be memorialized. There is a little guilt, too, in the action. There are so few pictures of Simon as a baby, as a child; their life here in the desert was only a month old when she became pregnant with him, and picture taking was low on the list of settling in, then caring for an infant, for two little girls, for house and husband, getting her practice off the ground. It's a reflexive, reflective act she tries to remember to undertake— to snap lots of pictures of her grandchildren—so while there is a noticeable absence of Simon in the family photo albums, at least there will be many of Lucy and Isabel, even if they never end up under clear vinyl, are only in that cloud her children talk about, where treasured memories are apparently saved forever these days.

She tiptoes out, and in the hallway emails the photo to everyone, herself included, because no matter how many times her children have shown her how to get her cell phone pictures onto her computer, she can't remember what to do, nor can Harry. Something with a cord, with a slot? Or are they automatically on her computer if only she knew where to look? Who knows and who cares. Another important thing she's learned about life all these years: beyond the indispensable requirement of mystery, one must figure out shortcuts for everything that is superfluous.

In the kitchen, she lifts out the jugs of home-brewed iced tea and fresh-squeezed lemonade from the fridge. She knows everyone would prefer she made the Arnold Palmers sweeter, but she likes it this way, a little tart, a pinch from summer.

Dulcet chirps coming from a cell phone. Not hers, which is on the counter, but another, behind her on the island. She leans over, looks at the screen, at a name that hugely intrigues, and though she will be taking an unsupportable liberty, will, without a doubt, be stepping over a very solid line, she is a mother, and the name represents one of those mysteries in life—*Valentine Osin*, about whom Camille reveals nothing—and she picks up her daughter's phone, and slides what she's supposed to slide, and says, "Hello."

The connection is bad, as if the caller is in a wind tunnel or phoning from a different galaxy, and Roma can't hear any voice on the other end, and she keeps saying, "Hello? Hello? Hello?" walking across the kitchen, intending to deliver the phone to Camille, but then she hears a click, and knows the call has been dropped, or the caller has hung up, and she looks at the phone in her hand, and debates whether to tell Camille that her phone was ringing, or that she missed a call from Valentine Osin, or that Roma answered it.

She puts Camille's phone down and decides to say nothing,

which agitates her because she counsels honest and open face-to-face communication. And her agitation increases because her ability to have that kind of communication with her children is limited to today and tomorrow. With Camille and Phoebe currently objects of fascination for Lucy, this would be an opportune moment to find out what Simon's exhaustion is about. Maybe Simon and Elena fell asleep after unpacking. Or maybe they're taking advantage of being together without children demanding their attention. Bravo for them, Roma thinks. Then checks the clock on the stove. This afternoon interlude of theirs has lasted more than an hour—enough already. She would like some time alone with her son, so where the hell is he?

SIMON IS ON THE bed watching Elena. She is naked, kneeling at her suitcase, tossing things out, searching for her one-piece swimsuit, which she finds and pulls on, and a long dress, which she drops over her head. Without looking at him, she says, "I'm going to swim laps. You can come if you want. Swim off whatever is going on with you, whatever this is."

At the door, she says, "I'm not mad," but her eyes are unblinking and this is what she says when she's furious. At home she would have slammed the door, but here she is circumspect, only the soft catch of the lock, and Simon is left behind with the clarifying awareness of the fear he's not wanted to broach, that Elena has pulled away, that all is not right between them, that all hasn't been right for a while, that things are not as either of them have continued to pretend that they are. A blatant awareness reiterated for him by the blinding sun crashing through the large windows, slicing through him like a heated blade.

In the hallway, Elena leans against the wall and closes her eyes. Exhilaration floods through her, then confusion, and neither emotion is what she would have expected to feel from her husband's abrupt interest in Judaism.

Does this mark the beginning of a midlife crisis? When the husbands of a few of her former editors hit forty, they bought themselves the clichéd muscle cars, screwed up their marriages with affairs; one gave his wife the passwords to all their financial accounts and disappeared, emailing pictures of himself on a tropical beach sporting a ponytail and a soul patch. But Simon is a decade away from forty. He's too young to be experiencing a need to remake his life. And if he isn't, if that need has hit him years early, she's not going to pretend she doesn't find those other alternatives preferable to what his proclamation about wanting to become a Jew might mean.

She is the first generation removed from Salamanca, Spain, piety imbued in its *plazas* and *campos*, its *capillas*, *catedrales*, *iglesias*, and *ermitas*, its *conventos* and *monasterios*. She was raised an excellent Catholic girl in Los Angeles, attending church sometimes thrice weekly, always with trips to the confessional; how could it be otherwise when her mother's maiden name is Abaroa, Basque for *refuge*, when her father's last name, her last name, Abascal, means *priest's street*. Her family home, where she remained until marriage, overstuffed with her parents and all four of her grandparents and an all-everything God.

The first time Simon brought her here to the desert, to this house, to meet all the Tabors, she was already in love, consumed, as she had not expected to be, not when she knew no Jews intimately, when her lengthy flirtation with Jesus was only a few years behind her. She had been anxious, but how quickly Harry had welcomed a Catholic into their Jewish enclave, as her own parents had not done immediately with Simon. She wasn't wearing her tiny silver cross that day, but Catholicism was imprinted upon her nonetheless, and when Harry asked, "Are you practicing?" Elena understood he was gently trying to assess the state of affairs between her and his son.

She had been lying when she said, "Only sometimes," but he had thoughtfully considered her answer before asking, "Isn't it something you either do or don't do, believe in or not?"

She had blushed, for how could she explain how conflicted she was, and afraid that loving Harry's son was reducing her love of God's Son, or how sheepish she felt in her confusion that a serious Catholic girl, raised to follow every one of her religion's precepts, was overriding those precepts, breaking the rules, because of love? She had wanted to say she believed all prayer, whatever its form, wherever it took place, was good, but she didn't, because she uttered those most important to her in church, and she wasn't attending as devotedly as she once did, as she always had, and she feared that loving Simon was diminishing her essential relationship to the Divine.

She hadn't known then whether Harry and Roma were serious Jews, or Jews mostly in name only, a fact about Simon she found infinitely comforting when thinking about where their love was taking them. There was enormous comfort, too, in learning that Simon was mildly resentful of the command-performance assemblies when the Tabors gathered together on a few of the Jewish holidays, saying he would only ask her to attend with him on the two important holidays that took place in the fall.

Of course, it's been more than that all these years—Rosh Hashanah and Yom Kippur in the autumn, Hanukkah around the Christmas season, Passover around Easter—and although she always feels a little traitorous to her own beliefs, she's enjoyed it more than she expected, because they aren't very religious and because even their serious holidays become parties, with food and wine and laughter.

Still, she's made sacrifices because of Simon, sacrifices she's not thrown in his face. Even today in the car, she could have said, "I hide going to church because I'm constantly debating whether I made the right choice marrying you, having children with you, and I question our ability to last for the long haul, and not just because we have different religious beliefs."

What she knows absolutely is that if Simon had told her at the start of their relationship that he wanted to live a Jewish life, she would have ended them, cast away whatever was forming between them, before it went any further. She did not want then, and does

THE FAMILY TABOR • 191

not want now, to take on Simon's lineage, no matter that it belongs to the man she . . . yes, *loves*, but not as much as she once did.

If Simon's midlife crisis behavior were to devolve into those stereotypical actions, she would divorce him instantly. She has no tolerance for such recklessness, for the excuses that invariably accompany the breaches of trust and of vows.

But if it's Judaism he embraces?

Does she divorce him?

Her family, what would they say? Irate when she married out of the faith, outside the walls of their church, they've come around because they are caring people, because they love her and their granddaughters, because they've learned to love Simon, whose undeniable charm was insufficient at first to overcome his not being a Catholic. If Simon becomes a serious Jew and she divorces him, they will be miserable, fretful about her place in the eternal afterlife, excommunicated for all time.

She pushes away from the wall, walking fast to the heart of the house, then slows her steps, commands herself to regain calm, to allow this time in Palm Springs to play out, to keep an open mind whenever Simon decides to articulate exactly what he means by that statement.

Perhaps she's wrong about what she imagines he wants. But it doesn't feel like she's wrong, and a crucial truth hits her: she's stepped too far away from her own religion and will not return to the arms of God in the guise of another. She does not want to be married to a practicing Jew, and her slow pace gives way, her feet speeding up with anger.

ROMA IS ADDING ICE cubes to the pitcher when Elena sweeps into the kitchen, her pretty face closed up tight as a fist, her turquoise caftan whipping to and fro, and Roma thinks of an ocean wave whose beauty alters when it crashes on the shore.

"Doesn't a midlife crisis happen in midlife?" Elena says in a clenched voice Roma has not heard her use before, and then her daughter-in-law is out the sliding glass doors, speed-walking to the far end of the pool, ignoring the girls' greetings and Lucy's "Mom-mymommy, MOMMY."

Roma watches Elena roughly pull the caftan over her head, throw it onto a chair, step onto the diving board, halt at the end, her feet curling over the edge, her calves flexing, her toes lifting up. Her dive is as refined and polished as a ballerina's, and yet the splash she makes is incredibly violent.

TWENTY-FIVE

*S*TERN *STERN STERN STERN stern stern stern*, the word is zing-ing from his brain stem through his thalamus to his cerebral cortex, like a shiny silver marble in a pinball game, and Harry wakes with a start.

Where is he?

In a bed, but not his own bed in his own room. This is a twin. He's in Simon's old room, where his granddaughters sleep when they visit.

Isabel. He put her down for a nap, and there is the slightest im-print in the sheet, the shallowest indent in the pillow, proof she had been here, but now he is alone. What did she think when she opened her eyes, saw her *sabba* asleep in her bed? He hopes she wasn't frightened. He hopes she giggled.

There is a curious hush in the house, as if an eon has passed, and his watch says he's right; it's nearing five. The afternoon has slipped away like a shadow.

A story. He had been telling Isabel a story, *the* story. He must not have reached any part unknown to him for he had fallen asleep, an impossibility if another atrocious truth had revealed itself to him. But it hadn't, and so he slept, and he feels calmed by these hours of repose.

But still, what point had he reached in the story before his voice trailed off and then ceased? He tries to recall, searches deep inside for that secret vault whose existence has shocked him and rocked him and altered his world, and the word that woke him up, *stern*, begins ricocheting again, this time in front of his eyes. His heart thumps hard in his chest, echoes in his ears.

Stern, as in the tone of a voice, the look on a face?

No, as in Stern, and Harry's not sure whether it's his own internal voice or that dry, unfamiliar one he's hearing, and a fine sheen of sweat coats him, and he sits up quickly, fighting to free himself from the tangled duvet, though he feels so very cold, inside and out.

Stern as in . . . ?

Come on, Harry.

I don't know.

Come on.

I really don't know.

Think.

I'm thinking.

Think harder.

I'm trying.

Oh.

Right.

Max Stern?

Right, Harry, Max Steeeeeerrrrrrrrrnnnnnnnnn.

Stern, wiped from his mind for more than thirty years, but Harry can picture him clearly. A tall man. Taller than most in the Hebraic tribe. Strong and solidly built stock by way of emigrated Poles who settled in New Jersey, and his personal accomplishments at Harvard Business School. Bright and sharp, quick with repartee, with witty life anecdotes. A colleague at the brokerage firm, arriving a few years after Harry. More than a colleague—with Max Stern's arrival, the Jews at the firm doubled. Two Jews who proved themselves smart, savvy, dedicated, and loyal. Consummate lieutenants, each rising to tandem positions one rung below their commander in chief. Flip sides of the same coin, both sides needed for the coin to function as currency, to get the job done. Harry was the trading authority: overseeing the stable of traders buying and selling stocks, bonds, gold and oil and all other commodities, options, futures, and derivatives, for the firm's clients; buying and selling it all for his personal clients, too. Max Stern was the wiring authority, in charge of settling all client trades. They had been close work friends, though neither needed to say that making themselves a tight-knit cabal wouldn't do.

Okay. Max Stern. What about Max Stern?

Think, Harry.

He remembers the afflictive slumping of Max's bullish shoulders, the hard chest concaving, the unexplained exhaustion, the dramatic weight loss, the diagnosis of leukemia, Stern on leave for the brutal treatment of his disease.

Yes, I remember all of that. I sent flowers. I sent books. I called regularly to check in, to ask how it was all going, to make him laugh. He always laughed when we talked.

A caring man, through and through.

I *was*, Harry says, to himself, to the dry voice in his head.

The timing, Harry, the timing was perfect for you.

Timing? What timing?

What was going on for you when Max Stern took a leave of absence?

The usual.

Nothing usual about any of it, Harry.

I'm thinking, I'm thinking.

Your thinking, what can I say, it's worth nil. I'll give you a nudge. You were wearing a new gray pin-striped suit. Narrow chalk stripes, first suit made to order, first time you were wearing it.

Harry remembers that suit, made for him by a tailor in a tiny shop in the city on Lexington Avenue, a costly birthday present from Roma. And the first time he'd worn it was when?

He closes his eyes, pictures himself in that suit. He was wearing a silk tie—he can see that. Blue and silver and white, finely checked. He was wearing that suit and that tie on a chilly fall morning. That's right. The trees were turning, leaves stippled in red, orange, and gold, muted in the uncolored dawn when he drove down the long drive of the Connecticut house, sped into the city.

He'd felt sad that early morning because—why? He pictures himself in that suit, in his silver Jaguar, turning on the news, shutting it off, feeling how long the next twelve hours would be because—because—because Max Stern wasn't going to be there.

Max Stern wasn't going to be in the office because the day before had been Stern's last day before taking medical leave. They'd thrown him a small best-of-luck party in the conference room, cake and scotch, and the chief had cocked his head at Harry, and in a corner said to him, "Meeting tomorrow in my office as soon as the market closes."

Right, that's right. And that day, ten minutes after the closing bell rang, Harry, in his new suit and that sharp tie, was in Carruthers's office, and Carruthers said, "Want to keep things working smoothly and Stern's gone for how long is anyone's guess, poor fucker. We've got feelers out for a replacement, but in the meantime, you'll take over settlement. Here's Stern's confidential access codes," and he handed Harry a slip of paper.

Correct. But what was happening right then?

I went back to my office, logged in with Stern's user name, plugged in his password, and settled the day's accounts.

Solomon, Moses, and David. Stop fooling around. What was already happening when the big man handed you Stern's information?

Harry feels cold sweat trickling down the back of his neck.

Oh, *fuck.*

That's right.

Carruthers.

Exactly.

I kept my mouth shut.

You did.

He remembered.

He'd already overheard the first of those insider tips. He'd already made a few cautious trades using those tips, was sitting on profits he hadn't figured out how to bring under his personal control, had only been able to segregate the money and park it in his private overflow account. Then Stern's illness, and his leave, and Carruthers giving him Stern's confidential codes, saying not a word about appropriately documenting that transfer of power, and Harry keeping his own mouth shut, and, snap of the fingers, he had the express and authorized ability to settle every trade, including his own illicit ones, without leaving a trace. That had been on a Thursday.

Yep.

On Friday, he canceled his dental appointment and, as he was forced to remember this morning, he made that trip to the Cayman Islands and set up the CST account, named after Cantor Simon Tabornikov. A day trip. Three and a half hours there, three and a half hours back. From the Caymans, he'd called his office, let them know he needed an emergency root canal, would be back in on Monday. Then he called Roma, told her to hire a babysitter for the girls, and by eight forty-five that night, they were sitting at a window table at the finest restaurant in their town, the sommelier uncorking a rich Barolo, filling their glasses.

What had Roma said when she lifted her glass? "What are we celebrating?"

And what had been his response? "Not a celebration, just a toast to the health of Max Stern."

That's right. But what were you actually thinking at that moment?

"Who could have imagined such a perfect confluence of events."

Correct.

But I didn't manufacture Max Stern's leukemia.

Of course not, but . . .

But what harkened bad luck for Max proved fortuitous, providential for me, putting me in control of both sides of the firm's legitimate activities, and my illegitimate ones—in charge of both the trading and the settlement. If not for Max Stern, then—

Exactly. And then what happened?

Harry shakes his head.

I don't know. You're asking me to remember what I don't re-member.

Try, Harry.

You showed me everything that happened on the day I quit and afterward. I quit and I never spoke to Max Stern again. I was gone before he returned to the firm. If he returned to the firm.

He returned to the firm.

Stern returned, which means Stern survived his disease, made a recovery, walked back into the firm and picked up his wiring reins. But that's wonderful, right? He didn't die.

Didn't die.

So he's not dead?

Not dead.

So why are we talking about Max Stern?

He didn't die, but for many years, he wished that he had—

He wished that he had what? What did Stern wish?

He wished the leukemia had carried him off.

Why? Why would he have wanted that? To be cut down in his prime? Come on, that can't be possible. I remember his password, *TJRTTT.* I didn't know what those letters stood for, but knowing Stern, I figured it was something like "The Jew rockets to the top." A man with that password wouldn't have wished to be carried off.

Come on, Harry. You know.

I don't know.

You know. You know. You know.

I don't. I really don't know.

Impossible . . .

Impossible? What's impossible? Impossible what?

Impossible that you don't know. Impossible that you never took a minute to discover what had become of him. Impossible to think you never gave him a single thought again.

But I *didn't.*

Out of the twin bed, through the sun-shot house, which seems hollowed out, emptied of everyone but him, into his study, to his chair and his desk and his computer. He types in *Max Stern.* A raft of articles about various Max Sterns—a philanthropist, a poker player, an artist, a composer, a newly deceased WWII veteran of the Battle of the Bulge, a movie producer, the lead singer of a Midwestern rock band, the name of an athletic center home to the Yeshiva University Maccabees, several dog lovers, and many, many lawyers are named Max Stern—but none of them is his, or rather that, Max Stern.

He types in *Max Stern* and the name of his old brokerage firm. Not nearly as many as are devoted to the Yeshiva University Maccabees, but there are several archived articles about the right Max Stern, and Harry pulls them up and begins reading.

Time slows to nothing, his breathing catching and stopping, until he must take several lung-filling inhalations, and then his breathing catches and stops again. He has no idea how many times he repeats that same cycle, but there is a rhythmic phrase hammering in his head: *You are a bad man. You are a bad man.* It goes on and on and on, until his own name is appended to the end of the phrase. Each time he thinks *You are a bad man*, he hears *Harry*, and that emphasis makes sense, because now he knows the full truth of what his actions wrought, what he wrought, the anvil he'd unwittingly brought down, because of what he had done.

It dawns on him that someone else is calling his name, not himself or the dry voice in his head, and he yelps like a frightened dog when a hand touches his shoulder and looks up to find Roma's smile fading, her eyes confused by his reaction. He automatically closes the computer.

"I've been calling you for nearly three minutes. What are you reading so intently? You need to shower and dress. We leave in thirty minutes. Blanca is already here for the girls. Come on, put yourself in gear, hero."

TWENTY-SIX

DO YOU REMEMBER . . . ?"
This is what Phoebe and Camille kept asking each other all afternoon. After Roma shepherded Lucy into the house for dry clothes and what she calls *savah* time, and Elena finished her bout of quick, hard laps, and said no, she didn't know where Simon was, and she'd be on the back patio if anyone needed her, it was just the Tabor sisters roasting under the sun, drinking down fresh Arnold Palmers, the cubes melting fast in the heat, weakening the strong tea and the sourness of their mother's undersugared lemonade.

"Do you remember when we were young and this desert and this house were new to us?"

Camille had been struck by the palm trees that didn't exist in the place she had thought was still home. It had taken her a long time to understand *this* place was now *home*, and not some strange vacation they were on, that they wouldn't again experience winters with snow falling in their own front and backyards.

Phoebe had loved how her and Camille's new bedrooms were linked by an immense bathroom that became a magical realm when the doors were left open. Their beds were against the abutting walls, and at night, after being tucked in, lights turned off, bedroom doors closed, they'd tell each other secrets. Sprawled on their stomachs, their spiraling voices would sail past the white shower, the white tub, the white double sinks, the tiny room inside the big bathroom where the toilet had its own door, knowing that whatever was said in their post-bedtime hours would end up in the other's ears. Sometimes they met in that sanctum, their pale nightgowns floating in the dark, and they'd sit on the cool white tiles, staring up through the skylight, wishing on the stars their father had given them.

"Do you remember how Mom would laugh because we always wanted to brush our teeth at the same time, and take showers and baths together?" Camille asked.

Phoebe did remember, and she also remembered turning sixteen and rearranging her bedroom, putting her bed on the far wall, insisting the bathroom doors be kept closed at all times, setting a rotating schedule for brushing teeth and washing faces and showering before school, and for baths at night, so she could be in there alone, inspecting the changes to her face, to her body, out of reach of her younger sister, who, at fourteen, seemed far too young to be her friend any longer.

Camille was only inches away on her chaise when Phoebe realized it was her fault they'd lost their sisterly closeness, that all their intricate talk about their hearts and dreams had stopped. She had thoroughly altered the nature of their relationship when she shut her bathroom door on her sister, created the distance that still existed between them, and she wanted to change that, wanted them to be best friends again, wanted her sister to be the person to whom she told all of her secrets. But she wasn't sure what to say, and so she said nothing, and they talked on about unimportant things.

When it was time to think about preparing for the evening, they swam a desultory lap, then saronged themselves in their towels and carried the glasses and pitcher to the kitchen sink. They walked together to their bedrooms, and Phoebe said, "Do you want the bathroom first?" and Camille said, "No, you go ahead. I'll lie down and close my eyes. I think the long drive took a lot out of me."

Phoebe washed and dried her hair, put on her makeup, spritzed herself with perfume, then knocked on the internal door to Camille's room.

"All yours."

Camille walked in and said, "It smells lovely in here."

"You can borrow my perfume. It's right there on the counter."

"Thanks. But I never use it."

Phoebe had nodded, then asked, "Do you want this door shut?" hoping her sister would say no, but Camille said yes.

Camille used to sing from the moment the bathroom was hers, silly songs she made up, songs sometimes with made-up words, and standing on the other side of the closed door Phoebe had waited, hoping to hear Camille singing again, but there was only the roar of the water, then the whine of the dryer.

When the bathroom was quiet, Phoebe tiptoed through it, quietly turning the doorknob on Camille's side. She planned to say, "Hi, I want us to return to those old times. I want us to tell each other everything again," but Camille stood naked, staring at the flowers and palm trees outside her bedroom windows, her body marbled by the late-afternoon light. Phoebe watched her unmoving sister, aware she hadn't seen her fully naked since they were teenagers, and even though she recognized the constellation of freckles just below Camille's right shoulder blade, Phoebe knew she could not intrude, could not simply alter their pattern by walking in unannounced, that she'd have to figure out another way to revive their prior closeness, and tiptoed back into her own room.

AT HALF PAST SIX, Phoebe walks down the hall. Camille's bedroom door is already ajar. Her sister is again at the windows, her dark hair long and shiny. She is dressed in the white satin suit she told Phoebe about. Sunbeams catch its slight iridescence, flaring a rainbow around her.

Camille turns and sees Phoebe, and the look that comes over her face is a plea for approbation, tinged with fear, and Phoebe knows she's probably entirely responsible for this insecurity of her sister's.

She would have shortened the white satin trousers so they struck above the neat turn of the ankle, and she would have tailored the jacket so it fit snugly, but she will not make those useless suggestions to Camille, who has tried hard to pull this look together, and has done a commendable job.

Phoebe smiles. "You're right. I love that suit. And it's perfect on you."

"Really?"

"Really. Where did you find it?"

"I got it at a boutique," Camille says, and Phoebe senses she's lying.

Camille pulls up her pant legs. She's wearing high-heeled sandals dotted with silver rhinestones. Phoebe would actually have bought them for herself. She wouldn't have painted her toenails gold, not with those sandals, but it works pretty well.

"Wow. They're fabulous. *You* look fabulous."

"I do? Really? What about the earrings?"

Made of finely spun silvery mesh, they remind Phoebe of waterfalls. They, too, sparkle in the early-evening sun when Camille pushes her hair back from her shoulders.

"The whole look is outstanding. Do you feel great? You should."

"I feel okay. Do I need more makeup?"

Camille with her au naturel look, who doesn't understand that au naturel requires a talented hand and something more than the minimal, does need more makeup, and Phoebe debates whether to say what she thinks.

"Your tan looks great, considering how pale you were hours ago. But yes, maybe, come on, I'll do it for you. I've got a lipstick you'll love. And a tad more mascara. And I could line your eyes, just a little. Make everything pop a bit." She can't stop herself, wanting only to help, for Camille to feel her absolute best. She used to do this for Camille when they were in high school, she a senior, Camille a sophomore, until Camille said, "Makeup is for frauds."

Camille hesitates. "Okay. But not too much. Not too heavy."

"Is my makeup too much or too heavy?"

"No. It's perfect."

"Okay then. So can you trust me?"

For a very long moment, the sisters stare at each other. Then Camille shrugs and follows Phoebe, trailing behind exactly as she always used to do as a kid, and Phoebe thinks, *It's a start.*

TWENTY-SEVEN

ELENA HAD ASKED HIM to do up the long secret zipper of her gown, the knitting of the teeth like a scream, and Simon imagined a knife brutally sundering skin, as if that was the damage those few words he spoke hours ago had inflicted.

She is at the bathroom mirror now, brushing her hair, the blush-colored chiffon revealing her body's lush curves. But her spine is staunch and straight, and it alarms Simon how quickly Elena has erected a protective wall, laid mines at her feet. The electrified force field around her is more impermeable than that of an upset woman indicating she wants to be left alone for a while, that her husband not trespass, that she is exercising decorum at her in-laws' by not instigating the fight they are going to have down the road. It feels ominous, the sexy shroud she has wrapped herself in, the crackling air.

He brought this on, never anticipating that what he thought was a rekindling of their love in this room, on that bed, at the height of the afternoon, could shrivel up and die in no time at all. But that's the thought in his head, its validity thudding hard in his heart, and he knows that his potential new terms—though as yet neither disclosed nor discussed—are already not agreeable to her, and perhaps not the old ones either, not anymore. Her posture states she will be making her own determinations going forward. That perhaps she's been making her own determinations for far longer than he's been aware, that what he's been sensing in her, with her, the division between them, wasn't a pathology of his sleeplessness at all.

He needs to say something, to break this poisonous spell, but the only thing she might want to hear is that he didn't mean it, that nothing will change. And that he can't say, surprised by his certainty.

And he is surprised again when she doesn't tightly coil her hair, when she abandons the pins that litter the counter, when she lifts the mass and lets it fall, as if setting loose a dark cloud.

"You look spectacular," he says, and it's true, and he hopes the compliment will soften her. Her black eyes are gleaming, but not with pleasure, and she offers him the tightest of smiles. She arches her trim feet and steps into her sandals, silk blush-colored rosettes across her toes as if she walks in a garden, the heels so high she nearly reaches his height.

"You look nice, too," she says, without looking at him in his tux, refusing to allow her eyes to be caught by his. "Shall we get on with it. Your mother said pictures out by the meditation pool."

"Are the girls—"

"They're wearing the matching dresses your mother gave them on her birthday. I told them they can swim again after, if they want to. Your mom hired Blanca and she said she'd go in with them."

"That's great. About Blanca, rather than a stranger. Did you ask if she might be—"

"It seemed premature. After all, we may not need her."

She does not speak these short sentences quickly. Instead, she permits their meaning to stretch out. And Simon understands that the trip together to Colombia may be off the table, that his idea of the two of them there, finding their way back to an earlier happiness, making love morning and night, sightseeing during conference breaks, drinking *aguardiente* or Cuba libres together at charming outdoor cafés, like the one in his story, may not happen, will definitely not happen, unless he backtracks completely.

Elena is making things perfectly clear: if he insists on exploring Judaism, everything they have been to each other is in jeopardy.

TWENTY-EIGHT

ROMA REFRAINS FROM ACTING on both her professional and wifely instincts. Tonight is not the night to ask Harry what's troubling him, to have him explain his curious detachment in the pool and at lunch, his irregular nap with Isabel, when the few times he's ever napped he was knocked out by the flu, the trance she found him in staring at his computer. Something is afoot, amiss, out of balance, but she will put on a happy smile and they will experience this memorable evening unmarred by the loving interrogation in which she'd like to engage.

"This is me," she says, twirling around in her gown, and Harry, standing in the bathroom, looks at his wife. She's arranged her hair, *bohemian* she calls it, tendrils falling around her face, and the yellow diamond drop earrings he gave her on her sixtieth are aflame, her eyes lit up. Her silk gown as magnificent as she is, narrow sleeves to her elbows, the eye-catching long V down her back, sculptured drapes falling around her, grazing her toes. She is a goddess, a golden statue in a golden dress, a treasure. She takes away the little breath left in him.

"You're ravishing. Breathtaking. Can I meet you outside? Give me ten minutes?"

Breathtaking is what he said, though he seems out of breath, a slight rattling wheeze Roma's never heard him make, but he smiles at her and she smiles back and twirls around once more. Then she is picking up her golden wrap, her golden bag, blowing him a kiss, and is out their bedroom door, calling to their daughters as she naturally would, asking who's ready.

HALF DRESSED IN THE wing collar shirt, bow tie already in sharp triangles around his neck, he stares at the hanging tuxedo, loath to put it on. But he must, and when he does, the soft, rich fabric stings him as if made of nettles, sits like a lie upon his skin.

He imagines himself as the fly that could have been caught in the web. Standing in his spacious bedroom in his palatial desert house wearing a tuxedo, he is a free man because the web captured another and the spider gobbled that other up and was sated.

He is devastated by those articles, about events that occurred only after he traded in his old life, extinguished his memories of that year, settled his young family in Palm Springs. He possessed absolutely no knowledge about any of it, but there could be no question the blame was his to bear. What he read defied comprehension; crucial questions remain unanswered.

There had been a joint FBI and SEC investigation into five years of the firm's activities. It was in the fifth year that Harry had made his illegal trades while Max Stern was out on medical leave. Had every one of those five years been of interest, or was the expansive time frame federal subterfuge and they had been focused only on that last year?

When the investigation began, Max's leukemia was in remission and he had been back at the firm six months. Named by Carruthers as the liaison to the federal agencies, Stern was beginning to produce subpoenaed files when a death temporarily halted everything. Going 120 miles an hour on a summer night in his new cherry-red 1987 Ferrari F40, Carruthers hit a concrete bridge abutment, died on impact in that single-car crash.

The articles didn't hint at what Harry was still pondering: Had

Carruthers been engaged in his own insider trading? Had he been facing arrest? Had he deliberately killed himself? Had he given Harry the settlement authority, without any corporate record of that action, without obtaining board approval, in order to set Harry up as a potential patsy, if things went wrong? Is that why Carruthers never hired someone new to take over for Stern? Or had Carruthers not cared who might be the patsy, so long as he had someone, and he already had Max? Is that why he didn't change Stern's confidential access codes when he put Harry in charge, so that every settlement looked as if it had been executed by Stern? And during the six months between Harry's resignation and Stern's reappearance, had it been Carruthers settling trades under Stern's name?

After the funeral, the investigation geared up again. Stern complied with all the court orders, turned over every file, and then, in short order, was arrested, on the hook for having held all settlement authority for the years in question. Arrested despite his yearlong medical leave, despite his exhortations that he had no personal knowledge of the trades under examination. The evidence was damning—Stern's name on settlements totaling $41 million in illegal profits from suspected use of verboten insider information. What wasn't reflected in that total was Harry's own illicit money, the $18 million he sent through the convolutions of the black market banking system, where it eventually wound up in that CST account in the Caymans. He was stunned to learn about the $21 million found in offshore accounts under fake names, and the $11 million found in secret firm accounts that seemed to belong to no one, and the puzzling $9 million idling in several of the firm's overflow accounts with blank paperwork and no signatories at all. He had been in charge then and had not comprehended the nature of those trades, that his money wasn't the only dirty money at the firm that he'd settled, sent out into the yonder.

Why hadn't Stern mentioned Harry when he was being interrogated by the authorities? Had he not known? Had Carruthers not told him? Harry had never mentioned it during those calls when he checked in on Max that year of his illness, but wouldn't Stern, when he returned, have insisted on learning who had been executing his job? Harry would have, but Stern, who knows—having risen from his sickbed, perhaps his relief at being able to suit up and return to work was all he could focus on.

It hadn't mattered that Stern signed an affidavit attesting to his medical leave, as did his oncologist, who detailed the many rounds of chemotherapy and radiation he had endured, as did the nurses and technicians, as did his family and friends, swearing he'd been hard at death's door: Max Stern's user name and password had been continuously active, without any break in the pattern, and no one would say otherwise. The firm's traders refused to exonerate Stern. The trades were settled, they said, and no one else had the authority—what other conclusion could be drawn? Harry understood the impulse, to protect their own skins, but why hadn't they angled the interrogative spotlight on *him*? It was common knowledge he settled trades during Stern's absence, yet nowhere in the articles did the name *Harry Tabor* appear.

It made no sense, until it did. It wasn't that he'd been given a pass by those blond, pale-eyed men, not at all. It was, instead, that despite his years at the firm, despite once being their boss, despite his warm and frank personality and his bonhomie, he was never a member of their closed universe, and with his absence, he slipped from their minds, as if he'd never been.

He saw it starkly: those traders, bosom buddies since their days at private kindergartens, at boarding schools, at the top Ivy Leagues, stamping their feet and bumping their pugnacious fists together in some private ritual by which they chose their scapegoat. Harry was long gone, but there was Stern, a man without standing, for he, too, was outside their tight world, and how easily they fingered the one remaining Jew at the firm, that rarest of creatures, a wholly innocent man, captured for slaughter, or at least railroaded into jail.

Stern had insisted on a polygraph. When the results were inconclusive, his lawyer argued that expert medical testimony would prove that long courses of chemotherapy and radiation and daily medications to fight against the recurrence of a life-ending disease altered one's heartbeat, one's breathing, the production of sweat from one's glands. Only an innocent man would demand the pneumographs wrapped around his chest, the blood pressure cuff around his arm, the electrodes attached to his fingertips, to be tested to see if he was lying. And it was Stern, not the FBI or the SEC, who demanded the first polygraph, then the second, then the third, and when the results of all three were identical, the lawyer argued that this was a surfeit of proof that his client was innocent, that the chemo, radiation, and meds were responsible for the precisely repeated anomalies. Guilt in this case could not be inferred from an inconclusive test. His client was not only entitled to the presumption of innocence; he was, in fact, an innocent man.

The traders all accepted plea deals—limited to the payment of fines and the suspension of their licenses until they completed the terms of their mild probations—but Stern refused to negotiate. He had been wrongfully ensnared in a scheme he had no part of, had not known existed, for which he had not financially benefited in any way, the transactions occurring in his absence, while he was fighting for his life, and he wanted his day in court.

A monthlong trial on numerous charges of insider trading, wire fraud, and civil money laundering, and then that innocent man was found guilty on all counts. The trial judge stated that five years of records told an incontrovertible truth, and handed down a jail sentence incongruous at the time for white-collar crimes. Twelve years for Max. Harry saw photos in those articles of Stern handcuffed and escorted out of the courtroom. He pictured Stern in a crummy van, in leg irons, attached by a heavy chain to real criminals, violent criminals, being taken upstate to prison.

Stern's wife divorced him and returned to her maiden name; his sons and daughter refused to visit. Harry and Max used to privately wish each other *Shana Tovah* when the High Holidays came around, they'd been the same kind of Reform Jews, but he read that Max Stern had undergone a prison transformation, had immersed himself in a serious course of Judaic instruction, had converted to Modern Orthodox, and inside his imprisoning home, in a special ceremony held in the visitors' room, he had been ordained a rabbi. Which also made no sense.

Harry had never given Stern another thought when he walked away from Carruthers Investments, and these revelations about Stern, they are still walloping him, hitting him hard as a boxer's punch, sending him reeling from this final fillip of upheaval in his personal universe.

While Stern was locked up, Harry was building a new life from scratch and flourishing—that aberrant year extinguished entirely from his mind. He was loving his family, watching his infant son crawl, then walk, and every morning, overflowing with confidence, enthusiasm, and energy, he drank his coffee, then drove to the building he had purchased, pushing open the doors of his brain-child CST, where with beneficent élan, he was releasing Jews from their own imprisonment, lifting them out of their villages, towns, and cities, in countries with oppressive regimes, flying them to this promised land in this desert, helping them build from scratch *their* lives in this new world about which they had dreamt for so long.

HE TUCKS HIS WALLET and cell phone into the inside pocket of his jacket, his emotions cresting to the surface in this bedroom where such great love and so much life has taken place, memorizing what he sees—that drawing in luscious verdigris tones they bought for their tenth anniversary, that twined and braided bronze sculpture for their twentieth, that black-and-white photograph of spectral calla lilies for their twenty-fifth, that massive painting over the bed, like an explosion of energized stars, for their thirty-seventh, that large pulsating piece for their most recent anniversary, blown by distant Polish lips into a Mobius vase, the glass so vibrantly red it might have been mixed with fresh blood.

He feels his hesitation, the reluctance of his steps through the house, a man heading to the gallows when he enters his study once again. He monkeys with the computer, then shuts it down entirely. From the desk drawer, he retrieves the speech he labored over for weeks and weeks, thanking the city, the nominating committee, everyone, for the Man of the Decade honor, gingerly holding it, then folding the paper into the tiniest, tightest square he can, palming it hard, before putting it into his breast pocket. He can't imagine reading it aloud to the gathered, estimable crowd.

But right now, it's picture time.

And there is the family gathered around the meditation pool.

Esmeralda's daughter Blanca, whom he has known since she was a toddler, is shooting photos like a professional, with the camera Simon and Elena bought him for the big 7-0 and he's not yet used. All of Blanca's life is ahead of her. She wants to be a child psychologist like Roma, is eager to transfer from the College of the Desert to UCLA, and Roma has written her a recommendation, and when Blanca is ready Roma will provide introductions to her colleagues in Los Angeles. He is focusing on Blanca because it is too difficult to think of his children. But he must.

He looks carefully at each exceptional one, how radiant they are, living amazing lives each and every day, their futures expansive and infinite. And his granddaughters, already peerless so early in their young lives, though he is aware he lacks any ability this moment to see into their futures, to imagine anything concrete so far in the distance.

The chatter dies away when he appears. Their faces a collective of smiles and gleaming teeth and sunned cheeks, excitement sparking off every last one. They have been waiting for the man of the hour, of the decade, of nothing.

"You all look smashing," he says, his thoughts bucking, wanting to stampede past all of this, to what might lie ahead, but then Roma catches his eyes.

At the long, narrow pool, lavender under the softening sun, he takes his place in their midst and prepares to be photographed, smiling a Harry Tabor smile to hide his juddering distress, his internal tumult, his deep remorse. This man, whose world has spun off its axis, is smiling as hard as he can.

TWENTY-NINE

THE STRETCH LIMOUSINE SENT by the city seems as long as any Bronx city block Harry once walked as a kid. Roma and Elena are providing last-minute instructions to Blanca. Lucy and Isabel are racing around their father and aunts, and Harry, stifling inside his tuxedo, looks at the pinking horizon. He has relished the desert heat all these many years, but tonight he finds it vibrational, frightening, parching the last of the air in his lungs.

The driver says with a slight bow, "A pleasure to meet you, Mr. Tabor."

"Sorry, sorry," Roma says, "I'll be right back," the click of her heels changing tunes as she moves up the drive and into the house, and Harry feels simultaneously marooned and relieved to be free of her exacting stare.

"Dad, you look very handsome," Phoebe says, and the only response he can locate in his brain is "It's very hot," which sets off a chain reaction—the driver waving his hand at his shiny chariot, saying, "Please, it's much cooler inside," and Elena shrugging her shoulders, climbing in, followed by Phoebe, the two women arranging their gowns at their feet, followed by Simon and Camille, who cross their suited legs, and Camille pats the space next to her and says, "Here, Dad," and he feels unhinged making his way in, his hands grasping the leather, his feet slow to follow, and when he's nearly seated, the little girls stick their heads through the open door, almost butting his chest, Lucy chanting, "Party, party, party, party."

"Say good night to everyone," Blanca says to the girls as she takes their hands. They twist their necks, calling out, "Night-night," and then Lucy is saying, "Pool, pool, pool, pool," identifying a place Harry would rather be, the word fading as Blanca leads them away.

"Dad," Camille says, "this afternoon Phoebe and I were wondering whatever happened to our dogs? To King David and Queen Esther?"

Startled, Harry stares at Camille. This minute she's asking him about those loving, low-to-the-ground dogs he recalled so vividly this morning, when he had not thought of them in more than three decades? Will he start crying right here and right now? He might, he feels the tingling in his eyes, but the salty tide reverses course when Simon says, "*What* dogs? When did we have dogs?"

"Camille and I had dogs in Connecticut," Phoebe says to Simon, then turns again to her father, but whatever she is about to ask him is lost when Roma reappears, holding her cell phone aloft. "Sorry, everyone, I forgot this." She enters the car quickly, lightly, taking her place across from Harry, smoothing her golden gown around her, thanking the driver shutting the door.

The limo rolls slowly down from the house, proceeds along Agapanthus Lane at a stately, processional pace, and then attains a smooth speed on Ramon Drive, and Harry tries calming the rapid beating of his heart, certain his family must hear the blood racing in his chest, spiraling through his veins. The air-conditioning, reviving at first, makes him shiver, and then conversation springs up, and he misses whatever they're talking about, but he hears clearly when Roma, smiling hugely, says, "Who's ready for this experience? For this once-in-a-lifetime night?"

THIRTY

THE STARLIGHT TERRACE IS a voluminous open-air expanse shimmering under intricate strands of golden twinkle lights, perfumed by bounteous arrangements of cut flowers, aurally enhanced by an orchestra playing violins, violas, cellos, basses, and flutes. Already crowded with men in black tie, and women gowned and bejeweled, milling and sipping as young waiters glide through the gathered, proffering icy uncorked bottles of champagne wrapped in fine white linen or swaying glasses on silver trays. Under the feet of the cocktailing denizens, a gleaming stretch of black dance floor, and beyond, tables set in platinum and gold, silvered desert ferns as centerpieces.

Harry hears the titillating hum of hundreds of excited conversations, spies an enormous photograph of himself on a golden easel, a life-size image of his personage displayed like precious fine art. And he falters. The aroma of the flowers is suddenly too cloying, too pungent, nearly putrid; his smile at those shaking his hands, clapping his shoulders, congratulating him on this honor, is counterfeit. The salutations being offered him are kind and sincere, but he deserves none of it. He, who caused the devastation of another's future, of Max Stern's future, deserves not champagne, not an extravagant meal prepared by one of the top chefs in the city, not this dramatic location, not this endless stream of compli-

ments, not the evocative music penned centuries ago by a famous
composer, not the laudatory speeches to come, not the eventual
dancing, but a dry piece of bread in a cell. Are there any words he
might speak that will not increase the breadth and depth and scope
of the false life he had not known he was living? Is there any way
for him to say anything in light of what he has learned about his
commission of ghastly actions, his express utterances that contained only lies, all these unbearable truths about himself?

He reaches for Roma's hand, then stashes his fist in his trou-
ser pocket, and hopes she didn't notice. He is no longer entitled to
her comfort, or to their hallowed connection, for he has fooled her,
too, made her an unwitting dupe who has believed in a promise
he hadn't remembered making and never kept, hiding from her
the unknown realities of the man with whom she's shared her life
happily. A brimming glass is thrust at him, his fingers automatically closing around the stem, the tiny bubbles somehow loud
over the din, and it feels like sacrilege, as if he will be struck
down, perhaps by God himself, if he were to lift the crystal to his
lips, if he were to take even the slightest of sips.

The rolling sea of bodies, the grinning faces of all these cele-
brants, Roma's dark eyes holding in abeyance questions he can see
she's not sure how to formulate—he must look away from it all and
he stares up at the darkening sky, at the ribbons of fiery red dressing the mountains, at the white stars above starting to shine, at the
blinking blue lights of a climbing plane. Palm Springs International
Airport is nearby, but far enough away that the plane makes no
sound at all, and Harry wonders where that soaring jet, that cylin-
drical tin balanced high up in the cold, dry stratosphere, is headed,
who on board is happy, and who is not, who is heading toward
something, and who is escaping, who, at the other end, will be
greeted upon their arrival, and who will feel the solitariness of their
lone and echoing footsteps.

And he thinks: *Dear God, tell me what I should do.*

And at the commencement of this evening, this blasphemous
honorific evening set to cap off this monstrously strange day of

emotional hurricanes, here is another one: that in calling out to God, he, Harry Tabor, is praying a third time. He is aware of that fact, aware he has just done that which he has long thought he does not believe in—but if not God, whose voice has been entering his head at will all of this day?

And now that he has beseeched, now that he has called out for aid, now that it feels impossible for him to take any volitional action, not even one more step, without some semblance of guidance, will the voice, whoever's voice it might be, come to him?

"Darling," Roma says, holding up her phone, "the mother of the little girl who's stopped eating is calling. Stay where you are so I can find you again," and Harry nods once, his eyes never leaving the jet in the sky that is moving in a way that seems to him both swift and as slow as an inching snail, unaware when Roma disappears from his side.

And then he hears that dry voice now familiar, that could belong to the God he implored, and he waits for what it might say, the knowledge it might impart, and his heart clamps tight, fizzles up, then releases, the blood flowing fast when the voice says, *You already know what to do, Harry. I know that you do.*

THIRTY-ONE

"M OM AND DAD GOT swallowed up fast," Camille says, hating the shakiness she hears in her voice. She used to like big parties where she didn't know anyone, where she could figure out, first from afar and then closer up, the leaders, the satellites, the contingents on the fringes, the connections and disconnections, the similarities and dissimilarities, the various motivations and ethos at play. Perhaps it's the huge crowd, in noisy constant movement. Perhaps it's that she's out of practice, her sorting abilities rusted from those months of isolation in her apartment, and not fully exercised in her one-on-one interactions at Lilac Love.

She would like to be back in Phoebe's room, in the chair at the vanity, with her sister's hands gently cradling her face. She had known Phoebe was going to offer to "make things pop," and she had steeled herself to refuse, to fend Phoebe off, but then something in her relented.

Camille hadn't expected that Phoebe's steadiness, their sudden intimacy, would bolster her from the inside, but it did, and she surprised herself by willingly following Phoebe's directions.

Phoebe told her to relax and trust her, and Camille relaxed and trusted her, and what calming solace that had provided.

Phoebe had said, "Pucker," and Camille hadn't felt foolish puckering up, her sister leaning close, gliding the lipstick on.

Phoebe had said, "Close your eyes," and Camille had done so, and her sister was careful with the mascara, the liner, the way she delicately blended shadow with the pad of her pinky.

When Phoebe said, "What do you think?" Camille had opened her eyes and Phoebe's beauty was right in front of her; then Phoebe stepped aside, and her own was reflected in the mirror. Her eyes mesmerized her, seeing within them the trust she had just given to her sister and the trust the Trobrianders had given to her. And she understood that she needed to trust herself again, and in that moment, she was thoroughly convinced she *would* pull herself out of her morass.

The crowd is ahead of Camille. Her sister and brother and Elena are next to her, but she is wavering, would like to reverse course, find that limo driver, go back home, climb into the bed in her childhood room and sleep, find herself in the surf of those islands in her dreams.

"Camille and I are going to wander and assess who we might choose as our minions. This is our night to be the princesses of the king," Phoebe says, and though it sounds idiotic to Camille, her sister's voice settles her, and though it surprises Camille, she's the one to take her sister's hand and hold on tight, surprised when Phoebe holds on just as tight.

"I think that makes you the royal couple in waiting," Phoebe says to Simon and Elena. "So off with you. Accept the adulation, as we will. See you later at the table."

Simon doesn't know what Phoebe is talking about—princesses and minions and royal couples in waiting—but he wants his sisters to stay. If his sisters abandon him, then what he fears is happening between him and Elena might actually be happening, but then Phoebe, a knockout in a gown the color of blued ice, and Camille, a beacon in heavenly white, vanish into the crowd.

His breath catches when Elena permits him to take her cool hand, lets him lead her in a different direction. He's not sure where he's heading, but so long as they are joined in this smallest of ways, perhaps he can turn this evening around.

"Simon Tabor, is that you?" and Simon finds himself clasped in a bear hug by a thick man with a shiny face and nearly no hair left on his head, and although he is still holding Elena's hand, can feel its coolness giving way to incipient warmth, she pulls free. Pulls free of him, from him, on this terrace where they married.

"Oh, *boychik*, I've startled you. Apologies. It's me, Levitt, your father's pal and tennis competitor. Let me look at you. No fattening at the trough of marriage, I see. My first marriage, I gained a quick thirty in no time flat. But not you, lean as a racehorse. I hear you have two daughters now. Mazel and all. So where's your gorgeous bride?"

Levitt has Simon enveloped in a hard embrace, and Elena looks back at him, just once, before sweeping away.

THIRTY-TWO

I N A TERRACE CORNER, under a halo of golden lights, watching her husband gazing intensely up at the sky, mindless of the horde swirling around him, Roma answers her phone. "It's Dr. Tabor, Jeanine. Is everything all right?"

"She's eating," Jeanine says. "Exactly the meals on the menu, but she cries with each bite she takes, her eyes shooting daggers at us. At dinner yesterday, she screamed at us before putting the food to her mouth. But we stayed firm. And it was the same this morning at breakfast and again at lunch, but she's stopped talking to us entirely, hasn't said a word since this afternoon. We want to know she's okay, but she refuses to look at us. Just now, she ate her dinner slowly, head down, one arm limp in her lap, then she dropped the plate into the sink, marched away and slammed her bedroom door."

"Has she eaten all the food she agreed to eat at each meal?"

"Yes."

"And do you and Steve sit with her while she eats? Talk to her even if she doesn't respond?"

"Yes."

"And are you doing what I suggested, telling her how much you love her, that her health requires that she eat, that you are doing this to help her, not harm her?"

"Yes."

"I know it's difficult, and heart-wrenching, but you're doing well. It will take time. I'd like you to call me again tomorrow. Will you do that?"

"Yes, of course, and Steve would like to meet with you. The two of us coming in to see you together. We're hoping Monday, Dr. Tabor."

"When we speak tomorrow, we'll arrange a time. Stay strong, Jeanine."

Roma is pleased by the McCaddens' courage, by Jeanine's call, and she turns around, looking for Harry in the spot where she left him, but her husband is no longer there.

THIRTY-THREE

FOR YEARS, CAMILLE HAS indicted her sister for her perfection, but now she finds warm security in that perfection.

Phoebe is charismatic and engaging, and sincerely interested in everyone they talk with: "Are you still involved with that charity?" "How is business treating you?" "You haven't aged at all!" "I'm so glad they stayed together, it's inspiring when couples can make it work." "We're so pleased you could be here to celebrate him." "My whole family agrees, what our father has accomplished in his life *is* incredible!" "Yes, Simon and I are lawyers, lovely of you to remember, but it's Camille who's the special one. Oh, you don't know, she's a *social anthropologist*, spent years in Melanesia. She's writing the most brilliant book about her experiences there. Camille, this is—"

And Camille is saying hello, and hello, and hello to people she doesn't know, or to people she vaguely recalls from childhood, thinking, *Does Phoebe really see me this way?* She had no idea.

When there is a conversational lull, when Phoebe is leading her forward to the next well-wishing group, Camille whispers, "I'm not writing a brilliant book. I only wrote a dissertation." And Phoebe whispers back, "But you will write a brilliant book. If not about your islands, then about some other magical place you'll go and about the fascinating people you'll meet there."

An ancient man, with the faintest of stoops and a deep desert tan, wraps an arm around Phoebe's bare shoulders.

"Hello, lovely Tabor daughters. The successful lawyer I know, but not the famous social anthropologist."

Phoebe's certainty has bucked Camille up, and with a fullness to her voice, she says, "It's a pleasure to meet you, Baruch. Yes, I'm Camille."

"If I could begin life over, I'd want to do what you do," he says, then turns to Phoebe. "You understand your sister has the right idea, to find worlds beyond what we can imagine."

"I know," Phoebe says. "I've always known it."

"So, Phoebe," the old man says, "by any chance are you still single?"

Phoebe can't hide her confusion.

"Oh, not me, sweetheart, but I have a very handsome grandson named Aaron, just your age, I think."

For a splendid moment, Phoebe imagines herself a double con-jurer: Her pretend lover at last drawing into her orbit a potential soul mate and *beshert*, justifying all her lying by manifesting the man of her dreams, serendipitously also named *Aaron*. She wants to say, "Yes, Baruch, introduce me to your grandson! And here are all the ways I can be reached!" but of course she can't.

"What a coincidence. Phoebe's dating an Aaron," Camille says.

Ancient Baruch pushes back his silver swoop of hair, and says, "Wouldn't that be a hoot if my Aaron was already your Aaron. It could be, he lives in Los Angeles, too. Aaron Gold?"

"Not Gold, but Green, Aaron Green," says Camille, smiling as if she's saved Phoebe. The last time Camille saved Phoebe, they were kids, sisters on the same side, in each other's corner.

Phoebe thinks, *Damn you, Camille*, and says, "I'm so flattered you would think of setting me up, but my sister's right, I am com-mitted," and Camille takes Phoebe's hand again and squeezes tightly.

THIRTY-FOUR

W HAT ARE THESE PEOPLE'S names? And what have they
been talking about? Elena has lost track of everything
and she needs to track everything because she is one of her father-
in-law's representatives tonight. The foursome surrounding her is
nodding, and Elena follows suit, nodding along, waiting for a conversational pause, and here it is, and she smiles and says warmly,
"It was lovely to meet you all, but will you excuse me? I should find
my husband."

There's no *should* about it. Walking away from Simon as she
did, pulling her hand from his, it's something Lucy might have
done, but she can't face him yet. In the distance, at the edge of
the terrace, that's where she wants to be. A new glass from a passing waiter, and she is sidling through the crowd, then away entirely, settling down in an orphaned chair, the heated air a little
cooler here, the lingering taste of champagne on her tongue, her
mind puzzling the tangents.

It isn't completely true what she said to Simon in the car this
morning. Yes, she considered marrying Jesus when she was a girl,
but only in the beginning had she thought of becoming a nun,
when marrying the Son of God seemed far more intriguing than
marrying a regular man. But then that secret lesson imparted by
one of the nuns, that Elena didn't have to marry at all, not ephem-

eral Jesus, and not an earthbound version either, and that knowledge had unleashed and untied her, given her the courage to dream of a traveling life. And she'd pursued it, earning serious journalism degrees. It wasn't domestic or international politics, or the intrigues at the Vatican, or serial killers and crime sprees, or personal interest stories that interested her, but where to go, what to see, what to experience, that absorbed her attention. It was always about travel. She imagined being alone in foreign locales, languages she didn't speak singing past her ears, and she making her way armed with a few linguistic basics in whatever native tongue was required: *Please. Thank you. Where is the bathroom? How do I get to—*

What she had also yearned for were the hotel rooms. Trawling through expensive pages of travel magazines late at night, she stared at those rooms. Whether cut-rate or costly, they all had big, clear windows letting in the sun, highlighting the whites, the creams, the occasional pale grays of the walls, and the furnishings in those same relaxing palettes. So vacantly inviting. Her family home, purchased before she was born, recalled Salamanca for her *mamá* and *papá* and her *abuelitos*—walls of roughened stucco, thick-leaded windows, subdued interior light, not anything like the houses of friends she visited growing up, or later the hotels in the glossy guides, or still later the hotel rooms she temporarily inhabited. Her in-laws' house is like a series of massive hotel suites, lustrous perfection, palely luxurious. The house she and Simon bought, though small and in need of repair, has many windows, and every wall, at her insistence, was painted cloud-white. But she misses, longs for hotel rooms, where she was whomever she wanted to be.

Over the last year, she's thought that if she could begin traveling again, living out of those pristine hotel rooms, writing articles about what she experiences far from home, she'd bounce back. Bounce back from the truth of their marriage, likely any marriage—the way the deep and resonant timbre of love alters with the daily ordinariness of it all. She knows from her parents, from both sets of grandparents, from the Bible, that all marriages have a meandering course, slipping down into troughs before rising up once again and finding a high spot on a hill with a splendid view. But it's hard being literally grounded and raising their children mostly on her own. When they married, Simon traveled maybe four weeks a year, but now so much more. Really, she and the girls don't see him all that often. Really, she's nearly a single parent. This last year, she determined that if both of them were working, traveling for work, it would reset them, require them to find parity—both making sacrifices to love their children while they pursued their careers. Of course she understands the importance of what Simon does, his work is consequential, significant, impressively humanistic, and she can't compete with that, but her own work used to matter on a small scale, and disappearing from home for a little while to ply her dormant talents, earning money they could use, would remind him that when they married he was the one left behind while she was gone for weeks, traveling a large part of the year. She wouldn't want to leave the girls for too long, just a few days every several months so she could reengage in the outside world, beyond the caring and feeding and loving of their young.

"Yes, please," she says when a waiter asks, "Another glass?"

Love. So much love. She has so much love for the Tabors, so much love for her children with Simon, Simon when she married him, and even though it's not been full strength for a while, she does still love him. So how will she explain to him, to them all, that if Simon is serious about this Jewish business, she will divorce him.

She can't articulate her reasons for this vehement reaction she is having to the very notion of her husband's desire. Her father-in-law has spent his life bringing Jewish families here—is being honored for it tonight. And how many stories has she heard about how often he has stepped in, as umpire, as referee, mediating between the older generations he brought over and their children, and then their children's children, when the older generations want the younger—those too young to remember the old country and those born here—not to abandon the old ways. And yet she, raised with the old ways, cast them aside for love. She's been a member of Harry's tribe, and leaving Simon would be a willful discarding of that tribe, and the heritage braided into their beings, whether tightly or loosely it doesn't much matter; she will be rejecting all of them, the ancestors and the survivors, too.

She's been a loving wife, daughter-in-law, and sister-in-law. She's attended the Jewish holidays with a smile and interest and cheer. She's learned to eat lox and red onions with bagels and cream cheese, to not mind the sweet kosher wine served at Passover. But does her prior acceptance now require she accommodate her husband's potential religious conversion, from a lackadaisical Jew to a Jew who is all-in?

She's always thought herself free from prejudiced beliefs, considers herself open and accepting, so what should she make of her abject refusal to experience any of what Simon might be after? To not at all want him to check it out, try it on? What does this anger, this negation say about her? That she's heartless, shallow, mean, unyielding, unmovable, or something worse? Or does it speak only to the inherent differences that have always existed between them, and not just regarding religion? Church is where she goes for herself, and she knows Simon was hurt by her secret, but it's a private place where she examines the issues—hers, his, theirs, the present and the future—directly when she can, obliquely when she fears the answers she might be given.

These Jews she loves subscribe to a compassionate God, while the God she grew up with was uncompromising, unyielding, wrathful, a hand lifted to heaven or aimed at hell. How can she tell them she prefers a bright line between right and wrong, the black and the white of rules, being cleansed of her sins, that their God is not for her, that she doesn't want to be immersed in Jewish life, that her soul will not permit it.

Their children can be part-time Jews with their father, she wouldn't be able to stop that from happening, but they will not be Jews when they are with her. She doesn't know if she would begin taking them to church, have them baptized as they weren't at birth, set them on the path to their First Communions and confirmations, how she—they—would manage not merely shuttling the girls between separate houses, but between conflicting versions of God. All those peregrinations, too much to consider now, will eventually have to be considered.

She looks up at the velvety blackness of the sky punctured by stars. Where does the rest of the moon go when only half of it is visible? Simon would know the answer to that, but it's something she might have to learn on her own, when the question is one day posed to her by Lucy or Isabel.

She feels a slight loss of balance, though she's sitting. Is she tipsy? A little or a lot? Three champagnes shouldn't be enough to do her in.

There's Harry, walking slowly. The vitality she associates with her father-in-law seems to have deserted him, a slump to his shoulders that always seem capable of supporting whatever might come. He is diminished on this of all nights, and the thought that he might be ill crosses her mind. She nearly raises her hand and calls out to him, but then doesn't. She can't tell where he's headed, but she watches him until he passes out of her sight.

Maybe it's not so complicated after all. Maybe Simon's desire to be a Jew is simply the opening she hadn't known she was seeking. That's not true. She's been thinking about the kind of opening she needs to unwind, perhaps, what they have created. How easily she pictures herself alone with their daughters in the house she would arrange differently, breathing more easily in a space cleared of Simon's intensity. And that thought, that she might breathe more freely without the husband she once adored, settles so strangely, so comfortably, into her heart.

She must be tipsy, otherwise why are these tears trailing down her cheeks? This morning she would have jostled herself into a better humor, told herself she didn't have anything really serious to cry about, and now there are so many reasons.

THIRTY-FIVE

ARE THEY REALLY AT the end of something here? Because Simon expressed for the very first time an interest in possibly being a true Jew? It can't be that, he thinks. Of course not. And yet watching his wife from a distance, chatting, smiling, responding, sipping from her glass, greeting those who were strangers to her, at ease on her own, he'd been unable to guess what was in her mind. Once, they would have known how the other responded to conviviality, unhappiness, a crisis, but that's no longer the truth. How strange that after years of being joined together in the exalted and the mundane, they might now be on opposite sides of the moon. One glance away, and Elena was gone when he looked again.

He needs a break from this gaiety, this loneliness in a celebratory crowd. He wants space and quietude. He should wander downstairs and find someone out front who's smoking a cigarette, ask to bum one and inhale the toxins into his fastidious body, now all sinew and muscle from his running and running and running, and exhaustion from his enduring failure to sleep. No, he shouldn't do that, shouldn't engage in a self-hating act; he should instead find his father.

He has been rooted in one spot, but now moves, purposefully searching for that fine man who, tomorrow, will listen to Simon's questions, and with his deep well of knowledge and experience, his intellect, his compassion and empathy, his ability to see past and future, will provide answers that will help Simon solve everything.

He winds his way in front of the orchestra, through the many, many knots of gregarious people, across the dance floor, around all the tables, past his father's photographed self, sidestepping the waiters pouring, but Harry is not to be found.

Where is his father? Was he also in need of a little solitude, and is now beneath the entrance awning, taking a breather? That would be very unlike Harry, who is always the last man standing at a great party, and objectively, aside from Simon's personal emotional conundrums, this is a great party so far.

But there is his mother, corralled into a corner by a tall young man who is talking quickly, and she is nodding, holding her empty glass, quickly glancing around every few seconds as if she needs either more champagne or to be saved.

"Could I ask for that bottle?" Simon says to a waiter, and when the icy bottle is in his hand, Simon makes a beeline to that far corner where Roma and the young man are standing.

"Simon," Roma says when he reaches her, "this is Owen Kaufmann."

THIRTY-SIX

CAMILLE'S STOMACH IS GROWLING, her head buzzing from champagne drunk too quickly, and Phoebe is in animated discussion with a woman in advanced middle age who's interesting to look at. Skin slipping ever so slightly off her sharp cheekbones, lips overly bright, tiny rivulets around the mouth splintering the coral shade, coral dress with too little fabric and too many flounces, naked knees entitled to sympathy.

There are several more just like her, a passel of them only a few steps away, so close to one another they could be the aging petals of a single flower past its prime. She is curious, and this is the curiosity she used to love, analyzing elements that comprise a tribe's commonality. What would she call this peculiar tribe? Fluttering Women, perhaps. Yes, she likes that name very much.

She cants her head to eavesdrop just as one of the women says, "We're like dogs at a pound," and the others nod and nod, mouths turned up in forced smiles, eyes lowered to fingers naked of those symbols of marriage.

How would Camille describe them to Professor Jin and her fellow social anthropologists?

"The Fluttering Women are women lost since their men died, who, with grimacing smiles, joke they are no longer the cute little puppy dogs in the window, but have been relegated to the lost and found, wagging their tails at those checking them out, praying they'll be taken to a new home before they're put down."

That very lyricism, permitted and encouraged in her field, so long as it's based upon evidentiary facts, makes her want to explore them in more depth, uncover everything underneath, what rules might have emerged among them.

She is further intrigued when several older men begin walking past, and the Fluttering Women begin fluttering more, encircling a few of those older men, breaking them off from the herd, surrounding them entirely, until the men, eyes darting, seeking an escape route that no longer exists, are imprisoned. These must be widowers, and those who have been allowed to pass untouched must have wives who are still alive. What strange ritual is she observing? Avoid ethnocentric conclusions, she cautions herself, seemingly strange behaviors have pragmatic functions and must be understood on their own terms—Malinowski's warnings that she never forgets.

The Fluttering Women are batting their eyelashes, their hands touching the widowers' sleeves; then sharply manicured fingers are moving through the air, emphasizing their words.

What are the women seeking? What reward do they want? That these men flatter, compliment, communicate, ask them for dates? Is this an idea for a study? The mating rituals of the widowed, old, lonely, and sad, who, refusing to relinquish hope, dream of a second or third or fourth act of love that will see them gratefully to the grave? She feels her brain tingling, wishes her small evening bag held a notebook and pen, and not just Phoebe's lipstick that is on her lips.

The excitement within her nearly catches fire until she thinks, is this how she'll end up if she marries Valentine Osin and he dies? She might, if she marries him in the state she's in, if the state she's in prevents her from being out in the field. Unless she can return to the field as quickly as possible, her life is over. And if her life is over, she may as well forget about everything, including Valentine, and move back here to Palm Springs, ensconce herself in her old bedroom permanently.

"CAMILLE? WHAT ARE YOU staring at? I can see your brain moving under your hair."

The excitement the Fluttering Women stirred up in Camille has already leached away.

"Those women," she says to Phoebe. "They're all dressed up and pretending they aren't dying for love, when it's what they want most in their lives. Do you think we'll end up like them?"

Phoebe looks over at the women, avid in their attentions to the men in their crowd, remembers her last date when she was trying too hard and couldn't find a thing to say, and she thinks she sees what Camille sees.

"Absolutely not," Phoebe says emphatically, then grabs Camille's hand and starts walking. "That won't happen to us. I'm sure of it. Let's go find everyone, find out when dinner's going to be served. I'm starving."

"Me, too," Camille says, wondering why Phoebe did not hold up Aaron Green and Valentine Osin as proof they already have love in their lives.

THIRTY-SEVEN

THE OPTIMAL WAY TO apprehend the beauty of a crowd is from above; an overhead perch provides the monumental view, the essential perspective. Eight hundred people RSVP'd yes to the gala and all are present, except for eight kept away by summer colds, migraines, gallstones, a last-minute change in plans. Seven hundred and ninety-two people on a twenty-thousand-square-foot terrace lit up by golden lights is a prismatic sight to behold. The vast array of hair color alone is arresting, and the lackluster labels of black, brown, blond, auburn, red, silver, gray, and white fail to do justice to the range of human plumage.

And look, from up here, one spies Phoebe and Camille Tabor turning on their heels, eager to seek out their family members, to discover when dinner will be served; and Elena Abascal, her emotions under control, cheeks dried, but flushed from the heat and the fourth glass of champagne she has rashly imbibed, is leaving behind her remote post, her orphaned chair, having decided it's time to locate her husband, though she has not figured anything out; and Roma Tabor, relieved to be away from Owen Kaufmann, who told her he interviewed Harry on Monday for the *Palm Times*, a fact Harry neglected to share, wants only to find her husband, whom she has not seen in the last fifty minutes; and Simon Tabor, wondering why he is discomforted by the young man's stare, leads his mother away, out of that terrace corner, back into the fray, responding to her whispered question with a shake of his head and his own whisper, "I haven't seen Dad since we came in."

At this very moment, the orchestral music alters, only the flutist plays on, his melodious notes ringing like dinner bells, and the enormous terrace shimmers with movement, as if the jovial, delighted, slightly inebriated guests have grown fins and tails, as if they are an enormous school of ebonized fish, flowing quickly, sherbet flashes of colors from the women's gowns like the rippling and glinting of scales. The school re-forming and re-forming as people peel away, find their tables, take their seats.

Phoebe and Camille are joined by Elena, who appears at their side. "There's Mom and Simon," Camille says, waving her hand, catching their attention. Roma's hand chops at the air.

"Is she saying something?" Phoebe asks.

"I think so," Elena says. "But I can't tell what."

And then these Tabors converge, at the special table set center stage, marked by a stiff silver flag that proclaims *Man of the Decade & Family.*

Roma, the hem of her golden gown clutched tight in one hand, is staring at her daughters, at her daughter-in-law, at her son; then she is looking beyond them, over the crowd now all seated, and the waiters lined up off to the side, and the musicians stowing their instruments in their cases while they enjoy their own dinner break. There is no Harry Tabor striding toward them, prepared to revel in the next stage of the festivities. Roma scans every inch of the terrace, but Harry is nowhere.

Her voice, hushed and hollowed, is unheard by anyone not a Tabor, but it has a metallic atmospheric reach, as if Roma Tabor is sending an electrical transmission far beyond where planes fly. So few words, but she is trembling when she says, "*Where is Harry?*"

From this lofty advantage, it is arresting to see seven hundred and ninety-two heads turning as one toward that center table, where the Tabors stand perfectly still, their own heads turning every which way, searching for the man who is not there.

VALLEY OF
THE SHADOW

THIRTY-EIGHT

SEVERAL MEN, INCLUDING SIMON and Levitt, went looking for Harry and returned shaking their heads—he wasn't out front, or taking a walk nearby practicing his speech, or in the men's room.

Now there is tumult all around Roma, as Police Chief Hernandez, in black tie, quiets the crowd. "In this unusual situation, I'm asking you to organize into temporary search parties to help scour the resort." By which he means the golf courses, the sand traps, the water traps, the ponds, the pools, the waterfalls, the cabanas, the restaurants, the cafés, the bars, the spas, the gyms, the locker rooms, and all of the bathrooms. "Once my force mobilizes, we'll take it from there."

Her children are together, holding hands, nodding at the directives, casting their glazed eyes and encouraging smiles at her, and she knows what they are trying to say: everything is going to be fine. Harry Tabor, husband and father and Man of the Decade, has merely wandered off, perhaps taken a fall, but will be discovered catching his breath somewhere on these groomed grounds.

Weak of limb, Roma sits at the special center table blaming herself. He was troubled all day and she had not investigated, had not wrung from him a confession about what was upsetting him, and her failure has brought this about.

Despite the heat, someone has wrapped her gold shawl around

her shoulders. Someone has replaced her champagne with medicinal scotch that burns on the way down. Someone has flicked off the twinkle lights, and glaring white bulbs bomb the terrace and patches of the desert. But most of that wild terrain is folded away into the deepest of blacks.

This lovely alfresco location, up from the ground, nearer to the stars, golden twenty minutes ago, has turned into an antiseptic and terrifying place.

The presidents of CST Property, Educate! and Lend, along with their wives, approach her, lean over her, putting hands to her shoulders, and she says, "Thank you, but please, you'll be of more use if you help with the search," and they nod and retreat, joining the others.

Roma shuts her eyes against the lights, the commands, the frenetic activity, and in the distance is her *baba* Tatiana, returned as flesh and blood, waving her pale, blue-veined hands. Roma's fingers tingle and she is again twelve, her hand within that soft and boneless grip.

Tatiana taught her to love dusk on Fridays, calm Saturdays, Saturday evening suns slipping behind the curved horizon, and she, so young, was enraptured by the soft sound of pages turning backwards, her grandmother exhaling incantations.

"Prayer is as elusive as snowflakes, fingerprints, the dreams we each have," Baba would say before opening the prayer book and reading aloud the Hebrew Roma had never been taught. And Roma listened to prayers that were haunting chants, dirges, exultations, a musical susurrus.

During one of her monthlong visits, Tatiana said, "We are ringed by fragility, so listen, Roma, listen well, because this is my gift to you. Do you see the white trilliums, the pink daffodils?" There was no vase of flowers in the guest room where Baba slept, and the garden was two floors below, but Roma nodded, and when Baba closed her faded eyes, she closed her own.

"*Meyn lieb*, can you imagine somebody you love? Can you imagine the rain on your bare skin? Can you imagine what I am saying when I talk in a language you do not know? This is what I want for you: to learn to read the truth struggling inside that person you love; to see the colors disguised beneath a rainbow; to listen to my foreign whispers and understand, without knowing the words, that I, your old *baba*, am flying toward the Almighty, toward transcendence. I may not reach that light, but my own father and mother raised me to believe in its existence, and I do, despite the dark world into which I was born."

The next year Tatiana had gone into the ground. The insects coming in waves, scuttling through the white pine box, gnawing the white funeral shroud to shreds, feeding upon the aged breasts that once had somehow managed to nourish Roma's mother, devouring the eyes that had seen and recorded for posterity the horrendous, rejoicing in the leftover flesh of the lips that had recounted the brutality and miracles she had witnessed. Her down-and-up life whittled into bones. When she was young, Roma had imagined her grandmother's bodily dissolution that way, her own body rigid with terror before the tears came. But on this terrace, with her hand on the glass of scotch, her eyes sealed shut, Tatiana's face is not bone scraped clean, but ivory flesh with the familiar etched whorls and crosshatches, the skin surely still satiny, the eyes clouded by cataracts, a wan blue that could blister to a stormy navy, all primal potency, the all-seeing power of an ancient who would not, would never be annihilated.

What is she to make of this visitation? That praying might make a difference? That having faith might stave off some abysmal end for her husband? Should she try to pray, take comfort in a way she's never needed before?

Roma brushes her tongue across her teeth, tastes her frantic worry. She presses hands to ears to muffle the strident desperation and fear, the sound of all those feet in dress shoes and fragile high heels moving across the terrace, to the elevators, to the stairs, to begin trawling all of this space. People already calling out "Harry," "Harry," "Harry."

This is the first hour of her life when everything is different, the dividing line between before and after, between then and now. She knows this with absolute certainty.

She is sinking, sagging, disintegrating, her sixty-eight years at last catching up to her. Taut skin collapsing, honey-colored dye striping right off her graying hair. Vivacious, effervescent, ebullient at the start of this evening, she is now crushed, and old. She feels so very old.

After Tatiana's funeral, she and her parents attended Friday night services as they never had before. In the car before sundown, heading to the synagogue, her father said each time, "This is simply to honor her. We believe in none of it. Understand, Roma, nothing exists out there that might help you at some future time." And yet her parents had been able to read easily from the prayer book, had known the Hebrew, had closed their eyes and swayed as the cantor sang.

She had understood her father meant nothing existed the way Tatiana believed it did, that there was no God watching out and watching over, but how else to explain her own life, with its marvels, and the luck her grandmother and her mother taught her to trust in?

But right now, that luck she considers first when she opens her eyes, that balance she maintains about its nature, that luck can offer her nothing.

How she desperately wishes she could believe as Tatiana believed, with unbreakable faith. But Roma's mind, always her guide, is telling her that whatever Tatiana relied upon to see her through, it's not out there.

What her mind is telling her is that even if she prays, spends hours and hours baring her soul, promising everything, it would come to nil.

What her mind is telling her is that even if every square inch of the desert is searched, Harry will not . . . *No, no, no*, that's a place she refuses to go.

THIRTY-NINE

R OMA? ROMA? I'M SORRY to intrude, but I'm constructing a
timeline. When did you last see Harry?"

She can't open her eyes, and she can't place the voice, though she's
heard it recently. It's not the voice she was expecting, the low rumble
of Chief Hernandez, gala guest, guest in their home over the years,
father of five, his eldest son a childhood friend of Simon's, the man
now in charge of figuring things out. This voice has a vacillating
quality that exposes its owner's insecure complex of youth and ego.

"When did you last see Harry?"

She looks down at her wrist, for her watch, and finds it bare.
Then she looks up, into pale eyes that belong to Owen Kaufmann.
Yes, she had pegged him right, just from that voice.

"What time is it now?"

"Eight thirty."

"We arrived at seven. We were together until—"

She takes her phone from her purse and checks the incoming
call log.

"We were together until seven fifteen, when I had to take a call. It
couldn't have lasted longer than two or three minutes, and when it
ended, I looked for Harry, but he wasn't where I had left him. I didn't
think anything of it. I assumed he was caught up greeting guests."

"So you didn't see him after that?"

"No."

"Your daughters and son say, after you all arrived, they didn't see him again. Your daughter-in-law says she saw him around seven thirty, but she didn't see where he was going. That's the last sighting we have."

"The last sighting? People must have seen him. Talked to him. This party was for *him*. There were hundreds of people here."

"Seven hundred and ninety-two, to be exact. We have the guest list. About three hundred reported seeing him early on, in that seven-to-seven-fifteen range, saying their hellos, offering their congratulations."

"Yes, there was a lot of that going on, of course."

"They all said he smiled, but said nothing in response to their greetings."

"He said nothing? That can't be true."

Roma pictures entering the party with Harry. He reached for her hand and the champagne glass got in the way, but was that then, or later when they were making their way through the crowd, or just before Jeanine McCadden phoned?

"I can't imagine him *not* talking, he's a talker. But maybe he didn't. I just don't recall. Then I had that phone call. And after that, I was waylaid by you."

Owen Kaufmann bows his head in an apology of sorts. Earlier, before all of this, when he'd been telling her about interviewing Harry, his height made her mistake him for a man. But he is a boy, skinny and wiry, face still caught in his sullen, pimply teens. Only his hands have a maturity, and a familiarity with hard labor, and belong to the adult he might grow into.

"Who was the call from?" he asks her.

"A patient's mother."

"Who?"

"Confidential and not your business."

"Was Harry feeling well?"

"Are you asking if he's ill?"

"Yes."

"No. He's in perfect health. He played tennis this morning. Everyone was at the house. We swam, ate lunch. He put one of our granddaughters down for her nap. He slept, too.

"Mr. Kaufmann, are you asking me these questions in a professional capacity? Have you been deputized by Chief Hernandez?"

"In a professional capacity, yes, as a reporter. But not deputized. Just doing my job."

"I don't think—"

"What?"

"I don't think this is a proper use of your time."

Owen Kaufmann looks up at the stars, then back to Roma.

"I think I feel guilty."

"Guilty? About what? Did you see him leave? Do you know where he's gone?"

"No. But I interviewed him and the story will be in tomorrow's paper."

"What does that have to do with this?"

"I don't know. Maybe nothing."

"Is there something you need to tell me? Is there something you know that will help? If you do, tell me right now."

For a moment, they stare at each other, and she wishes her mind were clearer so she could interpret his eyes, his body language.

"No, there's nothing," he finally says.

"Do you need anything?" he asks.

"Just for him to be found."

Owen Kaufmann nods and Roma looks away from him, into the impenetrable desert.

There is a hovering pause, then his tread across the wooden terrace, the planks creaking.

She is alone. She no longer hears the search parties, their calls of "Harry," no longer hears anything at all.

SHE DOESN'T KNOW WHEN the sounds reach her, of nocturnal animals awake and alert and busy in the desert. Out there in the night, a coyote yips sharply. Then a second one. Then a third. And it's a concert of yips and cries, and she listens and listens, considering the incremental differences in tone, wondering what they could be saying to one another. She hears hysterical human laughter from a great distance, and it goes on and on and then cuts out, as if a hand has been pressed over a mouth. She pictures her family in the future: Phoebe a bride, Camille in love, Simon rested, Elena happy, Phoebe pregnant, Lucy speaking without repetition, Isabel cuddling on her lap. She focuses on the sensation of time passing, but can't distinguish one minute from the next. The thought she has refused to consider, that she hoped she banished, circles and circles, buzzing all the while, and when it lands, she thinks of a wasp going in for the sting, and she feels faint with knowledge.

Then Chief Hernandez is kneeling next to her, taking her hands in his large calloused ones. He is not calling her Roma, and he is not calling Harry, Harry, but rather Dr. Tabor and Mr. Tabor, and his peculiar formality soothes, when she would have expected the opposite, for calling friends by their full names when one is missing surely is a sign that all is not well.

She holds her breath, preparing herself for whatever he has come to tell her. But it's nothing like that, no specific bad news, not yet, only that the search has been under way for eight hours. Detectives and uniforms were brought in immediately, to formalize the search for the guest of honor and take statements from the partygoers, who were sobered up with coffee, and then sent home.

Roma looks up in surprise, that eight hours have vanished, that Harry has been missing for at least that long.

"I'm sorry," he says. "I wish I had something solid to tell you. But we'll keep on until we do."

She wants to tell him they might as well stop the hunt, that they are all wasting their time, that the search will prove fruitless, but she cannot speak at all, cannot utter the words she knows to be true, that Harry Tabor will not be found.

FORTY

THE GLOW FROM THE half-moon and the high beams of the two cars barely dent the darkness. There are five Tabors returning home, detectives chauffeuring. She and Simon in this car, Phoebe, Camille, and Elena in the one behind. Her son is holding her hand, his body angled toward her, as he stares out his backseat window, just as her body is angled toward him, while she stares out hers. The tires on the macadam *sss-sss* when they run over squiggles of tarred repairs, but otherwise there is only the sound of air rushing past the windows. She wonders if the girls are silent and holding hands, too.

This is the long stretch between Rancho Mirage and Palm Springs—land that is indomitable, inhospitable, defiantly unpicturesque, unflagging in its ability to wear down human ingenuity.

Did Harry fall and hit his head and wander off? Is he somewhere out there, in one of those dry riverbeds prehistoric creatures might have stomped through? Is he trudging through gritty sand in his patent leather tuxedo shoes, his Luigi-made jacket catching on scrub? Is he aimlessly seeking shelter, lost in misdirection, unaware he is moving farther away from where he wants to be? Has he lost his memory, his wits, his mind? Will he be consumed by this flat desiccation that wins again and again? Hours ago, on the reverse drive, she thought about how much she liked nature besting man in this place she has long called home, but now everything out there is horrific. There are no words for her alarm.

Desert and more desert.

Then a clustering of palm trees announcing domestication.

A development with black roads winding around low boxy homes, each thinly aproned by velveteen grass. Grass, when the nearest body of water is the landlocked Salton Sea, its high saline content rendering it unusable. In the summer, the algae dies off and stinks. There is the entrance, the houses dark, the people within safe in their beds. A tennis court off to the right, the net an ethereal lattice caught in an arc of momentary light.

Desert and more desert.

The four-lane road divides, a meridian with twiggy-armed scraggly trees. Did someone plant those trees? Or were they always here, pushing themselves up through the poured concrete, as if to say, "This was my home before you, *Homo sapiens*, and will be my home after you"?

A professional plaza expertly landscaped. Rows and rows of magenta flowers caught by the car lights, a colorful false barrier against the unremitting desert that stretches as far as the eye can see.

Civilization—if that plaza was civilization—recedes again, and the San Jacinto mountain range looms up. The peak is ranked sixth among prominent peaks in the United States—Roma knows that. Harry and Simon have regularly hiked it, but from the back of the detective's car, the range looks flat, shorter than the ten thousand feet it actually is at the escarpment.

Tall wooden poles to the left strung with telephone wires.

The elevation changes, hiding the mountain range, leaving only a single hump visible in the distance. Is that actually the peak, like a tooth worn down? She doesn't know.

The Agua Caliente Indian Reservation off to the left.

Billboards on poles anchored into the shifting sand announce the tribe's Casino Resort Spa has Seafood Fridays, famous magicians, a revue of half-naked men from Down Under. A Vegas vibe to the signs, but the casino-resort-spa is a squat sixteen-story monolith plunked alone in the endlessness. The parking lot is mostly empty, the casino doors shut tight.

Desert and more desert.

A billboard of an embracing gray-haired couple happy to be living in the rental community being advertised, and Roma thinks, *Maybe they aren't selling a community of rental homes, but a community where you rent people to bring into your narrowing world, to help avert the next and lonelier stage of your life.* Then she thinks, *Please don't let the next and lonelier stage of my life be upon me.*

Every so often, a green speed limit sign stating *50*. On this stretch of uncultivated land that naturally slows down time, the detective is gunning the engine, and they are moving incredibly fast, but even if they were going 120, this trip, under these circumstances, would be ceaseless.

Desert Memorial Park cemetery.

She and Harry have never been to a funeral there. Everyone they know is healthy. No one has died. The last funerals they attended were those of their parents. Harry's parents died within months of each other; hers a short time later, two years apart. Death is never easy, but all four parents died painlessly, no agonizing, debilitating illnesses, no illnesses or diseases at all. No last days hopped up on opiates, thrashing and groaning in hospitals, or motionless in vinegary, claustrophobic homes for the aging, the decaying, the dissolving. Peaceful ends in their own homes, in their own beds. If there are lucky deaths, then they had them, in recompense, she's always thought, for what had gone before. They went to sleep and ended up in some form of eternity.

The land here falls into three categories: untouched desert; or tilled acreage that reaps the citrus, mangoes, figs, and dates for which the valley is famed; or golf courses, evidence of man's desire to force the sand to submit.

The airport.

Wasn't Harry staring up at a plane when she received the call from Jeanine McCadden? She had seen the lights and thought he was looking up at them, but who knows what her husband was looking at.

The San Jacinto mountain range grows large again through the windshield.

On either side of the highway, ruler-straight streets lead to man-icured colonies where people in their beds dream.

How many of them will remember their dreams?

As a seasoned psychologist, she is used to remembering her dreams—those of her grandmother and mother, or of people she doesn't recognize, or of animals she can't describe, or of oceans in which she swims and swims. And she is used to her rarer night-mares, which lack any coherent precision. When she comes to, pan-icked or gasping, the air tastes sweet when she realizes that she's awake, that it was only a nightmare, already evaporated, the tough bloody edges gone. She wants this to be one of those nightmares, but it's the waking kind, from which there will be no liberation from the fear.

Desert and more desert.

Then finally the outer edge of Palm Springs. She's never truly noticed how empty and uninteresting it is at the start, nothing to look at, no one out at all.

Sunny Dunes Road, Mesquite Avenue, Morongo Road, Camino Real, Sunrise Way. Who decides what is designated *road*, *ave-nue*, *camino*, or *way*? City planners, she knows that, but what is their criteria? What distinguishes one from the other from the other?

There is the adobe building where CST is based on the top floor, the five-story building she and Harry own, that will eventually be-long to their children. Rectangles of windows all the way up. The lobby is lit, as it always is, but she'd been hoping, when they passed, that CST's windows would be, too, and she would know Harry was in there, for whatever reason—she wouldn't even care why. But everything is dark.

The detectives turn onto Agapanthus Lane, then up the drive, the roar of their souped-up cars reduced to purrs.

When Roma steps out into the very early morning, the night is beginning to fade, the stars slowly retreating, the air cooler than it was when they left the resort, twenty-eight long miles ago. She thinks of Noelani McCadden's slow and sleepy movements dissipating the moment her tiny tennis shoes slap the pavement, the girl running at an unbelievable speed, the wind she creates blowing back her fine loose hair.

"You're staying, right? Of course you're staying," Simon says to the two detectives, whose names she can't recall.

"Yes," the tall one says. "We're going to do a thorough search here."

"I'll put on coffee," her son says.

Elena says, "I'll check on the girls," and disappears into the house.

Roma does not need to be led into her own home, but her daughters insist, hanging onto her wrists, taking her through the wide entry, into the living room, placing her on one of the deep white couches, never letting go.

One of the reasons she excels as a psychologist is because of her ability to burrow into the minds and bodies of her patients, regardless of their size, the inarticulateness of their thoughts. Never once has she ever wanted to actually experience what they do, but she would like to be Noelani right now, racing away.

And there's the epiphany: if the McCadden house is a safe and happy home, Noelani would first have to overcome the tug to turn around and return to that embryonic environment, before finding her stride. That's what Simon tells her he needs to do when he sets out on a morning run. One only takes flight at full speed when a house is not a home. And that's what Jeanine said Noelani does, runs fast straight out of the door, as if being pursued, running those seven miles at breakneck speed, a slow returning walk only at the last block, before putting her hand on the knob of the McCadden front door.

That definitiveness of Noelani's actions tells her everything:

Noelani *is* running away from something, *not* running toward something.

The mystery of Harry is up in the air, but this one she has solved, though is that something Noelani fears real or imagined or a heightened collision of the two?

She looks from one daughter to the other. "I can't sit here like this. As if I, all of us, are waiting for the heavens to crash down on our heads. I want to be in the pool."

"You want to swim?" Phoebe asks.

"I want to be submerged in water."

Phoebe looks at Camille, who nods her head, then up at the tall detective, who nods, too.

"Camille," Roma says, "I have to tell you something. Your phone rang yesterday afternoon and I answered it."

Camille glances at Phoebe, who raises her eyebrows.

"That's okay, Mom," Camille says.

"It was Valentine Osin."

"Okay."

"The connection was bad. I couldn't hear anything. I need to know. Is Valentine a man or a woman?"

Camille looks at Phoebe, puzzled. The two detectives look at each other, and then at the sisters.

"Valentine is a man, Mom. You know that."

"No, I didn't. You've never once used a pronoun to describe Valentine. But now I do. Thank you."

Roma shakes off her daughters' grips, stands, touches their heads, takes a few uncertain forward steps and turns.

"Phoebe. What kind of fight did you and Aaron Green have?"

Startled, Phoebe says, "No fight, Mom."

"Then why isn't he here?"

"Work, that's all."

"You should let him know what's going on."

If he existed, Phoebe would. Or she thinks she would. Maybe she wouldn't. It's impossible to imagine what she would do if he were real.

"Why don't Camille and I go in the pool with you," she says.

"That would be nice," Roma says.

BLANCA HAS LEFT ON the hall spotlights, just as Roma does for Harry on Friday nights. She wishes she hadn't sometimes pretended to be asleep when he climbed into bed so carefully, had instead embraced him. But she didn't, and now all those Friday nights when they could have been talking about the thoughts he has under the moon, or making love again, are gone, at least for now. She won't do that anymore when he returns. She'll roll over and hold him.

They left their bedroom neat and orderly. Bed made, pillows fluffed, the drapes opened wide. There are her palm trees and her flowers and the still water of her meditation pool, but the early light coming in seems new to her. How has she never seen that the white light of desert dawn has an omniscient force?

What is her advice to the parents of her patients when they are facing the unknown, when the therapy for their children has only just begun and there are no answers yet to their questions? That they must ground themselves while suspended in confusion, welcome a nebulous existence. Advice she herself must follow.

In the bathroom, she notices Harry's closet door is closed, perhaps the first time ever in all these years in this house, and she inhales a faint hint of his spicy cologne, and when she feels a scream gathering power, she focuses instead on what she has learned: Phoebe has no boyfriend. Camille is not gay. Simon and Elena did not comfort each other while Chief Hernandez issued his search-party instructions and they rode home in separate cars. Her husband is missing.

She rips herself out of the golden gown, bites hard at the fabric, gnashing at it with her teeth, gnashing as the insects must have done with Tatiana's burial shroud, until one seam finally splits, the cleaving so neat anyone handy with a needle and thread could repair it in minutes.

Why did Phoebe think she had to lie about her love life?

Why did she think Camille was gay?

What has gone wrong in Simon and Elena's marriage, and is it minor or major?

Why isn't Harry here to share, if only in a metaphysical way, this calamity?

Why has he left her?

Is that what she really thinks?

That Harry has left her?

It's a vertiginous thought that doesn't make sense. It doesn't make any sense at all.

Not once in their long marriage has either of them contemplated leaving the other.

Except.

Except.

Except once she did.

Once she did.

When Harry came to her and bowed his head.

When Harry came to her and told her about the shortcut he had taken, the wrongful act oft repeated, then bowed his head and gave her rationales for what couldn't be explained—the loss of his moral fiber, the perversion of his strong ethics.

She had been appalled. Speechless on the couch, she had wanted to escape the sordidness and the secrets he laid at her feet, his misery and contrition, his useless apologies.

She had wanted to hit him, then pack up herself and the girls and drive away in the snow, but she imagined them lost, or stuck, the girls cold and crying in the backseat, the three of them freezing to death, not found until the snow ceased, the roads cleared. But one only ran to preserve the sanctity of life, and she was not entitled to such an irresponsible action. What Harry told her did not threaten the actual existences of herself and her children, only what they were creating together—love, family, future.

As he sat with his head bowed, the rationalization of his actions concluded, he had waited for her to respond, and she thought then of telling him to leave, to walk out the door and never return.

And then she had hesitated again, when she thought of Phoebe and Camille fatherless, lacking his deep paternal love during their growing-up years, knowing what that lack would cost them and the ways in which it would alter them. She knew, because of what Tatiana and Inessa had told her about being fatherless, because she saw it in the children she treated.

And out of that hesitation came her recognition that if he had a plan to rectify his mistakes, she would consent, on the condition he give away every last dollar.

And he did have a plan, and she said that if he held onto any of the money, she would take the girls and leave him, wherever they might be living. But he had donated it all, and she hadn't had to leave him, and they had moved to this desert, and then that awful time was in the past, behind them, and they'd never spoken of it again, and life had resumed. In fact, this morning was the first time she's thought about it, and only because the Man of the Decade honor was evidence of all he has accomplished since then, of the man he has become.

They've been very happy all these years, facing the expansive future together, and she wants that expansive future with him.

Did he not want that expansive future with her?

Is it possible that his disappearance wasn't involuntary, as she has been assuming?

That he has disappeared voluntarily? If so, then why?

Did turning seventy impact him in ways that went unnoticed, that she didn't notice? Did he grow tired of helping so many others for such a long time and wanted it all to cease, to be left to himself? Did he want his freedom and so effected his escape?

If he did, what better way than with a public disappearance? He's told her the plots of enough of the crime novels he reads, and she's seen enough thrillers, to know people do that.

What she's contemplating feels wrong and incomplete, with

dangling narrative strands she doesn't know how to connect and read.

That she should know how to connect and read.

That's hubris, she admonishes herself. A lifetime excavating her patients' interior realms, their hidden pockets, has taught her that such protracted diving into the depths of others can't be sustained outside the therapeutic environment. In real life, relationships, always tenuous and tremulous no matter their apparent strength, would crack under the weight of such incessant mining. We bind ourselves to others in the heat of love, and the intimacy convinces us we know everything about the other. But we don't. We never do. We never can.

For a moment, she forgot that salient and distinguishing truth between therapy and life.

As close as she and Harry are, as well as she might understand him, she's thinking like a fool. What he once kept from her proves she doesn't know, could never know, what goes on inside of him at a cellular level.

Other cryptic secrets might be deeply buried, secrets to which he himself may not be privy.

She ought to be doubting the extent of her Harry-centric knowledge.

Whatever explanation she's reaching for is irrelevant, because there is only one actual fact: despite all the eyes of that large crowd, her husband is missing, vanished, gone, and she is in the midst, they are all in the midst, of the direst emergency.

What happens when the sun comes up? What happens the rest of this day, and all the days to come? If Harry isn't found, or doesn't reappear on his own, or she's wrong about the nature of his disappearance, then what is she to believe?

Her children are exhausted from searching. She is numb. Despite the desert heat, she is looking at an icy blank space that can never be filled. She thinks of Lucy and Isabel in Simon's old bedroom, asleep and dreaming, as she had hoped she was in the detective's car and knew she was not. They are in their twin beds, protected all these last hours from what the future may hold. If she can do nothing else, she would like to keep them innocent forever, splashing in the pool, the sunshine warming their heads.

On the bathroom floor, her golden gown is caught in that omniscient white light. Like a dead fantastical creature, like a phantom of happiness.

FORTY-ONE

SIMON IS CHANNELING HIS mother, carrying the red lacquered tray he remembers her using with his father's business colleagues when he was a teenager. Coffee pot, mugs, and the only sweetener he could find in the house, green packets that purport to be just like sugar. He did not bring milk in a pretty pitcher, as his mother would have. He wants these detectives highly caffeinated. He wants them working with speed and intensity, and he wants them to provide answers.

"I can make more coffee," he says as he sets the tray on the stone cocktail table. "I'm sure there's leftovers from lunch, and cookies, if my father's still eating them, so if you're hungry, just say so."

Elena has not returned from checking on the girls. Phoebe and Camille are catatonic on a couch. He doesn't know where his mother has gone. And the detectives don't react when he waves his hand at the tray. He wants to shake a mug at them, tell them to drink up, get moving. He fills mugs for his sisters and hands them over. Pours one for himself and takes a gulp that sears his throat.

Why aren't the detectives doing anything? What are they supposed to be doing? He wishes he knew.

"I'm sorry. I've forgotten your names."

"Detective Peter Zhang," says the short one, burly with a clean-shaven head, and the green markings of a neck tattoo peeking out of his collared shirt.

The other one reminds Simon of Victor, the very tall waiter in his story, the story he told Elena only yesterday afternoon, when time was moving properly, neither conflating nor telescoping, when his father was not yet lost or missing or worse.

"Detective Aaron David," the tall one says, and Phoebe knocks over her mug, the extra-strength coffee spilling and splattering. To the three Tabor children, it happens in slow motion, a black plume rising and falling.

Phoebe grabs the stack of napkins piled on the red tray, scrubbing and scrubbing at the couch. "Goddammit," she says, and runs into the kitchen.

"So what happens now?" Simon asks Detectives Zhang and David.

PHOEBE FINDS A CLEANSER under the sink that claims: *All Stains Gone!* She's got the can in her hand, and takes a step, then finds herself sitting on the floor, staring at her filthy feet.

Her feet are filthy because she took off her heels to search, pushing her way beneath bushes, hugging tree trunks to look up at their arms, to see if her father had climbed them. Stepping back and brushing bark from her dress and her hair when she grasped he would not be hiding in the branches like a Boy Scout gone crazy, run amok.

All that time searching, she feared she would be the one to find his body splayed out, his energetic brown eyes wide-open and unseeing, still and unmoving as he's never been in life. But he wasn't anywhere at that resort. He was just gone.

She doesn't want these awful images in her head. She doesn't want to return to the living room, to hear Simon and the detectives speaking about the next steps. She needs her cool, analytical self to return so she can do whatever's required to bring her father back.

She breathes in and out, and the names *Aaron Green, Aaron*

Gold, Aaron David slither through her brain. Could this detective, with his first name, be important? Another Aaron manifested out of her never-ending lie?

She knows from her mother this is avoidance coping, and it's no more useful than her attempt to draw love into her life.

She wipes away her tears. She is prepared to clean up her mess, and figure out how to help, but then she's sobbing again, and all she can do is sit there on the kitchen floor.

FORTY-TWO

During her first month in the Trobriand Islands, three people went missing at sea off Vakuta. Two sank, but one crawled out of the water. Camille was on the beach with their clan when they hauled the survivor onto the sand, slapped his chest, ocean spurting out of his mouth, a man transformed into a whale transformed back into a man. In the hours before, she had watched the Vakuta islanders performing Trobriand rites and rituals, invoking magic to reclaim them all. They only reclaimed the one, but it had been cause for a subdued celebration.

Camille only needs to reclaim one with the Kilivila words the islanders intoned, the dances they performed, but whatever is still stored in her brain is crowded out by memories of the funeral she attended not long after, on Kitava. The village had been thronged with three distinct groups: the general mourners—heads freshly shaved, bodies thickly smeared with soot, howling like demons, though they were not the dead man's matrilineal kinsmen; the true grievers—who were the dead man's kinsmen, from his clan, not shaved, smeared, or howling, not costumed or ornamented to declare their mourning, but composed, only a few softly weeping, and aloof from the corpse because of the express taboo that if they touched the body, the deceased's spirit might infect them, causing illness or death; and the dead man's widow and her children—who were considered neither kin nor clan, and under the Trobriand moral code, their grief was not considered spontaneous, but an artificial duty springing from acquired obligations. They were displaying the required histrionic version of bereavement, sitting closest to the body, to the grave, bearing witness, but nothing about their manic demonstration spoke of true heartache and sorrow. She stayed on, through all the elements of the mortuary ritual. She'd read about it in Malinowski, but still was flustered when the remains were constantly worried—the body buried and twice exhumed, then cut up, some of its bones peeled out of the carcass, given to one party and then to another.

"Do you know the password to your father's computer?"

What Malinowski had also written about in *The Sexual Life of Savages*, Camille personally viewed: the strictest and heaviest shackles of marriage were laid on the wife after the real tie was dissolved by death. The widow was not set free by the event. She was required to play the role of chief mourner, to make an ostentatious and onerous display of grief for her husband from the moment of his demise until months, perhaps years, afterward. She had to fulfill her part under vigilant eyes, complying fully with the demanding traditional morals, suspiciously surveilled by the dead man's kin, who would have regarded it as a grievous offense to their clan's honor if she flagged for a single moment in her duty and performance. Camille returned to Kitava many times during her two years in Melanesia, but once, near the end, expressly to see what had become of the widow. Nearly twenty-four months later, she was still dramatically grieving. And Camille had said to one of her colleagues, "This breaks my heart. When are you allowed to forfeit a dead love here?" The answer: apparently never.

And now her mother is in the bedroom long shared with her husband, pulling on a bathing suit so she can submerge herself in water. Is this her mother's own rite, ritual, or magic to bring Harry back?

The very tall detective is at the wall of her father's books. He pulls one out, holds it by the spine, lets the pages fall open. What is he expecting to find?

The other one is leaning over her father's desk.

"I'm sorry. Did someone ask me something?"

"Do you know the password to your father's computer?"

Zhang, that's his name. She doesn't know what he's talking about and it comes to her that she needs to stall.

"The password?" she says.

"Do you know what it is?"

Camille shakes her head. "I don't."

"Can you write down the family's birthdays, and your parents' wedding anniversary. It's usually one of those."

Although her father never hid himself away in here, she thinks of it as a sanctuary, peaceful in the dawn light. Paintings on the walls, books on the shelves, several now stacked on the floor because of what the tall detective is doing. The room is organized. Nothing out of place. On the neat desk, only a leather cup filled with pens, a stack of pads, and the laptop he finally purchased a couple of years ago. When she's checked her email here, she plops down in his chair, bellies up to his desk, and opens the lid. Never has she had to find him and ask for a password.

But Detective Zhang has just said it's password protected. What does that mean? That her father's now hiding something? If he is, what it could it be? And if he is, maybe everyone is looking at this disappearance the wrong way. She's not sure what the proper perspective might be, but if she reveals the password is new, and what it might suggest, will the detectives decide this is a voluntary act by a man of sound mind, a family matter, not for the police?

She reaches for the pad on the desk, *Harry Tabor* across the top in blue ink, clicks the pen hard, *CST* running up its side, and begins writing.

FORTY-THREE

ALONE IN THE LIVING room, Simon watches the sun dispelling the cold pewter light, rendering sharp what has been indistinct, bringing forth the reality of this new day. His thoughts refuse to align; they circle, skew, loop, jump forward and back, head in one direction, then reverse course, and he reins them in repeatedly, starts over again and again.

If Harry had taken a fall, or fallen ill, or had a heart attack somewhere at the resort, he would have been found. The gala guests or the police search teams would have located him and called for an ambulance. There would have been the wail of the siren, the glare of the rotating red lights. The party guests would have lined up, watched EMTs placing Harry on a stretcher, sliding the stretcher through the opened back doors, the van roaring off in screams of sound and color. Chief Hernandez would have arranged transportation for the Tabors to the hospital, and they would be sitting in Emergency or outside the ICU. But they are here on Agapanthus Lane, waiting. Waiting to learn something, or for something to happen, everyone gone to their separate corners. Neither his mother nor Elena has reemerged. Camille is still in their father's study, where she led the detectives at their request. Phoebe is still in the kitchen, or she was; she could have gone to her bedroom through the kitchen's other door without him being aware.

For a while, he heard her crying, but even that sound has disappeared.

The white couch is a Rorschach test of spilled coffee. He knows it's too late, those splotches are permanent, and unless the couch is sent out for professional cleaning, or the fabric replaced, those stains will return them repeatedly to the previous night when the jubilance died, to this morning of bewilderment.

He looks at his watch. It's six thirty. He had expected them all to be happily groggy a few hours from now, at the table at the big pool, their hangovers doctored by Harry's Sunday mimosas, laughing and talking over one another as they dissected the evening, Harry perhaps carrying out to the table whatever commemorative piece had been ceremoniously given to him. The fresh bagels from Baum's on East Sunny Dunes Road would still be warm and easily torn by their teeth, the bowls of different kinds of cream cheese fluffy, knives speared into the mounds. He expected to draw his father aside, suggest that hike, ask him for his steadying advice. Instead, the family is scattered and this trauma is surreal.

He searches his mind for past traumas visited upon the Tabors, to remember how everyone behaved, handled it, got through. His mother's *baba* and mother had suffered greatly before she was born, but that was a long time ago. And if he doesn't count the deaths of his mother's and father's parents, deaths in the normal course, deaths that occurred when he was too young to stand at the graves, this, he realizes, is the first one. And that fact dumbfounds him, and he's unsure if it's gratitude he should feel or mortification that their great luck means there is no one inherently capable of leading the rest through whatever might come. He knows how to take control in a courtroom, at the negotiating table, but this situation is neither of those. For this, he is unprepared, ill equipped. How different he might feel if he had nurtured his spiritual self all these years, found sustenance in a rabbi's words, in prayers read collectively, the feeling of community when seated in a synagogue. If he had worked at a belief in God. He tests himself, psychically pressing hard on the frangible spots in his brain, to see if yesterday's decision to investigate his Jewishness has been blanched away by his father's disappearance. It hasn't. Instead, there is a small seam of strength running inside of him when he thinks of finding answers in the Torah about what is happening, will happen. But still, where his father might be remains an unsolvable question.

When the sun glints off his tuxedo trousers, he walks to the front door and opens it. There it is, the mezuzah on the outer doorpost. In Hebrew school, he must have learned about it, but he recalls nothing. Later, whenever later arrives, he will research the mezuzah thoroughly.

He looks at the flowers and thick shrubs, at the Margaret Mead palm tree reaching to the sky, then along the long, curved driveway. The newspaper has been delivered, but he heard nothing, no slight thwack when it landed, though he was sitting near the living room windows. It's the local Palm Springs paper for a population that numbers under fifty thousand, no thicker than he remembers it being in his youth. Not all that much happens here, at least until last night. Then he's thinking about Elena, the tension between them while dressing, and at the party, and how they joined different search teams instead of searching for Harry together, and rode home separately in the detectives' cars.

He carries in the paper, drops it on a small white stone table next to the ruined couch, and feels as if a match has been set to his heart. For a moment, he's able to smother the flames, but then he breathes, and mixed with his own oxygen, those flames burst into higher heat, boiling into livid colors.

No, he won't wait. He'll research the mezuzah right now on his phone; maybe what he learns will provide aid or comfort.

What he reads is only partially helpful—for the mezuzah's power to be effective, one must touch it upon entering and when leaving the home, and recite the Shema, the most famous Jewish prayer.

He's never done that, never known to do that, and likely his family hasn't either. Do any of them know that prayer by heart?

His father surely, maybe his mother. But he does not. The mezuzah has been nailed there since he was a boy, but they are all a day
late, or decades late, and if he'd known this yesterday, known to do
this yesterday, who knows? Its power, the Shema's power, might
have been invoked, and his father would be here at home where he
ought to be at this hour.

He touches the mezuzah, then kisses his fingers, as the article
suggested. He imagines buying one and affixing it to the door of
his and Elena's house in the hills, reciting the Shema each time he
leaves and returns, praying that God will keep those who live within
safe and well. A brief punch of shock when he imagines himself no
longer living there, forced by Elena into exile.

He dials his father's cell phone and an anonymous digital female voice announces the number Simon has reached. His father
never figured out how to personalize his voicemail, which means
if he is gone, or for as long as he is gone, Simon has no recording
anywhere of how his father sounds.

Shattered by tiredness, by fear, by the remnants of the adrena-
line from this very long night that has now turned into day, he refills his coffee mug and pours one for Elena, and goes looking for
the woman who is still his wife.

FORTY-FOUR

CAMILLE UNHOOKS HER FEET from the stiletto sandals, unbuttons the white satin jacket, steps out of the trousers, drapes the suit on her bed, and looks at it. Did she learn anything in Melanesia about the Trobrianders' views on handed-down clothing? Did they believe that a previous owner's bad juju settled into the weave and thread? Did they have special bonfires for burning what is contaminated?

In the past, Camille always politely declined whatever her friend Marni was handing out, and maybe she should have this time. Marni thinks herself a generous person, but her generosity arrives with false cheer that does not completely hide her not-so-faint condescension. Maybe that satin suit retained the bad parts of Marni, and Camille carried those bad parts into the gala, and Marni's bad juju ruined everything.

She will give the outfit away. No, she'll throw it out, let it go to the dump, or the landfill, or wherever, be buried under tons of garbage where it shouldn't be able to do any more harm.

Perhaps that's what she should do with all the furniture in her apartment, and all of her clothes, with everything she owns that once belonged to others. The expensive sandals she'll keep. Only she has worn them, and until last year, she'd thought her juju was of the best kind.

She crumples up the suit, stuffs it into the bag that held her toothbrush and soap, knots the handles tightly. She will toss out these cursed clothes immediately.

She picks up her phone. If it is just past sunrise in Palm Springs, it is past three in the afternoon in the Cradle of Humankind, where Valentine Osin is working at the Dinaledi Chamber, the "chamber of stars" complex of limestone caves where fifteen skeletons and fifteen hundred other fossils of an extinct species of hominin were recently discovered and provisionally named *Homo naledi*. At three in the afternoon he'll be at the paleoanthropological site, dating and tagging or brushing away what might be two-million-year-old sand from skeletons or fossils, deliriously happy to be working with the most extensive discovery of a single hominid species ever found in Africa. The phrase *deliriously happy* she added herself.

Yesterday, he'd written her: *We are all still amazed that the* H. naledi *appear to have intentionally deposited the bodies of their dead in the remote cave chamber, because we previously thought such behavior was limited to humans. And the find is also remarkable because of the light it will shed on the origins and diversity of our own species.* Reading that, she had curiously simmered with outrage for that hominid species, who might very well have had their own name for themselves, who might very well have always protected their dead from scavengers, who might very well have viewed the retrieval of the fossilized remains of their fathers, mothers, siblings, children, as a prohibited exhumation, a deconsecration, who might not have liked or wanted to be known forevermore as *H. naledi*. Valentine's emailed excitement transmitted itself despite his scientific distancing, and she had felt a wave of disgust for the arrogance of scientists, a group in which she herself would be included, notwithstanding current personal struggles.

She looks at the phone and doesn't think it's Valentine she wants to call to tell of her father's disappearance. Still, it's true that tragedy clarifies—she can't keep pretending with him that her old intensity might return. It is her intensity he adores, and it's unfair to leave him hanging, waiting for that to occur. He should be free to give his rapacious energy its lead, to bestow his special love on someone who hasn't lost her way and sense of herself. Is she considering refusing Valentine Osin's proposal of marriage, his descriptions of their children? Those big questions are not for now, and she tucks them away.

It's Lilac Love she wants to call, Patty Donaldson she wants to talk to, with her broad smile and her electric-colored outfits and that laugh of hers and her daily whisper into Camille's ear, "How's my favorite social anthropologist?"—a fact Camille has kept from everyone else there. Patty is at her desk every day at eight on the dot, and it's Patty she'll call, when it's no longer dawn. Not to tell her what's going on here at home, but to say she's been delayed, won't be starting the drive back to Seattle this afternoon, won't be back at Lilac Love on Tuesday as planned. And to ask Patty how her favorite dying people are doing, if they're wondering where she is, if they're missing her, have letters they want her to write. She's not ready to lose their quiet wisdoms, their hard-won certainties, that experiencing all of life's mysteries is worth the attendant suffering that becomes embedded in the skin, the organs, the heart. She'll ask Patty to implore the nurses and the volunteer physicians to keep them alive until she returns.

In those lilac-painted rooms, Camille has seen how death, whether prolonged or rapid, becomes another kind of living, contains the zenith of humanity. She has been privileged twice so far to watch death growing close: the quieting, the last preparation, the decision at the final moment to go alone or in the presence of a chosen other, the breathing changing, growing shallow, then shallower, as the immediate world recedes, and the eyes turn inward, focused only upon the internal, in a place seen only once and so very briefly. She does not want any of her people to die without her holding their hands, without knowing they are leaving behind a loving witness to their souls fleeing their earthbound existences. She wants to thank them for allowing her entry into their worlds, diminished as they are, into their last days, their last hours, their final seconds. She wants to thank them for their wisdom, and make them a promise, that she will not waste or fritter that wisdom away. She wants them to know their time together is transforming her.

When her father is found, as a corpse, or physically damaged, or mentally altered with retrograde amnesia, or somehow hale, hearty, and healthy, with all of his memories intact and explanations crucial, her own world, all of their worlds, will be radically different. However this ends, nothing will be the same again, but her dying people, hopefully they will still be in their beds, turning their faces to the light, waiting for her to return, to listen to their stories, to be a comfort while they nap, to feel her touch, to know they are seen and heard and loved.

She drops the phone on her bed and looks at the bikini she was wearing yesterday. Hanging from the closet knob, it's twisted into something tiny and warped, but aromatic with Hawaiian Tropic suntan oil, the scent of her youth. She stretches it out, then puts it on, because if her mother wants to be in the pool, then Camille belongs there, too.

FORTY-FIVE

They are sitting on the third stair in the pool, lined up in the same order as yesterday. Yellowy light is washing over the mountains, slowly flowing across the whitened water. In a few minutes, they will be caught fully by the day.

"I think," Camille tentatively says, "that Dad might be hiding something. Did you know his laptop has a password on it?"

"Would Dad even know how to set a password?" Phoebe says.

"He must, because there's one on it now."

"What does that mean?" Roma asks.

"I don't know, and the detectives don't know I was surprised by the password."

"We should tell them it's new," Roma says.

"I'm not sure we should. What do you think, Phoebe?"

"I don't know. Why are you asking me?"

"Because you're a lawyer."

"A lawyer who represents artists, Camille. I don't remember most of the criminal law I learned in law school."

"Criminal law?" Roma asks Phoebe.

"If we don't let the police know the password is new, we could be obstructing justice, which is criminal."

"But if we tell them, I'm worried they'll stop looking for him."

With Camille's unthinkable prediction, the brief conversational flurry ends.

Roma wants to fill the void, to say out loud to her daughters that their father's disappearance might be deliberate, that as inconceivable as it may be, he might have left her. But as a mother and a psychologist, she knows healthy parent-child relationships require certain inviolable boundaries. The marital relationship, for example, is off-limits, its inner workings never discussed with the children, no matter their ages, unless life-altering events are truly looming, like divorce or death. This is the advice she gives to the parents of her patients. But does a disappearance, without any facts, qualify as one of those events?

Not yet, she decides. Not when she knows absolutely nothing, not when she has trusted the strength of the loving bond she and Harry have shared, not when she has been unaware of any thorny marital issues, not when she is in the dark as to the origin of those unknown issues or their compelling nature that would warrant such a draconian exit.

And if Harry has left her, and in this way, then he has left his children in this way, too, and she does not want to add to the fearful turmoil.

She leaves her daughters perched on the step and wades out. Only at this hour is the overheated pool warmer than the air. By ten, it will have reversed. She wades until the water slices across her neck, until head is separate from body, mind separated from emotion, then goes under. Never in her life has she cried underwater, and the tears, she feels them distinctly, despite the hot water in which she is submerged. She presses her hands to her eyes, feels flicks at her cheeks, touches her ears. She is still wearing her yellow diamond birthday earrings. When her lungs are begging, she rises, gulps in the dry air, looks at fingers streaked black with last night's mascara.

It hadn't crossed her mind to first wash her face, to remove the expensive gems from her ears, to extricate the pins from her hair, now a wet, matted mess on top of her head, to brush her teeth before keening in the pool. And she is keening, she must be keening, because she doesn't recognize the sounds she is making, like an injured porpoise or dolphin or whatever other aquatic mammal she was thinking about yesterday when she was swimming her morning laps.

Then her daughters are pressing against her, hugging her tight, these bodies she has held since they were slippery and fragile, since heads had to be carefully cradled, tiny pursed lips seeking that which only she, their mother, could provide, these beings she and Harry had such tremendous fun creating.

"Why is Savah crying? Why are you crying, crying, crying, Savah?" It is Lucy, sleep-tossed and naked, looking down upon her grandmother, who is clutched between her aunts, and then throws herself in.

She sputters up and flings her arms around Roma's neck. Over her niece's head, Camille whispers, "What about his safe?"

"I'm safesafesafe," Lucy says.

"You are," Phoebe says. "So, so safe. You want to play a game with me in the shallow end?" Lucy grins and swims sloppily, and Phoebe nods at her sister and mother, and follows Lucy back to the steps.

"Did you check the safe?" Camille asks Roma. "Would you know if anything's missing? If he'd taken anything out recently?"

"I would," Roma says, "because I took these out yesterday," pointing to her earrings. Then she is climbing the silver ladder out of the pool and dripping her way through the house, to their bedroom, to Harry's closet. Is this why he closed the closet door last night, as he never has before?

She punches in the combination—the numerical months and days of their children's births—and pulls everything out. A large assortment of small boxes filled with her fine jewelry. Mordy and Lenore's marriage license. Her mother and father's marriage license. Their own marriage license, their flowery *ketubah*. The originals of their social security cards. Copies of their children's birth certificates. The ten pounds of shrink-wrapped bills, in ones, fives, and tens, that she knows total $100,000, the flight money Harry insisted they keep on hand after 9/11, what he calls "our survivor cash." The wrapping is a little dusty, but intact, no tears in the plastic at all. If he'd willfully escaped from this life, from their life, it would have involved premeditation, planning, and Harry is a planner. He would have needed this money, would have taken this money; otherwise what would he use to live on? He'd know the police monitor usage on credit cards, withdrawals from bank accounts in a suspicious circumstance like this. That the money is here, her jewels are all here, slightly eases the pain in her soul. But it's a mixed blessing. Not even mixed, not really any kind of blessing. If Harry doesn't have the money, then he didn't plan to disappear, and if he didn't plan to disappear, then his disappearance means something else. She doesn't know what it might mean. She doesn't know what that something else could be.

FORTY-SIX

I THANKED BLANCA FOR sleeping over and tried to pay her, but she said your mother already did before we left last night. She knows something's wrong and wanted to stay, but I thought she should go. I didn't tell her what's happened."

"When did she leave?"

"A few minutes ago."

"Does she have a car? How is she getting home?"

"I don't know. She didn't say."

"I should see if she needs a lift."

"If she needed a ride home, wouldn't she have said so?"

"I don't know."

He ought to find Blanca, make sure she has a ride, or a car, or drive her home himself if need be, but exhaustion overwhelms him, and he stays seated at the edge of the bed next to Elena, holding his mug of coffee as tightly as she is holding hers, and he wonders why hers, that he poured at the same time as his own, still has rising heat. In the detective's car with his mother, he'd felt volcanic, as if he could erupt in molten, boiling lava, but now he is ash that is graying and cooling, turning cold even hot coffee.

"Are the girls still sleeping?" he asks.

"Yes. Lucy was starting to turn over, so I left, hoping she'd stay asleep.

"Simon?"

"Yes."

"I feel terrible. When I saw Harry last night, I let him walk by. I didn't go and join him. If I had, maybe I could have prevented this whole thing."

Maybe. Maybe not. They might never know. And he backs away from that thought. But Elena's waiting for him to say something, perhaps to absolve her of whatever she didn't do that she should have done, and he says, "It's not your fault."

She moves closer, lays her head on his shoulder. Is this an apology for yesterday or the provision of comfort or a wordless declaration that their love is still intact? Whatever the reason, he'll take it.

"Simon?"

"Yes."

"I'll do whatever you want, but should the girls know Harry is missing? Be in the middle of everything with the police? Should I take them home? You don't have to decide this minute, but think about it. And I'd like to find a church this morning, go to a service, or just sit alone and pray for him."

He looks at her, then says, "I think the girls will be a diversion for my mother, for all of us. Maybe we'll know something by this afternoon. Maybe he'll have been found. And if not, then yes, you and the girls should go home."

"What if they ask where Sabba is?"

"We'll tell them he's at the office."

Elena takes his hand and holds it tight. "It's going to be all right. Everything is going to be fine."

He'd like to believe everything's going to be fine, but he thinks he disagrees.

They hear something, someone calling out from a far distance, and Simon is up and through the door, down the long, long hall, a right into the other hall, hoping it's the detectives looking for him, telling him they know where his father is. But it's not. It's Isabel, standing in his old bedroom, rubbing her eyes, calling out,

"Sabba." He looks to the other bed, where Lucy sleeps. It's empty, the covers thrown back.

"I'm here, honey," he says, lifting Isabel into his arms.

"Not you, Daddy. Sabba. Sabba, another story now."

FORTY-SEVEN

PHOEBE AND CAMILLE ARE keeping Lucy entertained, timing her as she attempts to breaststroke across the pool. Lucy, kicking hard, swims one way, then the other.

"She's a windup toy without any sense of direction," Camille says.

"Every lap she swims is like four," Phoebe says.

"You know the sad irony? Mom always wants us to stay and we never do. We've never stayed longer when everything is great, and now we will, and for such a terrible reason."

"I know," Phoebe says.

Lucy grabs onto the far ledge and laughs. "Sososo fast, right, Auntie Phoebe?"

"So fast is right! Thirty seconds! Outstanding!"

"Nownownow?" Lucy screams.

"Do the butterfly," Phoebe calls out.

Lucy shakes her head.

"Do freestyle."

Lucy shakes her head again.

"What the fuck is it called?" Phoebe whispers to Camille.

"The crawl."

"Do the crawl. Ready? On your mark. Get set. GO!"

And Lucy is off again, on a slow and circuitous route back to the shallow end.

"I'll get her dried and dressed after this. Do you want to set out breakfast for the kids? They'll be hungry," Phoebe says.

"Maybe I should go get the bagels and everything, like we would have had this morning, if . . . Take both of the wee ones with me. Give you time to talk to Simon about Dad's password, and see how Mom is. See when the detectives are going to leave."

A tall shadow falls across them.

"I wanted to let you know we're leaving now, taking your father's laptop so the techs can break the password," Detective Aaron David says.

"Did you find anything that will help?" Camille asks.

"No, but the investigation has only begun. I promise, we're going to do everything we can to bring him back to you."

He's very serious, and professional, and handsome, and his eyes lock on Phoebe's and hang on a little too long, and she knows it's not an accident. How bizarre if love were waiting for her in this incomprehensible situation. But it's not, or at least not for her, not in these circumstances, not when the love would always be inextricably linked to whatever kind of tragedy this is.

"I'm ready," Simon says, coming through the glass door, breaking the connection between the detective and Phoebe. "Your partner is out front. And I have keys."

"You're going? Where?" Camille asks.

"To CST. See if there's anything there that might help."

"Auntie Phoebe, how long, how long, how long?" Lucy screams from the shallow end.

"Thirty seconds again. Fantastic!"

"Great job, Lucy," Simon calls to his daughter. Then he kneels at the edge, says quietly to his sisters, "Two things. Sabba is at the office if she asks. I've already told Isabel that. She wanted Sabba to tell her a morning story. And Elena is going to church."

"Church?" Phoebe says.

"Church," Simon reiterates dryly, then stands back up.

"Ready?" he says to the detective.

Detective Aaron David nods at Phoebe, and then at Camille, and follows Simon out through the gate that is hidden by heavy greenery.

"Church?" Camille says to Phoebe, and Phoebe says, "I never thought of going to temple. Should we?"

"Dad wouldn't be there," Camille says.

"Not to find him, but to pray for him."

Lucy throws her arms around Phoebe's neck, then lifts her head and freezes.

"What is it?" Phoebe says.

"Lions, lions, lions."

"There aren't any lions here," Camille says.

"*Shhhhhhhh*," Lucy whispers loudly at her aunts.

And they hear what Lucy heard before them, the catlike roar of the detectives' cars speeding down the curving driveway. Then the hushed engine of Elena's SUV.

"The lions are going to eateateat," Lucy says, her whispering quieter now, as if she is truly afraid of lions springing over the fence.

Camille is about to say something, and Phoebe shakes her head at her sister. She's disconcerted by Lucy's ferocious face, her intent stare into the distance. She doesn't want Camille to encourage this, but Camille asks, "What are they going to eat?"

"Bad, bad, bad people," Lucy says without any hesitation.

"Honey," Phoebe says, "there aren't any lions here and they aren't going to eat anyone."

"Wrongwrongwrong. There are always lions and they always eat people. Yum, yum, yum, yum, yum, yum."

Phoebe stares at her niece, and it hits her: the Tabor constellation depends on all of its stars—what will happen if one is lost for good, fallen out of the atmosphere? Then Lucy presses her face to

Phoebe's, wet cheek against wet cheek, and says, "I lovelovelove you, Auntie Phoebe. I didn't know you're a scaredy-cat."

"I didn't know either," Phoebe says. "But I guess I am." She tries smiling at Lucy, who is smiling at her.

"We're all scaredy-cats sometimes," Camille says.

"Not me, me, me," Lucy says.

FORTY-EIGHT

The sky is not yet a saturated blue, the sun still ascending. That it could be any midmorning of any day has unmoored Roma's sense of time, rendered it amorphous. She needs her working structure, its tumbling, humbling division into hour-long increments, or she will end up flat on her back replaying her life with Harry these last eight months, last year, all the way back to their beginning.

The truth is she has already been replaying every word and conversation between them, every look they gave each other and distinctly understood, the times when she thought she had interpreted correctly an unspoken thought in her husband's eyes. She has been engaged this way since ripping off her gown, tearing it with her teeth, crying in the pool, reviewing the contents of the safe, showing the detectives into their bedroom, into Harry's closet, pulling apart her husband's suits to show them the modern push-button panel, pushing the buttons again and opening it wide, letting them sift through her boxes of jewels and their official nostalgic papers, finding nothing of use for the investigation. Before the detectives stood at the master bedroom door, she'd hidden the shrink-wrapped survivor cash under a stack of blankets on the top shelf of the closet in Simon's old room.

An ancient prudence dictated Roma's action, an inherited

defensible fear that being found to possess an abundance of crisp cash might insinuate guilt about something, though the insinuation would be unwarranted and wrong. But she is the sole granddaughter of Tatiana Kahanevna Marat Jacoby, who in 1881 was five years old when her father, Kahan Kahanovich Marat, was dragged from his lecture hall at St. Petersburg University, where he taught taxonomy and was called *Professor*, tossed out onto Universitetskaya Embankment and badly beaten. The day before, Tsar Alexander II was assassinated at the Mikhailovsky Manège, where he attended the military roll call every Sunday, and the Jews were being blamed.

A week later, her black-and-blue father locked the door to their nice home, and in three droshkies, with one leather suitcase apiece, her father, her mother, her two older brothers, her two older sisters, and Tatiana rode to Nikolaevsky Station, and then traveled seven hundred and fifty-eight miles by rail to family in Kiev. Her father managed to secure another university position teaching young men the science of defining groups of biological organisms on the basis of shared characteristics and giving names to those groups. His students were a rowdy bunch of privileged boys who heckled him mercilessly as he stood at the blackboard attempting to impart wisdom. He hung onto that position by his nails until late spring, when Alexander III issued the May Laws, which deprived Kahan Kahanovich Marat of his career, his family of his livelihood, and turned him into a cobbler's apprentice, for which he was ill-suited.

Three years later, during yet another massive anti-Jewish riot, eighteen days after Tatiana turned eight, she was raped and her father and brothers among the murdered. The destroyed bodies were irretrievable, no graves marking their deaths.

When Tatiana physically healed, the dwindling family reduced their necessaries into what one leather suitcase could accommodate, selling the other six for cash, boarding a series of shrinking trains that moved them three hundred more miles away, to Odessa, where one small branch of the family remained. Called the Pearl of the Black Sea, Odessa was no pearl of a city for them, despite its humid subtropical summer climate and its dry, relatively mild winters. The large house where they expected to stay, three stories with gracious rooms reverberating with the sound of the sea, had been usurped, their relations turned out. Widowed mother and daughters found a small attic room and slept together in one bed, spent their days as shopgirls in a department store, earning one rouble each a year. Life improved for them all when Tatiana married Baran Ivanovich Jacoby.

In 1905, the Storms in the Negev were blowing again, though they had never stopped blowing, were as ferocious as ever. Tatiana was then twenty-nine, an eight-year wife and the mother of one-year-old Inessa. Out all together for a late-afternoon walk, her fine, intellectual husband and her loving mother and sisters were massacred by a mob incited by the authorities, led by priests, ignored by the police, the crowd crying, "Kill the Jews," and Tatiana saw them and the rest slaughtered like lambs, saw babies ripped from their mothers' arms and torn to pieces in a bloodthirsty frenzy. She pulled Inessa from her carriage, shoved her inside her coat, and fled. Of their belongings, she would miss most the ethical value of her father's prayer book, and the sentimental value of the novels by the Jewish and Russian writers she adored—Babel, Aleichem, Pushkin, Gogol, Chekhov, Tolstoy, and especially Turgenev—their pages her personal Torah, softening those harrowing years hour by hour when she fell into them. To return to the three small rooms where they all lived in penurious harmony—where she had been surprised to find she could love, where she was treated with devoted gentleness, never berated for her body's difficulty in carrying a child to term, her husband crying tears of happiness when she finally delivered a baby—would have meant certain death, and so she, an unlikely survivor, deserted the city along with the others, leaving it empty of them and their kind.

She walked with her daughter in her arms for a very long time—days, weeks, a month, she never knew for how long, only that when she no longer smelled the salt of the sea, she lay down under a tree, her child at her breast, prepared for them both to wither away and die. A farmer roused her at dusk. He did not ask what had brought her to this tree in the countryside, some thirty miles from the coast as the crow flies. At his farm that first night, he gave them only a plate of bread. The second night only a plate of salt. On the third night, he finally dropped on the worn table plates of both bread and salt, the simple Russian offering of hospitality, but by then she already knew his true nature. By then, he'd already flung himself on her with a harsh "*Krahseevahyah*," and she, a grieving wraith, had heard his Russian *beautiful,* closed her eyes to recall the love she had felt in her dead husband's arms, and understood the farmer's terms—the exchange required for a version of safety.

He laughed at her, but let her speak her prayers aloud on Shabbat, brought her beeswax candles to light, wine to drink so she could bless the fruit of the vine. She learned to shear sheep, to milk the old, thin cow whose milk was surprisingly sweet, to churn its milk into butter, to feed the scratching hens that laid large eggs, to assess the ripeness of fruits and berries growing in the farmer's small orchard. And when her work was done for the day, she placed her daughter on the old mare's back for gentle rides, and her daughter's baby teeth pierced gums that soon regained a fresh rosy hue, a bloom rising in her hollowed cheeks, her fragile bones lengthening.

Time passed in that false idyll, in a fraught charade, in a mockery of harmony, and one rainy afternoon the farmer displayed his treasure, eighteen gold 25 Rouble coins issued by Imperial Russia, of which, although she did not know this then, only one hundred pieces had been struck. He had been someone much grander before Alexander II's assassination, although he never explained what that grandness encompassed, or why he had given it up or had it taken from him, and said only, and only once, "I used to have the ear of the tsar in important matters."

For eleven years Tatiana was his helpmate, his servant, his partner in farming and husbandry, his lover forcibly taken only forty or so times. And never once did either she or her daughter ever call him by his name, or by any name at all.

And they didn't call him anything on a gorgeous August morning in 1916 when Russia's national flower, the chamomile, with their lemony centers and white petals, were swaying in the hot breeze, the purple crocuses with their yellow eyes not yet dying, the orange-pistiled arnica waiting to be picked for poultices, and in the small orchard, the apple, peach, pear, plum, and cherry trees and the raspberry bushes were all denuded, Tatiana and Inessa having picked them clean, wrung the juice into liquid *kompot*, stewed the skin and the meat into thick compote they bottled.

That morning, as he had never done before, the farmer turned his eyes on Inessa, whose name meant *chaste*, his red-veined piggy eyes growing round and large and glazed, and he licked his bovine lips, and Tatiana understood, as she always had, the ever-increasing price of survival. She moved slowly into the barn, picked up the sheep shears, and came back into the warmth of the sunshine, and smiled at the farmer, and came close, right up to his chest, as if to kiss him, and she felt his prick, already risen from his lascivious thoughts about the girl he liked to think he raised, and Tatiana leaned in close, and she touched him, then rubbed him, and when he let out his horrible *hmmmmmmm*, she stabbed him through the heart, watched him fall, his prick deflating like one of the old cow's emptied udders.

Then she removed the gold roubles from their secret place. Mother and daughter packed their few belongings quickly and left, the coins jangling in Tatiana's pockets as they began the long walk back to the Pearl of the Black Sea for the first time since the terrifying flight Inessa was too young to remember. For some time, the farmer's vizsla trotted alongside. This same dog was with the farmer that long-ago dusk, when he found her and her baby under the tree. When he had pointed and said, "This is Turgenev, the love of my life," she had hoped that a man whose dog shared a name with her favorite author might be decent, or at least decent enough.

As they walked on, away from the farm and the orchard and the barns and the small wooden house, Turgenev refused to turn back even when Tatiana barked the farmer's commands she had never needed to use, and finally she had no choice; she bared her teeth until it tore off for home, unaware it was now alone, and she wondered how much time the sheep, the cow, the mare, the hens had left, how vicious that kind dog would become when it finished gorging upon the farmer.

She sold the coins for nearly their value, and paid their way out of hell. Up the gangway they walked, boarding the white ship anchored in port, missing the Revolution of 1917, and all the following revolutions and the subsequent battles and skirmishes that would alter repeatedly the country in which Odessa was located, see the ongoing persecution of the Jews, and the internal exile of anyone not considered a true Russian patriot worthy of the name *comrade*.

Steerage, the between deck, the tween-deck, was where they slept, but Tatiana had enough cash to keep their bellies filled, and the waters were calm as they sailed away from their abortion of a motherland, to a distant country in which all were, ostensibly, welcome.

Somehow, mother and daughter managed to prevent the infection of hatred, the wallow of sourness, and in their adopted America, they learned how it felt to smile authentically, to laugh, to make money, to buy clothes and find friends, but not to forgive.

Never again did Tatiana or Inessa speak a word of Russian, not even a *nyet* when they refused to teach "that ugly rambunctious language" to Roma. Never again did Tatiana or Inessa raise a glass of fruit juice to their mouths, or bite into an apple, a peach, a pear, a plum, a cherry, a raspberry.

This was the totality of Tatiana Kahanevna Marat Jacoby's life story, which she parceled out to her granddaughter in tiny chapters when she came for her monthlong visits. She attained the climax, the murder of the farmer on whom a name would never be bestowed, when Roma was twelve, the same age Inessa had been when Tatiana prayed to God and then did what she had to do to save her daughter for anything that might be better in some other world. The telling of the denouement took the next half year, in elegant words that could cut the carotid, and then the brave woman Roma called Baba was dead.

The guilt, about surviving when every member of her family did not, about killing the farmer who once was someone grander, whose attempts at foreign kindness never outweighed his frank brutality, the fear of being branded again, blamed again, made a target again, revisited nightly in excruciating detail while Tatiana tossed and turned in an imitation of sleep—that history was passed down from Tatiana to Inessa to Roma, who is now sixty-eight, with a husband who has gone missing. A man who is a Jew who has helped Jews for three decades.

That's why Roma hid the survivor cash.

HER NEED TO REVISIT all of her history with Harry, to unravel this catastrophic mystery, is reaching obsessive proportions: her brain is locking down, traveling the same territory, already, so soon, too well rutted. It's the road to a certain form of madness. She's seen it, treated it, and *heal thyself* is what she commands, or all will be lost. Follow Tatiana, she thinks, who returned to her past only when telling Roma her tale.

Here is Elena, coming from somewhere, sandals softly tapping the concrete, kissing Roma on her cheek, hugging her tight, kissing Lucy and Isabel, then Phoebe and Camille, taking a seat at the table by the big pool.

Roma sees in Phoebe, Camille, and Elena fragility, vulnerability, and fear identical to her own. Their smooth faces seem to have aged since seven o'clock last night, light wrinkles where there were none before, a bruising staining their clear and radiant skin. They are all shaky, the firm ground swaying and threatening to give way beneath their feet. This is an earthquake for them all.

Her granddaughters in swimsuits, shorts and tees, are quiet, aware of the tremors in the air, too young to understand what they are sensing. Perhaps years from now, they will revisit this moment, wonder about it, and Roma breathes in hard, hopes it will remain merely a moment of interest to them, for which they will never find any clues.

Bagels and cream cheese that hadn't been in the house have been set out prettily. Camille must have picked up these things, sliced the onions, cut the tomatoes, poured glasses of orange juice for the girls, fresh coffee for everyone else. There is no platter of lox, which Harry likes to slice until one can see through to the other side, no pitcher of his mimosas, no centerpiece of silvery ferns from last night's truncated gala, no Harry, no Simon, no men at the table. They are like Tatiana and her mother and sisters, facing each other in tragedy.

A warm, comforting yeastiness rises from the large basket in the center, the aroma of onion and garlic, the scent of normalcy. For her own mental health, and for that of her children, they must not sit here stunned, unspeaking, pondering endlessly.

Lucy and Isabel glance up at their mother, a plea for their hunger to be recognized, those bagels sliced open and spread thickly with cream cheese. Elena reaches for the serrated knife and begins cutting.

What direction can Roma take to bring Harry into the conversation without frightening the little ones, who know nothing, will know nothing about their *sabba*'s disappearance—unless there is no other option?

She intended to take her children aside one by one today, to understand what is going on in their lives, using a mother's love, a psychologist's acumen, her personal insights as a scalpel, if needed. She knows more than she did yesterday, though not from their own lips, but this is not the time for that. Asking for a revelation of truths here and now would not effect what she is after. If only she knew what that was.

And then she understands how to bring Harry into this day, as if he is indeed just at the office, handling last-minute issues for his newest wave of émigrés coming from—? She can't remember where the three families are coming from, although she knew at the beginning of the week.

Her breath stills. CST without Harry? CST is his baby. It has never been merely an organization, but one made of frail flesh and spillable blood, people's lives, their chances at measurable happiness, all dependent on Harry. What will happen in his absence? The men who have recently come aboard CST are intelligent and far-thinking, but do they possess the hearts to become its loving foster parents?

The locks in her brain are turning, then lifting, letting her out of the cage. She is thinking again of others, and although the foreseeable future only extends to the duration of this breakfast, not fully en famille, she formulates in her mind what she wants to say: "I'd like to ask each of you to share a special personal memory of your father and your *sabba*. A conversation that was of import, or amusing, or an experience shared by just the two of you, and that you have carried in your hearts. Which of his lessons have meant the most, that you haven't forgotten, that you find yourself using daily?" She wants to make Harry a living presence gone only temporarily, soon to return. But will her request be interpreted as a memorial? That's not her intent, and she is concerned her children might think she's already assumed the worst, that soon they will be burying him, which is not what she is contemplating at all, not what she wants them to contemplate either. Is there a different way to spin this, to get what she needs, a way to quell her desperation by hearing her children expressing their love for their father?

It is her eldest who clears her throat, as if intuiting her mother's wish. Phoebe, who requires more security than her upbringing would have suggested or demanded, who needs to renew within herself the sense of thrill she has not experienced nearly enough in her still-young life, who might be lying, Roma thinks, about the state of her love life.

Phoebe's dark eyes, even darker than Harry's and Simon's, roam across the faces around the table, briefly meeting everyone's eyes, and then she says, "In light of last night's Man of the Decade honor, I want to tell a story about Harry Tabor, husband, father, father-in-law, and *sabba*.

"He once told me that one could not assume the big world meant your own world was large. He said that to make your world large, you needed to hold something back, to keep some things for yourself. If everything about you was known to another, you would feel smaller than you actually were, and you would come to accept that smallness, and in turn, you would inevitably shrink. But holding close to your heart your hopes and your dreams was like owning the key to the universe. He said, 'Certain secrets you must not keep, but other secrets are liquid gold, manna from heaven, will serve to create infinity within you.'"

When Phoebe finishes, her mother is staring at her, her sister clutching her hand. Until she opened her mouth, she'd forgotten entirely that conversation with her father when she was in law school, in love with Elijah, debilitated by the split she saw in herself, her inability to break free of the shackles she had placed on herself, her reluctance to soar.

A percussive bolt of truth runs through her.

She is aware, her mother and sister and sister-in-law are aware, of the meaning of what she has shared, what it says, not about her, but about the loving husband and father and *sabba*, the absent Harry Tabor, a counselor, it seems, of secret keeping.

The young women look inward, contemplating their own private secrets.

Roma stares at her daughters' fingers knotted tightly together.

The heavy silence continues until Lucy breaks it, quietly asks, "Savah, can it be my turn now?"

Roma looks at the child and inhales and nods.

"One time Sabba took me for a long drive in his convertible," Lucy says, speaking with a new overt confidence.

Have the disturbances in the air shaken something out of Lucy, set her free? Are Elena and Phoebe and Camille hearing what Roma is hearing?

She waits for the next sentence, wondering what might happen, if Lucy's tongue will catch and trip again, or instead glide the words into the air.

"We drove way out in the desert."

There it is, and joy expands Roma's constricted heart.

"It was sunny and hot."

This is Lucy speaking perfectly constructed sentences, using the punctuating period, no longer a wound-up parrot worrying a captured word.

"It was last year when I was four."

No one else seems to be noticing this miraculous alteration in Lucy's speech, this developmental leap that Roma was concerned wouldn't arrive, a leap that might coincide for all time with Harry's disappearance.

"He told me a story."

No, they are entirely missing this astonishing phenomenon, too rapt in Lucy's story that winds and wends and winds some more, but makes perfect sense about everything her *sabba* told her, the entire mythology of her birth, the origin story about the day she was born.

FORTY-NINE

Breakfast is long over, the dishes cleared, the uneaten food put away, but only the children have left the table. Lucy and Isabel are sitting on the side of the pool, splashing their feet in the water, occasionally giggling.

Elena looks at them and quietly says, "I'll get the girls out of the way. So you don't have to be careful talking in front of them. I'll take them to that hotel with the purple pool and the waterslides. They can play, and I'll give them lunch there. I'll need to borrow a car, Simon has ours."

Phoebe and Camille nod, and all three turn to Roma.

Roma is in her chair at the table, but somewhere else entirely.

"I'll put the extra car seats in mine," Phoebe says. "Why don't you and Camille put together what you need." She excels at orchestrating plans, getting things done, and to be away from the table is a reprieve.

From a closet in the laundry room, Phoebe pulls out the car seats her parents keep for the girls, and drags them to her car parked at the top of the drive. Five attempts and a slightly smashed thumb before she figures out how they work and snaps them in.

Elena is right to whisk the girls away, but what is the hotel's liability if a child drowns in that dark royal-hued water, which renders the pool bottom invisible? How can anyone tell if a child's gone under?

She lifts and lowers her shoulders, twists her neck, wanting to release the tension from her body and the prospect of death from her mind. But death is jammed in tight, forcing her to view even a pool with purple water through its lens.

"They could stay away a week," Camille says when she appears. Tote bags hang from her arms and she plops them into the trunk.

Lucy and Isabel are skipping, and Lucy runs to Phoebe and says, "We're going to the purple pool," and Phoebe picks Lucy up and says, "Say that again."

"We're going to the purple pool."

"That's what I thought you said. And what are you going to do there?"

"Play on the slides."

"You're going to have the best time," Phoebe says, then secures Lucy into her car seat, while Camille handles Isabel's.

Elena hugs them both. "You'll call if anything—"

"Of course," both sisters say.

"Bye-bye," the girls yell, waving madly out the windows, and Elena gives a soft toot of the horn, and down they go and turn onto Agapanthus.

ELENA AND THE GIRLS left for the purple pool a while ago, but Phoebe and Camille are still at the top of the drive.

"Did you notice Lucy isn't repeating everything she says?" Phoebe asks Camille.

"It started at breakfast."

"Really? Why didn't I notice?"

"Because we're all very emotional and because you're used to her repeating everything. The ear fills in what's missing."

They look at each other.

"What do you think has happened to Dad?"

Camille exhales. "I don't know. My mind goes in circles."

"Mine, too. When we were searching last night, I kept seeing him dead, and I was sure I'd be the one to find him."

On the kitchen floor this morning, she'd been calmed only by the thought that her father might have believed she was in love with Aaron Green, that there was the possibility she wouldn't be alone all her life. But since then, Phoebe keeps seeing him on a coroner's slab, with a tag around a toe identifying him as John Doe.

How long would it take before they figured out that body was Harry Tabor?

Camille touches Phoebe's shoulder. "That must have been awful."

Phoebe shudders. "It was. It is."

"Earlier, with those detectives in Dad's study, I was thinking about the Trobrianders' rites of—"

"Rites of what?"

"Too complicated right now. But at breakfast I kept thinking of Dad taking us with him to visit some of his families, how he was as gentle with the parents and the children as he was with us. And how the kids didn't seem very different from you, me, and Simon. Then he'd take us for ice cream sundaes and explain how difficult their lives had been in their own countries, and describe the new careers the parents were making for themselves, and how well the kids were doing in school."

Phoebe thinks of Camille, at eight, and ten, and thirteen, with her notebook and pen asking the children questions and writing down their answers, wanting to know the underlying stories of everything. Sometimes the kids were their same ages, sometimes older, with thicker accents, and Camille wasn't afraid of them the way Phoebe was. Phoebe had hated those visits.

"I remember," she says. "But last night, he didn't even get to be named Man of the Decade. If he's dead, do you think he'll still be honored? In some kind of posthumous dedication?"

"Don't think that way, Phoebe."

"I can't help it."

"Try. I don't know why I'm having this feeling, there's no basis for it one way or the other, but I don't think this is going to end in tragedy. In confusion maybe, and a hell of a lot of explanations, but not in tragedy. Or at least I keep sending that hope out into the universe."

Phoebe should be sending hope out into the universe, but her line to the universe is very weak. She sent out hope with fictional Aaron Green, and that has failed to bring her something simpler, like love, so how will her hope return their father?

"I will," Phoebe says, closing her eyes, thinking Camille has always been more naturally optimistic than her. "I'm sending that hope out right now."

Then Phoebe opens her eyes. "You don't think Dad deliberately left, do you? Is that what you mean by confusion and explanations?"

"I don't know what I mean. They didn't find him at the resort. He's not in any of the hospitals. And I can't see him ever leaving Mom, or Mom leaving him. So where is he? People like Dad don't just disappear like this from their lives."

Camille may have been considering living like a native on the Trobriand Islands, but even she would not disappear this way.

"People *don't* just disappear from their lives like this," Phoebe says with vehemence. "Families don't just find themselves in the midst of a mystery."

"You're right," Camille says.

SUNSHINE BEATS DOWN ON their heads as they watch their mother across the pool. Roma is still at the table, silent, motionless, hands folded together in her lap. Her face, Camille thinks, is a sort of death mask, full mouth in a straight line, a frown puckering her forehead. Camille watches until she sees her mother's chest rising and falling, and then feels her own doing the same.

"I can see her breathing. But she hasn't said anything since we cleared the dishes."

"I know," Phoebe says.

"She hasn't moved either."

"I know."

They approach slowly, not wanting to frighten, placing light hands on their mother's shoulders.

"Mom?" Phoebe says gently. "Why don't you go inside and lie down? Try and get a little sleep. We'll wake you if anything happens."

Startled, Roma looks up at her daughters. "I can't go into the house. I don't want to be in our bedroom. I don't want to see my gown on the floor. I keep thinking about sitting alone on that terrace last night seeing Baba Tatiana and wishing I could believe the way she believed."

She hadn't meant to say any of that. She meant to say, "We're all going to be strong. We're not going to contemplate the unknown particulars. If we do that, we'll make ourselves crazy spinning on the wheel of conjecture. So let's just be together right now."

But perhaps they ought to contemplate those unknown particulars. Perhaps she ought to tell her daughters that her mind has ricocheted from fear, to confusion, back to fear. Last night, she was sure something terrible had happened to Harry. At sunrise this morning, she wondered whether he might have left her. Now, with all these hours gone, and all their calls to his cell phone picked up by voicemail, and the survivor cash intact, which the children know nothing about, she's terrified again that something terrible has happened to him. Perhaps she ought to tell them she keeps imagining the detectives arriving with solemn faces and whispered condolences, bringing with them the altered contours of her future, of all of their futures.

No, no, no.

"Then, how about a chaise, Mom?" Phoebe says. "You'll be more comfortable. We'll all lie in the sun."

"Yes, fine," she says and finds herself upright.

It's automatic, Roma thinks—their arranging three chaises with breathing room between them. It's the gene that Tatiana possessed, and passed down to Inessa, who passed it down to Roma, who passed it down to Phoebe and Camille. A shared gene that, in times of trouble, or conflict, or dissension, or an unprecedented major crisis, like this one, demands simultaneous closeness with a touch of physical distance. It isn't the kind of gene that splits on gender lines, and yet it is missing in Simon. If he were here, he wouldn't be giving himself extra room. He'd be a restive, inquiring dog, pacing, and insisting on discussing everything, saying, "Can't we be closer together so it's easier to talk?" and flummoxed when his mother and his sisters shook their heads.

"I'll get you something cold to drink," Phoebe says.

Camille floats towels onto the chaises. "Take off the caftan, Mom," and Roma finds she's wearing Harry's caftan, and underneath, her bathing suit from early this morning.

"I don't think I washed my face. I didn't take off my good earrings."

"It doesn't matter, Mom," Camille says, taking the caftan from her. "Sit down."

Roma sits.

Phoebe reappears with a pitcher of Arnold Palmers and pours Roma a tall glass. "Sweeter than you like, but you need the sugar now, so drink."

Roma drinks as if she's been parched for years.

"Lie down, Mom," her daughters say, and then she is prone.

HELL IS DISCONCERTINGLY VACATION-LIKE, the temperature hovering at a comfortable hundred degrees, the flowers bright, the bees busy, the blue water of the pool inviting. It feels so very wrong to be stretched out like this, as if it were a regular lazy mid-August Sunday.

What would she be doing today if her husband were not missing? Reading the newspaper, or reading a book, or reading session notes about tomorrow's patients, or talking to Harry. Since the children are here, conversation would revolve around their interests, and she would carefully extract from them the state of their lives, explore a particular spot of concern, but the only subject of interest is the one she wants to avoid.

She instructs herself to stop thinking, to concentrate on the vitamin D she's taking in. A body absorbs that vitamin best not from a pill, but direct from the sun. Most days she tries to sit outside for fifteen minutes because she is the age that she is and vitamin D regulates the absorption of calcium and phosphorous, aids the blood and the gut, averts the weakening of aging bones, reduces the risk of developing multiple sclerosis or heart disease.

Her sense of time is still absent. She's not sure how long Simon has been gone, or how long ago Elena and the children left, or how long she has been out here under the sun's undiluted rays. She can feel her skin crackling. She needs sunscreen, but the girls are as inwardly occupied and quiet as she. She doesn't want to disturb them, and can't rouse herself. Her thoughts are cacophonous, and she hushes and hushes herself, until the noise calms, converts, becomes a wobbly internal blankness; then she hears Camille whispering to Phoebe, "I wonder if she really saw Baba Tatiana on the terrace."

Roma thinks about that, because the question is absurd, because her brilliant daughters sometimes say silly things, because no matter how clear-eyed they think they are, they should recognize the truth when they hear it. Roma never needed to teach them about luck—*that* belief they adopted naturally—but she passed down to them something else she was taught: to listen for the truth. And Roma was listening for the truth about Harry's disappearance when Tatiana appeared on the terrace. Of course Tatiana was on the terrace last night, in some form or another. It's true she's never appeared outside of Roma's dreams before, but last night she did, as she had to, because the past is always part of the present.

FIFTY

S IMON IS GROWING UP: he is a boy with a kite; a teen with long
hair and fingers raised in an old-fashioned peace sign; a very
young high school graduate grinning in gown and mortarboard; a
college freshman on his dorm-room bed, knees poking through
jeans; an eager law school student pointing to a high tower of
first-year case tomes from which he would begin to learn juris-
prudence; a married man of five seconds, holding his happy bride
in his arms; a proud father, with one, then two daughters on his
lap. There are photographs of his sisters, too, sporting evidence of
their own crazier rides through those stages. Under glass, the
three Tabor siblings mature in black and white and Kodak colors
somehow still vibrant. He doesn't recall these shelves of remem-
brance, but the last time he was here, he was maybe nine.

He is at CST, in his father's office. The late-morning sun through
the windows illuminates another set of photographs pinned to an
enormous white corkboard that runs the length and height of an
entire wall. There must be twenty thousand passport faces hanging up there, of all the people Harry Tabor has released from their
exhausting existences, brought to Palm Springs in twos, threes,
fours or more. Simon used to think of the planes by which they
made their escapes as airborne arks, his father as Noah. How often
has his father looked up at these faces when he's on the phone

arranging their transport, or fighting with foreign authorities to free them, his people?

The bookcases are crammed, too: history, geography, ancient civilizations, and what Simon would call miscellany, and then a large assortment of language-translation dictionaries—from English to Serbo-Croatian, Slovak, Russian, Romanian, Moldovan, Lithuanian, German, Hungarian, Czech, Bulgarian, and standard Chinese.

He removes a scuffed black book, its spine bare. It's a prayer book, inscribed:

TO HIRAM TABOR
IN CELEBRATION OF YOUR BAR MITZVAH
LOVE YOUR PARENTS

The handwriting belongs either to grandfather Mordy or grandmother Lenore, and one of them was not simply inscribing an important gift for an important day, but issuing an order, a directive, a reiteration of one of the Ten Commandments: *Love Your Parents.*

He finds himself laughing, and then he actually can't stop laughing, and then he's crying, stumbling to his father's worn leather chair, elbows on his knees, head in his hands.

"HEY, MAN. LISTEN, WE'RE going to figure out what's going on," Detective Aaron David says when he walks into Harry's office and finds Simon sobbing.

Simon feels the detective's hand on his back, patting as he would a child, humming "Twinkle, Twinkle, Little Star," which is Lucy and Isabel's favorite lately. Simon's face is wet with tears, and he says, "I sing that to my kids. Drives me crazy, but, you know, it really *is* calming."

"Part of my repertoire. My sister's got four under the age of six."

"Tough."

"Brutal. Listen, my partner called. The password on your father's laptop is probably nine characters. Without a brute-force program, it can take up to five days to decode something that long, but the techs are confident they'll figure it out by this afternoon.

"I'd like to check this computer of your father's, but I can give you more time."

"No, take the seat."

The detective sits, rolls up to Harry's long gray desk and powers up the computer.

"No password here," he notes.

"Exactly. He's never had passwords, so I don't understand why he had one at home."

The detective opens Harry's browser and scrolls to *History*.

There's nothing listed under *Earlier Today*.

There's nothing listed under *Saturday, August 18*.

He moves down to *Friday, August 17*.

"Okay, on Friday he checked out something called the *Cactus to Clouds Trail*."

"That's a hiking trail on San Jacinto," Simon says. "The steepest day-hike route in the country. Net elevation gain of ten thousand three hundred feet. It's a hike I've always wanted to do with my dad, but the thought of it makes him seriously nervous."

The detective looks up. "He's an avid hiker?"

"Avid to the extent that we've hiked some part of San Jacinto together at least once a year since I was a kid. But always an easy trail. I was going to suggest the two of us take a hike this week-end . . ."

"Maybe he was going to make the same suggestion?"

"Maybe. But he wouldn't choose *Cactus to Clouds*."

"Would he hike San Jacinto on his own?"

"Never. He always says, 'The mountain's inherently dangerous no matter how easy the trail.'"

"He's right."

The detective scrolls to the next entry and Simon looks at the screen.

"He was looking up Leonard Cohen?"

"I would say he looked up a lot about Leonard Cohen," the detective says.

> The Official Leonard Cohen Site
> Leonard Cohen—Wikipedia
> Leonard Cohen Dead at 82—Rolling Stone
> Leonard Cohen Makes It Darker—The New Yorker
> Leonard Cohen, Epic and Enigmatic Songwriter, Is Dead at 82—The New York Times
> Leonard Cohen Explains "Hineni Hineni / I'm ready, my Lord"—Cohencentric: Leonard Cohen Considered

"He must really like Leonard Cohen," Simon says quietly. "I didn't know that."

"Whoever knows anything about his father? I sure don't," the detective says, then taps on the music icon.

Simon leans in closer. His father last played a Cohen song named "You Want It Darker."

"Did he listen to anything else?" Simon asks.

The detective checks. "No, only this one," he says, and hits Play.

Naked melancholy stripped to the bone, haunting music with a chorus singing, "*Hineni, Hineni.*"

Simon's heard that phrase before, the doubled word emerging soundlessly from his own lips, keeping time with the singers. How does he know the word? Where has he heard it?

When the song loops around again, the detective checks the next site Harry visited, and Simon's question is answered.

> Hineni: On Yom Kippur, during the Kol Nidre service, the Cantor will chant a tremendously powerful prayer called Hineni. Translated, it means "Here I am."

Yes, of course, at Palm Springs Synagogue on Yom Kippur, Simon's chanted, "*Hineni, Hineni*," his voice joining those of his family, the rest of the congregation, the old, old cantor.

The detective opens the next site.

> "Hineni" means "Here I am!" But you've got to watch out how you say it, because it is a way of expressing total readiness to give oneself—it's an offer of total availability.

Simon looks down at the top of the detective's head, at the dark curls, a few wiry sprigs of white. "Did you read that one?" he asks.

"Yes. What're you thinking?"

"'A way of expressing total readiness to give oneself'? What does that mean to you?"

From the tinny computer speakers, they both hear, "*Hineni, Hineni,* I'm ready, my Lord . . ."

The detective looks up at Simon. "Hey, it's okay. We don't know what this song means to him."

"But you heard that, right?" Simon says. " 'I'm ready, my Lord.' "

"I heard it."

"What do you think it means?"

"What do *you* think it means?"

"Suicide?"

"Would he be considering that for any reason?"

"No. Absolutely not."

"Then he probably just wanted to know what the word means in English."

Simon prefers that explanation to the one gaining purchase in his thoughts—that there is something he doesn't know about his father, that perhaps no one knows, like the rapid onset of a fatal illness or a form of inoperable cancer he has learned about, but has kept to himself.

"Look at these other sites he visited. They also seem to mitigate against the idea of him harming himself." And Simon looks:

Archaeological biblical routes through Israel
Walking the Bible: A Journey by Land through the Five
Books of Moses
The Exodus Route: Walking It!

Is his father planning to undertake some crazy walk through a distant desert? Do these sites, with pictures of happy people pointing at the sand dunes around them, then raising glasses to each other at sunset on terraces of nice hotels, mitigate anything, as the detective has suggested? Simon isn't sure; his father could do away with himself along the way. Under an incessant sun, he could find himself a sandy hole, sit down, and wait for the carrion birds to come.

"Your family ever been to Israel?"

"No."

"Is he planning a trip there?"

"He's never had any interest."

"It's the first tangible we have to go on, so we'll run it down. If your father bought a ticket to Israel, or to anywhere out of the country, and if he used it, he'll be registered on the global APIS."

"Registered on what?"

"Advance Passenger Information System. It's tied into DHS, and it takes a little time to get the information."

"It doesn't make sense that he would have left his own party to fly anywhere," Simon says. "And his car's still at home."

"Taxi or private car service could have gotten him to either the Palm Springs airport or LAX."

"What about the limo driver who took us to the gala?"

"Cleared. He was driving all night, jobs we've confirmed."

"I'm trying to picture my father as the wandering Jew in a whole other desert, one with bombs and guns and armies and Israelis and Palestinians. But I can't see it."

"Enough years in the job, I've seen people do things you can't imagine."

"So I've got to go back to the house and tell my family what? That it's possible our very own Man of the Decade has taken a runner, might literally be following the edict of 'Next year in Jerusalem.'"

"Edict?"

"Jews who aren't already in Jerusalem say it at Yom Kippur and Passover," Simon says, surprised by this information he finds in his mind.

"Listen, go be with your family. I'll come to the house as soon as we've learned something. I'll lock up here when I'm done."

"What my father was looking at yesterday doesn't add up to much."

The detective nods. "That's true," he says.

SAN JACINTO IS RIGHT in front of Simon, so close he could run his car into this part of the base.

He should have gone right back to Agapanthus, but instead, he left the sleek part of Palm Springs far behind and below, and drove up and up and up a long thin road, watching the mountain growing larger and larger as he approached. Then he pulled over.

The neighborhood is dingy, small houses in need of repair and repainting, porches with sun-faded chairs unoccupied in the afternoon heat, but all the front yards shimmer and shine with fields of white sparkling stones. He cranks up the air-conditioning and leans into the vents. The last meal he ate was lunch yesterday and he's starving. And he's still wearing his tuxedo shirt and trousers. He looks at the clock. Seventeen hours he's been in them. He needs a shower and clean clothes and food and the sleep he will never have again. What he needs more than those creature comforts is to understand whatever knowledge can be gleaned from those bits on his father's computer at CST.

A pack of teenagers skateboards past, a thundering wave that flushes out a flock of tiny birds. Why aren't their wheels sticking in the softening tar? He can see the heat rising off the pavement in waves, and if he stepped out, his own shoes would sink, leave behind marks that he was here. The skateboarders whiz around a corner and the street quiets down, the birds finding their roosts again, a slight flapping of delicate wings, and then somnolence returns.

The first time he and Harry hiked a portion of San Jacinto, they took the aerial tram, exited at Mountain Station, and climbed to the high point of the range. It was a mild climb, only twenty-four hundred feet, and his father told him the heart of the mountain was a batholith, made of slow-cooled viscous magma that began below the earth's crust, pushed up over millions of years, that the size was directly related to the intensity of the rock folding and crumpling, and it didn't have a definite floor, the idea of which confused Simon entirely. His father said the light-colored rock was Mesozoic granite, and along the eastern edges, the second most abundant rock was metamorphic, and that this was a sky island, far more humid than down in the valley, averaging fifteen inches of rain each year while the desert got only six, and there were flora and fauna up there that couldn't survive below in the triple-digit heat. He was eight and the luckiest boy because his father knew everything there was to know. They did that climb many times, and when they climbed it to celebrate Simon's twenty-first birthday, he asked his father how he knew so much about the mountain, whether he had wanted to be a geologist when he was young. Harry slung an arm around him and said, "You're so smart, I thought you'd have caught on long ago. When you were a kid, I bought a book about it, and each time we do this hike, I read a new chapter in advance. I'm about five chapters from the end."

Simon stares at the mountain, remembering that birthday hike, and his father's explanation. He's always seen it as endearing—his father educating himself geologically on a hike-by-hike basis, advancing in the book slowly so he could teach Simon new things each time they hiked up there. But now Simon wonders if he should view it in a different light. It's odd that his father would have kept his reading of that book a secret. And odd that he kept something so minor a secret for a very long time. He's never imagined his father as a keeper of secrets, or as any kind of cheat, but that's where his contemplation is taking him.

He knows his father as a straight shooter, frank, honest, a man who faces everything head-on, who would not have vanished as he has. How does Simon string together the steep hiking trail, Leonard Cohen, the meaning of *Hineni*, and biblical walking tours? He deals daily in the complicated and the convoluted, but there are always some facts at his disposal, while here there are none.

He stares at the front yards of shimmering white rocks, at the drowsy houses, at a row of short cacti. It's always amazed him how they seem to pull their arms in close to ward off the sun, to keep hydrated as best they can. When his phone rings and Detective Aaron David asks where he is, Simon's heart freezes.

"Twenty minutes from the house."

"Can you pull over?"

"I'm already stopped. What's going on?"

"We're into your father's laptop. Yesterday—"

Simon exhales.

"You okay?"

"Yeah, I thought you were going to tell me he's dead."

"No, sorry. I should have led with that. Here's what we—"

"Wait, what was his password?"

"I'll spell it. *M-A-N-Y-O-V-O-T-H*."

"*Manyovoth*?"

"Yes. Make you think of anything?"

"I don't even know what language it is."

"We don't either. But he was looking up articles about—" And the detective explains to Simon what the police have learned.

When the detective finishes, Simon says, "None of that makes sense to me."

"We're heading over to talk with your mother."

"Did he purchase a ticket, get on a flight?"

"We're waiting for return calls from DHS, and bank and credit card companies, but in my opinion, I think he did."

The connection breaks off and Simon stares at a blood-red seam winding through the rock of the mountain.

Yesterday at home, his father researched a man named Max Stern, Carruthers Investments, and the laws for asking for forgiveness on Yom Kippur Eve.

He should be feeling hopeful. If Harry has taken a flight to Israel, then he's not dead. Or unconscious somewhere still on the grounds of the resort. Or lost out in the desert. But what purpose, reason, or need would his father have to fly to Israel? It's all unknowable, unknown, as if his father's incomprehensible actions lead to a door behind which can be found all the mysteries of life, only Simon doesn't have the key.

He becomes aware of his breathing, his stomach rumbling with hunger, the weight of his tuxedo trousers on his skin, the heat against the SUV's windows, the cold air blowing at his neck, and that he's thinking: secrets, cheating, and the Yom Kippur laws he's never heard of, about asking forgiveness. That holiday is a time of repentance, but he didn't know that repenting in one's own head was insufficient.

Then he's speeding back down the long thin road, watching the immediacy of San Jacinto diminish, even as it expands.

ZHANG'S MUSTANG IS PARKED behind a fat cactus on Agapanthus, before the drive up to the house. The detectives, waiting in the cool of the car, open their doors and step out. Detective Zhang is holding Harry's laptop, Detective David a sheaf of papers.

"Your father *is* on a plane, nonstop to Tel Aviv," Detective David says. "These are printouts of his laptop searches."

Simon takes the stack. Among these papers, there must be facts he can analyze, no matter how complicated or convoluted. He needs to read quickly, to be able to provide his mother and sisters with answers, or a cogent theory about Harry's bewildering actions, or at least possible interpretations for his behavior.

"Are the Jerusalem addresses you said he looked at in here? In case I need to fly there and retrieve him, hear directly from the source the meaning of all this?"

How would Elena react to his going? A day ago, her automatic response would have been, "Of course, go, you've got to find Harry." But now? He knows how she thinks—she'll link his father's absconding to Israel with his own nascent interest in Judaism. And he sees again that look on her face when he said, "I think I want to be a Jew." Words that seemed to be a kind of killing stone.

"Everything's in there, including the addresses and instructions for a bus from Tel Aviv to Jerusalem," the detective says.

Simon nods. A bus is what his father would take; he likes moving around a foreign city like a local.

"I need ten minutes before we head up."

He shuffles through the pages and stops at the printout of "Laws of Asking Forgiveness on Yom Kippur Eve."

> 1. It is absolutely imperative that one receive forgiveness for sins committed against other people. Even if one is full of remorse, Yom Kippur will not bring atonement for such sins unless one has appeased the hurt party and obtained his forgiveness. This includes all forms of interpersonal offences, hurtful remarks, slander, damages, overdue debts, dishonesty in business, not respecting parents and teachers—

The list is lengthy and eight additional laws follow, but Simon stops there.

Why was Harry researching this? Did one of his families reach out to him and say, "I need to repent and I don't know how to do it?" and Harry went looking for guidelines that could be followed? Or was Harry expecting someone to ask *him* for forgiveness? Or does Harry himself need to atone for his sins against another?

Simon can't imagine that at all. His father is a man of casual but direct rectitude in all of his actions, choosing his words with care, so as to elucidate, or illuminate, or suggest, or prod, but never to hurt.

He skims through articles about Carruthers Investments, the Manhattan investment firm where he knows his father worked before having a change of heart that culminated in a migration, as in the old days, from East to West, or that's how Simon has always thought of it. Carruthers, where his father's life had once been about money, and where he made his money, money he used to create CST. "My true calling in life," his father has said often with pleasure and pride.

He reads the few articles about a man named Max Stern, the only person at Carruthers to be jailed for insider trading, and he calculates the dates—it was after his parents and sisters had moved here to the desert.

Then another article about Max Stern becoming a rabbi and moving to Jerusalem, nearly twenty years ago.

Is this who Harry is on his way to see?

It must be. But why after so long? What precipitated this irrational trip? What was so calamitous, so grave and essential, that his father needed to immediately see a man from an ancient time in both of their lives? Harry's actions have stunned his family, which likely means that Max Stern, whoever he may be, whoever he is to Harry, will be stunned, too, when Harry shows up.

Simon shivers in the heat, feeling a cold wind from nowhere suddenly blowing through the leaves of a tree he didn't realize was there.

FIFTY-ONE

R OMA WANTS TO GO to Odessa.
If it still exists, she wants to find the farm where her *baba*
and her mother once lived, to see the trees in the orchard whose
fruit they picked and wrung for eleven years and then never ate
again. She wants her whole family to take that trip. She hopes Harry
will be with them on that trip.

And then Phoebe is whispering into her ear. "Mom, are you
awake? It's not Dad, but your cell's ringing."

"I'm awake." Roma takes the phone from her daughter, looks at
the screen, stands up, and clears her throat. Walking through the
courtyard to her study, she answers, "Hello, Jeanine."

"Hi, Dr. Tabor."

In the background, Roma hears the laughter of a young girl
and a man, which has to be Noelani and her father. Is that laughter
a positive sign? How she wants it to be for the McCaddens, and
perhaps, vicariously, for the Tabor family, too.

"How is everything today?" she asks.

Jeanine sounds happy when she says, "She's eating. Not a lot,
but not just what's on the list. And she's drinking water, but insists
it be warm. And she's stopped screaming at us. And she didn't run
at all this morning. She curled up on her daddy's lap and said it
hurts to drink anything cold because it feels funny when she

swallows, and when she eats even only a little bit, sometimes her stomach hurts a lot."

Roma sits down on her pale blue sofa. Has she overlooked something important, something easy to overlook when a young female patient presents as Noelani presented?

"Jeanine, I'm going to give you the name and number of a pediatric gastroenterologist. You'll make an appointment first thing in the morning. I'll call and ask her to fit you in and tell her what I'm thinking. That Noelani needs to be fully examined for primary achalasia and esophageal achalasia. In a nutshell, they'll test how well her esophagus and stomach are working. If there are peristaltic compromises in these structures, it might explain her food and liquid issues. This would be an organic problem, rather than psychological, and usually fixable. It doesn't explain her obsessive running, but could explain some of the other behaviors we discussed. Do you have a pen and paper handy?"

Roma leaves a comprehensive message with the doctor's service.

Hoping she has overlooked something.

Hoping that Noelani will have the chance to return to being a regular eight-year-old girl who eats and drinks without fear and pain, whose anxiety, anger, impulse control, and lying will turn out to be connected to the achalasia, and resolved by surgery.

It is more than possible. She's seen such behaviors disappear entirely when the achalasia is successfully treated.

And the running could have been Noelani compensating, expelling the energy of confusion. If Noelani doesn't run tomorrow, or the next day, or the day after that, it could be good news—in her experience, a child running to outdistance a monster within the house never stops until the threat is eliminated.

Regardless, Roma must place all her assumptions back on the table, including what the running might signify, and reassess Noelani from scratch.

But for this single moment, she wants only to imagine that on this day of all days, everything will work out for another family because she has righted a rare misstep.

Misstep, she thinks, what an odd word it is. And how many must we make without knowing we've erred? She turns the word around in her mind, and wonders again if Harry has run away. Not to escape, she's not thinking that now, but perhaps because he made a misstep of his own. It is, marginally, a better thought to consider.

"Mom, where are you?" Phoebe's imploring shout sends Roma running into the courtyard. Her daughters are standing at the pool, sundresses on, watching Simon and the mismatched detectives coming through the sliding glass doors.

Her son and the detectives aren't smiling, but none has the downcast eyes, the hesitant approaching gait, the voice sympathetically lowered to deliver the fateful news she's been dreading. And yet it is impossible to gauge the kind of news they are bringing her.

"PLEASE. TELL ME."

"The good news is that Dad's not dead," Simon says.

Roma finds herself sitting on a chaise, her body, spring-tight and coiled since last night, violently releasing the tension, limbs shaking as if palsied. Seconds until her arms and legs still. Phoebe and Camille are instantly on either side of her.

Simon sets a chair down in front of hers. The black around his eyes has darkened, his demeanor like the restive, inquiring dog she was thinking of earlier, but he is her Simon when he leans forward and takes hold of her hands.

"The strange news is that he's on his way to Israel," he says.

She can only stare at her son.

It is Phoebe and Camille who say, "What?"

The tall detective crouches down. "Dr. Tabor, your husband purchased an El Al ticket for the one p.m. nonstop flight to Tel Aviv, and this moment he's sitting in an economy class seat on that flight. He'll be landing at one forty-five tomorrow, local time in Israel."

"I don't—"

"I know, Mom," Simon says.

"Dr. Tabor, we think Jerusalem is his final destination. We have no way to confirm that, but we're confident the assumption is correct. We understand his leaving like this, without disclosing his plans, is out of character. We're very sorry about what you've all been dealing with. Unfortunately, there's nothing more for us to do. He's an adult and, as you've all indicated, physically healthy and mentally competent, and his record is clean, there are no outstanding arrest warrants we could act on, so our work ends here. We understand this information leaves you all with many questions, but now it's a family matter."

FIFTY-TWO

AT THE FRONT DOOR, Zhang shakes Simon's hand and Detective Aaron David claps Simon on the shoulder, holding his hand there for a while, before saying, "I'm really sorry."

"I am, too. But thank you for getting us this answer so quickly."

In the guest room, he strips down, runs water over his face and hair, pulls on shorts and a T-shirt, and finds Elena's note that she and the girls are at the hotel with the slides. He is glad they are gone, out of the way, his children having some fun.

In the kitchen, he guzzles a bottle of water, and finds his hunger gone. Staring through the glass doors, he watches his mother and sisters huddled together on a single chaise, their shock mirroring his, but he's more than an hour ahead of them in considering Harry on a plane to Israel. He wonders if they understand Harry's not been airborne for long.

His mother looks up then, and when their eyes catch and hold, Simon realizes why he feels he's stepping into a very delicate interrogation, where he must take it slowly, ease carefully into the little he's learned. It's because *she's* the one here with the institutional knowledge, the only one who can possibly make connections between the links. He walks back out into the heat, thinking, *She's our best material witness.*

THERE'S A SHARPNESS TO Simon's bearing that Roma doesn't recognize when he sits facing her and his sisters. The planes of his face have hardened, he looks older than he did yesterday, and the image that comes to Roma is of an asp, and she thinks perhaps she doesn't know the kind of man her son is when he's being a lawyer. She's never observed her sweet youngest child in action, but she sees now how he must be in the courtroom, implacable and relentless, a quick tongue flicking, the words seemingly easy, but impossible to understand, and her fleeting thought is whether he shows that implacable face to Elena, asks her questions intended to confuse, uses that particular tone with her, if that's why her daughter-in-law was upset, is upset, with him.

She's never imagined Simon could be this way. She's never heard this soft voice from him, never seen such a flat stare, as if she ought to know what *manyovoth* means, as if only her explanation will spring her from a strange trap it feels like he's setting.

"I've never heard that word before. What is it?"

"It's the password Dad put on his laptop yesterday. I hoped you would know what it means."

"I don't. It sounds made up."

Camille has been tapping on her phone and says, "It's not one word. It's two: *many ovoth*. *Ovoth* is a Hebrew word that means *ghosts*. So Dad's password was *many ghosts*."

"Does it make sense to you now, Mom?" Simon asks.

"It doesn't. It means nothing to me. And I don't know what it would mean to your father. He's not a believer in ghosts."

"I'm sorry," she says, wondering why she's apologizing, why she sees disbelief in Simon's eyes. "Simon, I really don't know what it means."

"Fine," he says, clipping the word. "So we'll move on. On Friday, Dad was looking up articles about Leonard Cohen in his office."

"Okay," Roma says.

"Do you know he likes Leonard Cohen?" Simon asks.

"We all know he *loves* Leonard Cohen," Phoebe says.

"His voice, his truth-telling skills, his poeticism. For not changing his name as Dylan did," Camille says. "We've been hearing
those reasons for years."

"I didn't know that," Simon says.

Roma thinks, *How do you not know your father likes Leonard
Cohen?*

But she says, "How is Leonard Cohen relevant to any of this?"

"Dad played a particular song of his on Friday, and looked up
the definition of a word in that song."

"What song? What word?" Roma asks.

"'You Want It Darker' and the word was *Hineni*. The word
means—"

"I know what *that* word means."

"You do?"

"I do. *Here I am.*"

"What do you think it means to Dad?"

"Simon, just tell us what you're thinking," Phoebe says.

"I thought maybe Dad was sick and hadn't told us. 'Here I am'
could mean being ready for death."

"If he were ill, I would know," Roma says.

"Are you sure? Maybe taking off this way is a symptom. Maybe
he has early dementia."

"Based on all of this, he may be crazy, but he's not physically ill,
and he doesn't have dementia."

"Has he ever talked to you about walking a route through the
Bible?"

"One of those walking tours through Israel, Egypt, maybe
Jordan? Corresponding to Bible stories?" Camille asks.

"Yes."

"No," Roma says. "Why?"

"The Cohen song goes, '*Hineni, hineni, I'm ready, my Lord.*' I
thought it was possible he was sick and wanted to go there to kill
himself."

"Simon, your father isn't sick and he would never do that to us."

"Well, he left us without a word."

The tentacles of that truth spread among them; then Roma says firmly, "There has to be a reason."

"That's what I want us to figure out."

"Then ask helpful questions," Phoebe says.

"I'm trying to piece together my impressions based on what I saw on his office computer and what he was researching on his laptop yesterday here at home."

"Fine," Phoebe says. "Continue."

"I was thinking of the hikes Dad and I used to take, and how every year he knew more about San Jacinto."

"He bought a book about it when you were eight. It's here in his study, underlined, highlighted. He used to make notes for himself. Why is *that* important?" Roma says.

"Why would he hide the fact that he was studying up on San Jacinto on the fly? Because he *did* hide it."

"He wanted to keep you interested, Simon. He wanted to impress you. He wanted you to want to keep taking that hike together."

"Do you think Dad tells lies?"

"Simon, enough. What are you getting at?"

"I'm not sure yet. Please answer the question, Mom."

Is her son interrogating her?

"It's human nature to lie," she says. "Even when we think we aren't lying. And when we know we're lying, most of the time it's to save someone from hurt, or to save ourselves from idiocies that mean nothing."

"Do you really believe that?"

"I do. I see it every day in my work. The self-protection afforded by lying starts very early in life. In a world of deliberate, or unintentional, or unknowing lies, you have to filter out the irrelevant. Your father and that book, he thought he was doing the right thing, so move on."

"Yesterday, Dad researched the laws for forgiveness."

She's lost trying to understand the connections her son is making.

"I've never heard of the laws for forgiveness," she says.

"About how to ask for forgiveness on Yom Kippur from someone you've harmed."

"Are you saying your father needs to seek someone's forgiveness?"

"Maybe."

"Your father has done stupendous work in his life. Who would he need to seek forgiveness from?"

Simon leans in closer, stares at her intently.

"Maybe from one of the many ghosts?"

"Simon, there aren't any ghosts."

"Maybe there aren't, but maybe there are. Does Dad know a man named Max Stern?"

It isn't, immediately, a name that she recognizes.

And then she remembers the man. A lovely man, with a nice wife. Her name, too, began with an *M*. An old country name: Masha? Magda? He belonged to a time in their lives that has no meaning for Simon—he wasn't even a thought back then. For Phoebe and Camille, that time has probably been reduced to the old Connecticut house, the huge tree out front with a swing attached to a heavy branch, the snow, and the tiny dogs.

What does Max Stern have to do with anything?

"Max Stern?" she asks.

"Yes, Max Stern," Simon says.

"I haven't thought of him in years. Why are you asking about him?"

"Did Dad and he work together at Carruthers Investments?"

"They did. The only Jewish men there. Then Max got very sick. That was hard on your father. He would call Max often."

"So Dad kept in touch with him?"

"Yes. But then we moved here."

"And when you moved here?"

"Not at all."

"Why?"

"I don't know. Distance probably. Back then, men didn't call each other up on the phone to chat or write each other letters."

"Not even email?"

"There was no email then. No one had their own personal computers. Cell phones weren't common. But what does it matter? Max had leukemia. He had been out on medical leave for quite a while when we moved."

She feels bombarded by Simon's questions. When he looks away, she finds her breath, until he stares at her again.

"Has Dad ever kept a secret from you?"

She understands immediately what Simon is asking. Has Harry ever kept something secret from her that she now knows? That long-ago time she hasn't thought about in nearly as long, when Harry confessed his secret, it was clear as crystal this morning. But that's not Simon's business; it's none of the children's business. A man makes a mistake, rights his ways, he's entitled to keep that mistake private.

"That's an impossible question to answer. By its nature a secret is kept hidden, so how can one ever know if they know it?" Her statement is objectively true.

"Listen, Simon," Phoebe says, and Camille hears the lawyer-voice her sister uses when she wants to be heeded, when she's impatient. "We all keep secrets. I'm sure you've got some secrets. Why would Dad be any different than the rest of us? What exactly are you getting at?"

Roma has always been able to read her children's thoughts, but, this moment, Simon's are impossible to decipher.

His voice is soft again when he asks, "Do you know what happened to Max Stern, Mom?"

"I told you. He had leukemia. I'm sure he passed away."

"I don't think he did," Simon says.

"Don't think he did what?"

"I don't think he passed away."

"Why?"

"I think he ended up in prison."

"Simon, where are you getting this from?"

"I keep telling you, from the articles Dad was reading on his laptop yesterday."

Roma closes her eyes. "It was before we left for the gala. I had to shake him, tell him to get ready."

"So now we know when," Simon says.

"What were the articles about?" Phoebe asks.

"About Carruthers, and an insider trading case, and Max Stern."

"It can't be the same Max Stern," Roma says.

"I think it is, and I think he's still alive."

"Alive? More than thirty years ago, Max Stern's prognosis was dire, he was given less than a year."

"I think he's alive, and he became a rabbi."

"A rabbi? Those articles must be about a different Max Stern. The Max Stern your father worked with loved what he did. And he wasn't religious. No more religious than us."

"I think it is the right Max Stern. And that Max Stern went to prison. Then he became a rabbi. And now he's a rabbi who lives in Jerusalem."

"Simon—"

"I think it's possible Dad needs to seek forgiveness from him."

"Why?"

"That I don't know. But I think Dad is on his way to Israel to ask Max Stern to forgive him. What that something is, or why that something propelled him last night to take action, that's anyone's guess."

He pauses, and Roma can see her son pausing dramatically like this in a courtroom, and then he says, "I think someone needs to go find him. And I think it should be me."

She needs space from Simon's challenging tone, a chance to think quietly, to read those articles for herself, to see whether Simon's interpretation of whatever Harry was looking at is correct.

The only thing any of them knows for certain is that Harry is on a plane to Tel Aviv, perhaps headed to Jerusalem.

Simon's conjecture about Max Stern must be wrong.

But she knows she's not thinking clearly. The momentary respite she felt learning her husband is not dead is curdling into ferocious fury about his disappearing this way, all the hours that passed without a call to allay their worries, to explain himself. She has an overpowering need for violence, to slam doors, rend her hair, scream like a banshee, destroy whatever is in her path. Because it feels as if Harry, with his singular action, has torn the strings of their hearts.

A CREAK AND THE hidden gate swings open revealing Elena and the girls, and the courtyard grows noisy with her granddaughters' laughter, their small feet slapping across the concrete, yelling, "Hi, Savah, hi, aunties," racing into their father's arms. Simon lifts them and carries them to Elena, standing motionless at the gate, a remote and unhappy sentry.

She is too far away to overhear what Simon is saying, but Elena's tight face begins to relax, then neither says another word. Finally, Elena lifts her hand toward Simon's cheek, but it comes to rest instead on Lucy's head.

Whether Max Stern is real or not, Simon is right: he should be the one to find Harry in Israel. It can't be her. She needs the distance that exists between them right now, and Simon needs distance from Elena. Sometimes distance is the only thing that can clear the vision.

The violent compulsion has drained from her body; only her fingertips are still tingling. Tingling as they once did when Tatiana held her hand tightly while incanting the Shabbat prayers. But that tingling was about love, and this tingling is about the opposite, and Roma imagines raking her nails down Harry's face until he's bleeding and scarred.

FIFTY-THREE

Yesterday afternoon, Elena couldn't have imagined holding herself aloof from the Tabor clan, but today she can. And she is. Alone at one end of the table near the big pool, empty seats down to where Simon sits, flanked by his sisters. They have been discussing the mystery of her missing or lost or presumed-dead father-in-law, who apparently is in none of those states, and she understands nothing; it's a foreign movie she's watching, trying to construct the story from hand gestures and facial expressions. The three siblings have bonded into a tight triumvirate. She wonders how to make it a quartet, how to become one of them again, if only for the short term, but she doesn't know the words to cross the divide, and if she did, she's not sure she would use them.

"I think I need to go there now," she hears Simon say.

"*Where* do you think you need to go now?"

Only when they turn to her does Elena realize she's spoken aloud. And like a delayed echo reverberating up from a deep chasm, she hears the anger in her voice.

"I haven't filled you in on everything, sweetheart," Simon says. "Want to take a walk?"

Elena doesn't, but nods.

"Will you check on the girls?" she asks Phoebe and Camille. "They're in their bedroom changing."

"Of course," her sisters-in-law say in unison.

SIMON LEADS THE WAY through the hidden gate, past the open-air carport, where Harry's old gold coupe sits regally, down the winding drive in their usual tandem, past the enormous Margaret Mead palm tree, past all the flowers, their colored petals soaking in the late-afternoon sun.

When they reach Agapanthus Lane, Elena turns right and Simon follows.

"I'm glad you and the girls went to the hotel."

"I thought it was the right thing to do."

"Did they have fun?"

"Isabel was brave. She went down the baby slide by herself. Refused my hand. And Lucy went down the biggest slide this time. She was nervous at first, but then I had to pull her away to eat lunch."

"Something's changed in her."

"It happened at breakfast," Elena says. "She was talking in regular sentences. Not repeating a word over and over."

"That's amazing."

"I know. I don't know why, though."

"Is that important? To know why?"

"Wouldn't you like to know what's changed inside of her?"

"Yesterday, I would have said yes. Today, I'm only grateful."

Elena looks at him. The Simon she knows doesn't talk in platitudes. Nor does he let anything go until he understands every facet. She thought her anger had cooled over the afternoon, but it's again white-hot.

"You don't want to know what's changed inside of our daughter? Well, I do, Simon. Just like I want to know what's changed inside of you. But first there's Harry to talk about. What happened last night? Where did he go and why? And where are you planning on going?"

Agapanthus Lane ends in a cul-de-sac guarded by an enormous bristling cactus. In all their years taking this walk—dating, engaged, newly married, new parents pushing Lucy in her stroller, then Isabel—they always reach out and touch one of its rubbery green leaves, careful of the thorns. Elena watches Simon touch a leaf now, but she doesn't. And she notes that he notes that she doesn't, and her refusal to maintain their small ritual is a meaningless act, but she wants to hurt him however she can.

They turn around and walk back down the lane, and Simon tells her what he learned and what he thinks he's figured out, and to Elena his explanation goes on forever, until he finally says, "That's everything and that's why I have to go find my father."

At the entrance to the Tabor drive, Simon asks, "Do you want to head up?"

"No," she says and deliberately walks faster to make Simon catch up.

When he does, she says, "So Harry is not actually missing. He was never actually missing. Instead, he has taken an inexplicable flight to the Middle East."

"To Israel."

"He has taken an inexplicable flight to Israel. Where he is hoping to find someone he may have wronged a long time ago."

"Right."

"And you want to go to Israel to find him."

"He's alone there. Under some kind of intense personal duress. You know him, Elena. It's completely atypical behavior. He doesn't go crazy. He doesn't run off. He plans the trips for the people he brings here meticulously, no detail overlooked, everything plotted out well in advance. He does the same for the trips he and my mother take. But he had to go right then, so instantly he told none of us about it, and didn't call when he might have. And now, when he's completely unlike himself, doing things he has never done in his life, he needs someone in his corner. He needs one of us. And it should be me."

"Are you going to come back a Jew?"

She sees Simon is startled by her question, but it's the one that matters if they have any kind of a future. She thought through all of that this afternoon.

"I am a Jew. You told me that yesterday."

"You know what I mean."

"I do."

"I don't want that." She decided this afternoon to be clear with him, so there are no misunderstandings down the line.

"I know."

"But you might."

"Yes. I might."

"More than might."

"I just want the opportunity to explore it for myself."

"I want you to hear me, Simon. I do not want to live in a Jewish household, beholden to rules that have no meaning to me."

"I know."

"I don't want to be married to someone I may no longer recognize."

"I know. But exploring my religion isn't going to render me unrecognizable."

"It will."

"Why do you think that?"

"Because I do."

"That's not an explanation, Elena."

"Drop your 'That's not an explanation,' Simon. We both agreed on a definition of marriage. Two paths side by side, walking in the same direction."

They've reached the far end of Agapanthus Lane and Elena turns swiftly, pulling ahead, forcing him again to increase his pace.

"I know," he says, jogging up next to her. "I still agree with that definition."

"We're married and building a life you now want to change. And to change in a way that doesn't work for me at all."

"But it might not change."

"Simon, your exploration will lead you somewhere. Your explorations always do. You took up yoga and biking, now you run. And with each pursuit, you explored it deeply, and got deeper into it, and made a lot of alterations that might seem little to you, but have affected us all. The food we have in the house, the dinners we eat, the fact that you and I rarely have a glass of wine together anymore, the fact that when you *are* home on a weekend, your pursuits gobble up hours you ought to be spending with our children, or in an activity we all do together. And I've made all those adjustments. Because all those pursuits made you less antsy, slightly more content. But this is something else. You're asking me to be open to a potential tectonic shift in our lives, and I'm not. I'm saying no, and it's not a matter of whether you become slightly more observant or fully observant. To me there's no difference at all. None of it is for me. And it's not how I want to live my life. But the choice is yours."

Elena goes silent as they pass the Margaret Mead palm. Usually, like Lucy, she says, "Double M," but not now. Now, she's staring ahead, a sheen of sweat on her forehead, her breath coming fast.

He wishes he could tell her what she wants to hear. But he can't. What astonished him twenty-four hours ago feels like accepted truth today. In telling Elena that story yesterday afternoon in bed, he finally heard what his body's been insisting he attend to, the sleeplessness merely an ironic way to wake him up. An enlightening imperative was handed to him, and a mighty comprehension lit him up from within—that finding his people, learning about his people, perhaps becoming one with his people, might ground him in new and essential ways, allow him to uncover or recover the inner stability and happiness he has been missing.

He wonders if yesterday will mark the last time he and Elena make love, the last time they are naked together. Whether their bond—already weakened, he understands that now clearly, she has affirmed that now clearly—will eventually collapse, that collapse traceable back to today.

But he doesn't have a choice.

She does, and he can't blame her, and he decides he won't blame her, will never blame her, for planting her feet, closing down her mind and heart, threatening consequences if he explores this new aspect. He has seen her like this before, over conflicts far less severe, not at all momentous. She is immoveable, unswayable; never once has he been able to sway her, to persuade her. Trying to convince her to give him the chance to make his discoveries about Judaism would be a hopeless endeavor.

At the front door, Elena reaches for the knob. "What do you want..."

He waits, hoping she will finish her sentence. But she doesn't. And the air rushes in between them, marking both the infinity and finiteness of everything.

He thinks of what he wants—to have her understanding, her faith in their future, to understand that if he embraces his spiritual, their marriage would not be diminished, might instead be enhanced. But he doesn't have any of that, and will not have any of that. And love has nothing to do with this impasse. Their failure to discuss their upbringings before falling in love—he'd been concerned only yesterday it would rise up and bite them. It's risen and it's showing its fangs and he's the one who introduced it into their reality. And the rift it's already causing between them, simply by raising the notion, will not be solved or resolved or handled or fixed, not even quickly patched up, by the time he steps aboard a plane tomorrow. Whether he stays or goes, they aren't the same people they were a day ago, or a year ago, or—no, he won't keep fooling himself about this—they aren't the same people they were in the beginning. And if he can't solve it all now, he might as well go. To hesitate at this juncture, to refrain from acting, it's a temporary repair that in the end probably won't save them.

"What I want to do is book a ticket to fly out tomorrow. Then drive home. That guy is coming to fix the ceiling crack in the morning, and I'll handle that. Then I'll take a cab to the airport."

Elena's nod is sharp and quick. "Fine. I'll pack up the girls."

She steps through the door, then faces him directly. "I love him.

You know that. I'll always love him. And I'm really happy he's alive, wherever he is." Then she disappears inside the house. The sun is bright, but from where he stands, the wide entry is caught in shadow, as black as a hidden cave.

SIMON LOOKS AT THE mezuzah, then sits on the wide front steps. This is the intimate remembered view of his life: San Jacinto in the distance, clustered houses dotting the desert floor, the green gem of golf courses, cacti to the horizon, the sky china blue.

He wonders what he will learn in Israel about his father and his past. And what he might learn about himself. And how he will feel exploring the possibility of becoming a real Jew, when he is in the country meant, despite everything, to allow Judaism to exist. And how he will feel when he returns home with those different kinds of knowledge.

He thinks of teaching himself and his daughters what it means to be Tabors, Jews in this day and age when the hate is again growing loud and vicious. They are the most recent descendants of the original Tabornikovs who stood as one with their people, perishing because of what they were, or surviving only because of luck, and he wants his small tribe to anchor their feet in the sand along the continuum of the millennia of history to which they belong.

He wonders how long he will be away. He wonders if he should contact Altan Odaman and say he's unable to attend the ILC conference in Colombia, but hopes he will be included again, or if he should not make that call and assume he will go from Israel to Palm Springs to Los Angeles and then to Medellín—alone, but prepared to discuss his legal approach for recovering the Goya paintings hidden for decades in catacombs beneath a mansion once usurped by Hitler's men, priceless paintings stolen from the family herded into a metal train car and, at the final stop, lined up at a mass grave and gunned down.

He wonders what he should say to his fellow partners about his hasty disappearance, the cases he will have to put on hold, the frustration his clients will feel with this delay, when they have waited lifetimes for justice to right the wrongs they have endured.

He stares at the sky until he sees visions of the future, not a future he would have foreseen, or wanted, but a future perhaps meant to be.

There he is, with his daughters at Friday night services at the progressive synagogue high up in the canyon. A young female cantor is on the bema, her breathtaking voice touching again and again the highest of notes, beckoning the wildlife close, as if the coyotes and the deer and the rabbits are listening, as if they, too, are gaining something from those prayers.

And there he is, returning the girls home, finding Elena in the kitchen, dishing up bowls of ice cream for them all. She swirls on whipped cream and hands tiny cherries to Lucy and Isabel to put on top.

And after the desserts have been eaten, they put their children to bed, like the attentive parents they have always been. Stories for Lucy, no stories for Isabel. Hugs and kisses for both. Nightlights turned on, moons and stars going round and round on the ceilings.

But he and Elena don't ascend to the marital bedroom, do not climb into the marital bed. Instead, they sit in the living room, Elena on the comfortable couch, Simon in the uncomfortable armchair, or they are out by the small figure-eight pool, with the glasses of wine she says they don't drink together anymore, looking back at all that happened this weekend, all that happened in Israel, and all that happened after he returned from that other desert, that land of the ancients, with the Tabor paterfamilias in tow.

Wherever they are sitting that Friday night in the future, they are past negotiating the need he has for himself and their daughters, to instill in them a newfound love for his—for their—religion. Those discussions will have concluded without a tenable answer, as they both knew such discussions would end, but the heat of animosity will have cooled into warm understanding, an acceptance of the

decision they made, that they saw through to the terminal sever-
ing. Each of them cherishing their marriage as both momentous
love affair and aberration.

Elena will say, "It's late, you should go," and they'll walk out
together.

Above them, the night won't be as starry as it is in this desert or
in the one far away that Simon will have seen up close. Below them,
the lights of the city they live in will glitter, and they'll stare into the
distance, at the dark bands that are the uncountable sand and the
never-ending waves of the Pacific.

They'll hold hands for a while, because they are modern, because
they are committed to raising their children with love and mutual
respect, because they have become gentle with each other in the af-
termath of their eventually empathetic and caring divorce. She will
kiss his cheek, and close the door, and do whatever she does when the
girls are asleep and she is on her own in the house they once shared.

He sees himself touching the mezuzah he bought in Jerusalem
and nailed to the doorframe, reciting the Shema, the important
prayer he learned there, that he's teaching to Lucy and Isabel.

He sees himself driving away, thinking how he and Elena are
creating their own new worlds, underpinned by the original worlds
from which they came. The despair will have dissipated by then,
and he will gather close to his heart the past, present, and future of
his family, the obligations he has to them, and to his people, having assumed his place within the Judaism he'd once thought was
not for him. And this last year, when he couldn't sleep one night
through, when he needed to find something more in his life, everything he didn't know he was seeking in yoga poses, or biking, or
running ten miles each morning, will seem far away. For hopefully
he will have found it.

And someday, the two of them, long ago a couple happily married and in love, will take other new steps, will open their altered
hearts and spread their changed wings, begin searching for their
own kind, remembering the hard lesson they have learned, that

love, no matter how real, no matter the passion that birthed it, is not always enough.

Simon stands then and heads inside.

To make his flight reservation.

To speak to his mother about anything else she has remembered from that time when Harry Tabor and Max Stern worked together in New York City, because there's more there, he's certain.

To speak to his sisters about staying on in Palm Springs until he returns with their father.

To pack up the car and watch Lucy and Isabel being kissed and hugged by their aunts and their *savah*.

And then to make the return trip from Palm Springs to home.

When the white noise of the tires on the highway has rocked the girls to sleep, he will pray, invoking that act with specific intent, that this desire to explore his Judaism, and what might result, will give him the needed strength to handle the future he and Elena will face.

FIFTY-FOUR

CAMILLE WATCHES HER SISTER watching their nieces in the pool.

When Simon and Elena went for a walk, and their mother went to rest, they kept an eye on the girls, and exhausted every avenue of discussion about their father, until Phoebe said, "I don't get why you're not as angry with him as I am. As Simon is. As Mom must be, even though she's hiding her feelings." Then she stormed off to sit on the pool steps.

Camille *isn't* angry. She can't help how she sees things. Their father's impulsive flight to Israel, his disappearance without a word— the rest of them insist on analyzing his actions through their prism of acceptable behavior. She understands that, as well as the anger that's biting on the heels of the fear. But what fascinates her most about all the indigenous tribes she's studied is how their own prism of acceptable behavior includes acts and beliefs and rituals and magic that alter the commonplace and render the quotidian mystical. It seems to Camille that perhaps her father is seeking exactly that. The rest of her family doesn't understand it, nor do they understand that the search for the mystical doesn't come with a schedule; it can't be discussed and mutually agreed upon. The one who hears the call is compelled to do whatever he must to experience it.

"I'll be back," she calls to Phoebe.

THE TALL DETECTIVE LEFT her father's books in stacks on the floor and Camille begins reshelving them.

Last night, she was intrigued watching the Fluttering Women with their tuxedoed widower prey, and this morning, she could not allow herself to contemplate her mother as a widow. But this afternoon, now that the worst has not transpired, what could have befallen her family has sharpened her focus.

What kind of widow would her mother make, and what would be the nature of her grief?

When Camille turned thirteen, Roma said to her, "Make thoughtful decisions from your head, rather than automatic ones, perhaps from your heart, whose underpinnings are harder to understand," and a woman who thinks that way would not fall apart, prostrate herself on the grave, lose her will to live. Her mother would cry and grieve and then unpack her unconquerable strength and move forward. She would not follow the mandates of widowhood as prescribed by the Trobrianders, nor would she join the ranks of the Fluttering Women. And Camille finds that reassuring.

But the Fluttering Women represent all those other women who might not negotiate widowhood as Roma would. Aren't they trying to alter the commonplace of that diminishing state? Aren't they seeking the mystical in the quotidian, as her father is trying to do?

Shelving the final book, sitting down at her father's desk, Camille thinks that they are.

Studying those lonely women at the gala last night, gathered in a circle, presenting as a tribe, she felt that lost vibrant hum of intellectual energy she dreaded had dried up.

She taps one of her father's CST pens on the wood.

She puts one of his *Harry Tabor* pads in front of her.

Then she writes: *Fluttering Women Research Study.*

She trawls back through her master's and doctoral programs for anything she learned about widows and widowhood, and writes:

1. *Many societies delineate the different roles of widows and widowers, concentrating on the functional aspects and the inheritance of property as historically transmitted through the men. The Trobrianders were a rare exception, everything notched to the matrilineal line.*

2. *The widow commonly plays the central role in funeral and mortuary rituals, arranging for the burial, the services, caring for the soul of the dead spouse.*

3. *In some societies, widows may be forced to remarry, or prohibited from remarrying, or required to self-immolate, joining the dead spouse on his funeral pyre.*

That is everything she recalls.

That might be all she ever read.

That might be all there is.

Is it possible she has arrived at a topic that deserves true exploration?

A topic rarely studied and largely absent from the research literature?

A social anthropological study exclusively about widows, funneled through a variety of perspectives: societal, familial, the nature of solitary or communal housing, the ways in which a complete and thriving life can still be enjoyed—and that's just off the top of her head.

There are parallels she sees: her family is still experiencing a liminal phase, each one of them already being transformed by Harry's actions no matter what happens next, no matter what happens when he returns, just as death transforms, just as the widow is transformed through the reevaluation and redefining of herself, her life, her place in the family, in society, and how she, in turn, is reevaluated and redefined by others—a complete reconfiguring in that space and time of bereavement and then afterward.

Such a study has depth and longevity, potentially extensive ramifications.

Such a study could eventually be calibrated into a book for a broad audience. Without exploiting the subject tribe, without needing to turn herself into a character. Dr. Jin would be pleased.

She writes: *The American Widow.*

She writes: *status, gender distinctions between widows and widowers, discrimination, socialization of widows within their kinship units, socialization outside kinship units, sex and the widow, remarriage.*

Then she lifts the pen from the pad and chews on the end.

Does this mean she would stop pining for that one wild and untouched tribe at the end of the earth that no one else has ever studied?

No.

But the abundant widowed population could be a different kind of wild and untouched tribe that no one else has ever studied.

And unlike the Sentineli, this tribe is contactable.

She would concentrate on widows in the first world, rather than the obscure and unfamiliar. And that might be the right thing, or at least the right thing for now.

Last night, when she imagined moving permanently back into her old bedroom in this house, she thought it self-defeating, but was it actually prescient? Returning not out of failure, but staying with a three-pronged purpose: to observe how her father is transformed by his journey of discovery, to analyze the alterations that will occur in her family as a result, and to study the Fluttering Women of Palm Springs.

There is much she will need to do and she dashes down:

* *Figure out the ethnographic model, research design, research methods, and data analysis.*
* *Talk to Dr. Jin about university underwriting, access to resources, grants, assistance from current master's or PhD students.*

A smile blooms on Camille's face. For just this moment, she will relish remembering what she's about and congratulate herself for recognizing something of serious professional interest. There is strength in her still. And the future, how much brighter it seems than yesterday on the final leg of her trip home. How wonderful to feel she has options, that she doesn't have to draw lines through anything, and that time, which has felt like her enemy, has returned as the friend she recalls.

How miraculous that the great things in her life are not behind her, but ahead of her.

FIFTY-FIVE

CAN CAMILLE BE RIGHT? That their father's journey is about seeking the truth?

If she is, then Phoebe should be worrying that there is a genetic component to secret keeping, and that she inherited it from him. The evidence certainly points in that direction. She can't fathom her father's secrets, but she knows her own, and she would like to be free of the lies, free of her deception about Aaron Green. Maybe there is no *one* for her, but better to walk alone forever with a clean soul than to keep on as she is.

Her nieces, asleep together on a lounge chair, are brown as berries, but she gently presses each of their arms, to make sure they aren't burning. Lucy opens her eyes and says, "Hi, Auntie Phoebe," then snuggles closer to Isabel and is asleep again.

The sky is a weightless blue, without a single cloud. She was only six when they moved here, but she often thinks of the Connecticut sky, its low ceiling, its alabaster clouds, the feeling she had of being safeguarded and protected. The sky here is so large, so limitless, as if everything one wants in life is out there, but so far away it's impossible to capture.

She must stop thinking she is waiting for things to happen. She's in charge of living the life she wants, and that means living honestly.

She wishes Camille were sitting with her, their mother, too. She would say to them, "I've broken it off with Aaron. I've been considering it for a while. His constant travel means the relationship is always starting and stopping. I need someone who is really here, present all of the time."

It would be the truth.

Not exactly the truth.

Not the truth at all.

But they wouldn't need to know she's ending her relationship with a figment of her own creation.

Yes, she will tell her them she's broken it off with Aaron. She will come clean, or clean enough for her purposes, her needs, her sense of holistic peace and well-being. A simple statement without embellishment.

She imagines her mother saying, "Sounds like a very wise decision. You're entitled to want someone *who is really here*. Someone who is present all of the time. Trust me, my sweet, it will happen. I promise you that." And Phoebe would wonder if her mother already knew the truth. And if she did, what would she advise? "The energy we put out into the world returns to us. Happiness equals happiness. Sadness equals sadness. Mistrust is matched with mistrust. If you keep your heart open, if you find satisfaction in who you are, if you don't manufacture another false love, then absolutely, love will find you."

That's exactly what Roma would say.

Phoebe finds her phone and returns to her step in the pool, dialing Raquel to see how Benny is doing without her, to see if Raquel will care for him the next few days.

"HE'S FAB, TOTALLY FAB," Raquel says. "No prob. We're besties now."

And Phoebe wonders if Raquel has moved Benny to her own apartment, is spending hours with him on her lap, tickling him under his chin, stroking the soft fur of his ears. If she did, if she is,

Phoebe hopes her little love isn't fickle, will understand Raquel is only his temporary caretaker, will not sleep on top of Raquel's head.

"Everything there A-OK?" Raquel asks.

Phoebe hadn't decided whether she would explain to Raquel her reason for staying.

Listening to the girl's chirruping, her ceaseless happy nature bouncing from satellite to satellite, she offers a different confidence in exchange.

"I broke up with my boyfriend, so I'm staying for some extra mothering."

"Oh, Phoebe, I'm so sorry. I know how rough it can be. You're lucky to have a mother to help make you whole again. Mine died when I was young and I still miss her so much."

She's not been kind to Raquel, at least not in her heart; she summed her up, and wrote her off, without thinking that perhaps Raquel keeps reaching out because she's alone. And Phoebe's touched that when heartbreak is the topic, Raquel expresses herself in whole nouns and verbs.

"This might make you smile a little," Raquel continues. "Someone sent you flowers yesterday. A huge bouquet. I hope it's okay that I brought it into my apartment. Just until you're back. It seemed so sad for those flowers to be sitting alone, not enjoyed. And Benny eats leaves, doesn't he? I thought it was better he couldn't get at them."

So Benny is in his home, on his heating pad and his pillow, drinking his tap water, eating from his bowls on the black and white tiles, stretching out his small body in a square of sunlight. And Phoebe is touched again.

"Raquel, you keep the flowers and enjoy them. But was there a card?"

There was a card and Raquel reads it to Phoebe: "'To the woman at the Shell station this morning. I don't actually think you're French, but I'll forgive that little white lie if you'll have dinner with me. By the way, you forgot to pull your gas receipt from the machine.' It's signed Marc Weiss, and he included his telephone number and his email. Kind of cool, Phoebe."

And it is kind of cool, and it is also kind of stalkerish, that he retrieved her receipt from the machine and used it somehow to track her down, and she wonders if she will agree to a date, and if she does, how that date would go, and she wonders if Marc Weiss is Jewish, and she says to Raquel, "That's a surprise."

Has she been too dogmatic? That's her thought when she and Raquel hang up. She's wasted time wanting love before children. That life she's longed for hasn't materialized, so why not table love for now, bring the baby she wants to the center. Figure out how to become a mother first. Maybe then love would follow.

She will abandon her expensive weekends away and instead come to Palm Springs for long weekends, come for a month. Spend more time with her own mother and father. She would like that. She will do that. And she gives a little prayer of thanks that the choice is hers because her parents are alive and her father will be home soon. Because the worst thing in her world hasn't happened.

THE GLASS DOOR OPENS and there is Camille, with a hat on her head, and one for Phoebe, and a pitcher filled to the brim, the ice clanking.

"Please tell me that's not another vat of Arnold Palmers."

"Just lemonade," Camille says.

Phoebe takes the offered hat, sticks it on her head, finds empty glasses for Camille to fill, then sits again on their regular step in the pool.

When they are sitting side-by-side Phoebe says, "Maybe you're right. Maybe anger isn't the right emotion now that we know where he's headed."

Camille's genuine smile shocks tears into Phoebe's eyes. She forgot about the purity of comfort that comes from being with her sister, someone who's known her for all but two years of her life.

"I want to tell you something, I've ended it with Aaron."

Camille nods, then touches her glass to Phoebe's.

She forgot this, too, about Camille, that her sister doesn't care for superfluous talk, that she takes those she loves at face value, that she would never ask for details, or offer up the trite, like how sorry she is, or that she's sure someone better will come along.

"I'll tell you something, too. I've decided to get rid of everything I've ever bought at a flea market, charity shop, garage sale, that's ever been handed down to me from another. Any supposed treasure I picked up off the street. It's time that whatever I own, whatever I wear, holds only my own essence."

"I think we'll both be much happier," Phoebe says.

"Can we play the swimming game again?"

It's Lucy, standing naked behind them.

On the chaise, Isabel is still asleep, next to Lucy's yellow bathing suit.

Camille puts down her lemonade and wades into the water. "Come on, Lucy. I'll time you."

"You have to play, too, Auntie," Lucy says to Phoebe.

Her niece resembles Phoebe more than she does Simon or Elena, the long curls they both have, though Lucy's are nearly black, the golden gild of their skin.

"Of course, I'll play," Phoebe says, and splashes out into the middle of the pool.

"Are you ready to leap, Lucy? *One. Two. Three*—"

And Lucy leaps into Phoebe's arms.

FIFTY-SIX

I N THE BEGINNING, ROMA didn't know.

She left her family in the courtyard. She needed some quiet and rest. But her thoughts would not quiet. Her upset would not rest.

So she unloaded the dishwasher.

She stuffed pool towels into the washing machine.

She made her daughters' beds, and then the beds of her granddaughters, neatened the clothes around their sparkly suitcases.

Then she retrieved Harry's survivor cash from the high closet shelf. Its square, solid weight reminded her of a reliquary she had seen in an antique shop years ago, when she'd brought Phoebe and Camille into the city for lunch with their father, an outing that had excited the girls so much. She bought winter coats for them and wandered through stores, while Harry fed them hot dogs at his favorite stand, and showed them the trading floor, the men yelling, waving arms and tiny pads and pencils, and the girls had opened their mouths and yelled into the noise, then laughed because no one had heard. When she picked them up, they were spinning in Harry's leather chair, talking to each other in their secret language. In the year before they moved, Phoebe would say, "No story, Mommy, but listen," and then translate for Roma that secret language she shared with Camille.

She opened Harry's closet door, opened the safe, and replaced the package. It was when she heard the lock set that she knew.

Not all of it.

Not even most of it.

Not at all how Max Stern fit in.

But she knew suddenly and absolutely that Harry's disappearance had something to do with that other money.

And she knew suddenly and absolutely that Harry had not donated it as he swore that he had.

She was on the floor of his closet, looking at the safe, at his shoes, at the suits he wore every day, at the garment bag imprinted with *Luigi*, at his swim trunks on the hook, and the clear drawers where his ties were neatly arrayed, her fury burning her up from the inside.

She had threatened to leave him unless he gave away every corrupt dollar. She had trusted him when he said, "It's done." She had viewed his confession as a cleansing, a secret Harry had kept, then revealed. Doubt had not been part of their marriage before and doubt wasn't part of their marriage after. But she should have doubted.

She should have demanded evidence that the money was gone, had not accompanied them from their old life to their new; she should have asked additional questions; she should have probed so much harder, forced the truth out of him. If he had lied to her then, she would have seen it in his eyes, heard it in his voice, and she would have taken action.

But she hadn't. And because she hadn't, he'd never needed to lie to her outright. All these years, his lie has been one of omission.

Which meant she herself was not completely innocent.

What now?

Does her discovery constitute the destruction of everything?

Is his disappearance an elegy for them, for this family they have created?

Is there a statute of limitations on the commandment of honesty?

Is there a statute of limitations for whatever crimes he committed? Should she turn him in?

Should she execute her ancient threat and leave him, end a marriage she wouldn't have thought of ending yesterday?

This morning, she wanted their expansive future to continue, and whether it continues or not, that decision is now in her hands.

And the money? Where is it?

It's never figured into their lives, but are there clues about its existence that she should have seen and missed?

"MOM, WHAT ARE YOU doing in the closet?"

Roma looks up at her son. He's not the asp she imagined him to be, but it's always the news-bearing messenger who first bears the brunt.

"Looking for something."

"I want to talk to you about my plans," Simon says, and holds out his hand.

He leads her to the back patio, where she sits in the chair Harry favors during his solitary hour on Friday nights.

Her son sits across from her once more.

"I've booked a ticket to Tel Aviv for tomorrow. Elena's packing up the girls. We're going to drive back now."

Where *is* the money? They have never lived other than within their means. They arrived in Palm Springs with solid bank accounts, with the beginnings of college funds for the girls and retirement savings for themselves, and when they bought this house, real estate here was cheap, they couldn't give away homes, and there was vacant office space on all the main avenues. Harry had earned substantial money, and she had sold her practice in Connecticut for a tidy sum.

"Mom, have you remembered anything more about Max Stern, about what he might have been doing at Carruthers that sent him to prison?"

The money Harry used to found CST, it had belonged to them both. She saw the checks for the purchase of the building, for paying personnel here and abroad, what he paid himself. In those first years, she was privy to all the financial information—the large payments made to CST by countries effecting political relocations, the payments made by families already here and wanting to bring out relatives left behind, donations made by individuals and corporations wanting to help. From its inception, CST had a stable of certified accountants. Tax returns filed, taxes paid. The inflow and outflow of funds managed to the penny. It expanded. And expanded again. Its mission: to save people. But the organization was not a charity; it was profitable from the start.

"I don't know anything else about Max Stern. Everything I know, I've told you."

"Are you sure, Mom?"

About that, Roma is sure, and she says so, matching Simon's interrogative tone with a finality in her own.

"What do I say to Dad when I find him? The father I thought I knew would never run off this way."

She teaches her patients how to assess their own actions and those of others. To gain balance, to accord the proper weight to their upset, to put everything into the proper perspective. She teaches them what Tatiana taught her—that a person's actions do not sum him up, that seeing the whole of a person is an impossibility. When Tatiana told her story, Roma was twelve and viewed the world simply. Tatiana had said, "What I did was wrong, but it was also right. You will grow up and come to recognize that every negotiation between human beings, every aspect of human reality, consists of a range of colors, all of them shades of gray, all those shades representing the truth, and the many variations thereof." She has lived sixty-eight years thus far, and she knows from her own experience that Tatiana was right.

"Simon, a person's actions do not sum him up, seeing the whole of a person is always an impossibility."

Every aspect of human reality does consist of shades of gray, so where on that spectrum should she put Harry's moral failure thirty-plus years ago? Where should she put his failure, when he had not stolen money from another, but instead used information to create it, when his actions were disgraceful, but had not deliberately harmed another, when he has nurtured, helped, aided, and transformed so many lives since then?

And where does she put her own failure, her long-ago silence?

"If it's true that your father is headed to find Max Stern to seek his forgiveness, isn't seeking forgiveness the very definition of a light shining in the world? Attempting to right the wrong? This is what Baba Tatiana would have said: forgiveness can be granted or not, mistakes can be fixed or not, but if one is lucky, those streaks and stains and holes can be cleaned up, buffed out, filled in, and life can go on."

"So we're supposed to look at this as something noble Dad is doing?"

"Who among us is ever as good as they can be, as they want to be? And isn't the effort what's most important, the pursuit in that direction, that the good we discover in ourselves we claim, or reclaim, and use wisely and well, and spread it around, pass it on?"

"You sound biblical, Mom." And then her son is crying, tears like small gems glittering in the sunlight, and Roma pulls him up and hugs him as hard as she can.

If she had only questioned Harry all those years ago, as she always has with her patients, with her children, they might not be where they are today. But *this* is where they are.

And this is what she knows: however different life will be when Harry returns, she will not leave him, and she will not tell their children the truth. Harry can, if he wants to, but she will not be the one to puncture their belief in him, their faith in his virtue. For now, it will have to be enough that she knows what Harry did, and what he failed to do, and the role she herself played.

FIFTY-SEVEN

YESTERDAY, A MONTH AGO, since last summer, Camille would have felt a prick of pleasure that Phoebe's relationship with Aaron Green is over—love ever the stumbling block, the sole malfunction, in her sister's perfect life. But that envy has lost its power.

So what if Camille's most important possessions could fit into one box? So what if that box would hold only the groundbreaking ethnographies written by the once-upon-a-time stars who founded and dominated her field, their work, lives, and deaths of little interest to others who aren't Camille, or nascent anthropologists? So what if the first editions she searched for in antiquarian bookstores over the years, since Margaret Mead entered her life, could probably now be found on Amazon, some third-party seller asking seven or eight bucks, plus the ubiquitous $3.99 for shipping?

What did any of that matter?

Her most valuable possession is her mind. And that mind is working again, the flexibility and suppleness she had always relied on, returning, revealing to her a new vista, new paths to explore.

No matter how long her visits home, she has never once unpacked. She lives out of her suitcase, as if prepared for a quick getaway. She doesn't want to make a quick getaway now, and though she traveled light for this weekend, she begins hanging her things in the closet, folding them into drawers.

When her phone rings, she answers and says, "Are you in the Cradle of Humankind?"

"I was, but it's midnight here, so I'm in my hotel room in Johannesburg, drinking a beer. You haven't responded to my last three emails and I was worried about you."

It's hard to remember her sluggish mind, because it's moving now at Mach speed, and Camille thinks: *He'll be on this dig for five and a half more months, and in that time I will have assembled my proposal for the American Widow study, and convinced Dr. Jin to give me what I need, and thrown out all my used clothes and furniture, and perhaps sublet my empty apartment, and turned down any offer from the Peace Corps, and hugged those I have come to love at Lilac Love goodbye. By the time he returns from the Cradle of Humankind, I will be myself again, or a new version of myself, living in a vibrant new future. And I might want his love, his ring, his children, in that vibrant new future. Or not. Who knows? I don't have to make any final decisions.*

I can wait.

I should wait.

I want to wait.

"It's been a little crazy here," she says. And she tells Valentine about her father having gone missing, but that he's safe, on a plane, an unanticipated trip, and when he returns, she thinks he'll have marvelous stories to tell.

And then she tells him about her drive to Palm Springs, and her thoughts on the drive, and about the Fluttering Women at the gala, and how those women have given birth to a potential study she's contemplating. "That's great, Camille. *Really* great," and she hears her enthusiasm reflected back to her.

And when he asks, "Is there a substantial enough population in Seattle for your needs?" she knows she has five and a half months and so doesn't answer his question directly—"I'll figure out the geographical considerations,"—and that suffices for her bearded physical anthropologist with two-million-year-old sand under his fingernails, who says, "I miss you, Camille. I won't push about marriage, just know I want to be with you for all time."

After she and Valentine Osin say their goodbyes and disconnect, Camille gathers her few toiletries together, to set out on the bathroom counter—the moisturizer she has begun using, the under-eye cream, a lipstick in the most unobtrusive shade she could find, the round pot of blush and the brush Phoebe insisted she buy the last time they were together in Palm Springs and went wandering around the better outlet mall.

When she opens her bathroom door, she is surprised to find that Phoebe has left her own open. It is an invitation, she realizes, to continue the conversation that has begun again between them, that hints of intimacies that might be shared. Tonight, when they are both in their beds, she'll say, "Phoebe, can you hear me?" and she imagines their whispers once again traveling through the tunnel of gleaming tiles, their words reaching each other's ears, finding safe havens.

FIFTY-EIGHT

"EVERYTHING'S IN THE CAR except for our suitcases," Elena says.

The sun is moving across the sky, rays lighting up the bed that separates them. The next time Simon is here, when he has brought Harry home, will he stay in this room that has become theirs, or return to the room of his childhood? He doesn't know.

"Everyone's heading outside to see us off," she says. "We should get going. Traffic's going to be bad."

She is looking around, at the agapanthus duvet, at the large picture windows, at the cacti beyond, and Simon's heart stutters. This might be the last time she's here with him.

A turn, and she's moving, through the doorway, into the hall, lost from his view.

The suitcase wheels are quiet on the marble floors as he heads into what Elena has always called the heart of the house. He hears his family outside. His mother is talking and Lucy is answering, and Elena laughs, and he wonders if only he is aware that her laughter is forced.

The newspaper he tossed onto the stone table is still there. Into the side pocket of his suitcase, something easy to read while waiting tomorrow for the plane to take off. Already he's thinking about what he needs to bring, wondering if their shelves at home hold any books about Judaism or Jewish history. Yes, there's one, a fat tome he's never cracked, bought because he heard the author on NPR: *The Story of the Jews*.

He lifts their bags into the back of the SUV, then hugs each of his sisters, and Elena does the same, and Lucy and Isabel are up in their aunts' arms, then kissing their *savah*, then in their car seats; and Simon is hugging his mother, telling her he'll call when he lands, will keep her informed every step of the way, and she says, "Chief Hernandez just phoned. Upset about Harry. Wishing us all luck. Wishing you luck." Then Simon is in the driver's seat, securing his seat belt, checking on his smiling daughters. He releases the emergency brake, coasts down to Agapanthus Lane, and turns left.

THERE IS A LATE-AFTERNOON perfume rising from the cacti flowers, and inside Roma's chest tiny birds are batting their wings.

"Mom, both of us are staying. I'm staying until Simon and Dad are back," Phoebe says.

"I may stay longer," Camille says. "Would that be okay?"

"You can stay forever. You both know that," Roma says, and pulls her daughters close.

"Let's go in. I'm going to open some wine and Camille and I are going to make dinner," Phoebe says.

The house is mellow with sunlight.

The kitchen is clean and not the way it usually is when her family has come and gone. They've eaten only two meals in the last two days, and no one has cooked anything.

Phoebe plunges in the corkscrew, a neat yank, and she's pouring, handing a full glass to Roma.

Camille is taking stock of the contents of the refrigerator, setting out green cartons of vegetables that no one consumed, the salmon steaks that were never grilled. The island fills with cutting boards and knives, a colander dripping water when Camille finishes rinsing the mushrooms, the scallions, a red pepper shaped like a heart.

Soon, her daughters are cutting and slicing and dicing and chopping, seasoning the salmon.

These last two eventful days seem to have reconfigured them. They have a new rapport, or perhaps regained the old, before their differing personalities formed a distance greater than the actual mileage that separates them. Phoebe presents herself as thoroughly modern, when she isn't, not truly, whittling away these past years at her natural softness in order to find the sharp angles she thinks she needs to survive. Camille, at the forefront of her personal vanguard, donning the role of a solitary, when really she aches for closeness, a desire she refuses to acknowledge, as if by acquiescing to sustained intimacy she might lose sight of herself. They work well together, swapping between chef and sous chef, preparing a dinner Roma can't imagine eating, but will, to please them.

"We'll call when it's ready, Mom. About an hour, right, Camille?"

And Camille says, "Exactly."

"We love you," they say when she leaves, glass in hand, the wine kissing the rim. She hears Camille asking Phoebe if they should lighten the mood, play some music, flip on the kitchen speakers. Even with this new or renewed spirit of friendship between them, some things never do change, the younger always first requesting approval or dispensation from the elder before doing what she wants to do. Roma is down the hall before Phoebe responds.

SHE THINKS ABOUT GOING into her study and calling Jeanine McCadden again to set up an appointment to meet with Noelani tomorrow, to begin a new assessment of the girl, to determine if there is a monster in the house or not. But she doesn't. She lacks the energy, and her voice will betray that she isn't her usual calm, controlled self.

She thinks about returning to the back patio, sitting again in Harry's favorite chair, but she doesn't.

Instead, she makes her way to their bedroom, places the wine-glass on his nightstand, sits on his side of their high bed.

Harry is not dead. He's alive, on a plane that touches down to-morrow afternoon Israeli time.

In a few hours, Simon and Elena and Lucy and Isabel will wind up the curvy road to their house. A trip made in silence, she's certain, though she's uncertain as to the reasons.

She thinks about how family is an amalgamation of the solid, the liquid, and the vaporous. A shambling creature made from accidental love, a meshing of beliefs occasionally disarrayed by inevitable bafflement, and the creation of others adorned with names signaling hope for their natures, prospects for their futures. Whether there is love, happiness, contentment, success, health, and satisfaction, or sadness, trauma, and tragedy in any family, so much is dependent on ephemeral luck.

And she thinks about primal wounds. Of the wounds her family has suffered as a result of Harry's flight from home, of the psychic repairs that will be necessary; of the wounds Simon and Elena's family will suffer, if they cannot right whatever is wrong; of the wounds Jeanine's family has already suffered because of Noelani, and will continue to suffer if her psychological issues are not fully resolved by the hoped-for diagnosis of achalasia and its surgical mending, and if Roma doesn't immediately determine what the running means to the girl. Before their first session, she researched the number seven and also the meaning of Noelani's name—*mist of heaven*. How does that little girl's name, how do the meanings of all of their names, figure into the composition that becomes *family*. Melodiously symphonic at the best of times, atonally dissonant at the worst.

In German, Harry's name means *home* or *house ruler*. It also might have a Phoenician origin, although in Hebrew, it means *exalted brother*. It's also the name of the king of Tyre in the Old Testament.

In Hindu mythology, *Roma* is an alternate name for Lakshmi, the goddess of prosperity.

Phoebe is Greek, and means *shining one*. In Greek mythology, it is one of the names for the goddess of the moon. In poetry, Phoebe is the moon personified.

In French, *Camille* means *young ceremonial attendant*. In Latin, *virginal, of unblemished character*.

Both daughters were made in the countries from which their names were selected.

Simon's name, taken from Harry's deaf ancestor, means *one who has heard*.

Elena means *shining light* or *bright one*.

Lucy's given name is Luz, meaning *light* in Spanish, taken from the title of the Virgin Mary, *Nuestra Señora de la Luz*, Our Lady of the Light.

Isabel, a Spanish variant of *Elizabeth*, is actually from the Hebrew *elísheva*, meaning *God is my oath*.

None of this gets her any closer to some unclear truth she's seeking.

Camille's idea of music. That's exactly what Roma wants to do, listen to Harry's favorite, hear Leonard Cohen singing the song with *Hineni* in it, immerse herself in the music Harry was listening to before he fled—if only she remembered what the song was called.

His bedside cabinet is well organized. His CDs lined up. Stacks of stapled articles he's printed out on his laptop, returned by the detectives and sitting on the coffee table in the living room. She glances through a few of the older articles, recognizes those he's shared with her at night when they were reading in bed. She pulls out the Cohen CD with "Hallelujah" on it. She's never told Harry that she thinks other artists have rendered that song far more exquisitely than its creator. She finds the track, and when it begins, she picks up the latest article in Harry's stack, one from the *New Yorker*, and reads a random paragraph.

"There again, it's a beautifully constructed melody that steps up, evolves, and slips back, all in quick time. But this song has a connective chorus, which when it comes in has a power all of its own."

She goes back to the beginning. It's an article about Leonard Cohen, and the strange serendipity does not completely surprise her. Those were Bob Dylan's words about Cohen's "Hallelujah."

She flips ahead several pages.

"Some nights, one is raised off the ground, and some nights you can't get off the ground."

Cohen's words about a concert he gave in, of all places, Jerusalem, when he was having problems on stage. By then his songs were personal meditations, but that night, he couldn't find his natural depth and stopped. And tried again. And stopped. And tried again.

"I turned around and the band was crying, too. And then it turned into something in retrospect quite comic: the entire audience turned into one Jew! And this Jew was saying, 'What else can you show me, kid? I've seen a lot of things, and this don't move the dial!' And this was the entire skeptical side of our tradition, not just writ large, but manifested as an actual gigantic being! Judging me hardly begins to describe the operation. It was a sense of invalidation and irrelevance that I felt was authentic, because those feelings have always circulated around my psyche: Where do you get to stand up and speak? For what and whom? And how deep is your experience? How significant is anything you have to say? ... I think it really invited me to deepen my practice. Dig in deeper, whatever it was, take it more seriously."

She's hearing this analytical rumination in Cohen's worn voice, confiding, intimate, "a fantastical growl . . . lordly," just as the journalist wrote.

On the last page of the article, she reads:

> "What I mean to say is that you hear the *Bat Kol*." The divine voice. "You hear this other deep reality singing to you all the time, and much of the time you can't decipher it . . . At this stage of the game, I hear it saying . . . 'just get on with the things you have to do.' It's very compassionate at this stage."

Is this what happened to Harry Saturday night? Did he hear the *Bat Kol*? Did he hear a divine voice singing of a deeper reality he couldn't decipher, that he desperately needed to try to understand? Was it a compassionate voice? Despite her fury, she hopes that it was, that whatever lifted him away, spurred him on, spurred him forward, came to him in love and light, with kindness and compassion.

She looks out the large windows. She's lost track of the sun, missed it bursting into primary colors, fading into pastels, then setting.

There is a quiet knock at the bedroom door and then Phoebe and Camille are on either side of her again, their arms wrapped around her again.

"Come join us," Phoebe says and kisses Roma's cheek.

Camille kisses her other cheek. "We're listening to the same Leonard Cohen song in the rest of the house."

Family is the "connective chorus"—a Dylan phrase about one of Harry's favorite Cohen songs Roma will honor by appropriating for them all.

Phoebe lifts the untouched wineglass from her father's nightstand. She takes a sip, hands it to Roma, who does the same, who passes it to Camille, who sips, too.

They leave the dimming room, moving toward the soulful music, the instrumental notes swelling and rising, that eroded voice lifting them up, replenishing their strength, imbuing them with a sense of the eternal. Forward they go, as if on their own quest, out of the darkness and into a splendor of light. It is not the white light of omniscience that dazed Roma this morning, but another variety, love-filled and containing a rainbow, and she looks into the reflection, the refraction, the dispersion, for the colors beneath the rainbow that Tatiana once told her to look for when she was a child, and though she doesn't see them, not yet, she hopes all that bright purity marks their safe passage through limbo.

SACRED
GEOGRAPHY

FIFTY-NINE

*Y*OU ALREADY KNOW WHAT *to do, Harry. I know that you do.*
Staring up at the blue-lighted plane traveling across the blackening sky, he had called out to God, and those were the words that he heard, resounding in his head, in that dry voice turned familiar. And his life simply halted, as if suspended, as if he were suspended in air. It was not the clout of death, nor how he thought death might be, only a cessation of everything, an overwhelming absence that rendered him both deaf and blind. He was terrified at first, but as the terror lifted, he calmed, and with that calm came a clarity pure as a diamond: the truth of how life worked, how it had worked for his parents in the Bronx, for his grandparents and great-grandparents in the Pale of Settlement, for all the Tabornikovs in all the past centuries. Truth made of a substance finer than any crushed mineral. He believed in the big bang and in evolution, in science and rationality and logic, but discovered, with an absence of surprise, that he could believe in something more, something else, in an alternative universe in which one's spirit, one's existence, the living of that spiritual existence, obeyed more poetic rules. He felt that finely crushed substance sifting into him, marking the beginning of time, the choosing of his people, landing softly upon those rocks of hard knowledge now wedged into the spaces of his soul he hadn't realized were empty until today, empty since he

made that first trade and then said *genug*, back in another life, in a forgotten year that belonged to the prior millennium.

That finely crushed substance, weightless though it was, was potent, magical, altering him, returning to him sight and sound, but changing how he was seeing, how he was hearing, a levitation, an ascension of sorts, and it was then that he assumed the profound duty he owed to the person he had wronged, the authentic, existential, and cathartic need to repent for what he had done. An unassailable obligation, despite his committing those wrongs so long ago, regardless of having spent his life since then altering the impoverished existences of so many.

Staring at the sky, head tipped back, motionless on that terrace, he was no longer seventy, not yet a man at thirteen, but a young boy on a red velvet seat swinging his legs, Mordy and Lenore stilling him, whispering, "Listen." And he listened to the rabbi instructing the congregation in the ways of atonement, explaining the Torah's requirement to ask for forgiveness in person, specifying the sin, as soon as the harm had been inflicted. That the Jewish people were born possessing innate kindness, knowing the nature and the power implicit in forgiving, in the act of seeking and providing it. That if the wounded, the offended, the hurt, the victim, the transgressed, refused at first to forgive, one had to continue on, facing the pain he had caused, facing himself, returning to atone again, and again, and again, each time in person, each time speaking original words of genuine, earnest, and candid apology. That path toward atonement, it was intended as a deliberately humbling walk, and one had to keep walking forward humbly, until forgiveness might be granted.

And he knew he was humbled, and he was prepared to step onto the path, to follow it on and on until he reached its end, where he would atone with every fiber of his being, and hope that Max Stern would find it in his heart to forgive him. Only then, bathed in the virtuousness of the man against whom he had so thoroughly transgressed, would he be cleansed of his misconduct, his malfeasance, the harm he had unwittingly inflicted, freed of this choking shame, this self-loathing consuming him, this impotence pinning him down.

In those long moments when the past and present collided, he was both the child he once was and the man he was at last becoming, and he understood.

And it was true. Harry Tabor understood.

From that perch high above, there was approval for the way his mind was working, the way his being was accepting all he had learned about himself, not feigning ignorance, not shunning it, but facing it, his newfound strength not weakened in the least, not swept away, by the gala celebrating him. Approval, too, for what he had decided to do, for he was and had always been a man of action, and action was what he would take.

Harry Tabor was experiencing supreme lucidity, attaining the essential perspective, stepping into the holy. His free will was restored to him then, and he lowered his head from the dark night and the stars, and moved across the terrace, seeing nothing except that path he would take, no light yet at the end. Down the steps he went, and it seemed as if the cab was waiting for him, idling there at the entrance, the driver's face hidden in shadow, and he said, "Palm Springs," and he was racing through the night, lowering a window, feeling the rushing of the heated air, tossing out his cell phone, a quick puff of rising sand marking its landing in the desert, where it will never be found.

He did not return home, for *home*, with its embracing love that he longer deserved, was not on the path. He rode the elevator up to CST, entered offices that were soundless and dark, confused about why he was there, until he sighted the path, and made his way to the hidden safe known only to him, opening it, stashing his passport in his pocket, taking cash from the roll he keeps on hand for families in need. He had never done anything like this. Had never not planned in advance. Had never disappeared for even an hour. Had never caused concern over his whereabouts. But it was not a time for explanations. If he explained, his family would stop him, and he could not allow anything to prevent him from fulfilling his profound duty.

He quickly wrote a loving letter to Roma, another to the children, and left the two envelopes on his desk to be found. In those letters, he did not mention Israel, or Max Stern, or that he had an address on a slip of paper in his jacket pocket that he hoped would lead him to where he needed to go, scribbled down just a few hours ago, while searching for answers to questions he had never known to contemplate. Nor did he write that there was a force guiding his actions. He told them he loved them. He told them not to worry. Beyond that, there was nothing else to say until he understood how Max Stern was, what the years in prison had done to him, until he asked for Max's forgiveness in person, specifically, heart laid bare, though decades late.

He didn't know if Max was still alive, but if he was, he would find the wrongfully convicted stockbroker turned Modern Orthodox rabbi living in Jerusalem.

And if the search was not easy, he would never give up, would continue looking for Stern until the finale of Harry's own days.

And if there was only a grave, he would find the rules for asking forgiveness of the dead, and go to the grave and do everything he needed to do, and do it again, and again, and again, and then lay stones on the stone, saying, "Forgive me," saying, "I remember you."

It was, for him, a vanishing act of life-saving consequence, both a distillation and concentration of the imperative to make amends to his old friend.

It would be, for all time, the single most important act of Harry Tabor's previously enviable life.

Though he's not quite sure how he managed to go from CST to LAX, or how he spent the time once he was there, he is now in a seat on an El Al plane that is twelve hours into its fourteen-hour-and-thirty-minute flight to Tel Aviv. He doesn't know what time zone he is in, only that it is one in the morning at home. Outside his window, the sky is whitening, cloudy wisps gliding alongside, as if outlining the path toward the plane's destination.

The first part of his journey, to this airline seat, should have been impossible, but it had been unfettered, aided, knots untangled, these initial steps on the way to atoning facile and smooth, as if his mission was anointed, for it was remarkable how the world embraced a broken man of handsome age, black-tie-clad, with cash in his pocket, his thoughts at last properly aligned. His economy-class ticket had been quickly rendered obsolete when the young stewardess, a golden sabra he could imagine expertly wielding an automatic weapon in the Israeli army, ushered him to the front, into platinum class. He tried to decline the upgrade, but with her strong arms, the sabra pushed and cajoled, and it seemed right to give in, to give her what she wanted, and her hand on his shoulder said he had made her happy. He declined, however, the wine and the cocktails, the small plates of olives and almonds, the dinner. When the sabra said, "All meals are kosher, if that's your concern," he thanked her and said he needed nothing, and he didn't. He was a man on a pilgrimage, traveling far away to make things right, to correct what he had deliberately obliterated more than three decades in the past.

He has been sitting all these hours like a statue in his seat, jacket on, hands clasped, barely aware of his fellow passengers slumbering around him. But the stale air is warming up, and he feels all the slowed breaths, the slowly beating hearts, the dreams in which they are engaged and encased, and he removes his jacket.

There, in the inner pocket, are two envelopes, their presence a shock.

The letter he wrote to Roma, the letter he wrote to Phoebe, Camille, and Simon, letters he thought he left for them on his desk at CST.

Instead, he has them, and is crushed by his discovery. And frantic, as they must be, too. He turns them over and over and over, hearing Roma's voice telling him that the workings of the mind are often unfathomable, and perhaps he unconsciously held onto them, and needed to contemplate why.

And so he contemplates. Perhaps the words he wrote last night in Palm Springs to those he loves were not the right words, were insufficient. Perhaps those envelopes ended up in his pocket because he will not know the right words until he has reached the end of the path and returns home to them as, he prays, an illuminated man.

He tears the envelopes and the letters within into tiny pieces, until he holds fistfuls of confetti, and watches them flutter into the bag held open by the sabra collecting detritus from her passengers.

He sets his jacket across his legs and closes his eyes. When all of the world's emotions roll through him, he finally understands that the past will always exist, and that the world will always defy comprehension, and that he is not, has never been, will never be, traveling all on his own.

Soon there is an internal rush of lapping oceanic waves pulling him under, into the ruffled layers of sleep, and the dream he has in his platinum-class seat on this El Al flight taking him to Israel, it has not been touched from above, belongs wholly and only to him:

Ben Gurion Airport. A cab to the Savidor Merkaz train station. Climbing aboard the right bus, an hour later stepping out into a city of ancient grandeur, of veneration and conflict for Jews, for Christians, for Muslims. A cosmopolitan medieval city, of walls and gates, and pink and white stone, looking down at the Dead Sea, across the Jordan River to the biblical mountains of Moab in the east, west to a coastal plain and the Mediterranean. It is a temperate seventy-five degrees, but the sun is hanging steep in the sky. Birds nest in the old walls. Hooded crows, jays, swifts, and bulbuls, though he doesn't know their names. He stands still for a moment, watching a flock of white storks flying overhead. The air is fragrant with the aromas of cooking, scented with spices. He is carried along by the crowds, awash in a myriad of languages, Hebrew, Arabic, English, he recognizes, but there are many more that he doesn't. Among the pageantry of secular garb and monastic vestments, of black hats and hijabs, and the splashy colors sported by the tourists, his tuxedo merits no second glances.

This is the Old City. There is the Temple Mount. The Dome of the Rock. The Jaffa Gate. The Tower of David. He passes synagogues and yeshivas, mosques and madrassas, churches and convents, bazaars and souks, hidden courtyards and gardens, all manner of dwellings. It is an architectural mosaic, continuously inhabited for five thousand years. Beyond, where he is not going, the ancient is replaced by the modern. And beyond the modern, the desert sands range from white to ochre.

He hears the peals of church bells, the calls of muezzins from the minarets, the chanting of Jewish prayers at the Wailing Wall. He is in Jerusalem, the city on a hill.

He follows the address on the slip of paper carried these seventy-five hundred miles. He circles and circles around tiny streets and finds himself in a narrow stone lane that opens into a large tiled courtyard. Sunny, but shaded by old trees, olive and fig. The crumbling walls covered by climbing vines. People on wooden benches raising their faces to the sun. He thinks they might be waiting to speak to the man who lives in that restored thousand-year-old house with the door that is painted such a particular blue he imagines stepping through it and reaching the sky.

He raps quietly, nervously, heart knocking in his chest, and then standing before him on the transom is a man who is Max Stern. And not. As tall as Harry remembers, but dark hair now white and wild, his once clean-shaven face hidden beneath the bushy long beard of a sage, a sublime light in his eyes. The force of him is extraordinary, and Harry understands that whatever Max Stern once was, he has been transformed into a powerful being.

There is no time to waste, no niceties that would make sense, and so he begins.

"I am here to seek your forgiveness."

Max Stern lifts a hand, the motion mysterious, the intent ambiguous.

"I, not you, deserved to be punished. You should have thrown me to the wolves. Why didn't you throw me to the wolves?"

And he is again that young boy on that red velvet seat in the synagogue, his parents imploring him to listen, and he hears his childhood rabbi say, "The sages taught whoever forgave the faults of others would have his sins pardoned by Hashem." Here in Jerusalem, facing the man he wronged, he prays it is true.

Max Stern says nothing, gives nothing away. Even his eventual smile gives nothing away. Finally, he steps aside and says, "It took you far longer than it should have. But I knew one day you would show up at my door. Come in, Harry Tabor, come in."

SIXTY

I T IS A QUARTER to four in the morning.

In his bed in his house in the hills, Simon is awake and staring at the crack in the ceiling. Elena is asleep; the girls are asleep. His bag for Israel is packed and at the front door.

Will he find his father?

Will he at last sleep, on the plane, or in his hotel room in Jerusalem?

Will he be transformed by this trip?

Will he find the truth of himself?

Will he find the hole he possesses filled up?

Will his wife still love him, though she has said she will not?

It's the unforeseen Elena doesn't want in her life, as if there could be no distinction between the internal and the external, which doesn't make sense in the context of her Catholicism, practiced all these years, with him unaware.

She turns beneath the sheet, and his automatic response is to hope, then to pray, Elena is turning toward him, despite all he has considered, all that he knows, all that she has said. But when he looks, he is confronted from a distance by the tight whorl of her black hair pinned at her neck. She's far away, at the very edge of their large bed, as if even in sleep, she is expressing both her literal and metaphorical position.

IN PALM SPRINGS, THE Tabor women are also awake.

They slept, but one by one they emerged from unremembered visions, padded out of their rooms, and gathered outside. Except for the occasional chirrup or hoot or quick high cry of the desert's night creatures, silence surrounds them as they toss away their night clothes and walk united into the pool. Under the silvery glow of the waxing moon and the plentiful stars, they float naked in water as warm as the air.

Phoebe is thinking of Lucy and wonders why. She does not remember it was Lucy in her dreams, grown into a young woman with flowing hair, speaking to a crowd in words liquid and fluid, her eyes never once straying from her aunt and cousin in the front row. In the dream, Phoebe had smiled up at Lucy, then leaned over and emptied her shoes of sand. Then she had kissed the small hand of her own daughter, a charming chestnut-haired little girl whom Phoebe had fairy-tale-named Tulip Tabor.

Camille is thinking of shoots of grass, and seas of flowers, and oceans of sand, and the way chocolate tastes in her mouth. There is a giddiness inside of her, of which she is barely aware, just bubbles of something traveling between heart and head. In her dream, of which she has no recollection, she was wearing a gauzy white gown, cradling a naked infant at her breast, walking alongside Valentine Osin, who was dressed in a white linen suit and clutching a book in each hand, one titled *The American Widow*, the other, *How the H. Naledi Changed My Life*.

It comes to Roma that she woke breathless, unaware she dreamt of a fruit orchard set in a desert, her feet mired in sand, trying and failing to reach the trees laden with fruit, round, and ripe, and alluring. When she sat up in bed, she had looked at the clock and seen it was half past three. She does not know it yet, but that will become her waking hour for the rest of her life.

Her hair glides on the surface, water beads slip across her skin, and she finally feels quieter, calm even, at one with the atmosphere and the future of her family, the connective chorus that they are, that they will remain.

She imagines Harry and Simon returning. The whole family around the table by the big pool, set with rose crystal goblets and rose-flowered plates. Harry, himself once again, with that big Harry Tabor smile, and the weight lifted from his shoulders. Simon, happy, rested, no longer restive at all. And she and Phoebe and Camille listening to the adventuresome tales told by husband and father, son and brother, about their separate journeys to Israel, about finding each other, their time there together. About all that transpired when Harry met Max Stern. Asking the easy question first: Is he really a rabbi?

When the tales of courage and discovery and insight slow to a trickle, she will suggest the whole family plan an immediate tripartite trip: to walk one of those biblical routes Harry had been researching; then to find that farm, once Russian, but Russian no more, where Tatiana and Inessa lived for eleven long years; then to find those former shtetls once located in the circumscribed Pale of Settlement, where most of their people lived their whole lives.

She wants them all to remember the Kahanoviches and the Jacobys and the Tabornikovs, their determination to survive, that determination giving rise to this Tabor clan, which will continue to exist. She can nearly smell the tang of the Black Sea, feel the fecund earth in the palm of her hand. She imagines them all together, reclaiming themselves, reclaiming their origins, demonstrating their profound gratitude for the immense kindness that has been visited upon them.

SIXTY-ONE

S IX MONTHS AGO, SIMON lost the sensation of time moving, how it felt when it raced or crawled, and although the days have progressed, for him, time instantly halted, turned inert and stagnant.

He has spent whole days in his office with his door shut and the *Palm Times* article on his desk. First read in his business-class seat, drinking his coffee, newly airborne on that Monday in mid-August. He opened the paper he'd taken on his way out of the house and saw the byline of Owen Kaufmann.

The name had called forth the young man who had cornered his mother at the gala, when the gala was still a party. He couldn't recall their awkward conversation, but he remembered his discomfort, and when he led his mother away, his impression had been that Owen Kaufmann did not like Harry, and he had wondered how that was possible, because everybody loved Harry.

He hadn't known then that Owen Kaufmann had interviewed his father earlier in the week. And he hadn't known then that Owen Kaufmann had misled Harry, telling him it was a profile about his Man of the Decade honor, rather than an uncharitable exposé masquerading as an op-ed.

That morning, on the plane, he read Owen Kaufmann's description of Harry, *a charming man, with smarts, and a can-do person-*

ality, and Simon wasn't sure if the inked sarcasm he sensed was real or not. But when the article applauded CST's valuable contributions to society and the people it served, he'd relaxed.

Then been gut-punched. Owen Kaufmann had written about Harry's time at Carruthers Investments, and the insider trading case that had ensnared Max Stern, and questioned whether Harry might have been involved.

And if Mr. Tabor was, then we must decide whether dirty money becomes cleansed, if magnanimously used thereafter, and whether lapses in personal morality and ethics can be erased by later benevolent acts.

All suppositions, not a single hard fact, and Simon's instinct was to sue the *Palm Times* and Owen Kaufmann for libel. But he knew a hack job cleverly posed as opinion that ended with a saving rhetorical grace—*But when so few help others, can we afford to condemn those who do?*—would be impossible to fight. He had stared out his window all the following hours.

Later, he wasn't sure if he was relieved or not that his own deep research shook loose nothing more than what his father had already discovered, and nothing about his father at all. He has never mentioned the article to his mother or to his sisters. And they have never mentioned the article to him. They would have, he's sure, if any of them had seen it, if it had been brought to their attention. Despite the influx of outsiders during certain months, Palm Springs was a small town, gossip quickly making the rounds. But in all their conversations since mid-August, it's never been raised, and he wasn't going to be the one to break their torn hearts, to ruin the historical view of husband and father. But he has had a difficult time coming to terms with the accusations Owen Kaufmann knifed into those lofty pretend questions.

He has joined a temple, and attends Shabbat services, to which he brings Lucy and Isabel, who sit quietly for the first hour, but then reach their limit. His newfound passion, though, is for the classes held in the rabbi's office, where he and other seekers study the Talmud. He has taken naturally to that remarkable compendium of

Judaism's written and oral laws that encompasses all of the authoritative Jewish religious teachings from what seems to Simon as the very beginning of time. He has emerged as a class leader because of his evocative questioning, and takes copious notes when the discussion bears down on one of the many specific questions he needs answered. He is finding solace in the deep philosophical arguments set out in the Talmud. There is no black-and-white world, as he had believed until recently. It is a world made of whole cloth sewn in shades of gray.

He has also spent several afternoons researching Einstein's beliefs about the fabric of time—that the past, present, and future all exist simultaneously, that there is no true division between past and future, but rather a single existence. That knowledge sometimes quiets his thoughts, affords him a temporary becalming, a brief cognitive peace.

But the yearning has been acute for at least a seasonal division between past and present. In the desert where he was born, and in Los Angeles where he lives, the sunshine has been a constant affront. He gritted his teeth through the end of summer, then the fall, and into the winter, desperate for an end to the sun's flared strength, its relentless glare, when he required atmospheric acknowledgment, the tempest of weather.

Now, at the end of February, as he searches for an uncertain address found folded in a suit pocket, the weather at last possesses the necessary gravitas. No frost, which would be appropriate, but vaporous fog, a chilled drizzle, a sulky, scowling sky, all providing the weight and angle of retrospect.

He steps into a large empty courtyard patterned in Byzantine tiles. The once-bright shades of turquoise, apricot, rose, and lemon, long bleached by the elements, have left behind ghostly colors.

The wooden benches are wet and empty.

The dusky leaves of the old trees are dressed in quivering raindrops.

The coiling vines are climbing the ancient walls.

The drizzle turns insistent and he shivers, but not from the cold. He never expected that weeping nature would return him to the immediacy of his existence, absent since mid-August, but it is returning, and returning here in this place. There are stirrings of faint hope, too, regarding the efficacy of prayers, that perhaps the fullest scenes of his life are yet to come.

He brushes the moisture out of his hair, straightens his coat, then knocks on the bright blue door of a small house in the Jewish Quarter of the Old City in Jerusalem.

He steps back when the door swings open. The man is shorter than Simon expected, spare but strong. Energy pulses beneath his plain white shirt. He wears black pants, but his feet are bare. His hair is white and wild. His beard is white and wild and reaches his Adam's apple. Simon is struck by the sublime light in the man's eyes, by his learned, prophetic force, the power bursting from his being.

"You look exactly as he did at your age."

"You know who I am?"

"I know your father is Harry Tabor. I always hoped he would show up one day."

"He tried."

"Tell me."

"Six months ago he was on his way here to find you. His journey ended on the tarmac at Ben Gurion. He died in his seat on the plane. I didn't know that, none of us knew that, when I flew here the next day. I was coming to support him. I never left the airport, simply turned around and took my father home.

"When he decided to find you, he told none of us he was going, and we still don't know the originating impetus, the catalyst. I've pieced together bits, but there's too much I don't know or understand, too much that's missing, and I'm hoping you'll tell me the entire story. What I do know is he believed he had sinned against you. And those sins were driving him here.

"I've come back to continue the path he was on, to complete

what my father started. To atone for his sins, the suffering he inflicted upon you, and perhaps to obtain your forgiveness on his behalf. For you to forgive Harry Tabor."

The man nods and tugs hard at his beard. "It seems we ought to get you out of the rain and introduce ourselves. I'm Rabbi Max Stern."

"Simon Tabor."

"Well, Simon Tabor, atonement doesn't quite work that way. A son cannot atone for his father. But come in. I'll make a pot of tea and we'll talk."

LAMPS ARE UNLIT, YET the house is filled with a glorious encircling light, white and omniscient. The home is ascetic, but far from austere—lifeblood rushes through it; the walls vibrate with the magnetism of an inquisitive mind. Open books are splayed throughout on pale-wood furniture, Scandinavian simplicity in this most complicated of countries. A Persian rug in muted jewel tones mirrors the faded courtyard tiles. A folded tallit crowns a bronze sculpture. On the dining room table, a glass bowl of dusty rocks and a vase filled with wildflowers are centered, as if in conversation. There are no personal pictures on display, but he senses love occurs in this environ, is given all of the time by the man who resides here, received by those who seek him out.

"Are you married?"

Simon shakes his head. "The divorce will be final soon."

"Children?"

"Two lovely young daughters."

"Are you observant?"

"Just before my father died, I planned to explore, and if it suited me, to immerse myself. After his funeral, after we sat shiva, I joined a synagogue, threw myself and my grief into it. Now I observe Shabbat, take my girls to Friday night services, and I'm studying the Talmud deeply. I'm here to atone, and also to learn."

Max Stern fills the kettle and settles it on the stove, the flame sparking blue before calming. He turns to Simon then, raises into the air a firm hand, veined and weathered, browned by the absent Jerusalem sun.

"We'll speak of many things in due course. But you've arrived at an auspicious moment. This, Simon, is where the lesson begins."

When they hear the first note, they lock eyes, in an intimacy at once instinctive and emotional, and together they listen to the exquisite cacophony Harry Tabor heard in his airborne dream: the peals of church bells, the calls of muezzins from the minarets, the chanting of Jewish prayers at the Wailing Wall.

"Yes?" asks Max Stern.

"Yes," says Simon Tabor.

ACKNOWLEDGMENTS

Huge love and deep gratitude to these amazingly talented people who believe in me:

At Flatiron Books, Amy Einhorn is a fabulous force and consummate supporter; Caroline Bleeke has the keenest of eyes; Conor Mintzer has the details down pat and wonderful cheer; Amelia Possanza, Nancy Trypuc, and Ellen Pyle are unflagging in their creative ways of bringing my work to the attention of booksellers, reviewers, and readers. And my heartfelt appreciation to: the copyeditor, Mary Beth Constant, who writes me funny notes in the margins and catches what needs to be caught; the production editor, David Lott, who lets nothing slip by; the interior designer, Donna Noetzel, who makes the visual experience of reading my work as good as my own words hopefully are; and the cover designer, Keith Hayes, who created a sparking great cover for *The Family Tabor.*

At The Borough Press, the whole team and especially Suzie Dooré with her sharp reads and emails that make me laugh.

At Trident Media Group, the fantastic and funny Erica Spellman Silverman, great literary agent and wonderful friend; and Nicole Robson and Caitlin O'Beirne, who so enthusiastically put their impressive talents at my disposal.

Independent booksellers are the marvelous bridge between author and reader. I am deeply grateful for all they have done to make *The Resurrection of Joan Ashby* a success. Please support your local bookstores. Enormous thanks to:

Liza Bernard
(Norwich Bookstore, Norwich, VT)

Zora de Bodisco
(Book Booker, Gulfport, FL)

Kenny Brechner and Karin Schott
(Devaney Doak & Garrett Booksellers, Farmington, ME)

Anmiryam Budner
(Main Point Books, Bryn Mawr, PA)

Nona Camuel
(CoffeeTree Books, Morehead, KY)

Bill Cusumano
(Square Books, Oxford, MS)

Kimberly Daniels and Angie Tally
(The Country Bookshop, Southern Pines, NC)

Jann Griffiths
(Booksmart, Morgan Hill, CA)

Anne Holman
(The King's English, Salt Lake City, UT)

Steve Iwanski
(Turnrow Book Co., Greenwood, MS)

Andrea Jones
(The Galaxy Bookshop, Hardwick, VT)

Pamela Klinger-Horn
(Excelsior Bay Books, Excelsior, MN)

Valerie Koehler
(Blue Willow Bookshop, Houston, TX)

Don Luckham
(The Toadstool Bookshop, Keene, NH)

Jessica Osborne
(E. Shaver, Bookseller, Savannah, GA)

Ellen Rodgers, Kelly Pickerell, Hillary Taylor, and Julia Blakeney
(Lemuria Books, Jackson, MS)

Nancy Simpson-Brice
(The Book Vault, Oskaloosa, IA)

Luisa Smith
(Book Passage, Corte Madera, CA)

Deon Stonehouse
(Sunriver Books, Sunriver, OR)

Susan Taylor
(Book House of Stuyvesant Plaza, Albany, NY)

Beth Wagner
(Phoenix Books, Essex Junction, VT)

To all the readers who have reached out to share their personal stories after reading *The Resurrection of Joan Ashby*, I'm honored by your confidences.

FOR:

Everything everlasting: Michael Dickes, my brilliant husband and most favorite person. NC, NL, ND, ND.

Laughter, love, and friendship: Claudine Wolas Shiva, Sherri Ziff, David Smith, Michael Stewart, Ginger Buccino Mahon, Atienne Benitez De Conciliis, Heather Macdonald LaMarre, and Gabrielle Massey.

Great conversations and constancy: Henry Wolas Dickes; and Pearl Wolas, who was with me through most of the writing of this novel.

The story about burning money: Jacob Mazon.
The banking tutorial (errors are mine alone): Neil Rudolph.

Leonard Cohen's remarks and quotes, read by Roma Tabor, come from the fine article by David Remnick: "Leonard Cohen Makes It Darker," *The New Yorker*, October 27, 2016 issue.

Writing is such a private and intense endeavor that sending a novel out into the world requires an enormous leap. Thank you so much for reading.

Recommend *The Family Tabor* for your next book club!

Reading Group Guide available at

www.readinggroupgold.com